FORCE PLAY

A Denver Bandits Novel

LO EVERETT

AUTHOR'S NOTE

This is the fourth book in the Mile High Hearts series which follows the Denver Bandits baseball team. It can be read as a standalone, but to fully appreciate the dynamic of the group, I recommend reading it as a series. Dom and Indie's story starts as a failed one-night stand between frenemies. Force Play has plenty of banter to keep you laughing, some heavy pining from our hero that will make you swoon, and lots of hot moments in between. But I'd be remiss if I didn't share insight into the heavier topics as well.

Force play also touches on topics of parental death, anxiety, grief and biphobia. The diagnosis and treatment of cancer and related fertility issues are heavily discussed as part of Indie's story.

Force Play [fawrs pley]

verb, baseball terminology

When the defensive team makes a play that leaves the baserunner with no control over being called out. Not to be confused with foreplay, which is also detailed in the pages of this book. For all the control freaks out there, this one's for you. May you find the person, place, or thing that calms your mind.

PROLOGUE

DOM

ONE YEAR EARLIER

My dad has always told me that the first time he saw my mom, he was drawn to her—that her beauty and her laugh mesmerized him. Although, he's never gone as far as to say it was love at first sight, probably because my mom would laugh her ass off at that.

The way *she* tells it, cheesy lines and charm weren't enough to win her over; she made him work for it. But they both agree that a love like theirs is a rare gift—the kind that comes into your life in a flash. And when you're presented with it, you should grab on and give it everything you've got.

If anything is missing in my life, it's what my parents have. For years I've dedicated myself to baseball, and while I haven't shut myself off from love like some of my teammates, I just haven't found that person yet.

Like that old, twangy country song, there's been plenty of faces, but they tend to be of the one-night variety.

I'm already riding high from our shutout tonight when I step out of the locker room and see a stunning, dark-haired woman standing against the opposite wall with my teammate Hendrix and his girlfriend Poppy. Big almond-shaped eyes the shade of dark-chocolate size me up, swirling with interest that she tries to hide behind crossed arms and a potent "don't fuck with me" expression. Long, toned legs give way to a pair of frayed denim shorts. She's wearing my team's jersey, and while I have no reason to believe my name is on her back, I'd love to find out if it is.

Call me a fool, but I don't expect to find my person by spending my nights alone. It might not be the love my parents talk about, or maybe it will be; I'll never know for sure if I don't shoot my shot.

When those soulful eyes find mine again, I smirk. Normally, that's all it takes to seal the deal, but she just rolls them, dismissing me, and focuses back on Poppy. Her curls are wild and even though I know nothing about her, I get the sense that they fit her perfectly. The bouncy locks shift, covering her face when she leans over to whisper in her friend's ear, making Poppy shake with laughter.

Funny, smoking hot, and not fawning over me—I already like her more than I should.

I'm not sure who this fiery woman is to my teammate and his girlfriend, but I'd really like to find out. Maybe figure out why she's looking at me like she wants to maim me on sight, and why I'm considering letting her.

"You coming to Dean's?" I ask Hendrix, the newest member of the Bandits and one hell of an outfielder. Our grumpy first baseman is opening up his penthouse for everyone to hang out—a rare occurrence—but everyone was in the mood to do something a little more low-key tonight.

He nods his head once. "We're heading there now. Want to ride over with us? I ordered an Uber."

I glance over to where the drop-dead gorgeous Medusa, with the nearly black hair, is leaning against the wall, her eyes cast down at her maroon nails, clearly bored. One look from her right now is sure to turn me to stone.

"Will you be there?" It's the wrong move and I damn well know it, but I'm dying to see what happens when I push her buttons.

"Mhmm." She doesn't bother looking up at me. "I'm going to use the restroom before we leave," she tells Poppy, giving me her back, which is currently sporting my best friend's last name and number. That's not ideal, but whoever *she* is, she's not *his*. Dean doesn't date.

All signs point to her being fair game. How pissed would she be if I called dibs?

Very.

It's tempting, but I rein myself in. It's a fine line between annoying her and making her hate me, one I need to tread carefully if I want a chance with her.

The next night, after sweeping the series against the Los Angeles Diablos, our favorite post-game bar is wall-to-wall with fans streaming in from the stadium. Wayward hands pat my shoulders as I pick my way through the cheerful crowd at Draft to the roped-off tables in the back.

There's no shortage of women here who would eagerly come home with me, but for the second night in a row, I can't take my eyes off the woman currently sitting across the table from me.

Tonight, she's wearing a short denim skirt that accentuates her curves, ending in a flap over her thighs. It has me dying to find out whether it's a real access point or some sort of optical illusion designed to intrigue me. The simple teal tank top she's wearing shouldn't be anything special, but its square neckline frames the swells of her breasts, making me want to know if they are soft as they look. Not to mention, it reveals a delicate tattoo that you would almost miss if you weren't paying attention.

Indie Moreno, the captivating childhood best friend of my teammate's girlfriend, is here visiting, and so far seems outwardly unimpressed with me.

Almost all of her energy has been directed at sparring with me and there's something about the challenge that has me hooked.

Except for last night, after the game, when she confused the shit out of me by flirting with both Dean and me. I'm almost certain she's doing it solely to fuck with me. And there's the fact that she let me buy her coffee earlier today. I think that was more for Poppy's benefit—to give her friend some alone time with Hendrix after we helped build her sound booth.

What really throws me off is the way she watches me when she thinks no one is paying attention. She hasn't figured out that the hot and cold game she's playing with me only makes me want her more.

Mostly.

Watching her flirt with Dean is getting old, painful even, but I plan to remedy that tonight—just as soon as I can get her alone. Right now she's sandwiched between my teammates, alternating between chatting with Poppy who's perched on her boyfriend's lap and flirting with Dean who's seated on the opposite side, leaving me across the table.

Cockblocking my buddy isn't normally my style—I prefer the role of accomplice—but this is going to be too much fun to pass up. I see right through Indie, and it's not really him she's after. If it were, her eyes wouldn't keep drifting to mine in the middle of their conversation.

A woman comes up to Hendrix, interrupting the conversation he's having and blatantly disregarding Poppy. Across from me, Indie freezes, her piercing eyes narrowing on the woman who's aggressively flirting with her best friend's man. Her knuckles turn white on her beer bottle as she watches the interaction, looking like she's ready to leap over the couple and come to her friend's aid at the first sign she needs back-up.

Fuck, why does that make her even hotter? Maybe it's because this team has become an extension of my family.

After Poppy effectively shut down the woman trying to stake a claim on Hendrix, the table cleared out, everyone opting to go their own way for the night. The happy couple was the first to haul ass out of here, leaving enough sexual tension in their wake to drown all of us.

"I hope you packed noise canceling headphones, unless auditory voyeurism is your kink," I tease, hoping she gives me another of those unguarded smiles.

"My kinks are none of your business," she tosses back at me, shifting in her seat, only to cross and then uncross her legs. I file away the fact that a little possessive display gets her hot.

"But you have them." I'm a sick man and this woman is my malady. I know I shouldn't push her buttons, but I can't fucking help it—not when she scrunches her nose like that at me.

"Down, boy. You wouldn't know what to do with me if you had the chance." This time there's a twinkle in her eyes. Maybe she's been infected with the same illness as me and enjoys this little game of verbal foreplay just as much as I do.

"Things are about to get interesting." Dean chuckles darkly next to her. It doesn't matter whether he's on her side or mine, because I'm on a fucking mission.

"Only one way to find out. What's it going to be? Are you going to chance it with the lovebirds, or are you ready for some fun?" I taunt hoping that it doesn't blow up in my face.

Cleavage peeks out of her tank top when she props herself up on her elbows, shrinking the space between us. I have to force my eyes up and the smirk I find on her plump red lips tells me I've been caught looking. "What do you have in mind?"

"Getting out of here would be a start." I look around the dark bar. Most of my teammates have cleared out, and this isn't the right atmosphere for the type of fun I want to get into with Indie.

"You know what sounds like a good time?" She licks her lips, looking between Dean and me, like a hungry lioness. Whatever comes out of her mouth, it's going to get the three of us in trouble. "Dancing."

Dean's grumble is so dramatic it's comical.

"Don't be a stick in the mud. The pretty girl wants to dance. Let's take her to Lark's." The upscale night club my buddy owns is perfect—especially the private VIP section. Maybe it'll give me the opportunity to get Indie alone for long enough that she'll let her guard down and give me the chance I've been vying for.

"I don't dance," Dean asserts. He hates Lark's, but he hates most everything, save for his cabin and baseball.

"Not even for me?" Indie gives him an exaggerated pout, showing off a playful side that I want to see more of.

"Not for anyone," he grumbles in return. Indie's pout deepens and Dean sighs. "You're just lucky I'm not ready to go back to my penthouse yet." He's got that petulant rich boy vibe down pat, standing from the table and shoving his phone deep in his pocket.

"I'm sure I can find a willing partner." Indie shrugs off his piss-poor attitude and joins him.

I think the fuck not. If anyone is dancing with this woman tonight, it's going to be me. Pushing up from the table I trail the two of them out to the parking lot.

Even as we wait for the car, I can see her relax a little more, her shoulders shimmying to the music playing on the outdoor speakers as she scrolls her phone, a smile tilting up her lips every so often. It's sexy as fuck. She's got a wide smile, the kind that shows her teeth, and I love that she doesn't try to dull it down or hide it. It's such a contrast to her prickly attitude, and I immediately want more. Not only that, but I want to be the one pulling it out of her, tearing down her walls one by one to see what's locked behind them.

Does she lounge around her house relaxed and happy? If I try hard enough, I can almost picture her humming when she's alone. Or is she the kind of girl that moans when she takes a bite of her favorite food? I want to know it all.

When the Uber pulls up a few minutes later, Dean takes the front seat and I slide in beside Indie in the back.

"Are you ready for me to win you over with my dance moves?"

She jolts in surprise when I playfully bump her with my shoulder, her warm skin on mine making me very aware of how close we are back here, just the two of us.

The lightness of her laughter washes over me and I make it my mission to hear more of it tonight, because when Indie laughs, it's the prettiest sound in the world. "What makes you think you can win me over at all, Domino?"

"My mom told me I can do anything I put my mind to, and I took that to heart."

"I fear she led you astray." Her hand pats my cheek, sparking a desire to capture it and hold it there. "I'm not one of those girls that's easily impressed by a pretty face, or the fact that you can swing a bat." The coldness that returns when she calls me out for my profession stops me from acting on the whim.

Interesting.

"So it's the athlete thing that bugs you. Is it just because I'm a better player than Dean that you don't mind flirting with him?"

"Fuck off."

In the mirror, I see the driver hold back a laugh when Dean flips a double bird in my direction.

Squaring up for battle, Indie turns towards me. "Nope, it's the way you strut around like a puffed-up peacock all the time. Being humble goes a long way."

"Humble, you think this guy is humble?" I point to the rearview mirror where a bored look settles over Dean's face. "Don't let him fool you, he does it too. He's just a modest strutter." I lower my voice. "Actually, we don't talk about it; his mediocre puffing makes him sad."

"Right here," he reminds us.

"Isn't it past your bedtime, old man? We can drop you off at home if this is too much for you," I quip at my friend, half hoping he takes me up on the offer.

When he doesn't answer, I turn back to Indie, brushing a wayward curl back so I can see those almond-shaped eyes. When I find them, they suck me in, making me feel like I'm tumbling into the abyss with little control over my landing. "I'm going to show you I'm not the guy you think I am. Except the pretty part—that is spot on." I wink at her.

"Not doing yourself any favors." The words are mumbled as she leans forward and talks to Dean over the front seat, blocking me out of the conversation.

My friend glances back over his shoulder, shaking his head at me. "Cocky is his default setting, but it's probably our fault for telling him how pretty he is too often."

"The roles of team grump and team dad were already taken by you and Cruz. I had to blaze my own trail. Besides, it's not cocky if you can back it up," I tell them both, pulling out my phone and firing off a text to my friend Topher, the owner of Lark's.

"You can pull around the back. We'll go in that way," I tell the driver, pocketing my phone.

"Frequent flier?" Even in the dark car, I can see the glimmer of hope in her raised eyebrow—like she's delighted that she just caught me.

"Something like that." From what I've gathered, Indie isn't going to take me at my word. She needs to see that I'm not just some cocky playboy.

Topher is waiting at the back door a minute later when I hold the door for Indie to join me. Predictably, she ignores the hand I offer to help her out of the car. When Dean joins us, they follow me to the VIP entrance, where my friend greets me with a handshake and then pulls me in for a hug. "Nice game tonight."

"Thanks, man. How's Lark?" I ask, stepping back so that I'm at Indie's side.

"Good, I saw her earlier. She told me she's looking for another shot at you on Wednesday."

The woman beside me scoffs under her breath, "Playboy." It's a whispered insult, one I don't think she means for me to hear.

"My bingo game is on a hot streak. Tell your grandma not to get her hopes up. It would kill me to break her heart," I say, placing my hand on Indie's back and leading her inside. She shakes it off, stopping and turning to face me in the narrow hallway, making Dean almost barrel into us from behind.

"I'm going to go get us a booth. Want anything to drink?" he asks, stepping around us, which gives me the perfect excuse to step into Indie's space.

"Tequila," Indie answers, her eyes not leaving mine. "His grandma?" she questions when we're alone.

"Not what you were expecting?"

"No . . . not exactly," she says, leaning against the wall, her eyes scanning me like she's looking for the lie.

"Good, there's a lot about me you don't know, but that's only because you're too busy flirting with my friend to distract yourself from what you really want." I move in closer, my forearm flattening against the wall next to her head.

She sucks on her cheek, but it doesn't cover the way the corner of her lip twitches. "And you think you know what I want?"

"Me," I whisper, my lips brushing the shell of her ear.

"Awfully arrogant. What makes you think that?" She presses her shoulder blades into the wall, tilting her chin up and pushing her chest out—fortifying herself.

"The way you're trying so hard to pretend you don't; flirting with my teammate, but only when you're sure I'm watching. Like last night at his penthouse, and again tonight at Draft. Not to mention the heat in your eyes when you're throwing your snarky comebacks at me." Her pupils flare as I step in closer. On every sharp inhale, I can feel her hard nipples graze my chest, but I won't point that out just yet. "Don't worry, I like it when you're mean to me, and I'm not afraid of a challenge."

"I'm not some conquest." Her posture goes rigid.

"No, you're not. You're so much more than that," I tell her, stepping back and sweeping my hand out. She pushes off the wall and glances over her shoulder before she leads me out of the hallway and into the dark club.

PROLOGUE

INDIE

ONE YEAR EARLIER

Tequila. What the hell was I thinking? I wasn't. That's the problem. I was distracted, caught off guard. It can't happen again. My body already wants to say fuck it and jump the cocky baseball player's bones. Right now my brain—my past—are the only things keeping me from doing something monumentally stupid.

That's not fair. I'm sure he's not actually stupid. I chuckle to myself at my little joke.

Dom directs me to the back of the club, where there's a roped-off section with a couch and table for the three of us; a tray of shots, limes, and salt shakers waiting.

Dean's there too, his arm draped over the back of the couch, looking serious when I take the seat beside him. Dom sits on the opposite side, sandwiching me between these two gorgeous men. I don't hate it. Not like I should. Terrible idea, I remind myself.

In need of a distraction, I reach for a shot glass, holding it out for a silent, solo cheer—*to bad decisions*—before tipping it back and swallowing.

"That's one way to do it." Dom's sitting so close that his warm breath makes my neck break out in goosebumps when he snickers at my expense.

He's always laughing, like life is just one big party. "What? Did I not take my shot right?" If this man has the audacity to tell me how to shoot tequila, I will knee him in the balls without an ounce of remorse.

"You can take it however you want. I just prefer mine salty." His hand closes around the shaker.

"Then show me how it's done," I taunt. "But I'm not holding the lime in my teeth for you."

"Do I look like a frat boy?"

"I don't think you want me to answer that," I volley back. He does not look like a frat boy. The word *boy* doesn't belong anywhere near this man. He's masculine, knowing, and right now with the way he's staring down at me, he's exuding so much undeniable sex appeal that it's a wonder I'm not pregnant from just the vibes he's putting off.

"All you need to do is sit still, not punch me, and maybe even enjoy yourself." His eyebrow cocks in question—no, in challenge.

Damn it. I'm so screwed. It's like he's reading right from an instruction manual—one with my face on the cover. Since we've met, he's known *all* the buttons to push. I'm too competitive for my own good, and he figured that out without even trying.

"Can't make any promises." Annoyance slices through me at how breathless it comes out. That was *not* the snarky comeback I was aiming for.

He dips two long fingers into the liquid, his thick thigh pressing into my leg as he leans in close, pushing the strap of my tank top down the slope of my shoulder with his dry hand. "I'm *really* going to enjoy this. It's not too late to back out if you can't handle it."

"Show me what you've got," I say, my stubbornness showing its ass.

Heat from his body wraps around me as he traces my collarbone with his tequila soaked fingers, making me warm and fuzzy before the alcohol has had a chance to take hold. My nipples pebble against my will as he drags the chilled liquor from the base of my neck and out towards my shoulder.

I must be on another planet because when he dips his fingers again and brings them to my lips, I let them part, my tongue darting out to taste it. "You're being so good for me."

The lust-blurred fog I'm in tricks me into abandoning the urge to bite his finger for that last remark. I'm so lost in the sensation of him caressing me that I don't even notice the salt shaker until he's sprinkling some over the sticky line he drew. His tongue darts out and his eyes flash to mine.

"Indie?" My name is a question—a chance to say no.

I don't; the request for consent is my tipping point. My head bobs of its own volition, giving him all the permission he needs.

His palm and fingers span both sides of my neck when he grips the back of it, holding me in place. Soft lips move over my collarbone, sucking, licking, and kissing before he pulls back with a satisfied smile on his face. Blindly reaching for his shot, he takes it, lime forgotten on the tray, and releases me, pushing up from the couch.

I'm still reeling when his rough voice breaks through my lust filled trance. "Dance with me." The playful tone he's used with me since we met gives way to something more gruff, and I find myself swallowing nervously.

If it wasn't for Dean reaching to grab his shot, I'd have completely forgotten he was a witness to the debauchery that I just allowed. "You're really not going to dance?" I'm stalling, trying to preserve my sanity long enough that maybe I'll come out of the hypnosis he has me under.

"No, you two have fun." The knowing smirk he gives me puts him near the top of my shit list; possibly even above his friend.

"Afraid if you dance with me, you might end up falling head-over-heels?" he taunts like the devil with a pretty face, his hand waiting to drag me down to hell with him.

But I bet it'd feel like heaven. I *know* it would.

I ignore it, or I try to, but my palm itches to reach out and take his. After that little stunt with the tequila, it's safe to say that my hormones have taken control. "Not a chance." Every reason I want this man is a stark reminder of the last time I got mixed up with someone like him. Handsome, easygoing, and on top of the world—deceptively wholesome.

"Then I guess you've got nothing to worry about." He waits, his hand still extended between us.

Dammit, this is one of my favorite songs. The beat is sultry, the lyrics a tempting tale about how blissful it feels when you give into your desires. And I *do* love dancing, which is the whole reason we came to this club.

It's not like dancing is a gateway drug to ending up bent over the bathroom sink.

His calloused hand closes over mine when I place it in his palm. Despite the roughness, it's warm and welcoming, putting me at ease. It's the self-assured smirk he gives me as he pulls me to my feet that makes me wish I would've stuck to my guns. Slightly crooked in a seemingly endearing way, it annoys me and sparks the desire to do something incredibly reckless at the same time.

Every brain cell I've got is screaming at me to flee; hyperaware of the situation I'm putting myself in. Consider it instinct. After years of avoiding athletes, or really anyone who reminds me of my ex and the worst time in my life, I can't help it.

My body, on the other hand, is begging me to stay and dance with him. It's dying to feel him pressed against me. I'm a weak bitch. Two full nights of fighting this tether that tugs me to him has worn me down, so I let him lead me to an empty corner of the dance floor.

Dom pulls me close, moving to the music and lining our bodies up perfectly. It feels good—too good. My eyes flutter closed and I focus on how all-encompassing it feels to be held by him.

There's no escaping him when he's this close, the corded muscles of his arms flexing and popping through this thin shirt as his hands find my waist, gripping me tight, like I might run. He's not wrong to hold me that way, because this is all too real with his cut muscles pressed against me giving me a good idea of what he's working with under those clothes.

My hands have no place to go but around his neck or on his chest. Choosing what I think is the safer option, I thread my fingers together behind his head, only to find the hair at his nape is unfairly soft—it's like a magnet for my hands. I can't stop them from exploring; my nails drag over his scalp, eliciting a deep rumble from his chest that cuts all the way through my weakened walls.

Goosebumps climb up my stomach when his fingers brush over my hip bone as we move together, our bodies working as one to the deep bass. "Fuck, Baby, you're killing me."

It's a throwaway term of endearment coming from most people, but the raspy way he says it, the unwavering certainty in his voice as he tugs me closer yet, makes it feel like honey melting against my heated skin. I can't brush it off. It's so damn sweet and I'm greedy to lap it up, getting drunk off the sugar and him.

His pretty words and the hardness of his body pressed up against me are a potent mix. They do nothing to dissuade the desire currently pleading with me to break all my rules about not hooking up with athletes.

I pull away when the song ends, determined to go back to the VIP area where Dean waits and get myself under control.

Or maybe control is the last thing I need. Maybe doing something reckless and stupid is just the thing that will break this spell he has me under.

Dom reaches for me, but I twist away, heading straight for his friend. Looking over my shoulder at him I wiggle my fingers. He says he wants me . . . just how far will he go to get me?

There's nothing he can offer me that his friend can't. The club and the lights are just messing with me, making this thing between us feel like more than just a physical attraction.

Dean looks like a king, his legs spread, one arm draped over the back of the couch, a whiskey tumbler resting on his knees. He's got the sexy, damaged thing going on that most girls are suckers for; a contrast to his best friend, who I can sense is hot on my heels as I cross the club.

The man tracking me is the boy next door . . . if your neighbor's a full-grown man, with a grin that melts panties, perfectly messy hair, and an ass that fills out baseball pants in a way that should be illegal. Everything he wants seems to appear at the snap of his fingers and he's never going to turn it down.

He's everything eighteen-year-old me thought she wanted, until I had it and realized that shiny things still tarnish.

Walking right up to Dean, I step between his legs, grabbing the whiskey dangling from his fingers and bringing it to my lips, draining the glass. Leaning in close, I kiss him hard and fast. And holy shit, the man can kiss. I lose track of everything around me, including the reason I started this in the first place until his hand comes up to my face for a moment before he pulls away and looks at me with skeptical eyes.

The kiss was impulsive, but the question I ask is not. I don't want to be here anymore. After dancing, I'm feeling overwhelmed, overheated, and overdressed. This will almost definitely blow up in my face, but damn, it would be a fun way to go. "It's crowded here. Why don't you two take me somewhere a little more . . . private?"

Carefree, flirtatious Dom is long gone, replaced by a possessive man whose grip on my hip sends a full-body shudder skating down my spine. My skin flushes hot when a growl vibrates along my neck from the man hovering behind me. "What the hell are you doing?" His tone makes my pulse jump and with how close he is, I'm sure he doesn't miss it.

"Having fun. Seems like it would be right up your alley, playboy. You want me? This is how you get me." Miraculously, I keep my voice steady even though I feel anything but. Bending so I'm floating precariously between the two of them, I find his friend's green eyes filled with uncertain curiosity. "What do you say, Dean, want to play? We could have so much fun."

"I don't think I'm the one you really want," Dean says, looking over my shoulder.

Teeth scrape across my pulse point. "Game's over. Let's go, Firecracker."

Dom's lips seal over the stinging skin, making my back arch involuntarily. "And what if I'm not done playing?"

"Then you can play with me," he says, turning me around in his arms. His fingers thread into my hair. "And only me." That playful boy-next-door is nowhere to be found right now. Those caramel eyes are stormy with desire that has me pushing up on my toes and doing the one thing I swore I wouldn't do with him: give in to the whirlwind of feelings he brings out in me.

Hope, lightness, longing for something easy.

Soft lips welcome mine. The man kisses like it's his favorite pastime, and damn it, I can't even be mad about it because it's *that* perfect.

It sparks a fire deep down that has nothing to do with the music or how he moves. It's all him. *All us*. And when he teases the seam of my lips and I open for him, it only gets better.

Our lips are still fused as he walks us backward. My feet tangle, but his hold on me is sure. He doesn't let it stop him from putting space between me and his friend, sending both of us a clear message.

Mine.

Slowing the kiss until I'm the one leaning in chasing more, he pulls away and rests his forehead against mine. "Ready to go?"

"Yes." It feels like more than just three simple letters and I can't put my finger on why.

It's only a few steps from the dark club to the waiting car, but the cool night air has chills racing over my skin, still sticky from sweat and tequila. Dom leads us to our ride and I follow, my legs wobbling from that kiss.

Like the gentleman I imagine he was raised to be, Dean opens the door, letting us in first. This car is larger than the one that brought us here and is set up like a limo, but is the size of a normal SUV. It's clearly not an Uber.

Dom takes a seat in the back, settling me in his lap, his palms splayed across my thighs, keeping me right where he wants me. Dean joins us, moving towards the front and speaking to the driver before turning back toward us.

"You wanted to play a game? Give him a show he'll never forget," Dom says, his voice strained with desire.

Stunned at what he's asking, I let him twist me in his lap, pinning my knees on either side of his legs. Immediately, I feel him grow hard, jutting up towards his stomach. Even with the layers between us, there's no mistaking how perfectly long and thick he is.

"What's wrong? Don't want to play anymore?" There's a dare in his eyes as he waits for me to make a move.

I shouldn't, but knowing Dean can see exactly what Dom's doing to me only heightens my need to be reckless with him. Matching Dom's taunt I look over my shoulder at his friend and rock my hips.

Once.

Twice.

And the third time, a whimper escapes me. I'm too turned on to stop now that I've started.

Pain bites into the swell of my hips where Dom's grip tightens and my skirt rides dangerously high, but neither of those things matter with how fast he has me climbing.

A pained groan behind me has my eyes straying before my head snaps forward, Dom's fingers pinching my chin.

"Eyes on me," Dom practically growls at me. "He can watch you, but you better be looking at me when you come, or this stops." He rolls his hard cock over my clit until I'm panting in his ear.

"Please," I whine when he stills underneath me.

"Tell me you're mine, and I'll let you make a mess all over me."

Delirious with the need for release, I say the one thing I shouldn't: "I'm yours."

CHAPTER 1

DOM

As the oldest child, a professional athlete, and all around pretty awesome guy, I'm not surprised to find my mom looking at me like the sun shines out of my ass. The Bandits just lost to the New York Metros in extra innings, but you would never know it by the way her eyes well with emotion as she looks up at me.

"No matter how many times I watch you play under the lights, it's still surreal," she gushes.

"For crying out loud, Kelly, he doesn't need you to pump him up. His ego is already the size of Texas." My dad's laughter booms through the concrete corridor outside the locker room as he approaches with my younger sisters. Even when he's teasing her, you can tell she's the love of his life. He stops behind her, wraps his arms around her waist, kisses her neck, pulling a pleased sigh from my mom as she relaxes back into his embrace.

"Can you not?" My youngest sister, Dottie, groans when he kisses her neck.

It's always been like this—the two of them being handsy and loving on each other. My childhood friends always questioned how I dealt with it, and teased me endlessly; especially when my mom showed up at my high school ready to pop with Dottie.

Trauma from that period of my life runs deep. I'm still haunted by the memory of one of my teammates walking up to my dad after a game and giving him a high five for giving her the "good baby gravy."

"Dottie, girl, my advice to you is to get used to this, and be thankful. You're here because they are gross," Daelyn says.

"Just think, I've been dealing with it for twenty-seven years. That's eight years longer than you." I level my middle sister with a look and then turn to Dottie. "And eighteen longer than you."

"Ew, you're so old."

"Daelyn," Mom scolds. "If he's old, what does that make me?"

"Oh, Mom." I cringe at the same time Daelyn laughs darkly.

"Ancient, Mom. That makes you ancient," my middle sister says with zero remorse.

"Don't talk to your mom like that. She's the most stunning mummy on the planet. Look at her all wrapped up." He wiggles the arms that are still around her to emphasize his terrible dad joke.

Beside me, Dottie just hangs her head, not impressed by our old man at all.

"Please get me out of here, before that new rookie comes out. I'll die of embarrassment, Dom." Daelyn tugs on my arm, leading me away from the locker room and towards the parking lot. I wasn't in a hurry, but fuck if we are staying here where she'll run into my teammates. She's only nineteen, way too fucking young for any of them.

Especially Braxton Hayes. His brother may have had a great reputation while he was here, but Braxton is the league's bad boy; just traded from Minnesota for his off-the-field shenanigans. And that means something coming from me.

That's not the kind of trouble she needs in her life.

"Yeah, let's go back to the house and we can order some pizza."

"You're not going out?" my dad asks, sounding way too eager to be rid of me.

"No, why would I go out when you guys are here?"

Daelyn's foot stomps next to me. "I was hoping you'd take me to Draft with you."

"You're not twenty-one yet, Dae." If she were a cartoon, there would be steam coming out of her ears. "We are all going back to the house, or stopping to grab pizza together. No one is going to Draft, and I'm certainly not going alone."

"That's settled then; pizza and back to the house to get this one to bed," my dad says, patting Dottie's head.

Her mouth opens in a wide yawn as she protests, "I'm almost ten. I can stay up now."

"Sure you can, sweetie," Mom assures her, wrapping her arm around my sister's shoulder. In front of her, Dae trudges through the parking lot towards my truck like a night in with her family is a death sentence.

"You know, you don't have to change your routine just because we're in town. If you want to go out with the guys, we can take the girls back."

"Are you trying to get rid of me for a reason?" I bite back, feeling a little hurt over his insistence.

"Not at all, I'm happy to spend time with you. And it means the world to your mom and sisters. But we have all day tomorrow too. If you have a date or something—"

Turning to face my dad I unlock the car so the girls can get in. "No date tonight." I grip the back of my neck. "Actually, I've been laying off the . . . um—"

"Dating?" my dad supplies, his eyebrow arching in amusement.

"Actually, I've been doing more dating, and less of the other stuff." My dad just stands there, his lip tipped up in a crooked smile as I fumble my way through this. "I want what you and mom have."

"And you just realized that you won't find that by fucking around?"

"Jesus, Dad," I choke out.

"I'm not stupid, son. I know what you've been up to these last few years. Is someone specific making you slow down your whore ways?"

"Oh my god, you did not just say that. Nowadays, we don't use that word as a put-down old man."

"That's weird. Your mom—"

"Finish that sentence and I swear I will barf all over your shoes. I'm going to have to bleach my fucking ears tonight as it is."

"So who is she?" my dad asks through laughter as I fight off a shudder.

Untamed curls, paired with dark eyes that seem to see right through me, and a soul she pretends is blacker than the coffee I know she drinks flash through my mind, stealing my attention like she so often does. From the start, I got a thrill out of the way Indie sparred with me, tossing around insults like they were candy at a parade. All our banter was just verbal foreplay leading up to the night that made me want more.

Between fucking and talking that night, we couldn't have slept more than a few hours. When the sun came up, she made a pot of the strongest, most disgusting coffee—seriously, that shit could have been used to neutralize nuclear warheads—and she drank it without even cringing. Then she disappeared from my house like I was the worst decision she's ever made, telling me, in no uncertain terms, that it was a one-time thing.

Indie Moreno is a liar. She's lying to me and she's lying to herself. What we had was more than just one night of mind-boggling sex. What we had wasn't just an itch you can scratch and walk away from. It could have been *everything*, if she would have just let it.

"It doesn't matter, she's not interested in me and she lives in Chicago." I'm temporarily resigned to that answer, unable to do anything. She asked me to let her go and I'm trying.

Since she walked away that morning, the appeal of hooking up has lost its luster, and it's really fucking annoying because I was good at fun. The best, actually.

Besides keeping things strictly platonic the last year, she lives halfway across the country. Instead of waiting around, I've been dipping my toe into dating. So far it's been underwhelming.

Everyone either wants to date me for clout or there has been no chemistry.

"There is this girl I met volunteering at Sunny Acres and I'm thinking about bringing her to Dean and Mia's house warming party next week. But I'm just not sure if it will lead to anything." It won't, but she's nice, and her interest in me is genuine, so I owe it to myself to at least try. *Right?*

"Still hung up on the one that got away? You know, being in a committed relationship isn't as easy as your mom and I make it look. It takes work."

"I'm not afraid of hard work." I've done the work once before; it didn't pay off. And since then I've made an effort to focus on baseball. "Have you forgotten what an excellent boyfriend I can be? Just ask Hazel. I was a textbook boyfriend, even from across the country when we were in college."

"Sure, next time I see her around town, I'll ask. I'm sure her husband would love that."

"Fucking Bryce," I grumble. My high school friend, the same one that congratulated my dad on getting my mom pregnant, married my high school sweetheart. They're both happy as can be, and in the end it worked out for the best, but fuck if it didn't sting for a while.

"Fucking Bryce," my dad agrees. "My point was that if you can't get this girl out of your head, maybe it's worth the work."

"I've watched you and Mom work through the hard stuff." And there's been struggles. IVF to get pregnant with Dottie. My dad losing his job right after Dae was born. Raising three kids. They always come out on the other end stronger. "I'm not afraid of the effort and commitment. A love like you and Mom have is worth it."

"Don't forget that if whoever *she* is gives you a chance," my dad says, patting me on the back before he rounds the car to slide into the passenger seat.

Following his lead, I drop my duffle bag in the back and then take my spot in the driver's seat. When I turn over the ignition, the radio blasts 2 Live Crew at decibels unsafe for anyone's ears, but especially my sisters'. Grappling for the dial, I crank it all the way down before turning to the back to find three sets of annoyed eyes on me.

"Sorry," I offer with a shrug, pulling out of the lot and heading towards my favorite pizza place.

DoughThugs and Harmony has the best garbage pizza in Denver, and dueling pianists that specialize in instrumentals of top nineties hits. But today is the thirteenth of the month, which means it's Swiftie night, and I plan to give Dottie full access to my wallet to request as many songs as her heart desires. Only for her, of course. No one else.

Putting Indie out of my mind, I focus on something I can control: spending time with my family and making my sister smile.

CHAPTER 2

INDIE

Jay Christopher should thank the god of whatever underworld he crawled out of that there's a conference room table between us.

The logistics of crawling across it in my skirt and heels are the only thing holding me back from strangling him.

When I was awarded this project, the previous chief human resources officer had told me it was the key to my promotion. Instead, my boss has taken a day that I've been looking forward to for the last year and ruined it.

This afternoon, I went in front of the board to talk about the early success we've seen since implementing the new succession planning model I developed for the company earlier this spring.

"Indie, you can't expect that someone with your attitude would be selected for a promotion. We need team players. Sure, your work is top-notch, but you're snarky, closed-off, and don't trust people to work alongside you."

"I don't trust *you*, JC," I hiss, my professional composure fucking off, just like I wish this asshat in front of me would. If I'm being honest, I've questioned my resolve to stay here every day since the retirement of my mentor, the woman who gave me the opportunity we are currently discussing. "But why would I when you've been peddling my work as yours for the last three years? If I was a man, we wouldn't be having this conversation. You'd pat me on the back while laughing at my *sarcasm*."

"We've talked about this before, Indie. And yet, I've never once seen you at happy hour, getting to know your colleagues outside of the office. You need to build rapport with them, make them *like* you."

First, *ouch*. Second, I think the fuck not. "I do that every single day with the ten plus hours I spend here. What they *need* is to see me doing my job; to trust that I know what I'm talking about. Not insight into my drink order at Willy's."

JC checks his watch for the dozenth time since we sat down. "Sorry, Indie, a promotion is not in the cards for you. Leadership is taking things in a new direction since Maggie's retirement."

Meaning the promotion I've been promised for the last three years is going to someone else. I've done everything he's asked, except the happy hour thing, because that's just plain stupid. I already give every ounce of myself while I'm here, and now they want my evenings too.

The slimy smirk that tilts up his lips makes my stomach lurch. Pushing back I rise, palms flat on the table, leaning over it so he can see the fire in my eyes. "Good luck taking credit for my work when I'm not there to explain the data and logic behind it." I smile and give him my pièce de résistance—flipping him off over my shoulder and walking out of this godforsaken conference room, heels clacking angrily until I drop into an empty bench outside the downtown Chicago office.

Holy fuck, I just quit my job. Walked out, with no notice, and burned my career to the ground. Swiping the hot angry tears from my eyes I order an Uber. No way in hell am I riding the L home in heels after today.

The anger coursing through my body has me on edge the entire ride, and when I finally get home, I know there's only one thing that will help.

The polished black skirt and off-white blouse I painstakingly picked this morning are crumpled in a pile on the bedroom floor, and are quickly replaced by a pair of bike shorts and a long sleeve shirt.

I can feel the rage and agitation crawling under my skin like hot snakes, ready to sear my skin from my bones if I let it.

On the way out the door, I snag a water bottle and a few other pieces of gear. With an unexpected afternoon off—or, more accurately, the foreseeable future off—I hoist my bike over my shoulder and maneuver it out of the building.

It takes some finagling, especially with the slight tremble of my hand, but after wrestling with my bike for a minute, I get it in the back of my small SUV. And as I pull out of the parking ramp and let the city fade away in my rear-view mirror, I can feel that uncomfortable fluttering in my chest easing.

Heading southwest, I crank the music for my forty-minute drive, letting it drown out the angry pulse still pounding behind my ears at the unfairness of it all. No, not unfairness; this was a choice, maybe not a super calculated one, but I was in control.

True unfairness is being diagnosed with cancer at forty. Or not having control over being sick as hell from the treatments. And then fighting with everything in you to overcome it, only for it to come back. Unfairness is having your life cut short and being taken from your family, from your daughter, when she needs you.

What JC did was bullshit, which is why I don't regret my decision, fair or not.

Quitting my job with no plan won't be the hardest thing I've overcome in my thirty years.

Besides, just because I don't know what comes next doesn't mean I won't figure it out. That's one reason my bike is shoved into the back of the car.

I think better out here, away from the city, with the trees flying by as I ride until my legs want to give out and I can feel every beat of my heart inside my chest.

Although, coming out here alone—knowing that I'll ride until dusk or beyond—is probably not the smartest thing I've ever done. I should text Brianna and let her know where I am. She's working tonight anyway, so she can't give me too much hell.

Not like my friends would.

She'll just want to know if I'm okay.

We've only been dating for two months and it's not serious, but she's unlike anyone I've dated. She actually cares, probably more than she should. Still, texting her is my best bet—safety and all that.

Poppy, my childhood best friend, gets my need to be a little reckless from time to time. But she would just tell me it's another reason I should be closer to her in Denver—that she would be here right alongside me.

Mia would scold me before offering to write JC into one of her books as an act of vengeance. But she wasn't there like Poppy was when my mom was sick. So I've sheltered her from this part of me, afraid that it'll scare her away.

Although, without Mia, I wouldn't have Brianna to text. Mia was in town for an event a few months ago when her own relationship was falling apart, and Brianna was a waitress at the Indian restaurant we went to. My observant friend caught me watching the redhead waiting tables and encouraged me to get her number.

For the first time since I hooked up with Dom, I felt a pull to someone new. One-night stands have never been a hang-up for me before, but I couldn't shake this one.

A week after seeing Brianna, I found myself back in the same place picking up an order of Murgh Tikka Masala. She happened to be working and saw me first, snagging my order from the hostess and bringing it over herself, along with her number. Unfortunately, our schedules make it hard to see each other as often as we'd like. Between waitressing and grad school, she might be busier than me.

Now that I'm unemployed, she definitely is. My hands twist on the wheel as I turn the car into the Palo Forest Preserve. Fresh air fills my lungs, and the events of this morning fade to nothing more than background noise as I unload my bike and strap on my helmet.

Before I start down the trail, I shoot off the text I've been procrastinating sending to Brianna, who I've decided is least likely to yell at me or judge me.

ME:

Pin sent: Palo Forest Preserve - North

ME:

My afternoon freed up unexpectedly.
Out riding. Call me after your shift?

BRIANNA:

Have fun! How'd the presentation go?

ME:

I'll fill you in later.

BRIANNA:

Is everything okay?

ME:

It will be. I just needed to get out of the city.

BRIANNA:

Who are you riding with?

I know she means well, but each response has my nerves ratcheting back up. My whole body is buzzing with the discomfort I had shed by simply being out here. I want to lie; tell her I'm with one of the guys from the crew I sometimes bike with. Her worry will only make this awful feeling of disappointment that I'm trying to get rid of worse. But she's too sweet to lie to, so I stick with the truth.

ME:

I'm solo. It was a last-minute decision.

BRIANNA:

Tell me you at least have your watch.

I look down at my bare wrist. *Shit.*

Several weeks ago, when I was in the heat of preparing for today's meeting, I took off after a particularly long workday for a solo hike. My phone had died, and I came home to find Brianna waiting for me by my door, wrecked with worry. After a hug that stretched on, she marched me inside and made me set up the emergency feature that would call my dad if I were to fall or crash my bike.

ME:

I didn't wear it today because of the meeting and I forgot to grab it on my way out.

BRIANNA:

I don't like this. Text me when you're done.

ME:

I'll be fine. Please don't worry about me during your shift.

BRIANNA:

Not possible. Stay safe, babe.

ME:

I will. Talk tonight.

With my feet on my pedals and my tires in the dirt, I feel grounded in a way that can't be replicated. Nothing else makes me feel this alive. Expect maybe really great sex. The pulsing, pounding feeling deep in my soul that reminds me I've survived everything life has thrown at me.

The future may be uncertain right now, but being out here feels right, and I want more of this. Less city, less corporate bullshit, less work that doesn't matter. More adventure, more meaning. Wherever I land will be *my* choice, not something I do because it's what I'm supposed to do. I'm done doing what's expected.

Dusk creeps in around me and my legs burn as I pedal the last few miles of the sixteen mile loop. Pushing harder, my light illuminates the narrow trail in front of me. It's been almost an hour since I've seen another rider and I know I'll find the parking lot empty when I get back to my car.

For most people, it would probably be nerve-wracking, but for the first time today, my mind is clear, and pieces of my plan coming together with each heart pounding climb. The picture of what's next crystallizes with every quick and twisty downhill section filled with berms and jumps. My fear over the unknown of it all left behind like the ground under my tires as I launch my bike over the small tabletop. I do everything right, sending my bike sailing through the air over the flat mound of dirt until I land on the other side.

This is what it feels like to be alive.

CHAPTER 3

INDIE

When I get back to the parking lot a little later, my car is the only one remaining, as I expected. The silence of the forest is a reminder that I'll be back in the chaos of the city soon, and I hate it, which is why I need to talk to Brianna, tell her about what I'm going to do. She's not going to like it . . . I just hope she understands.

After loading my bike, I connect my phone to the car and text Brianna asking if I can come over. All the peace that I found on the trail starts to fade as the city gets closer.

Chicago has been my home since I moved to the city from my rural Illinois hometown for college. After graduating with my master's, I took a job using my Human Resources degree that promised growth and development opportunities. One that would set me on a path to climb the corporate ladder, and would allow me to be self-sufficient. It was practical, with good insurance, but the work hasn't been fulfilling for years.

All I want now is to do something that would make my mom proud, and allow me to have more of the things that soothe me at my fingertips: my friends, the mountains, the wilderness.

Pulling into the lot near Brianna's apartment, I lock the car and cross the street to her building. Buzzing her apartment, I bounce on the balls of my feet. Not just because of my still-damp clothes from riding, or the temperature dropping with the sun going down, but from the nervous energy running through me, fueled by knowing the conversation I need to have is likely going to hurt both of us.

I like Brianna, she's smart and thoughtful, and easily the best person I've ever dated. She's gorgeous and there's chemistry between us—enough that neither of us are left wanting, but not the kind that burns the house down around you.

Like I had with him. Every time I let my mind wander to that kind of explosive chemistry, one person comes to mind. It was a slip; one night when I gave into our connection and let myself just fucking feel—something I never allow; not outside of physically exhausting my mind and body. Although, now that I think about it, that's exactly what he did, *several times*.

But I can't think about him right now. Not when the door clicks open to Brianna's apartment building. My hands twist together as the elevator carries me up to the third floor. Things are good and I'm about to throw a major wrench in them.

Brianna's dark red hair is piled on top of her head and her face is scrubbed free of makeup as she waits by her apartment door for me. Fucking stunning. How I got so lucky to spend the last few months with someone like her is beyond me.

"You're in so much trouble." She eyes my mud-splattered legs before her gaze moves up, roaming over my body, checking for damage and pausing when she sees the dried blood starting on my elbow and running down my arm. "What the hell, Ind?"

Her soft hands wrap around my wrist, gently turning my arm over in her hands, a frown tugging down those puffy lips. When she takes care of me like this it's easy to forget that I'm supposed to be the one that has it together. I'm six years older, and out of school. But as I stand bloodied and broken on her doorstep, I just feel like a failure. Recently unemployed and careless, making my sweet girlfriend worry.

"It's fine, I just grazed a tree, I'll tuck my elbow next time. Promise." I smile, hiding the wince when the pad of her thumb brushes over a tender spot that is certain to bruise by morning.

"This is not fine! You come back to me hurt after taking off by yourself. It was dangerous."

My lips roll together. She's not telling me anything I don't already know. This is who I am; who I morph into when life gets hard. This crutch has gotten me through cancer treatments with my mom, shitty exes, grad school, and grief. It's been like this for so long I don't know how to be normal anymore.

Her hand comes to my face cupping it. "Shit, babe. What happened today?"

I can't help it. Even knowing I'm about to dismantle us, I let her pull me in, melting as soon as her arms wrap around me. "Can we go inside and talk?" Closing my eyes, I press my face into the crook of her neck, trying to memorize how good it feels to be held like this.

"Of course, but before we talk, you're going to let me clean up this arm," Brianna says, twining her fingers through mine and leading me into her apartment.

I wait on the couch while she grabs the first aid kit from the bathroom. Looking around the apartment, my eyes settle on the picture frame on her coffee table. A familiar pain lances through my heart. Her mom is kissing her cheek, and there's bright smiles on both of their faces at Bri's college graduation—something my mom never got to see. By then she had lost her battle and it was just Poppy and Dad at my graduation, both of them doing everything they could to get even a hint of a smile out of me. As soon as they left after dinner that night, I went for a run; ten miles on the lakeshore trail, alone, tears streaming down my face the entire time.

Brianna comes back into the room and I pull my eyes from the photo, forcing a smile until it feels right. At least that part has gotten easier. I've learned how to mask my pain, hiding it so it doesn't make other people uncomfortable—or worse—worry about me.

The minty notes of her shampoo engulf me as she leans in close, cleaning my arm before she spreads a cool salve over it and covers it up with a large band-aid. Her tenderness with me only makes this harder.

"Feel better?" I take her hand in mine and bring it to my lap.

"Not really." Her laughter rattles around uncomfortably between us. "But that's probably not going to change until you tell me what's going on with you. What happened today that had you running wild?"

"I quit my job," I say aloud for the first time. The words don't shock me like I expect, and to Brianna's credit, she doesn't flinch. "Everything went perfect during the presentation, but afterward JC and I met to go over everything and he let me know I wasn't getting the promotion as promised."

"I hate that guy," Brianna seethes, scooting closer and gripping my face with both hands. "You earned that promotion. When you practiced with me last week, your delivery was flawless. Every single question I threw at you was answered with insight into the data and benchmarking."

"I know. Really, I do. That's why I quit on the spot, without a plan." This time it's me laughing, only instead of sounding nervous, I sound manic.

"That's okay. We can figure it out together."

Fuck. This next part is what I've been dreading, but I'm confident in my decision. There's just one thing I'm questioning: what happens with us.

"I sort of have a plan already," I start, turning towards her and facing this head on. "That's why I ran to the trails. To think."

"And what did you come up with?" she asks, nibbling the corner of her lip. Reaching out, I pull it free, dragging a sigh out of her as well. "Just tell me. Don't make me suffer."

"I'm moving to Denver. Things here feel stagnant. I've been in the same apartment since college and work so much that the only time I spend my hard-earned money is traveling. I want—no, I *need* to get out of this city. There's too much painful history. And this job was the thing that kept me here."

She winces, but I can't bring myself to apologize. It's the truth. I like Brianna, but we aren't in love.

"I've been chasing this promotion for years like it was the one thing that could make me happy, but it's not. Nothing about that job—the corporate world—has ever made me truly happy. Was it challenging? Yes. But that's it."

"What about me? Don't I make you happy?" The way she asks isn't desperate or clingy. Brianna is analytical, she needs all the facts. This is her gathering information, so she knows what she's dealing with.

"You do." I hedge.

"Just not happy enough to stay for."

"Would you stay for me?" I ask, even though I know her answer.

"No," she says softly.

"And I wouldn't want you to. If losing my mom taught me anything, it's that nothing in this life is guaranteed. Life doesn't care about the accolades you receive at work, or the money you have in the bank. It's cruel, and I want to counteract that."

"And you're going to do that by moving to Denver?"

"I'm moving to Denver for me, but my support system is there. Once I've settled in, I want to freelance for nonprofits. Starting over won't be easy, but it will be less daunting than staying here. Knowing they all have my back will let me focus on building something new, taking what I learned in the corporate world and creating volunteer programs, maximizing their human capital, whatever they need."

"You'll be great at that, but at the risk of sounding selfish, where does that leave us?"

"I don't know." I sigh.

"When are you leaving?" she asks.

"Maybe a few weeks. I have a few things I need to get in order before I can just pack up."

"Let's take things one day at a time. I'll be honest, long-distance this early in our relationship sounds daunting, but I'm not ready to just call it quits."

"That doesn't seem fair to you—"

"Don't pacify me. I know what I'm getting into. All I'm asking is that we are open and honest with each other. If at any point it's not working for either of us, we let the other know."

"That sounds practical."

"You know me. I'm nothing if not logical. Romantic, isn't it?"

"Well, no one's ever taken care of me quite the way you do. That's pretty romantic." Since my mom died and Poppy moved to Denver, I've been mostly on my own. But even though my dad and I still talk more days than not, and I drive home at least once a month to see him, it's not the same.

Taking my hand, Brianna pulls me up from the couch, leading me through the small apartment to her bedroom. With no job to rush to in the morning, there's no reason I can't stay the night.

Everything else can wait until tomorrow.

CHAPTER 4

DOM

Our season started hot with a nine game winning streak, but a roster shake up right before the All-Star Break threw our game off a little. Now we are trying to salvage our season with three new rookie teammates: Braxton Hayes, Montana Jones, and Dash Thomas.

Going into this away series in Chicago, we are on a seven game losing streak. I think everyone is a little uneasy about what the front office plans to do with the new acquisitions. And while I'm fairly certain our leadership is being proactive about some of our veterans nearing retirement, not everyone is adjusting as well.

But right now, it's not the recent additions to the team, the losing streak, or the fact that all the guys brought their girls along for the trip that is causing a distraction. It's the bomb Dean just dropped that has me acting like a headcase when I should be focused on getting ready to take the field.

Not a single one of my friends—if we can even call them that—saw fit to tell me that the reason their girls tagged along on this away-series was so they could help Indie pack because she's moving. *Moving.*

She was the one-night stand that blew my fucking mind, and not a single one of those pricks thought I'd want to know. What stings worse is that *she* didn't even tell me when I saw her just last month in Telluride.

Granted, she kept her distance the entire trip, like she has since the one and only time she let her guard down for me. And what a stunning sight that was, to see her the way she's intended to be: wild; but soft and vulnerable as she let me give her body what it craved. *Me.*

Dean stands in front of me, tugging on his neck. "Kid, you gotta chill. Your face is turning red."

"I don't care how Boston you are. Do not *'kid'* me right now. How many times have I called her my future wife to your face, and you didn't think I might want to be clued into the fact that she's moving?"

"At the risk of losing my balls, you also asked if I thought you should propose to Vivi because you liked how mean she was." Fuck, I hate he has a point. I said that when the director of Double Play, a charity that we all work with, read Xavier the riot act earlier this year. But I only said it because I was still going through withdrawals from Indie, and Vivi is almost as scary.

Not a single one of the guys understands how Indie turned me inside out. Mainly because she would literally do just that—make my entrails, extrails—if she thought they *all* knew about us.

"But you were there. You saw how we were together. Fuck, man," I remind him, letting my head fall against the bench in the locker room. I'm laid out across it like it's a couch because what the hell else am I supposed to do?

I've spent a year floundering, trying to date, but everything pales in comparison to the memories of that night. It haunts me. Starting with how she tried to make me jealous by kissing Dean. I've never shared a girl before, but I would have that night. If that was the only way she would have let me have her, I would have done whatever she asked. The way she squirmed on my lap as I made it crystal clear to Dean, the driver, and her that she was mine and only mine, is burned into my soul. And how, when we got back to my house, I showed her all the other ways I could make her shatter. All she had to do was just give us a chance, but it wasn't enough to overcome her fears.

The revelation that she's moving to god knows where is pushing me over the edge. I can't even think about the game I'm about to play.

"Please don't remind me." He cringes looking down at me from where he leans against his locker.

"You didn't seem to mind. In fact, I remember you being an active participant." I watch as his features twist.

"That was before," he says, exasperated with me and the conversation.

"Before you went and fell in love. And you'd begrudge me the same opportunity." Instinctively, my hands go to the firework print headband my friend, Lark, made for me. Not only is she the namesake for Topher's club, but she's also a regular at Wednesday night bingo, an ace with a sewing machine, and a way better compadre than Dean at the moment.

"No one is begrudging you anything—well, except, maybe her. She's moving and the girls are staying to help her pack up because she's dealing with some shit. What else is there to say?"

So much. Like where the hell is she going and what is she dealing with? There's a lot to unpack here. "Exactly. Don't you think I should know that?"

"Are you two even friends? You brought someone else to the housewarming party and the two of you have basically avoided each other since you hooked up. I thought you'd moved on from this."

And that's the crux of it. I've played it off like there's nothing better than playing the field. But Dean is my best friend; he knows better. Hell, he saw firsthand how unhinged this girl made me. "Moved on . . . I can't even with you. It was a few dates, and you don't just *move on* from a woman like Indie. Can you just fill me in? Where is she moving, and when?"

His face scrunches up like he can't tell if I'm being serious. For fuck's sakes, I'm laying in the middle of the locker room like it's a therapist's office. Except, my therapist sucks, because he's not giving me the information I want to hear, and I've got nuts and butts swinging in my face. *So unprofessional.*

"She's moving to Denver next week. You really didn't know this?" That has me sitting up so fast my head spins. Feet planted on the floor, I push up from the bench.

"No!" I throw my hands in the air, pacing like a maniac. And honestly, I might be one.

"Shit, maybe we're all a little too wrapped up in our own lives lately," my friend says, scratching his jaw.

"Thank you! Finally, we're getting somewhere."

I'm not trying to be needy, because these guys have had a lot going on. Between time with their girls, celebrations, and training, we haven't had much time just us guys. Probably another reason, now more than ever, I want what they have, someone to come home to.

Coach Wilson's voice echoes through the locker room. "Five minutes and I want everyone out there warming up. Our piss-poor play ends today."

Around us, the rest of the guys shut their lockers and get ready to head out. Cruz and Hendrix pass us as they make their way from the lounge area to the dugout. "You heard Coach Wilson, let's go, boys. It's our turn now," Cruz says, clapping me on the back.

"You good?" Hendrix asks, coming up beside our captain. "It feels like we interrupted something."

"I'm fine," I grumble, grabbing my hat from my locker and pulling it down on my head. "Will she be here tonight?"

Cruz and Hendrix look at each other eyebrows drawn together. "Indie?" Hendrix finally asks.

I nod in response.

"Yeah, she's out there with the girls right now." Cruz nods towards the tunnel.

"That's all I needed to hear. Let's do this fucking thing." I throw my arm around Dean's neck and pull him towards the field; ready to show her exactly what she's missing.

CHAPTER 5

INDIE

In the week since I quit my job in dramatic fashion, I've gone through the entire spectrum of emotions. There have been panicked moments where I questioned if I was really going to give up the stability of the corporate world. Guilty ones, such as when I told my dad. I mean, he paid for those fancy degrees—which are now packed up in the box the courier delivered—after all. And there's been nervous excitement about doing work that makes a meaningful impact.

In the chaos of the Comet's stadium, surrounded by the people who have supported me, I can't help but feel deep gratitude for each of them. Including Brianna, who's stuck by my side, regardless of the fact that I'm leaving. Walking away would've been the easier choice, especially considering we haven't been together long. But even now, with her hand on my knee, she's talking to Poppy, attempting to get to know my friends.

Introducing the two of them might be my only regret because they are currently exchanging stories about me. Some of which I'd rather not remember. Others, like the one they are in hysterics over now, warm my icy heart.

Poppy recounts the time I got suspended for shaving off Caleb Cummings's eyebrows because he told her she had a stick up her ass—just like her mom—when she wouldn't suck his dick on the back of the bus during a ski club trip.

Fall asleep on the bus after a stunt like that and you only have yourself to blame.

He was right about one thing: Beverly's an uptight bitch, and that's not even the worst thing about her. She's also a horrible excuse for a mother, which is why Poppy spent more nights sleeping at my house during the summer than her own.

Giving it my best effort to distract my girlfriend from all the ammo Poppy has on me, I lean forward in my seat, turning my body towards her. I don't miss the way her eyes drop to where my tits are pressed together.

"Game's about to start. Maybe we can take a break from story time for a few minutes," I say, running my finger up her arm.

"Sorry, Bri. I'm with Indie on this one. I don't want to miss Hendrix running out onto the field in those new pants they got this season," Poppy says on the other side of me.

"Ugh, I can't even fight you on that. The boys might hate the pants, but I have zero complaints." Mia lets out a long sigh, her eyes glued to the field.

"For real, it's like they used the crotch cover from the OB/GYN to make these uniforms," Delilah adds.

"Does that bother you?" I ask, trying to imagine how I'd feel if thousands of people were ogling Bri in front of me.

"People can look all they want, but they're coming home with us," Mia says with a lift of her shoulders.

The guys jog out onto the field, stopping all the chatter as Lilah whistles loudly at Cruz and Poppy and Mia stand to cheer. But when number four takes his spot in the outfield, it's no longer the woman beside me I'm picturing in see-through pants, it's the man with the cocky smile and pretty hair.

Distance and time don't seem to matter. As soon as those bright chestnut eyes find me, my stomach flips and I'm back in his bed with him.

"Is that him?" Brianna bumps my shoulder, jutting her chin to Dom, who's now staring at us like we kicked his puppy. His eyes are glued to where Brianna's hand is touching my leg. "Oh, he doesn't like this. *At all.* You really didn't do him justice when you described him. He's not a snack, he's the whole damn pantry."

"Meh." I do my best to sound indifferent, but seeing him out there on the field . . . it's always done something to me. Which is why I ended up in his bed, against my better judgment, in the first place.

And his lap. And his shower. And pressed against his bedroom window.

He doesn't move, he just stands there, frozen, while his team warms up.

All around me, the girls lose it when Hendrix runs up behind him and whacks him on the back of the head with his glove. It snaps Dom out of it and he readjusts his hat over the patterned teal headband he's wearing under it.

"He's not that good looking. It's the baseball pants . . . They do things to your brain. It's a proven fact, backed by research," I argue back.

"Seriously, did they put magic spandex in them? Why does Cruz's ass look so round?" Lilah's hand ghosts over her neck, her cheeks turning pink when we all turn to look at her.

"It's not the pants. Dean has them all doing this glute workout to help build their power." Mia bites her lip, her eyes never leaving first base where number forty-five is stretching. "It's really something," she adds on a shaky breath.

Whether it's the pants, or the lunges, or having the support of their women in the stands, the Bandits start off strong and keep the momentum going. By the seventh inning, they're up on the Comets six to two. Annoyingly, Dom is leading the charge. Maybe I'm imagining things, but I swear I can feel his eyes burning into me when he steps up to the plate to bat.

Brianna either hasn't noticed or is unbothered by it, but I wish he'd stop. I had a lapse in judgment that will never happen again. Which he clearly needs to be reminded of based on the wink he gave me over his shoulder when he took the field in the last inning.

Guys like him are a dime a dozen. Cocky and self-assured; floating through life. The fact that he's so blatant about his *feelings* for me—which don't extend beyond our compatibility in the bedroom—is one reason he'll never be more than a memory of one incredible night. No matter how much of that undeniable charm he lies on.

"You're awfully tense for a night of fun with your friends," Brianna whispers into my ear during a break in the action. My eyes drift to where Dom is taking off his elbow guard at first base. "Ignore him." Her hand smooths over my knee.

"He's trying to rile me up," I huff, annoyed that she picked up on it, and maybe a little more annoyed that she's unbothered by it.

"Clearly it's working." She laughs, dropping a kiss on my neck.

"Are you trying to make him jealous?" My breath hitches as her grip on my knee tightens.

"Do you want me to?" Her eyes glitter playfully under the stadium lights.

"Jealous or not, I don't care, I'm here with you and I'm leaving with you. He's . . . nothing." Except for that one night he felt like everything. But I can't dwell on that, because it'll drag me back under like a rip current if I do.

"That's my girl." Her lips brush my ear. "But if you want to make sure he knows that you're mine, I can make it very clear. Just so he knows he's *nothing*."

"Jesus," I mumble, suddenly feeling overheated in a way that has nothing to do with the warm night.

THE MYTH, THE MAN, THE LEGEND - DAD CHAT

DAD:

Nice game tonight, son.

Your mother and I are proud of you.

DOM:

Thanks for watching. I felt good out there.

DAD:

Just the Chicago air? Or is there another reason why?

DOM:

Jeez. Catch any fish with that bait, old man?

DAD:

You tell me.

DOM:

So this is where my obnoxious tendencies come from.

DAD:

Your mom thinks it's endearing.

DOM:

Wonderful, I have delusions to look forward to in my old age as well.

DAD:

So you weren't playing for anyone special tonight

DOM:

I didn't say that.

DAD:

Tell me more . . .

DOM:

You would get along great with the bingo ladies.

DAD:

You say that like it's a bad thing. Now give me the tea.

DOM:

She was there . . . with her girlfriend.

DAD:

Don't be a homewrecker.

DOM:

You know me better than that. I can be patient.

CHAPTER 6

INDIE

"Open up Indie. We've got coffee and donuts," Poppy hollers at my door as I weave through the chaos that is my apartment. Boxes and totes are scattered everywhere in various states of disarray. There's a pod coming tomorrow that will leave for Denver, and I'll follow a few days later. First, I'm making a trip home to spend a few days with my dad and go visit my mom. He insisted I come so that he could check my tires and change my oil—neither of which are necessary, but I'll let him poke around so he feels useful.

"Did you bring the good coffee?" I ask, pulling the door open.

"Is that a serious question?" Lilah extends the coffee carrier out to me and I take it from her, pulling my order out on the way to the counter.

"I can't believe you still drink black coffee," Mia says, making a face as I take my first sip.

"My soul won't tolerate anything else."

Working together and chatting as we go, we start in the kitchen, making a packing assembly line. Mia and I pull things out of cabinets and hand them off to Poppy and Lilah, who wrap and pack them.

After a dozen donuts and an absurd amount of caffeine, we finish in the kitchen and move on to the bedroom. This time, we split up, Mia and Lilah work on cleaning out the attached bathroom. Thankfully, I had the foresight to pack away my favorite toy which was charging on the counter before they got here. That would have been more than they bargained for.

While they pack up towels and hair products, Poppy and I sort through the closet, deciding what gets donated and what makes the cut for Denver.

"Is Bri working all day?" Poppy holds up a navy blazer for my perusal.

"Donate." I nod to the growing pile of business professional clothes I hope to never wear again. "She's in class now and then working tonight. Yesterday was kind of it. We won't see each other until she comes out to visit in a few weeks."

"And how are you feeling about that?" Poppy adds another almost identical blazer to the pile.

"Fine, I guess." My friend levels me with a stare that says *don't bullshit a bullshitter.* "It's weird. I figured we'd just call it quits when I told her I was moving. I'm glad we didn't because I like her, but I don't see how this is going to work."

"Do you want it to work?" Using every inch of her height she grabs a box from the top shelf.

"Of course." But there's not enough enthusiasm in my voice when I say it. Poppy holds out a shoe box lifting the top to show me the pair of ridiculous shoes that I haven't worn since college. "I almost feel bad about donating those knowing they will torture someone else's feet."

"I like her," she comments with a tiny lift of her shoulders. The next box she grabs has a pair of strappy sandals that join the others in the growing pile of clothes that have no place in my new life. "She's not as sweet as I first thought. There's a little fire in her that I didn't expect."

"Yeah there is." I was surprised by the way she egged Dom on last night knowing our history. "Long-distance just seems like a big ask. She's young and has a lot going on between school and work."

"You've never been afraid of doing hard things," Poppy comments as she digs around, straining to reach something on the shelf.

"This is different. We're both so hardheaded and goal-orientated that I'm worried neither of us will give up, even if we should. We agreed to just see where things go—one day at a time."

"What about this box?" she asks, finally getting her fingertips on whatever's stuck back there.

By the time I realize what it is, it's too late; she's got it down and opened before I can stop her. As soon as the lid comes off, we both sink to the floor, our backs against the wall, work forgotten.

Poppy lays her head on my shoulder, lifting the picture on the top of the box for both of us to see. "*Oh, Farrow.* She was so stunning and kind, just like her daughter. You know I loved her for the way she took care of me like I was her own, Ind." Her fingers brush over the edges of the picture. My mom is holding me on her lap in a rocking chair reading, *Love You Forever.*

"She was the best. Hands down." I reach into the box pulling out the next picture: my mom and I, side by side, on our bikes as we race them down the hill at the park. I'm older here, maybe thirteen, but those were the best years. I hadn't outgrown spending every waking minute with her, and she hadn't gotten sick yet.

"I took that one." Poppy takes it, flipping it over to see the writing on the back. "Summer days at the park with the girls are the best. July 2008," is written in the sloppy cursive that I'd recognize anywhere. The same curvy penmanship is permanently inked into the design on my shoulder. Her words to me, "have courage and soar," forever in the stars.

I pull out another one, this time of the three of us. Time slips away as Poppy and I stare at it silently. This was the day before she told us about her cancer. She took us both into Chicago and we spent the entire trip doing whatever we wanted. There wasn't a single time she said "no" to us that day.

It was the last time that life was normal for any of us.

Placing it face down, Poppy grabs the next one, unfolding where it's creased in the middle. "Way to ruin it, Jensen." My best friend snarls at the picture. It's my birthday, sophomore year of college, and it's the last picture I have of the two of us before the cancer came back. The last one where she has hair and looks the way I want to remember her—happy and healthy.

Unfortunately, my complete shithead of an ex is also in the picture. I fold him back so it's just mom and I before shutting the cover on the box and setting it aside so it comes in the car with me.

The air between is still heavy with grief when Poppy speaks with quiet concern. "You'll need a doctor in Denver. One who knows your family history and has a solid track record with these sorts of things—"

Ovarian cancer and the chances of it coming for me are the last thing I want to talk about, so I cut her off, knowing exactly where this is headed. "I'll find someone, I promise."

"Don't lie to me about this, Indie. It's too important." She grabs my hand, wrapping it up in hers. "*You're* too important. Promise me."

"Cross my heart." The cadence of my heart picks up, making me feel out of control at just seeing the worry on Poppy's face. I just want to make it stop.

"Have you given the testing any more thought? I know you didn't want—"

"Poppy, I love you, but please don't. I said I would find a doctor and I will. But don't push me on the rest."

"I love you, Indie, so I'll drop it. But only if you promise to listen to what the doctor has to say about it." She pushes up from the floor, giving me the space she knows I need right now. "I'm going to put this stuff with the others and then we can order lunch before we finish in the living room."

She leaves me sitting on the floor and I open the box, taking that last picture of the pile, turning it over in my hand.

Taking it by the edges, I pull, but not enough to rip it. Even after all these years, I can't bring myself to do it. I want him cut away and gone from the memory, but I leave him there, an omen of all the lessons he taught me.

He was my first heartbreak in so many ways. He let me down at every turn, yet I clung to him like a lifeboat in a storm because that's what my life was at the time. The boy in the baseball uniform stares back at me, as handsome as he was then, but now I know better. Behind that perfect facade is something rotten; a boy who pretended to love me all the while, weaponizing my sexuality. Using the fact that I'm bisexual as fodder for his buddies. Pretty lies don't hurt any less. And looking good when you crush someone's soul doesn't negate the damage.

"Never trust the pretty ones. It hurts worse when you don't expect it," I say to myself as I fold him back and tuck the reminder into the box for when I need it again. Carrying the box with me, I set it on the counter with the pile of stuff that needs to come with me in the car.

I find the girls in the kitchen pouring over the stack of takeout menus. "What are you hungry for, Indie?" Lilah asks as I slide onto the stool next to her.

"You guys can pick. You're the ones giving up your day to help me."

"How about pizza?" Mia suggests. "It's not moving without pizza and beer."

"Can't go wrong with that," Poppy agrees, pulling out her phone to order, her eyes sliding to me, silently asking if I'm okay.

I'm not, but I give her a weak smile anyway.

"Poppy was saying you were going to reach out to nonprofits soon to see what needs they had for volunteer coordination and staffing programs. Dean is on the board for Double Play. He could put you in touch with the right person," Mia offers.

"That would be amazing."

By the time the afternoon rolls around, the living room is packed and the girls need to head back to the hotel to get ready for the game tonight.

"You're sure you don't want to come tonight?" Poppy asks once more.

"I think our girl is ready for a nap." Mia tugs on her future sister-in-law's arm. "And she probably wants some alone time after having us in her space all day."

"I'm wiped. I couldn't imagine doing this without you all. Thank you for being here," I say, walking them to the door.

"Enjoy the time with your dad and drive safe." Poppy holds me tight, like she knows I'm seconds away from unraveling and her arms can piece me back together.

With the door shuts and the apartment is quiet for the first time since this morning, I look around at everything we accomplished.

I'm really doing this. Moving across the country with no job, no prospects, and leaving behind the only healthy relationship I've let myself have in years. For the first time since I quit, doubt creeps in. My eyes snag on the box of photos that Poppy and I looked through earlier.

Would my mom be proud of me? I think she would. Like I told the girls, I know what organizations I want to work with; free women's health clinics and cancer charities, for my mom. And places like GSA and the Pride Foundation, for me. Just like that, the doubt disappears, replaced by the determination that's gotten me this far in life, and a sense of purpose that is carrying me forward. Grabbing my running shoes, I lace them up and snag my keys, the trail calling out to me. Soon I'll replace the paved urban trail that hugs Lake Michigan with the dirt that always seems to ground me.

BINGO BITCHES DO IT BATTER

JANET:

I met an adorable single mom at the supermarket tonight. Are you over that mysterious dating slump yet?

DOM:

I seriously regret drinking Lark's homemade moonshine and confiding in you all.

LARK:

Don't tell lies, it's unbecoming.
You got several lovely dates out of that confession.

DOM:

I no longer need help with the matter.

LARK:

So you're out of the slump. Was it my Mallory?
Are you going to start calling me Gigi?
I'll set an extra plate at Thanksgiving for you.

STEPHANIE:

My money is on the preacher's daughter I set him up with.

DOM:

No, they were both lovely, but things have changed and I'm not ready to move on yet.

JANET:

Go get her tiger.

CHAPTER 7

INDIE

Every time I pull in the driveway of my childhood home, emotions steal the air right out of my lungs. I'm left panting, trying to calm myself before I head inside to see my dad. This place holds countless beautiful memories that I cling to, but the more recent ones hold tight to my still-bruised heart—unshakeable even after a decade of grieving. Not even the physical pain of being here without her can keep me from visiting.

"Dad!" I call over the thud of my duffle bag landing on the ornate rug my mom picked out.

"In the den." His deep voice echoes through the house. For a second it almost feels like nothing has changed, like he and my mom will appear together with hugs, welcoming me home. It's a shock I'll never get used to.

"How's the sudoku treating you today?" I ask as I round the corner to his favorite room in the house.

Just as I knew he would be, his feet are kicked up in his dark green recliner. The matching one next to him sits untouched. It's time to replace both of them; the velvety fabric is worn and discolored, but he's not ready for that.

"Keeping my mind sharp as a tack." The footrest clicks when he lowers it, setting aside his puzzle. "Need any help with your things?" He doesn't move as quickly as the last time I was home. He looks weary, and I wonder, for the thousandth time in the last few years, if being here alone is too hard for him.

"Nope, just one bag," I say, meeting him halfway.

"So a short visit, then." He frowns, pulling me into a hug.

"Yeah, I want to get on the road the day after tomorrow. Avoid a storm system coming through later this week."

"Well, I'm glad you're here, sweet pea." He kisses the top of my head. "Want to stretch those legs after your drive?"

"Yeah, that sounds nice." My inability to sit still isn't a secret. After the drive, the last thing I want is to be cooped up inside.

Our feet carry us the same way they always do; out of the cul-de-sac, past the elementary school, and down the path that leads to the cemetery. When we get to her plot, we take a seat, side by side, on the bench.

"You want to go first? She's probably sick of me by now," he says, sounding more at peace with being here than I feel. This is part of his routine. Every morning starts with a walk to see mom, rain or shine. It's his way of keeping her memory alive.

"Sure."

His hand covers mine, and he kisses my cheek before standing. "I'll give you two some time to catch up and take a lap around the path."

Starting is always the hardest, but once the words come, they pour out. Each word a nano stitch in the patchwork of my tattered heart.

It's been almost a year since I've visited her, so I have a lot to fill her in on. "I'm moving to Denver. Poppy's so happy . . . I'm dating someone—Brianna. You'd love her. She's sweet and nurturing without being a pushover. The two of you would be a pair . . . but . . . I'm not sure she's the one."

I share revelation after revelation, feeling lighter with each word.

Sucking in an uneasy breath, I gather myself because, up until now, everything has been surface level—easy—but I can't ignore the pull to tell her what's really going on with me. That's one thing that hasn't changed since we lost her;

talking to her still calms me in a way only she can. The only thing that compares is the peace I feel when I'm biking or running.

"I quit my job. I know you don't care where I work or what I do as long as I'm happy. And the truth is, I wasn't . . . not really. It was all about the hustle, but it wasn't fulfilling. Plus, my boss was a gargantuan ass-nugget. Denver will be different—better." It comes out in a rush, one long breath of admission. When I'm done, I feel more at ease than I have since my ride the other night.

Sitting in silence for a minute I listen to the birds, imagining what she would think of all this. She'd be glad I was following my heart, even if it's crazy. She'd tell me to embrace my whims because her faith in me was unwavering.

"I can't believe it's been ten years. Would you do it all differently if you could? You didn't know cancer was coming for you, but if you'd have known, would it have changed anything?"

The tears sting my eyes as they fall, my unanswered questions making them spill fast and hot.

"You couldn't have loved harder—you already did that so well. Even before the diagnosis, you never held back." Not like me.

All the ways I've been holding back flash like a slideshow in my mind. The testing. Staying in my job for as long as I did. Not moving out by Poppy sooner. Walking out of that house last year when everything felt a little too close to perfect. Leaving *him* behind.

"That last one is the one you'd give me the most shit about. And no, there's no chance of us getting together when I move, so don't even think about it. Smooth talk and pretty faces only lead to heartbreak; I learned that lesson the hard way. I won't be fooled like that again."

My dad comes into view as he closes out the loop. Swiping away the tears, I give her a private goodbye before he rejoins us.

"Did my girls get all caught up?" He tucks me under his arm and kisses the top of my head like he has since I was a little girl.

"We did." Usually talking to her gives me clarity, but I'm more confused than ever. "Do you think we could head back soon? I'm starving and a little tired."

"Yeah, sweet pea, let me say goodbye." Just like every time, he kisses his pointer and middle fingers, placing them over her name before he tells he loves her and misses her.

NAUGHTY SLIDERS AND TACO SLUTS

POPPY:

Hey Babe! How was the visit with Papa Moreno? Does he miss me?

INDIE:

Good. Of course he misses you. You give him fewer headaches than me.

POPPY:

Only because he didn't have to keep me when I was being a shit.

INDIE:

We both know I was the one that was always being an asshole.

MIA:

Not you, you're perfect.

INDIE:

Thank you! I'm glad someone finally noticed.

LILAH:

I bet teenage Indie was a trip.

INDIE:

You have no idea. I was very good at "advocating" for myself.

POPPY:

Like the time you got sent to Principal White's office after you kneed Leif McMiller in the nuts.

MIA:

I love story time.

INDIE:

He pushed me against a locker and stuck his tongue down my throat without consent. He was sweaty from football practice and I was not into it.

POPPY:

Principal White looked like she wanted to high five you for not putting up with it.

LILAH:

Go Indie!

INDIE:

I still got detention, but he did too.

POPPY:

Worth it.

INDIE:

Absolutely. It was a defining moment for me. While his slimy tongue was still inside my mouth, I remember thinking Larissa Kane would never.

MIA:

Awe. It's your bisexual origin story.

LILAH:

I'm proud of Baby Indie and so excited to have you closer.

POPPY:

I'll be there in two days! And then I'm going to recruit you all to help me move again.

CHAPTER 8

DOM

Our win in Chicago lit a much needed fire under us and our win against the Vancouver Tridents yesterday gives us five wins out of seven since our series with the Comets.

Today is an off day, and other than a quick workout this morning, we are free until our game tomorrow night.

With my hair still wet from the shower, I walk through the locker room to where a few of the guys are already dressed. Running the towel over my head, I drop to the bench and grab my bag to do the same.

"Want to hitch a ride over with me?" I overhear Hendrix asking Cruz as they both tie their shoes.

"Sure, I just heard from Delilah that Mikey is going to cover the shop so she and Willa can come help. Is Poppy already there?"

I pause, my hands on my knees shifting towards them. Dean drops down on the bench between us, a towel around his waist, blocking my ability to eavesdrop the way I want to.

"Are you going to meet us over there?" Hendrix asks Dean.

I open the door to Dean's locker, leaning over him until I can see myself in the mirror. "Whew. Not invisible. You guys really had me worried for a second."

All three turn to look at me.

"Anything you want to tell me?" I ask casually. "Or are you just going to leave me hanging?"

Dean raises his eyebrow at me. "I'm not sure you deserve to know if you're going to be dramatic about it.

I wave him off. "Of course not."

Hendrix coughs into his elbow. It's a weak-ass attempt to cover his laughter.

"The girls are over at Indie's helping unpack. We could use an extra set of hands with her furniture."

"I'd love to help. Thanks for including me." I slap him on the back, reaching into my bag and grabbing a fresh pair of undies. My afternoon off suddenly looks much more exciting.

"Just don't mess with her too much. I know the two of you like to toss barbs around like they're foreplay, but she just drove across the country, leaving behind a career, her girlfriend, and dad," Hendrix says standing from the bench and hoisting his bag over his shoulder.

"I think what Hendrix is trying to say is she might not be in the mood for your brand of flirting," Dean adds, rubbing salt in the wound.

"Got it, no flirting." I drag out the words, not liking them one bit. "Because she's got a girlfriend." Bitterness coats my tongue as I force the words out.

"I give him five minutes," Cruz says, following Hendrix out the door.

"That seems generous. He'll piss her off in three, tops." The door closing cuts off the rest of their conversation.

"You're both wrong. She's going to be pissed as soon as she sees me."

"Probably. But she knows how to handle you. I'm not worried," Dean says, pulling his shirt over his head as I finish dressing.

THE MYTH, THE MAN, THE LEGEND - DAD CHAT
AS READ BY: SIRI VIA DOM'S CAR

DOM:

You've officially moved up the chain from Dad Best Friend to Only Best Friend status.

DAD:

I'm honored by this development.
Who do I owe a fruit basket for screwing up?

DOM:

It's hard to pinpoint when they're all at fault.

DAD:

But seriously is everything okay?

DOM:

Fantasmical, bombastic, or as our forefathers might say, the bees knees.

DAD:

These fits of dramatics come from your mother's side.

DOM:

Liar GIF

DAD:

Me? Never. Just call me Honest Abe.

DOM:

No one is talking about you, Lincoln. This is about me.

DAD:

Right, proceed with this tale of betrayal.

DOM:

SHE MOVED HERE AND THEY DIDN'T TELL ME.

DAD:

Whoa. No need to shout.

DOM:

Agree to disagree.

DAD:

So what's your plan?

DOM:

Convince her she can't live without me.

DAD:

And what about the girlfriend?

DOM:

Shit. Is it bad that I hope they broke up?

DAD:

Don't besmirch your family name.
We raised you better.

DOM:

Excellent use of besmirch.
I don't like it but I'll be a gentleman.

CHAPTER 9

DOM

As expected, the first words out of Indie's mouth when I walk through the door of her apartment are edged with the fire of a thousand suns. *Burn me up, Baby.*

"I'm not babysitting him." She brushes past me, barely looking up from the box she's carrying through the small kitchen.

The greeting only makes my smile grow wider. "Missed you too." Grabbing the box out of her arms, I look down at the marker scrawled across the top. "Bedroom, perfect. That's where you like me best, anyway," I say, low enough that only she hears.

"Not enough for a repeat." Her voice is honey sweet with a hint of spice, just like the scent that swirls around us when she leans in and pulls the box out of my arms. Without a second glance, she turns away from me, treating me to an unforgettable view of her ass in a pair of tiny spandex shorts.

I choose to believe the sway in her hips is for me.

When she's out of sight, I move across the apartment to where Dean is talking to Poppy.

"The pod in the parking lot has all the heavy stuff. If you guys start on that, we can work on unpacking in here," Poppy directs, watching me carefully.

I get it guys, I'm the problem.

"Do you know where she wants things, or should we just get them inside for now?" Hendrix asks.

Poppy looks around the space. One wall is lined with boxes and totes, leaving the rest of the small kitchen and living room combo mostly empty. Beyond that, it's all clean lines and minimalist vibes. The balcony opens up to a view of the mountains. It's everything I envisioned for a woman like Indie. Nonsense and a little untamed.

"If Indie's busy, I can take an educated guess," she says, excusing us to start with the heavy lifting.

The four of us are able to empty the pod quickly and start on helping to reassemble things inside. Which is perfect because being sequestered outside is not helping me gain any ground with the woman I want.

Dean swipes his hand across his forehead as he puts together a small desk.

"I'm going to grab us some water." Leaving the bookcase I was setting up, I stand, taking a minute to stretch my back. My muscles are tight from being crouched over the project but I'd do it again in a heartbeat.

There's a little extra pep in my step when I find Indie standing by the fridge. Coming up behind her I reach around her, pulling out the waters one at a time, in no hurry to put space between us again.

"All this just to be closer to me? Moving seems extreme, but I can't say I'm disappointed." I step back just enough so Indie's not trapped and uncap my water.

Instead of shutting the door, she reaches back in and grabs another bottle. "Here you go." She presses the cold drink into my hand.

"What's this for?"

"Just figured hauling that ego around is a lot of work and you might need another one so you don't wear yourself out." The annoyance in her voice can't hide the gleam in her eyes at the insult.

"You already know stamina isn't an issue for me," I tell her, handing the extra bottle back. "But you might want it. You're looking a little flushed, just like you did when you came on my fingers." My smile grows as I add, "And my tongue and cock."

"You can't talk to me like that anymore. I'm seeing someone."

Swiveling my head, looking around the space. "That's funny, I don't see her."

"Just because she's not here doesn't mean anything." The playfulness gives way to a defensiveness that doesn't sit right with me.

"Are you trying to make me jealous, because it's working."

The confident mask she wears falters, and I see uncertainty flash in her dark eyes. "No. Why would I do that?"

"Maybe the same reason *she* was trying to make me jealous in Chicago." Indie brings the bottle I gave her to her lips, taking a long drink. "You told her about me, didn't you?"

The way she stomps off without another word is all the answer I need. If what we had meant nothing there would be no reason to share it.

Grabbing the waters from the counter I hand them out to the guys and then go back to the bookcase.

"Will you stop it?" Dean asks a few minutes later.

"What?" I know damn well what he's talking about, but it's more fun to push his buttons. Even if he's not as grumpy as he was before falling for Mia, his tolerance for nonsense is still low.

"You've been humming 'Happy' like you're yellow and wear bibs since you came back with water. What the hell do you have to be so pleased about?"

"Dude. I would pay money to see you curled up on the couch watching those little yellow fuckers causing mayhem. You're a changed man, you know that."

"Screw off. She lets me touch her boobs on movie night. *Every damn time.* I'll watch whatever she picks, and you would too." He glances over his shoulder. Whether he's checking to make sure his girlfriend doesn't hear or Hendrix, I'm not sure.

Screwdriver in hand, I pretend it's a whip, sound effect and all.

"Really looked like things were going so well for you with your *future wife*," he mocks.

"She wants me. Fighting turns her on," I tell him with a wink.

"Seems like it. Is that why she stomped away and you're out here putting her bookshelf together?"

He takes the pencil from behind his ear and raises it, but before he can flick his wrist, I slap it out of his hand.

"Do I even want to know?" a silky voice asks from behind us making Dean chuckle darkly.

The look I shoot him shuts him up. But it's not me he's afraid of. Dean knows just as well as I do not to mess with Indie.

"Mia sent me over here. Said you had something I'd want?" Her eyes flick to me and the corner of her lip twitches before she refocuses on my soon-to-be dead teammate.

"Did she, now?" he asks.

"Basically," Indie says, pulling her phone out of her pocket and unlocking it before handing it to him.

Without an explanation, he types something out on her phone before handing it back. "I told her you would be in touch. She'll be thrilled to hear from you; I think you're just what she needs."

"Fantastic! I'm excited to meet her," she says fucking beaming when she spins on her heels and walks away.

Blood rushes to the tips of my ears making them hot. "What the hell was that?"

"Not sure what you mean," he says in the flattest voice I've ever heard.

"*One.* She made it pretty clear to me she already has a girlfriend. *Two.* Why would you do me dirty like that?"

"Relax. I gave her Vivi's number." He must see something on my face that tells him I'm still not following. Shaking his head he continues, "Not sure this is any of your business if she hasn't told you."

"Suddenly you're too good for tea time because you've got a girlfriend?"

"You're exhausting, you know that, right? Indie wants to work with nonprofits, helping build volunteer programs and creating talent solutions for their full-time employees . . . or something like that."

"So you weren't *hooking her up* with someone."

"No. You've fucking lost it," he says adding the final leg to the desk.

We both stand and I help him flip over the desk he's working on, positioning it against the wall like Poppy instructed. With all the major projects done, and the day winding down, the group is gathered around a charcuterie board sipping on beer or wine. One person is notably missing.

Scanning the small apartment I catch sight of her dark hair gleaming in the late afternoon sun out on the balcony. Her head is tipped back and her eyes are closed as she sits with her legs pulled to her chest on the wicker lounge chair. She looks like she needs a friend. I may not be the one she wants, but I'm who she's getting.

Before someone can spot me or try to stop me, I'm slipping out the door to join her. When I step onto the balcony, her eyes are still closed as the breeze makes her curl bounce around her heart-shaped face.

"I'll be back inside in a minute—" It's a tone she never uses with me, soft and unguarded. And gone the instant she opens those big brown eyes. "I thought you were Poppy. What do you want? I'm exhausted and don't really want to deal with *you*."

"Ouch. After I gave up my day off to help you move." The glare she levels me with is cold enough to cause frostbite. "Not the right thing to say. Got it."

"Is there a point, or are you just trying to disturb my peace?"

"I want to give you this." I fish the piece of tissue paper I snagged from the box of kitchen plates out of my pocket and hand it to her.

"I already have your number."

"That's not what this is, but since you brought it up. Would it kill you to use it once in a while?"

Oof that eye roll almost looked painful.

"If it's not your number, whose is it?"

"That's my friend Lara's number. She's on the board of a few local charities. I heard you wanted to make some connections. If she doesn't sit on the board, she can tell you who does. Her father is the mayor, and she's been working with nonprofits since she was sixteen."

"The mayor's daughter. Why am I not surprised? I'm not sure she'll be much help to me. I'm looking at very specific charities—the kind that do meaningful work for youth, or focus on women's health and marginalized communities. Not just ones that throw fancy galas so they feel better about life."

Disdain drips off each word, reinforcing exactly what she thinks of me. It's never been a secret, but she's wrong on most counts. Not that she has any intention of letting me prove that, so I don't even try. Words don't mean shit to her. Whoever hurt her, they did a number. And if I ever find out who it was, I'll be sure to return the favor.

"You caught me. Super tight with the mayor's daughter. Practically gave me the keys to the city. I've even taken her to a few of those galas." She turns the piece of paper over in her hand. "Just call her. She's someone you'll want to know."

"And how should I tell her I got the number? If she finds out it's you, will she run in the opposite direction?"

"Nah, babe. She's always been satisfied with our encounters." I don't tell her it's because I let her win at bingo, know how to waltz, and write out checks every single time she asks. Indie can find that out the fun way.

"Gross. On all accounts. Don't call me 'babe.' And don't tell me about your conquests."

I chuckle and slip back inside, hoping she never realizes that when she's spicy, it makes me want her more.

CHAPTER 10

INDIE

Teal fingernails trace circles on the inside of my knee as the Bandits leave the field in the bottom of the sixth. It feels good in the way that someone scratching your back before bed does, but the spark that it would have sent through my body weeks ago is more on a fizzle now.

Brianna flew in yesterday. In the two weeks since I left, we've texted every day, but have only been able to video chat twice. It's no one's fault. She's swamped with her summer classes and I'm scrambling to make connections as fast as I can.

Thanks to the guys, I've got meetings set up all week to make introductions and share my ideas with several of the nonprofits I want to work with. But I've still got a long way to go, especially with researching grants and alternate funding, to help me from burning through my savings.

As much as I hate to admit it, Dom's connection with Lara seems promising. After my initial reluctance to reach out, I did some research and found her philanthropic involvement impressive. I could have done without seeing the photos of her and Dom together looking magazine ready in their gala best.

Weird jealousy aside, we spoke briefly on the phone and she was helpful, knowledgeable, and well connected—just like he promised—and there's no question he'll hold that over my head every chance he gets.

"Are you guys going to come out to Draft with us after the game?" Delilah asks, interrupting my thoughts.

I hadn't planned on it, but when I glance over at Brianna, her face is lit up at the idea. "Sure, we can come out for a little while." Honestly, I was hoping we'd have more time together to figure out if we can make this work long-distance, but she's already flying home tomorrow.

There's a lull in the conversation as Dom steps up to the plate, his smile never wavering as he gets in his stance. Where the rest of the guys look serious, number four always looks like he's having the time of his life out there.

Christian Damiano, the pitcher for the Boston Revs, shakes off the sign twice before he gets a signal he likes. The ball is screaming right over the center of the plate and Dom must like what he sees because he swings. The connection cracks through the stadium and sends it right down the first base line, burying it in no-man's-land by the foul pole.

"Holy shit, he's fast." My eyes track Dom as he rounds first before the Rev's even have their hands on the ball. Kyle Bosco makes the throw to the cutoff and by the time the ball is on its way to Emerson Knight, Dom is sliding into third, somehow managing to get under the throw.

"What the hell are those two cackling about?" Mia gestures toward third base where Emerson and Dom are hunched over laughing.

"Knowing Dom, he's probably challenging him to race after the game," Poppy says.

"More like telling him about his lucky thong," I comment off-handedly. Four sets of eyes swing toward me. *Shit. Shit Shit.*

If he finds out I said that he will never let me live it down. Our hookup from last summer is the worst kept secret, and up until now, I've never admitted to anyone here but Brianna.

"A thong, huh?" Brianna comments tilting her head and squinting her eyes like she might be able to see it through his pants from here.

"Where is the popcorn guy? I need a bucket to bury my face in." Thankfully, Xavier steps up to the plate providing a distraction.

The rest of the game is uneventful, meaning I manage not to make a fool of myself and the girls have enough tact not to dig for more dirt in front of my girlfriend.

By the time Brianna and I make the short walk to Draft, I need a cold beer and some space from both Brianna and Dom, who have waged some sort of silent war for my attention. She's always finding a reason to touch me, and Dom is just being Dom.

There is no way he needed to stretch that much before the top of the ninth. That's not how muscles work. They were plenty limber. He just wanted to make sure I was looking at his ass. Which I wasn't. *Not at all.*

My hand is linked through Bri's as she leads me through the building and out the back where there is a private courtyard that the guys rented for the evening.

"You look like you could use this," Brianna says, when she returns from grabbing drinks to find me alone at the table. Coming up behind me she rolls the bottle over my heated skin, dragging it over the pulse point in my neck making my nipples pucker under my thin tank.

"Oh god," I moan quietly, covering my hand with hers and holding the bottle in place. "That feels heavenly."

My eyes drift shut when her hand lands on the opposite shoulder, curling over it possessively. Seeing this side of her makes me glad I didn't cut and run the second I decided to move, even if things have been a bit off for the last two weeks. This teasing side she's letting me see more of is addicting as hell. I wish I had gotten to explore it before I moved.

"Fuck me." The rough curse from across the patio scraps across my skin. Hearing Dom's deep voice while Brianna's soft hands are on me has my blood pumping hot through my veins.

For weeks, months even, that gravelly voice haunted me every time I tried to erase the memory of the way he owned my body. But the way he said my name never faded, as much as I wished it would.

An amused chuckle vibrates against my ear. "You messed him up."

"Hardly. He's unflappable. Nothing bothers him and certainly not that he doesn't get to have me again. Fuckboy 101, thou shall not sleep with the same girl more than once," I say as he turns and disappears back into the bar, revealing the rest of the guys.

Hendrix has his arm looped over Poppy's shoulder. Cruz has his wife's hand clasped tightly in his own. And Dean drops a kiss on Mia's head before glancing over his shoulder at where Dom went.

"Indie," Dean greets, dropping onto the bench across from me. "Did you two break him already?" he asks, pulling his girlfriend down next to him.

"Ignore him," Mia says, swatting at his arm.

"He's fun to mess with," Brianna says, taking the seat beside me.

"You're evil." I lift a strand of red hair. "Where do you hide the horns? I know for a fact there's no forked tail back there."

Dom chooses that moment to come back, setting two pitchers of beer down in the middle of the table, making them splash with how quickly he moves. Without a word, he takes the seat at the furthest end of the picnic table, and Xavier lowers himself to the seat across from Dom, his hands raking through his hair and his eyes never leaving his phone.

"How'd you and Indie meet?" My spine straightens when the question comes from the end of the table. Dom's eyes settle on my girlfriend.

"I'd like to formally take credit for that," Mia answers from where she's encased in Dean's grip, the two of them leaning against the high-top table next to us.

"You'd what now?" Brianna looks from Mia to me.

"That first night I stopped in the restaurant with Mia, she told me I should get your number," I offer.

"The two of you were making eyes at each other all night. Like this." She half turns toward Dean looking up at him like she's about to drag him back to the hotel.

"Let's not," Hendrix groans.

"Don't even start. Kitchen fucker," His sister says, shocking the hell out of all of us and making Dean chuckle against her neck.

Hendrix opens his mouth, presumably to defend himself, but Poppy just slaps a hand over it. "You deserved that. Now take it like a man."

"But you didn't get my number that night," Brianna reminds me, pulling my attention back to her from where it strayed to the set of amber eyes that look more troubled than I've ever seen them.

"Also my fault," Mia chimes in again. "Well, actually, Dean's fault," she says, tilting her head towards her boyfriend. "She didn't want to rub it in my face while I was heartbroken over this one."

"Guilty." He doesn't even try to defend himself. Not that he could. The man was a giant asshole to everyone while he got his shit together. In the end, he needed that time to be the man Mia needed.

"I came back the next week for take-out and you gave me your number before I could ask."

"What was your plan if I hadn't been working?"

"I guess I would have been eating a lot of Indian food," I joke.

"Fuck," Xavier groans at the opposite end of the table, snatching his phone and standing. "Sorry guys. I've got to go deal with Kristy."

"I'm going to make sure he's okay." Dom's lips turn down in a frown and he stands, following Xavier to the alcove near the bathrooms.

"Fucking Kristy," Hendrix grumbles under his breath.

"Shush." Poppy nudges him.

"I'm just saying, she's looking for a meal ticket."

"Don't you think you might be a little biased?" Mia asks her brother.

"Biased, or qualified to call it like I see it," he retorts. "She literally only gives him the time of day when she needs something."

"She was a lot to handle in Telluride," I admit. Something about her rubbed me the wrong way, so I kept my distance from her and the house, spending most of the trip either with the girls or out exploring on my own. Although, Kristy's antics weren't the only thing keeping me away.

Every time I turned around, there was a reminder that Dom was nearby. His shoes by the door, the crisp scent of his shampoo in the bathroom, the coffee that was ready for me every morning—he was inescapable. So I did what I've done since the morning after we slept together, only this time I physically ran as an escape from the tension in the house.

"Everything okay?" Cruz asks when Dom comes back over.

"Not sure. He's all out of sorts, but he wouldn't let me leave with him." He props his elbows up on the table next to Hendrix. His eyes sweep over Brianna, who's standing behind my tall chair with her arms wrapped around me from behind.

"I'm going to use the bathroom," she says, dropping a kiss on my neck before she skips away.

Not surprisingly, Dom is by my side before the door to the bathroom has even closed, leaning in close so that I can't escape the minty smell of eucalyptus that I find undeniably sexy, no matter how much he annoys me. Admittedly, it's a little harder to be irritated with him than usual after he put in a good word with Lara for me. No matter how terribly I treat him, he just keeps trying—talk about emotional stamina.

"Lara said you called and you two are getting lunch soon. My favorite way to be thanked is f—"

Without thinking, I slap my hand over his mouth, silencing him. Under my palm, his lip spread in a smile before he nips at my hand. I tear it away from his face, shaking it off like it'll undo the zings of heat through my body.

"Why are you the way you are?" Something inside me begs him to never stop at the same time I will him to shut up. Logically, I know better. He can be playful and kind all he wants, it won't make a difference.

"Probably the same reason it's so hard for you to keep your hands to yourself when I'm around." He smirks.

I snarl back. "That was to stop the never-ending stream of stupidity that comes out of your mouth. Do you save it all for me? Or are you inappropriate with everyone?"

"I was going to say flattery. Although I'm definitely not opposed to the other 'F' word when it comes to you. Someday I'll convince you I'm not the villain you think I am." He doesn't wait for me to respond, changing the topic instead. "You and Bri seem happy. Is she moving out here?" An air of mischief dances around him as he studies me.

"Not that it's any of your business, but no. She's in school for another year and a half in Chicago."

"Hmmm . . . long-distance is hard," he muses.

I was prepared to fend off an advance or sarcastic remark—maybe an offer to warm my bed in her absence. Not thoughtfulness and so much genuine understanding. It takes me a second to recover.

"Um . . . yeah. We're working it out. Day by day," Bri says, saving me when she slips in the space between us. I'd been so wrapped up in fending off Dom that I hadn't even seen her there.

Her arm comes around my waist, outwardly making it seem like everything is fine, but I don't like the way she says it like she's uncertain if it'll work. I've had my doubts, but I thought she was pulling for us. What are we doing if neither of us is fully invested in making this work long-distance?

"We haven't officially met yet. I'm Dom."

Sticking his hand out, Brianna takes it, her hand fully encased by his larger one. "Oh, I know who you are." She looks him up and down with a laugh.

"Excellent." He tilts his head to the side, looking around Bri to find me, his hand coming to his heart. It's truly unfair that he can look wholesome as fuck and devilishly handsome at the same time. This is why the man gets whatever he wants. "See, Firecracker, this is the kind of 'f' word I was talking about—flattery."

"You're assuming that's a good thing." Warm laughter floats out of Bri. She's completely unbothered by this, while I feel like a tennis ball being whacked back and forth. "Indie wasn't lying. You *are* a handful."

"Well, that seems kind of personal to share. But I'm glad you think so."

"Oh my god." I let my head fall forward, pressing against my arms on the table. "Please stop. Why are you even still here? Don't you have an unsuspecting woman to pick up?"

"Nope. I've given up the hoe life."

"This is really entertaining. I'm glad I came." Lifting my head I glare at her. "Obviously. I mean because you're here. But he's just so . . ." Bri pauses, tapping her finger to her chin.

"Not. Helping," I bite out, no longer hiding my annoyance as they continue chattering, while I sip my drink, looking on. Outwardly, everything looks fine. Brianna's physically attentive, but she's spent more time talking to everyone around the tables than she has to me. The past two weeks apart feel like they've created a rift between us. Everything just feels too friendly. That passion I felt for her before the move is fading.

An hour later, I'm dragging Brianna towards the door to wait outside for our Uber home. All of the other couples left about fifteen minutes ago, leaving Dom and a few of the new guys—Braxton and Montana, I think—to themselves. My mind was distracted with trying to come up with an excuse to leave and then feeling guilty because Brianna was clearly still enjoying herself. Maybe I'm a shit girlfriend to fault her for enjoying herself. I just thought that after two weeks apart she'd want to—I don't know—duck out early and spend time together. Honestly, it's an exhausting cycle.

"You seem frustrated," she says when we step out into the dark night.

"I'm trying really hard not to be," I admit, checking my phone again to see where the driver is. Great, he's now seven minutes away instead of five. Closing out the screen, I look back to where Brianna is leaning against the brick wall, looking far more collected than I feel.

"These are your friends, right?" she asks, looking down at her fingernails.

"Yes," I say.

"Why are you so bothered by me making an effort with them? Shouldn't you want me to get along with them?"

My head pounds and I pinch the bridge of my nose. "Of course I do. This is just harder than I thought—managing long-distance with our schedules. When you said you were coming out here, I'd hoped we would have more time just the two of us. I'd hoped it would be like it was before I left."

"You're right, things have changed, and it's different than I thought it would be. I like you a lot, and I wish things were different, but between school and work, this is all I can give you."

"I'm not asking for more."

"What *are* you asking for?" She pushes off the wall, coming to stand in front of me.

I glance down at my phone. Six more minutes. "I don't know."

"It seems like that might be part of the problem. We barely got started and neither of us have prioritized this. You're about to take on a whole new career, and we aren't in a place to travel back and forth. It's okay if this doesn't work."

And that's the soul of it. We aren't willing to fight for this, and that tells me everything I need to know about what's next for us. For the first time since we left the stadium, my shoulder inches away from my ears, partially relieved that she's making this decision for the both of us. "I wanted it to work."

She shrugs. "You don't need to say that just to make me feel better."

"What if I'm saying it so I feel better?"

She steps into me laughing. "What now?"

"Take the Uber back to my place and stay there. I'll head over to Poppy's or Mia's and crash on the couch."

"No. I can sleep on your couch."

"Absolutely not. You flew out here to see me. I'm not making you sleep on a shitty couch." Even though I could sleep in the living room, it feels weird to go back with her.

"Everything okay out here?" Dom's deep voice asks from the door. When I turn to tell him to butt out, I find him watching us with his eyebrows drawn together in genuine concern.

"It's fine." The car pulls up and I grab my keys, twisting the small gold one off and pressing it into Bri's hand, along with a quick kiss to her cheek. "Please, just do this for me. I'll go stay with one of the girls."

She nods, ducking into the car. "Fine. Text me so I know you found a place to stay."

"I'll make sure she's set up," Dom says, keeping his distance even while inserting himself into the situation.

CHAPTER 11

DOM

Brianna's red hair disappears behind the closed door for a moment before she rolls down the window and waves.

The glow of tail lights disappear in the distance and we stand there silently for a moment, the air thick between us. Then Indie turns away from me with her head down and pulls her phone out of her back pocket. A wall of curls hide her face from me.

"What are you doing?" I've given her space until this point, not wanting to intrude, even though it's killing me to know what's going on in her head.

"Calling an Uber," she says flatly, still not letting me get a read on her.

I wanted her for myself, but never at the expense of her getting hurt. The thought that she's upset has me moving closer.

"And where are you going?" She takes a step away but I don't let her retreat. Placing a gentle hand on her arm, I turn her toward me.

"Poppy or Mia's."

Still, she refuses to look at me. "Hey, are you okay?" I don't dare lift her chin so I can see her the way I want to. She shifts on her feet.

"I'm fine, Dom. I just want to get out of here." No snark or sass, just resignation. Defeat—from her voice, to her folded shoulders, and her downcast eyes. Yet she hasn't called a car.

"Come on." Covering her hand with mine I lock her screen. "You know you don't really want to spend the night with the happy couples right now."

"Where do you expect me to go?" She slides the phone back in her pocket and I consider it a win.

"One of my perfectly good guest bedrooms. You can even take the one in the basement if it makes you feel better to have an extra floor between us." I point down the street. "My truck is right there. I know you don't like me, but right now, you don't have a lot of appealing options."

"That seems like a stretch. All it would take is a call to any of the girls and they would happily take me in for the night. No questions asked."

She doesn't move to follow me when I take a few steps towards my car. "But *you* would mind. Come on, you're not going to get a better offer."

Her feet scuff across the sidewalk, always staying a couple of steps behind me. When we reach the truck, I hold the passenger door open as she sinks back into the seat. I'm tempted to ask her if she's okay again. Indie's a little thorny, but that doesn't mean she's immune to disappointment and hurt.

"Don't look at me like that. It's fine. I'll be fine," she says, pulling her door shut and ending the conversation.

Shockingly, I hate awkward silence with a passion. Still, I suppress the need to fill the car with chatter, regardless of how badly my skin prickles. Indie's forehead is resting against the window, but outside of being less combative with me, she really seems mostly fine. There are no tears, no angry ranting, just acceptance of the situation. I heard enough of the conversation to know that she and Brianna mutually called it off.

Not that my feelings on the situation matter, but I'm not sure what to think.

On one hand, I'm not mad about her newly single status. Maybe I was jealous, especially of how she had her hands all over Indie the way I wish she'd let me touch her. But after getting to know Brianna, it was obvious she was a good person. Kind enough to take care of Indie the way she deserves, and strong enough to challenge her so she doesn't get bored. If she's not going to give me a shot, at least she was with someone that seemed decent. Still, you can't convince me that anyone is better for her than I am.

Now, if only I could make her see that.

Tonight's a start.

She's coming home with me, and I can give her a place to figure things out before she has to face whatever went down tonight. Like a wounded animal, Indie needs to be coaxed into trusting people and I plan on being on my best behavior; which is a side of me she hasn't seen yet.

Silence fills the car as we wait on the opening garage door.

Beside me, my passenger is slouched against the seat, squeezing her eyes shut. I can't help but hope she's remembering the first time she was here. The way she softened for me. Or the hours we spent talking between the sheets. How much more we shared that night than just our bodies.

Just like that night, I hold the door for her as she slips inside. Except tonight we are going our separate ways. There's no heated kiss against the wall, there's no tearing at each other's clothes in a rush of passion; but she's here, nonetheless.

"What's it going to be? Do you trust me enough to take the guest bedroom down here, or do you want to be downstairs?"

"Do I have to worry about you sneaking in during the night?"

"No. I wouldn't join you in bed even if you begged tonight. You might not think much of me, but I'm not a homewrecker, and until you know for sure that things are over with Brianna, you're off-limits."

"I'm off-limits anyway," she says, her voice lacking the normal venom as she rounds the corner, then turns her head the other way before finally tilting her chin up and looking beyond where I'm standing and into the open concept living room.

"Something I can help you find?" I ask, sucking on my cheek. Because despite looking worn out, there's a glimmer of trouble behind the sadness in her eyes that tells me she's up to no good.

"Your live, love, laugh sign . . . where's it hiding, Martha?" She sucks on her cheek, hiding the twitch of her mouth behind the move.

"Don't be ridiculous. I don't have a sign." I lean in close, lowering my voice. "It's tattooed on my ass."

Her composure falters, and I can practically see the wheels turning.

"Now you're picturing me naked, aren't you?" She gives me an eyeroll and I know she's going to be okay. "This room has an attached bathroom with a tub." I tip my head toward the guest room my parents typically stay in. "A nice, deep, soaking tub with lavender salts and everything." In a small way, this is me taking care of her, but it's innocuous enough that she might let me get away with it.

"In your dreams." She scoffs, her soft footsteps moving towards the door.

"Every. Damn. Night." Looking over my shoulder, I watch as her steps halt for a second before she shakes her head and seals herself behind the door.

Between the adrenaline from the game, having Indie in the stands, and now knowing she's right downstairs, I'm too amped up to sleep. Nothing has helped. Not the push-ups I did on my bedroom floor to wear myself out. Not the hot shower afterwards to calm me down. Not even counting Sheriff Sluggers, the Bandits mascot, leaping over my bed for the last twenty minutes, has helped to dull the spike of energy thrumming through me from having her here.

If I stare at the ceiling fan any longer, I might lose my mind. Resigned to a long night I slip out of bed and head to the kitchen for a drink of water. The whirling sound of the jets coming from her bathroom reaches me as soon as my feet touch the cool wood floor at the bottom of the stairs.

Fuck. She's in the tub. My tub. In my house. Wet, naked, and probably relaxed.

At least that means she wouldn't find me creeping around in nothing more than my briefs sporting a now fully hard erection, because I don't need to imagine what Indie looks like without clothes. That picture is etched in my memory, and it's currently starring in the reel of dirty thoughts running through my brain.

Backing away from temptation, I finish the task that brought me down here and grab a cup from the kitchen. Normally I use the fancy dispenser to get crushed ice for my water, but I need the blast of freezing air to cool me off more than I need those perfect tiny pieces of ice.

Not to mention, I can't bear the thought of her hearing the mechanical grinding from the ice machine and getting out of the tub to cover her flawless body with a towel. It might make me a masochist, but the idea of her bare and dripping under my roof is the most divine form of torture. Filling my glass, I bring it upstairs with me knowing I'm about to do something I shouldn't.

I drain the cup in one long drink, a last ditch effort to cool the inferno bubbling under my skin. It does nothing to take the edge off. Glass forgotten on my nightstand, the hard surface of the headboard bites into my bare back, and I palm myself through the black cotton of my briefs. Even if I wanted to think of someone else, it wouldn't work.

Trust me, I've tried, but she's the only one I want. It took fighting it exactly once before I realized it was going to be a thing. Since then, I've only spent time with girls that are the polar opposite of Indie. A fact that absolutely makes me a jackass.

Now she's here in my house, and I don't even have to close my eyes to conjure what she would look like. Fucking perfection.

Beads of moisture hanging from the dark curls sticking to her tipped back face. Her pouty, cupid's bow lips slightly parted as the hot water laps at the peaks of her dark nipples, the swells of her breasts floating near the top of the water and dotted with goosebumps.

I can picture it all, down to the sound of her breath hitching when I take her heavy breasts in my hand. Playing with them the way she loves—biting, sucking, pinching. It's almost enough to have me coming all over my stomach in record time.

My hand disappears under my waistband and my cock jumps at the contact. Being around her again and not being able to have her is like walking a fucking tight rope—each step is more precarious than the last. It's not until I smooth my palm down my shaft that I find my balance.

There's no substitute for her soft hands, but I wrap my fist around the base anyway, giving it a squeeze. My own touch is nothing compared to her—how she used both hands; her thumb smearing the bead of precum over the head every so often, the tip of her tongue darting out like she needed a taste.

My muscles tense and my strokes slow, drawing each memory out until the pressure turns to blistering heat at the base of my spine.

Her mocha eyes looking up at me when she fell to her knees and took me into her mouth for the first time. The disappointment on her face when I pulled her off, and how it morphed into a grin when I hauled her up off the floor and told her to crawl across the bed. How that smile stretched when I told Indie I had big plans for her and they didn't involve me coming down her throat—at least not right then.

My fist works faster, matching the need I feel for the woman in my mind.

Each memory is better than the last, but nothing sends me over the edge as fast as the memory of the way she melted underneath me, pliant and soft the first time I sank into her. I can still taste how salty her skin was when I kissed her shoulder as she cried out for me.

My thighs shake and my groan echoes through the empty room. Like always, it's mixed with her name as hot spurts of cum land on my stomach.

And just like every time it feels empty when I open my eyes and she's not there; coming to a memory of her is a shadow of the moments we shared in between the sex. Her sharp tongue, whispered stories about our childhoods, her dreams, the unhinged laughter she treated me to when we were watching videos of people getting hurt.

"Holy shit. I know I told you this was one and done, but what I really meant was one night. Or was that all you got?" Pushing her hair off her face, she rolls off me.

And then, like the devil she is, she chooses the exact moment I'm taking care of the condom to slip out of bed. Tying it off, I quickly reach out trying to snag her, but the only thing there is air. All I'm left with is her fading chuckles and the smell of her still floating in the room as she disappears into the bathroom.

"You weren't so snarky when you were coming all over my cock just a minute ago!" I shout towards the cracked bathroom door. Then, because I can't help myself, I pant, slapping my hand against the wall and chanting my own name, mimicking her smoky voice the best I can. Which, admittedly, is not well, because her little moans and grunts of ecstasy matched the poetic melody of the world's sexiest symphony, and I just sound like a terrible porn soundtrack.

Laughter bounces off the bathroom walls, letting me know I sound just as ridiculous to her ears.

"Just for the snark, you're going to take my cock all night long. And I'm going to make sure every time is unforgettable."

"Is that so?" The water running at the sink stops, and she steps back into the room, all my favorite parts of her right there, on display, in the moonlight.

"You'll be doomed to a lifetime of remembering how good I felt deep inside you, knowing your stubborn ass can't have it again because it was only one night. But first, I just need a few minutes to recover."

"A few?" she squeaks, but it doesn't stop me from lunging for her again. This time I'm faster and I catch her, pulling her back to me before she can run again.

"The MLPA requires I take a fifteen minute break between rounds, per our labor contract." I haul her against me by the waist as she squirms. *"So tell me something while we wait. What's your guilty pleasure—other than my dick?"*

"What do you mean?"

"When Indie Marie—"

"Not my middle name." Warm laughter tumbles out of her freely. Each time she makes that sound, my chest puffs up a little more.

"As I was saying, when Indie Jones needs to turn off her brain and relax, what does she do?"

"Wrong again." When she lifts her head from my chest, there's a gleam in her eye. *"Don't judge me. It's kind of evil."*

"I would expect nothing less." My teeth nip at her earlobe, making her squirm against me. *"Tell me."*

"Videos of people falling, tripping, colliding with things. If I'm feeling extra spicy, the ones with ball shots really brighten up my day." She reaches for my phone on the nightstand and hands it to me to unlock.

I pull up YouTube and she vibrates against my chest laughing at the home page which is filled with funny pet videos.

"Talk about predictable." The backs of her fingers run up my jawline before she pats my cheek.

Plucking the phone from my fingers, she taps at the screen. When she turns it back to me, I shake my head as the catcher on the screen takes a foul ball right to his crotch. *"That's not going to shorten my refractory period."*

Her unhinged laughter at the player's misfortune turns raspy when she runs her hand down my stomach. *"Hmm. What about this?"*

"Yeah, that'll do it. But you only get him if you can watch a video of a dog eating watermelon without laughing."

She cups me, a shit-eating grin on her face. *"So you're telling me that if I laugh, you won't let me wrap my lips around you and taste you? I've been dying to get my mouth on you all night."*

"You drive a hard bargain, but fine, my body is yours to use as you please. We don't even have to watch this." I drop the phone to the bed and roll her onto her back. *"That was close enough to fifteen minutes."*

Like I said, empty.

Physically, Indie and I are compatible as hell. Hands down the best sex of my life. But sex alone has never kept my attention, which is why I've been mostly single since college. Only having a few brief relationships as an adult, I've been biding my time for the person who would come along and make me want to chase the kind of devotion my parents have. Someone I could see being my best friend and challenging me every single day—not letting me get bored or complacent.

You'd have to be dead to be bored with Indie around. Even now, my cheeks ache from just reflecting on that night.

Finally, my eyelids are heavy as I pad to the bathroom and give myself a full service wipe down. This time, sleep comes easier when I fall back into bed moments later.

CHAPTER 12

DOM

All of my best dreams, for the last year, have featured the feisty stunner sleeping just below me, but last night, they were more vivid than usual—more focused—like the details that were getting hazy with passing time are now renewed at having her here again.

Loud banging at my bedroom door startles me, making one of those dreams where Indie was tracing the lines of ink on my thigh fade to black as I drag myself unwillingly back to reality. That is, until I'm alert enough to realize that the real thing is better, and waiting outside my room. My legs tangle in the sheets and I almost lose my front teeth when I tumble out of bed in my rush to get to her.

"Let's go, Sleeping Beauty!" calls the real-life version of my dream woman.

"Give me a minute." I kick my legs free, and the sight that awaits me when I twist the knob is better than I could've imagined.

Leaning against the doorframe, and looking as impatient as always, is Indie, swimming in a threadbare t-shirt; my high school baseball team logo across her chest. A rolled-up pair of basketball shorts sit high around her midsection where her waist narrows, making the curve of her hips stand out.

When my parents came to visit a few weeks ago, my mom brought some things from high school she thought I would want to keep and stashed them in that closet. Mostly awards and memorabilia from college, but there was also a stack of clothes that she said were too sentimental to get rid of. I hadn't planned to keep much, but now seeing Indie in them, I know this set earned a permanent pardon from the landfill.

"Can you give me a ride back to my apartment?" With her arms crossed, she drums her fingers against her elbow. Poking her tongue against her cheek, she looks me up and down. Her eyes linger momentarily over my black boxer briefs. "You couldn't put clothes on?"

"Good morning to you too. How did you sleep?" I ignore her question, pretty sure it was rhetorical since I clearly didn't bother with clothes, too fucking eager to get to her, but it worked out in my favor. Partially because I like the feel of her eyes on me, and equally because I wanted to remind her of everything she's missing out on.

"Fine, I suppose. The bath was nice," she admits with a shrug, her gaze squarely on my face now.

"Don't you want to know how I slept?"

"You look well rested. That's enough information for me."

"Do I now? Tell me more about how amazing I look."

"That's not—you know what, if you want me to go into detail, I'm happy to." Her overly sweet smile tells me I'm in for it and I can't wait.

"I really do."

"You have pillow creases on your cheek, so that was my first clue. But it's the drool crust on the corner of your mouth that really sells it." Her pointer finger lands on the right side of her face.

My fingers wipe the corner of my mouth. Sure as shit, there is crusty spit in the corner. "I blame you," I tell her, letting my eyes drop to where her crossed arms are pushing her unrestrained tits up.

"How is that my fault?"

"My REM sleep was filled with some *very* vivid dreams about how much you love my tattoo, and the way you draped yourself over me to get a closer look at it."

Her eyes drop to the art. There's no hiding the effect she's having on me as my cock swells, going semi-hard under her gaze.

"Those perfect tawny nipples brushing against my stomach as you kissed a path from there to my—"

"Enough." She catches me off guard when her hand comes up to cover my mouth. This is becoming a habit of hers, and I'm not mad about it. "I don't have time for this." Her hand stays clamped over my mouth. "Brianna switched her flight. I'm not sure if I should give her space or give her a ride, but either way . . ." Her words trail off and I wrap my hand around her wrist, kissing her palm before I remove it.

"You want to get out of here?" My hand stays where it is on her wrist and she doesn't move to pull it away until my eyes drop to the shirt again.

"What? Did you expect me to sleep in my jean shorts and tank?"

Probably not the time to tell her I'd hoped she'd sleep naked like she did last time. "No, of course not." I pull on my neck. "I . . . uh, should have offered you something."

"It's fine. Snooping was more fun. Frankly, I'm disappointed I didn't find anything incriminating."

"Let me make it up to you."

She rolls her eyes, probably expecting me to say something crass.

"I'll drive you home and take Brianna to the airport. That way, you two can do what you need to do, but neither you have to suffer through the awkwardness of the drive or drop off."

"Why?"

It's a single, loaded word. "Why not? It'll make your life easier, and I don't have to be at the stadium for a few hours."

"Such a boy scout."

"Do you want to see the merit badges I earned from eating your pussy? Camping and Geocaching."

"You were actually a boy scout, weren't you?"

I wasn't, but it's too much fun messing with her. "One for camping between your legs all night—best campsite ever, by the way. The view was better than anything I've ever seen. Twelve out of ten, would return. The other for finding that spot that makes your back arch and your eyes roll back."

"There's actually something wrong with you."

"But you're still going to let me help you because you know I'm right. That car ride would be brutal."

"Fine. Yes. But not because I want to."

"I got that." Laughing would only irritate her more, so I roll my lips together to stop it. As much as I love annoying her, I'm making progress. Not that she would admit it, but this is the second time in twelve hours that she's let me help her. *And* I did it all without the help of my dick. Which, up until yesterday, was the only thing she's ever wanted from me.

With her clothes from last night folded up in her lap, she sits stiffly in the passenger seat of my truck.

"Your apartment isn't in the city," I say as I drive towards her apartment building. It's not far from mine, something I immediately noted when I helped her move in.

"And your point is?"

"Coming from downtown Chicago, I just thought you might want the convenience of city living. But it makes sense, you're closer to the mountains, with adventure right outside the door."

"I guess." She glances at the mountain range out her window.

"It's okay if you tell me I'm right. It won't kill you."

"It might." Like I'd hoped, the corner of her mouth pulls up in a grin that she quickly hides before she turns to face me head on. "My life would be a lot easier if you stopped trying so hard to make me like you."

"For who? Maybe you haven't noticed, but I like your claws. And I can take anything you throw at me. But enough about me. What thrill are you going to chase down first? Besides me, of course," I deadpan before I continue trying to pry her shell open. "Climbing the 14ers, backpacking the Colorado trail, or mountain biking black diamonds?"

"You remember what I told you about my adventure bucket list?" That gets her to look at me.

"I think about that night every day. I couldn't erase it if I tried."

Her eyes flick over me carefully. "I haven't decided yet," she says, giving me her back again as she faces the window. "Turn here."

"It's a vault, remember," I tell her, tapping my temple with my pointer finger. "I'll wait in the car while you two talk." Going in with her seems invasive, and I'm not sure I can handle seeing it if they decide to reconcile. Or kiss goodbye. Just the thought has my knuckles screaming as I grip the steering wheel.

"Yeah, thanks." She doesn't look back as she walks to the front door of her apartment.

I'm distracting myself by scrolling when a shadow passes over my screen and I look up to find Brianna reaching for the passenger door. She pulls herself into the truck and drops a bag into the back before looking at me.

"So the ex is taking the ex to the airport. This should be entertaining." There's no malice in her statement and she looks no more broken up about it than Indie did last night.

"Yeah, I'm not sure she would consider me an ex. But when you say it like that, I'm not sure this is less awkward than her driving you."

"It's only weird if we make it that way. And you're right, 'ex' probably isn't the right word for you."

"I don't know how I feel about you knowing so much about me." I rub my palm over my jaw.

"Oh yeah, playboy? Worried she told me all your dirty secrets?"

"Nah. I have nothing to hide. I would tell you every filthy detail about the time Indie and I spent together if I didn't think she would kill me."

"I'll pass on the play-by-play." She grimaces.

"Sorry. You probably have no interest in talking about this. Are you okay?"

"Do you actually care? It's clear you still like her."

"Well, yeah, but that doesn't mean I'm heartless. Just because I want her doesn't mean I can't have empathy when you're both hurting."

"It wasn't that serious. It could have been if we had met at different points in our life, but right now there are too many external factors for us to overcome."

I don't miss that way she raises her eyebrow at me. "And what? I'm one of those?"

"Aren't you? You already admitted you aren't over her. We don't know each other well, but you're a professional athlete. It's a safe bet that you're tenacious. It seems like an essential skill for someone at your level."

My laugh is self-deprecating. "She must not have told you that much about me or I'm sure you'd know that she's not interested in giving me a shot beyond what I've already had."

"Oh no, she made that perfectly clear, but Indie doesn't always see what's best for her. She's reckless; it's how she copes with her past. Stubborn as hell, too."

"Yeah, I've picked up on both those things," I say, not sure where she's going with this.

"You probably confuse the hell out of her. You're everything she tells herself she doesn't want, and everything she probably needs. But the last time she trusted herself to fall like that, it backfired in the worst way.

"I don't think I like this."

"Hang in there, big guy. Our girl is not an idiot, she's self-aware. The reason she fights her attraction to you so hard is because she's over-compensating."

"So she wants me, but doesn't want to want me?"

"Pretty much."

"And how is that a good thing?"

"There's a fine line between love and hate. Let her think that she hates you. In reality, you're exactly what she needs, and if anyone can convince her of that, it's you."

"Why would you help me?"

"Same reason you're here right now. I want her to be happy. Just because we didn't work out doesn't mean I don't still care about her. Indie's special, captivating, enchanting. I've known that since the first time I saw her, but you know that already."

"Yeah, I do."

"She deserves to find her person. I wasn't me, but I think it might be you."

I pull up to the terminal, shift the truck into park, and grab Bri's bag for her. I meet her on the other side of the truck and drape the bag over her shoulder.

"Thanks for the pep talk," I say, meaning it.

"Just take care of her. She's as tough as she acts, but she shouldn't have to be. Give her a place where she can rest."

"I will."

"I know." It sounds genuine, which is more than I would expect given our circumstances.

As she walks away, I call out, "Hey, Bri."

"Yeah?" She hitches her bag up and turns to face me.

"Don't call her 'our girl' again. She's mine now."

I see her head bob in acknowledgement just before she's swallowed up by the crowd of people rushing into the airport.

THE MYTH, THE MAN, THE LEGEND - DAD CHAT

DOM:

I've failed you.

DAD:

I doubt that.

DOM:

Nope. I'm definitely a shithead.

DAD:

How big of a turd are we talking?

DOM:

She broke up with her girlfriend and I'm not sad about it.

DAD:

Is she sad about it?

DOM:

She seems okay.

DAD:

And you didn't contribute to breaking them up?

DOM:

No. As much as I would like to think she did it because she realized I'm the one for her, that isn't the case.

DAD:

I'm glad we don't have to write you out of the will for being the biggest turd in all the land.

DOM:

These are the affirmations sons everywhere seek. Thanks, Dad.

DAD:

Anytime. Now, go get your girl.

CHAPTER 13

INDIE

My head is tipped upside down as I scrunch my hair with an old t-shirt when the buzzer for my apartment blares. Irrationally, the first thought that pops into my head is that it's Brianna and it sends an uncomfortable tingling sensation up my spine.

If everything went as planned, she should be boarding now. I watched from the door as she climbed into Dom's truck without a backward glance. She's gone. I could see the finality in her eyes when we said goodbye.

In the end, we parted on good terms, agreeing that ending things was for the best. She didn't even balk at Dom's plan to drop her off. Of course, I'd never admit it to his face, but I'm grateful that he offered. It gave us a clean break.

Squinting, I peer through the peephole. My eyes take a second to focus, but when I see the coffee cup with the Buns & Roses logo stamped in black and pink ink, I open the door without questioning it.

Only it's not Poppy or Mia, or even Lilah on the other side of the door, as I assumed.

Wiping my palms on my thighs. I resist the urge to reach out and grab the coffee, which he's now dangling between us. "Why are you here?" I let my eyes drift from the coffee in Dom's outstretched hand to his face. My nails drum against the door in annoyance, he's wearing that stupid grin that always makes my stomach flip against my will.

We will not.

He's not even that attractive if you take away the smile, perfect hair, the damn tattoo, and the muscles peeking out from under the black Bandits t-shirt he's wearing . . . Okay, fine, he's damn near perfect.

He knows it, too, which is why he opened his bedroom this morning in nothing but those black briefs. I can still see it fresh in my mind—the swell of his bicep as he gripped the door, the ridges of his abs sharpening as he leaned in close. He did that on purpose and I hate him for it because now I can't get the nearly naked version of him out of my head.

Last time it took me months to rid myself of the nonstop fantasies it caused. There's no telling how long it will take this time. Now I have the added complication of being forced to see him more with us living in the same city. Before I'd go long periods of time where I could push him out of my mind. Maybe this was all a terrible plan.

"Brianna got to the airport fine, but that's not why I'm here. I just thought you'd want to know."

"Um. Yeah, thanks. Is that for me?" I ask, eyeing the coffee. Caffeine sounds pretty fucking good right now. And judging by my riveting linguistic abilities, I could use some of the good stuff. After Dom left, I headed straight out my door for a hike. It did its job, wearing my body out to release the anxiety I was feeling, but now I'm just exhausted.

"It might be. Are you going to invite me in? This hallway is nifty and all, but it's not air-conditioned and I'm a pampered princess."

"Coffee first." My fingers flex towards him making the universal signal for gimme. "Is it—"

"Black like your soul? Of course. I know what you like." The playful wink he gives me hits me right in the ovaries.

I bring the coffee to my lips, hoping it hides my reaction and I tell him, "Wink at me like that again and I'll kick you right back out."

He knows better than to wait for me to offer him a glass of water and goes straight to my cupboard to get his own. Hopping up on the counter I watch as he opens up every single cabinet but the one they are in. "Oh, for fuck's sake. I'll grab it." I hop down marching over to him, brushing against him in the process.

"Thanks." Smiling way too wide, he hovers, waiting as I stretch up to grabbing him a cup.

Realization hits me as I lower my heels to the floor, the glass in hand. "You did that on purpose."

"And it worked like a charm," he says, taking the glass from me, our fingers touch, when I jerk my hand back he just laughs and goes to the fridge. He messes around with the buttons, switching the ice maker from cubes to crushed. The grinding continues as he fills the cup to the very top with tiny pieces of ice before he fills it with water.

"I'll ask again, why are you here? Is it just to annoy me?"

He drains the whole glass while I wait. "Nope. That's just an added bonus." Refilling the glass halfway, a move I'm almost certain is engineered just to piss me off, he takes his time before answering. "Can't I just stop by to check on my friend?"

"We are not friends."

His dark eyes flash with hurt, and I feel a tinge of guilt in my chest. After everything he's done, I know I should be nicer to him. But it would only encourage him, and that's the last thing I need.

"Former lover, then?"

"Key word being 'former.'"

"You're lying to yourself again."

"About?"

"Us not being friends for starters, and the former thing seems a little premature. I still have time to change your mind about that."

I laugh so loudly it takes me by surprise, but it doesn't deter him. Instead, it has the opposite effect. He scoots closer until we are hip to hip, leaning against the counter, and shifts to face me head on. Not one to back down, I do the same, but regret it immediately. This close, I can't ignore the scent of him wrapping around me or the imposing presence he has over me. When he looks down at me, the swoop of long brown hair that's always got this irritatingly perfect wave to it, falls forward.

"You let me drive you back to my house last night and stayed the night platonically. That's something friends do. Especially when one of those friends is notoriously bad at accepting help."

Suddenly my fingernails are incredibly interesting. I study them, refusing to give him the satisfaction of admitting that he's really got me pegged there.

"Then you accepted my help again this morning, letting me drive Brianna to the airport. She's delightful, bee-tee-dubs. I'm going to miss her."

"Sure you are. But you're still wrong."

"Now we are in your kitchen sharing coffee. See friends."

"You don't have coffee," I remind him.

He reaches out, taking the cup from my hand and sipping. "I do now."

"Still not friends." When another silky strand of hair falls forward, I add, "You need a haircut."

"Are you going to cut it for me?" He hands me back my coffee and I bring it to my lips, ignoring the fact that his lips were just on it and I don't hate that as much as I should. In fact, I kind of like it, which is problematic.

"Absolutely not." My nerves flare at his absurdly broad smirk. It's trouble, I just know it.

"Then it's settled. I'm not cutting it until you do it for me."

"I hope you like long hair because that's never happening."

"You'll cut it before the season is over." Voice clear and steady with his confidence in his prediction, he steps back turning towards the door. "See you soon, *friend.*"

"You never asked if I was okay?" With his back turned away, I squeeze my eyes shut, quickly realizing my mistake. But it's too late to take it back, so I straighten my spine.

Long strides carry him back towards me and his fingers brush along my jaw. The cocky smirk and mischievous gleam to his eyes are nowhere to be found when he looks down at me cupping my face. "Are you okay?"

"F-fine," I stutter, not expecting that level of earnestness from him.

"You know you don't have to be. As a matter of fact, it's normal to not be. You've got the girls who'd be there for you in a heartbeat; even the guys consider you like family. And you've got me."

Emotion constricts my throat. "Yeah, thanks," I say and strangely, I mean it.

CHAPTER 14

INDIE

Turns out finding a doctor that would see me on short notice without requiring me to sell a kidney on the black market was a tall order. Lara was incredibly understanding when I texted her asking if we could move our meeting to this morning to accommodate the appointment I was able to get due to a cancellation.

Not that I have any immediate plans that require birth control, but my prescription lapsed, which means I'm also due for my annual exam. And given my family history, I need to get it taken care of quickly. Luckily, the free women's health clinic is in the same neighborhood as Buns & Roses.

The bell above the door chimes when I walk in, and I spot Lilah's blonde head bopping along to the music as she works.

"You seem extra happy this morning," I say, stepping up to the counter as she continues moving her hips to the beat with her back to me.

"Indie!" she exclaims, setting the pan down and coming around the counter to hug me. "I didn't expect it to be you."

"I have a meeting this morning and an appointment nearby after. There's no way I was going anywhere else for coffee when I was this close. What's got you shaking your ass this early?"

Pink stains her cheeks. "Folger's had it all wrong. I love coffee, obviously . . ." There's nervous laughter, and then there's the uncontrollable, bubbly giggle that comes out of Lilah. "But the best part of waking up is an orgasm before you have a cup."

"Ah . . . the world's best wake up call. I miss morning sex."

"Enough oversharing from me. Who are you meeting?" She grabs a mug and starts on my coffee.

"You're not even going to try to talk me into a fancy drink?"

"No, you're a lost cause where coffee is concerned. I've accepted that," she says, untying her apron and leading me to a table where she takes the seat across from me.

"Do you know Dom's friend Lara?"

"Yeah. She's come to a few events with him in the past. She's fantastic; you'll love her. He set you two up?" Her brows furrow.

"He introduced us," I hedge, thrown off by her wording. "Said she was well connected in the nonprofit space."

"That makes sense. Sorry, I think my husband fucked a few brain cells out of me this morning." Laughter puffs out of her and she adds, "She'll be a great resource for you. She knows everyone."

Before I can push for any more information, the door chimes.

Lilah's eyes brighten as she waves the tall blonde woman over. Standing from her spot she wraps her arms around the chicly dressed woman in the same greeting she gave me. "Indie was just telling me you were coming in. It's so good to see you again, Lara," Lilah gushes.

"Likewise. It's been too long. It's been all stuffy political events with my dad's reelection. Those are nowhere near as fun as having fancy dinners with you and the guys for a worthwhile cause." Even her laughter is refined as she jokes with Lilah.

Tightness creeps up my spine when she steps back from the hug. Lara is stunning and commands the kind of graceful poise that only the most self-assured seem to possess.

"Lara, this is my friend Indie. I think you'll love the ideas she has to help our local nonprofit organizations. You two are going to work so well together. I'm jealous he gets the credit for pairing you two up."

Crystal blue eyes sweep over me appraisingly. "Any friend of Dom's is a friend of mine."

Lilah leaves us to finish her baking and Lara gets right down to business. As much as I wanted to dislike her on sight—a feeling I'm not ready to dig too deep into—I can't. She's a fucking delight. Professional, clever, and has brilliant ideas that only compliment what I'm trying to do. Her immediate passion for helping me achieve my goals is invigorating. Knowing that I owe Dom for this introduction is the only dark spot in an otherwise bright morning.

We leave Buns & Roses together with a plan to meet again in a week, and a promise from her to share some of the work I want to do with her connections to assess their interest.

"Dom's a man of many talents, but professional matchmaking was not one I expected from him." Our light laughter mingles between us.

Checking the time on my watch I see that I only have about fifteen minutes before my appointment. "Shoot. I need to get going. I have another appointment." My brows draw together as I pull up the address on my phone.

"Of course. Do you know where you're going?" Lara asks, picking up on my obvious confusion.

"Well, I thought I did, but the map isn't loading. Do you know where the Downtown Women's Health Center is?"

"As a matter of fact, I do." She points down the block and gives me directions to follow. "If you see Maryann while you're there, feel free to drop my name. She's in charge over there, and they could benefit from your help."

"Thank you so much; for meeting with me today, the directions and the lead. Really. This whole idea—moving across the country and taking a risk on a career outside of the corporate hamster wheel—it's a little daunting. But it just feels right, you know?"

"If anyone can do it, it's you. You've got the vision, the drive, and an unmatched devotion to the cause," she adds softly, laying her palm on my arm. "And I'm here if you need anything."

My eyes drop to her hand and then slice back to her face. There's a tilt to her hand, the distinct look of interest that goes beyond working together. Delilah's confusion over why we were meeting crystallizes into understanding. I'm an idiot. Lara's not interested in Dom. The uncomfortable jealousy that was plaguing me earlier is long gone with the realization that Lara is queer. It's a piece of evidence I don't want to look too closely at for fear of what I'll find.

The walk to the clinic is short, but with the summer heat, my skin is sticky by the time I step into the air-conditioned building. Waving my hand in front of my face I step up to the desk to check in.

Glancing around the waiting room I notice the touches the staff has added to make the space more comforting. For a lot of patients, me included, being here probably feels a little overwhelming. Soft neutral tones and low, calming music help to make this all feel a little less harrowing.

Over the course of my life, I've always been privileged enough to have access to exceptional health care, and I've seen firsthand the difference that can make through my mom. The extra time we got with her as a result is a gift I will always cherish.

I just hope that by working with organizations like this one, I can play a small role in giving that same gift to other families. But that isn't what brought me here today.

"Indie Moreno." A slim man in dark scrubs calls out from where he's standing by the open doorway leading to the back.

"That's me." The vinyl creaks when I stand from the chair and cross the waiting room.

He gives me a warm smile and makes small talk as we weave through the hallways to a small examination room.

"Is it a requirement that all clinics are set up like mazes when they are built?" Nerves get the best of me, and I let out an awkward chuckle.

"It sure seems that way," he says, before running through my personal and family history. Asking some additional questions when we get to my mom's diagnosis.

"The doctor will be in to see you shortly." It's the kind smile, like the one he's giving me now, that emanates compassion and warmth that always makes my hands clammy. Especially in a medical setting. Does he feel sorry for me? Is he calculating the difference in my age now and when my mom was diagnosed?

Sixteen years, seven months, thirteen days. A fact I desperately wish didn't taunt me each day that ticks away.

Clocks in doctor's offices always seem to move slower than anywhere else. And right now it's painfully obvious. I fidget with the gown that doesn't cover nearly enough of me, tugging at the paper to keep the cool air circulating through the office from making me chilled. Eight minutes feels like a lifetime.

Finally, there's a soft knock at the door that practically has me jumping off the exam table.

"Sorry to keep you waiting. I'm Dr. Maryann Smith."

"Of course you are." To her, I'm sure the strangled laugh that comes out of me sounds deranged. I cover my face with my hand, not even sure how my invigorating and productive morning has turned into this. The woman I'm supposed to talk to in a professional capacity is about to be knuckles deep in my vagina. "Sorry. Nice to meet you. I'm Indie."

"What brings you in today, Indie?" Maryann asks, her soft gray curls are barely contained by the chignon she has her hair twisted into. Crinkles around her eyes deepen when she tilts her lips up in a polite smile.

"You're not what I expected." Coughing to cover her laugh, she waits for me to recover. "Oh god. I'm so screwing this all up. Do you know Lara Preston? She and I met this morning, and she told me I should speak with you if I saw you today about a project I wanted to partner on. I just didn't expect this . . ." My hand sweeps down my paper covered body towards the stirrups, which are already extended out. It's only a small miracle that my heels aren't in them yet.

"I planned to find you after my appointment, fully dressed and not all amped up on pre appointment jitters."

"Ah. Yes, Lara is wonderful. She helped us fund a trans health equity program. But why don't we start with those nerves around your visit? Then, when you are dressed, we can talk about everything else."

"Yeah, I think I can handle that. I always think better with my pants on."

"Don't we all. Nobody really likes these visits, but I'm glad you came in. Looking at your family history they're critical for you. I'd like to do a mammogram after your exam today. Have you had one yet?"

"Nope, not yet. But I have a feeling today is my lucky day. My previous doctor and I had discussed starting them before I moved."

"And that's okay. Your mom was diagnosed at forty, so this is when we would typically start them for someone with your history. Before I do your exam, I noticed you're also looking for birth control options. Are you using something currently?"

"With the move, my prescription lapsed, and my previous provider encouraged me to take it because of the potentially reduced risk of developing ovarian cancer. But I'm also newly single and conventionally unemployed, and not in a place to be raising a tiny, needy human. So all around, a good idea." As if being nearly naked with nothing more than a paper tablecloth draped over me isn't humbling enough, the man who has no business being in this room with me is filling up all the space in my brain that isn't currently being used for rambling. I push away the thoughts of his hands on my body and the way he looked hovering over me, his shoulders straining, because now is definitely not the time for a stroll down memory lane. It's just that he was the last partner I had that I needed to worry about any of this with.

"Let's get you back on oral contraceptives, just to be safe."

"Yeah, that's fine," I say as she washes her hands at the sink before taking her spot at my feet.

When she's done, she steps out for a moment, allowing me to dress. A few minutes pass before she slips back into the room; a sample pack of birth control in hand.

"This will get you started and we can get you a prescription moving forward. Remember to use a backup form of birth control until these are gone. Now that you have pants on, we have a few other things to discuss, and if you don't mind, I'd like to start by talking about genetic testing."

Dread creeps up my spine, making my neck straighten and the muscles snap tight. "Dr. Smith, you're wasting your time. I know everything there is to know about BRCA gene testing. I've gone over every single pro and con annually since I was eighteen. Each year I come up with the same answer: testing isn't going to keep me from getting sick. Nothing will. Not even daily appointments with you. The emotional toll of testing has never been worth it for me."

"Tell me something. Have you done your annual review of it this year?"

"No."

Her hand disappears into a coat pocket, and she pulls out a pamphlet. "There's a support group that meets here once a week. Come to one meeting and just listen. It's a mix of some women, like you, who have chosen not to get tested, and others who've gone through testing and received results on both sides of the spectrum."

"I don't know." The thin paper feels like a heavy weight in my hand.

"No one is going to pressure you either way. But you'll have a community of people who know exactly what you're going through no matter what you decide."

"I'll think about it," I tell her honestly.

"Now, onto the fun stuff. Whatever you and Lara have up your sleeve, I'm sure it'll be wildly successful because she's a powerhouse and, well . . ." She tilts her head to the side, considering me for a moment. "I just have a feeling about you."

When I get home from my doctor's appointment, there's a gravitational pull centering around my couch trying to drag my tired body towards it, but my mind just won't quit. Unfortunately for me, it's the worst possible circumstance. Mia and Poppy are traveling together for a book event. Lilah was alone at the store today and Willa is in class. The support system I moved here for is MIA and I don't blame them, *like at all*. But I need to get out of this apartment and do something before I lose my shit.

It only takes me minutes to grab my gear and ride my bike to the nearby trailhead. Starting off slow I pick an easier trail since I'm unfamiliar with the terrain and do a few shorter loops.

The more miles I ride, the more I think. Rationally, I know the support group Dr. Smith referred me to is harmless. It certainly won't change my mind, but maybe knowing I spoke to others in the same boat will dull the inevitable guilt that gnaws at me when I tell my dad and Poppy that I'm not getting tested this year.

With a renewed sense of resolution and pliant muscles, I veer off, following a fork to a more difficult loop. On my second time through, my confidence has me riding a little harder. Out of the saddle, with my weight back, I sail through a downhill section, letting the thrill of the ride push me harder. All the icky vibes from earlier drain from my body with each stroke of the pedal.

Out of the corner of my eye, I see a blur of brown fur. The distraction is just enough for me to take my eyes off the trail for a split second.

"Shit!" I yell as my back tire skids across the dirt kicking up dust when I try to correct and make the corner. But it's too late, or maybe it's just too much. I can't be sure with the trees whipping by and the ground getting closer.

Pain radiates through my whole body, but it's the worst in my ankle. When I crack open an eye, two things are clear. I'm no longer on my bike, and I fucking hate squirrels. Especially that one. Slowly, I push up on my elbows, rocks digging sharply into my skin. Above me, the reason for my current situation is clinging to the tree looking at me upside down like I'm the problem here.

Where the hell is my bike?

Before I can figure that out, my watch is going off.

Dad.

"Double shit," I groan out loud, laying back down and accepting the call. "I guess the crash detection works."

"Please tell me you threw your watch against a wall to test it and not yourself."

"It wasn't my fault, it was that stupid squirrel. Do you think squirrels taste good in soup?"

With that, the little fucker scampers off, but not before dropping the spit covered acorn he was carrying right between my eyes.

"I'm going to eat you for lunch, you fucking menace." Dirt stings my eyes when I reach up to rub my forehead.

"Indie, did you hit your head? You're not making any sense." Concern laces my dad's deep voice.

"No, my head is fine." I think. My ankle is fucked, but a quick check of all my limbs tells me everything else is okay.

"Where are you?" My dad's voice borders on too loud for the pounding in my head.

"You're probably not going to like the answer."

"Indie, I swear I'll get on a plane right now and scour the whole state."

"That's not necessary. I'll call—" My mind runs through all the options as I sit on the ground, caked in dirt, my ankle throbbing. There's no one to call. The girls are all gone or occupied. The Bandits flew home late last night from an away series and play again tonight. Hendrix naps with his phone off and even if I could get in touch with him, his first call would be to Poppy, who'd probably freak out and fly home. "I'll call a *friend*." I finally sigh, resigned to my fate. When I hang up with my dad, I swipe through my contact list and find him under, "Yours."

CHAPTER 15

DOM

Trying to clear the sleep from my eyes I rub them again, certain that I'm still asleep and dreaming. If not, there's something wrong with my eyes, because what I'm seeing isn't making any sense.

Last summer Indie didn't protest when I took her phone and held it in front of her face, unlocking it to add my contact. She was still a little sleepy and very blissed out from orgasms. Nothing like when the post-sex-high wore off and she flipped the switch, going back to not being able to stand me.

Fumbling with my phone, I yank it from the charger and answer, afraid she's going to change her mind like she did then.

"It only took you a year to use this number. I'd have bet my signing bonus that you deleted it the second you walked out of my house."

"The thought crossed my mind," she says, her voice unsteady.

Something's wrong. Indie doesn't show weakness, not with me.

"Things must be pretty serious then. What do you need?"

"Can you come get me?"

My throat thickens at the utter defeat in her voice. She sounds worse than she did after she and Bri broke up.

She doesn't have to ask twice. I'm up and out of bed pulling on a shirt and grabbing my duffle bag for the stadium in case I don't have time to come back.

"I'm on my way. Where are you?" Her breathing is labored as she rattles off the name of a recreation area that I recognize. "That's close. It'll take me maybe ten minutes. Are you okay?"

"No. My ankle is messed up. But I'm going to work my way down the trail. I just need to grab my bike and I'll meet you at the parking lot—"

"Sit down," I bark, interrupting her. "Find a rock and wait. What trail are you on? I'll come up to get you."

"But I have my bike."

"Leave it, I'll buy you a new one." My tone softens as I open the garage and jump into the truck.

"That's not happening," she argues back and dammit, I wish she was mine so I could fuck that sass right out of her. There's no telling how badly she's actually hurt. The stubborn streak that runs through her is as wide as the Rockies and is going to have her downplaying her injury.

"Then I'll carry you and it. Just don't fucking move." When she doesn't agree right away, my patience grows thin. "Understood?"

"Yes."

"I prefer a 'yes, sir,' but that works." Concern has me pushing the gas pedal down. She must be in bad shape if she's not going to snap back at me for that.

She stays on the phone while I drive but doesn't say much other than giving me short answers about what happened and where she is. When I pull into the parking lot, I take off at a run uphill toward the trail.

"Indie!" I call as I get to an area she described.

"Here," she says, drawing my eye to where she's tucked into a corner, her ass in the dirt and her ankle propped up on a rock.

"Shit, Baby." The term of endearment I've only used with her once slips out when I see the mottled red skin around her swollen ankle.

"It's not that bad." When she shifts her position, the wince on her face says otherwise.

"Let's get you out of here and to a doctor to check it out." Squatting down next to her I drape her arm around my neck, carefully helping her up.

"That's not happening. No doctor."

Arguing with her won't get us anywhere, and right now, I need to get her out of here and find ice for her ankle.

"You're not really in a position to fight me right now."

"I hate you." But even as she says it, she lets her head fall to my shoulder giving me more of her weight. Exhaustion makes her body sag, as the adrenaline from her accident ebbs.

"No, you don't, but it's okay. I like the idea of role playing with you."

"How do you plan to get me and my bike out of here?"

"Vampire style. Let's go spider monkey."

"As long as you promise not to bite me."

"But you like it when I—" *If looks could kill.* "Noted, not in the mood."

"How come that's never worked before?"

"Call it a hunch, but it seems like you have enough to deal with. Now, where is your bike?" She points to where it's wedged upside down between a few tree branches. "That's a funny place to park a bike."

It's everything I hoped it would be when she weakly chuckles against my chest. "Why don't you just take a load off for a second while I fish that out for you?" Easing her on to the rock she had her ankle propped up on, I hop over the brush to get her bike. With it out of the pickers, I prop it against a tree and help her on to my back. Reaching behind me with one arm I support her as much as I can so she doesn't jostle her leg too much.

"I'm going to go nice and slow for you, okay? You tell me if it's too much."

Her breath hitches against the heated curve of my neck before she nuzzles in closer, her lips brushing my neck from the position the helmet she's still wearing is forcing her into.

"I can take it."

"Don't I know it." I mumble, adjusting my hold on her.

"Stop," she groans, but I can feel her cheeks swell with a smile from where she's pressed against me.

The walk back to the truck is slow and my hand aches from having to hold Indie and steer the bike with one hand. Both Indie and I are covered in sweat from the blistering sun when we get back to the truck.

Opening the tailgate, I lower her to it, helping her lift her leg so it's not dangling off the back. For the first time since I found her on the trail, I get a good look at her. My knuckles graze her jaw as I unbuckle her helmet. Turning it over in my hands I look at the damage.

"You hit your head." There are jagged edges where her visor snapped. My teeth grind together, frustrated with myself, I should have checked that before moving her. Taking a spot on the tailgate next to her, my fingers comb through the damp hair stuck to her forehead and run my thumb over her temples. "I'm taking you to the stadium with me."

"What? No. That is not the plan." She tries to pull away from my touch.

"So damn stubborn. If you're not coming with me, then I'm going with you to the hospital. Coach will probably be pissed. I'll definitely get a fine . . ."

With a dramatic flare I would expect from me, not her, she throws her head back in exasperation. "And *I'm* the stubborn one?"

"You're right, we both are, but you owe me—your knight in shining armor—because I came to your rescue." Gently I brush some dirt from her shoulder making her bite her lip when it reveals another injury, this one a deep scrape.

"Jesus woman. What were you trying to do?"

"It was the squirrel, not me." Her head drops into her hands.

"Yeah, you're definitely getting checked out. A squirrel didn't do this to you. Maybe we should go straight to the ER, have them do a full workup."

"If I come with you, that's it, you used your one chance to hold this over me."

"Hmmm. Sounds reasonable, but I have some other demands." My eyes drag over every inch of her making sure there aren't more injuries I'm missing, but she's a mess, so it's hard to say.

"Not surprised at all," she deadpans. At least her spunk is intact.

"You'll let the trainer check you out. And you'll stay until the game is over."

"Then you'll bring me home and this will all be over?"

"Not a chance. We need to see what the trainer says first. You'll do whatever he recommends, even if that means you need help to do it."

♥

Coach gives me a look that I know means I'm going to have some questions to answer, but doesn't stop me when a hobbling Indie joins me in the locker room.

"Nuts and butts away. There's a lady coming in," I announce as I help Indie through the door. With her pressed to my side, my arm around her waist, I can feel the groan. But it's not pain, it's annoyance.

Indies eyes go wide with panic. "Not ready to face the music?" I guess.

"Not really." She scans the room, her relief palpable when she doesn't spot any of my teammates.

Thankfully, the training room is near the entrance of the locker room, set away from where we dress, and we're early enough that we don't see any of the guys. "Hey, Grant, give me a hand," I say to our trainer as I lift Indie onto the exam table.

"Great, twice in one day," she mumbles.

"What was that?"

"Oh, just my dignity being left on an exam table for the second time today."

"What's going on Dom?" Grant asks, drying his hand as he walks over and stopping me from being able to ask Indie what she means. "Oh, ouch that looks painful," he comments, placing a gentle hand on Indie's outstretched foot.

"She was mountain biking and—"

"A squirrel ran out in front of me. I ended up in one tree and my bike ended up in another," she cuts in.

"And she hit her head," I interject.

"My visor broke when I hit the ground. He's making a bigger deal out of this than necessary. It's feeding the hero complex that goes along with his Flynn Rider haircut." The exasperation in her tired voice is reassuring. She can't be too badly hurt if she's still fighting with me.

"Maybe we let the medical professional do his job." I tilt my head to Grant.

"Fine," Indie gives in, arms crossing over her chest and laying back on the table.

While Grant does his thing, I grab a towel and run it under some water. Stepping up to the other side of the table I gently run it over her arms. Each scuff and scratch I uncover only makes me want to pull her into my arms, and take her home where I can lock her away and take care of her.

When this is all over, we are going to have a little chat about what the hell had her thinking it was a smart idea to be out on that trail alone.

Lifting her hand in mine I wipe the dirt and pebbles off. The vibrations that come from the watch take me by surprise.

"Shit, that's probably my dad." Her eyes drop to where our hands are connected. "Well, either answer it or give me my hand back."

Pressing the green button I keep working, treating each finger with the same care.

"Hey, Dad."

"I'm an old man, Indie. You can't keep testing my heart like this and then not call with an update." Her dad's voice is filled with fatherly concern for his daughter.

"Sorry." It's the first time I've ever heard her sound so vulnerable, and part of me knows I should give her space for this conversation, but there's no way in hell I'm leaving her side until I know she's okay. "I'm getting checked out now."

"Do they know about the squirrel nonsense? Make sure they check your head. You know what, put me on speaker so they can hear me."

"You're already on speaker, it's a watch, Dad. And why does no one believe me about the squirrel?"

"Hey, sir. My name is Dom. I'm one of Indie's friends. We're getting her checked out right now." I lower my voice to a conspiratorial whisper, "We know about the squirrel." Building slowly it starts with rolling her lips together, and then spreads to the corners of her mouth before I finally get what I'm working for—a stunning smile, followed immediately by Indie's fist connecting with my bicep.

"I showed you the acorn. You said you believed me."

Grant shoots me a questioning look and I duck my head in a quick nod.

"Nice to meet you, Dom. Are you going to stay with her until she's cleared?"

"Wouldn't dream of leaving her side." If only he knew how true that statement is.

"Good," he says, pausing before he addresses his daughter again. "You and I aren't done talking. I want to hear about your meeting and your check-up today. Was everything okay?"

"Yeah, Dad, we'll talk later." She sucks in a sharp breath when Grant manipulates her foot. Which is now bare, and it looks even worse, the swelling and bruising extending to her toes.

"Without doing imaging, I can't say for sure, but based on what I'm seeing, it's probably a severe sprain. You should still go get it looked at," he cautions, moving on to her head, asking questions and checking her eyes. "You're going to need to stay off of it for at least a few weeks. Limit weight bearing activity as much as possible. Definitely no riding or any other high-impact activities. I'm not seeing any signs of a head injury, but someone should keep an eye on you."

"She's going to hang out here during the game." I look at Grant. Who nods. "Unless you'd prefer I see if I can get you in a box. I'm sure Lilah would join you."

"Here is fine. I'm not sure I'm up for much else." Peace of mind that she's going to be close by isn't enough to dull the sadness I'm feeling for her. She's the picture of defeat, her shoulders sagging and her eyes on her ankle. It's a look I've never seen her wear.

"Can I get you anything before I get ready for warm-ups? Grant, can you grab her some ibuprofen?"

He comes back with water for her to take the pills and wraps her ankle. "I'm going to set her up in the dark room. Can you check on her every so often? If she's feeling up to it later she can watch the game in the media room."

"What is the dark room?"

"Exactly what it sounds like." Scooping her up from the table, I'm relieved when she doesn't fight me. We pass Xavier in the hallway, and he gives me a questioning look. But he's smart enough to not say anything, for now. I'm sure it's coming. "We use it to rest before games or between practices, but tonight it's all yours. No one will bother you here. And Grant can help you if you need anything between innings." Lowering her to one of the couches, I prop her leg with a pillow and grab her a blanket.

"Yeah, okay."

"I'll see you after we win," I say softly, her eyes already heavy.

CHAPTER 16

INDIE

Leather sticks to my skin and I pull the blanket tighter around me, trying to get comfortable. The pillow slips and a zing of pain shoots up my leg in the darkness when I move to grab it. Slowly, I sit up, disoriented at first. My ankle throbs where it's propped up, bringing back the events that lead me to wake up on a cold leather couch.

The squirrel, the bike, Dom. It all comes rushing back.

Moving gingerly this time, I sit up. My eyes adjust to the low light and I see that someone left a pair of crutches for me, probably Grant. Judging by the thick grogginess that still clings to me I was out for a while and the game is probably well underway.

I hobble my way towards the light filtering in from the hallway and find Grant still in the trainer's office, right where I left him. Only now the TV is on, and he's engrossed in the game.

"You're awake. I came in to check on you a few times and had to make sure you were still breathing," he jokes, glancing from the TV to me momentarily before he stands and offers me his seat.

I want to refuse, but I'm still too tired and sore.

"It's already the eighth inning."

There's no point in trying to hide my yawn. He's seen me at my worst once already today.

"As I said. Out like a light." Grant rolls another chair over and helps me elevate my foot. "We should ice that while you're awake." He doesn't wait for me to respond, just grabs a bag of ice out of the chest freezer in the corner and fits it against my ankle.

Between the weight of the ice and shock from the cold, I hiss through my teeth.

"You really did a number on it. It's going to hurt for a while, and it'll heal faster if you stay off it."

Groaning, I let my head fall backwards, already feeling trapped by the stupid injury. "How long are we talking?"

"Oh, you're going to be one of those."

"One of what?" Goosebumps cover my skin and I cross my arms, attempting to stay warm. The closed off posture and my words give off defensive vibes. But I suppose I am.

"The kind that can't sit still and ends up hurting it worse."

"Is there anything I *can* do?" Nothing isn't an option, not when getting outside and moving my body basically keeps me sane.

"Swimming, but only if it doesn't aggravate the injury. Dom had a similar injury during spring training last year. He can show you the pool exercises he did. It's mostly walking and running with a flotation belt on until it's strong enough to swim."

Perfect. Where the hell am I going to find a pool? Especially one that I can use anytime of day and without dozens of other people around. That's the reason I run to nature when things in the real world get too hard. Solitude helps me think.

"Let me grab you a sweatshirt or something," Grant says, his eyes dropping to my bare legs. Between the ice and the dried sweat from my ride, I'm freezing.

He's back a minute later handing me an oversized black and teal hoodie. I don't need to see the number four stitched on the arm to know who it belongs to. The second I pull it over my head, warm amber and rich jasmine surround me. I hate the way it immediately relaxes me. And that it's so perfectly him—a little sweet, a little spicy, and so damn wholesome. It could be straight out of a cologne ad in one of my mom's *Good Housekeeping* magazines from the nineties.

Ducking my head I breathe it in one more time. That's all I'll allow myself. Despite my annoyance, the sweatshirt does the trick, helping to chase the chill away. With no other options, I watch the Bandits wrap up the game, narrowly beating the LA Diablos two to one.

It's a miracle I've avoided the other guys this evening, but I know the chances of escaping the stadium unseen are slim. It's not that I want to hide this from anyone, but I'm just not ready to deal with the explanation for why I was out riding alone in the first place. Not until I know what I'm doing.

When the door to the office bangs open, I'm so startled that I almost topple off the chair. Thankfully, I don't. But I do laugh when I see Dom standing there, hair still dripping wet and his joggers on inside out. All the humor quickly fades when my eyes settle on his bare chest, water droplets still clinging to his firm pecs.

"Ready to get out of here?" he asks.

I hear him, but I can't pull my eyes away from the rivulet that is slowly running down the valley that splits his stomach, heading straight to where his perfect dick is outlined by his sweatpants. *Did he forget his underwear in his rush?*

"Can you check her head again? There's got to be something wrong with her if she's openly gawking at me."

And that does it. I give my head a little shake freeing it from its lust-addled state. "Maybe check *his* while you're at it. All of *my* clothes are on the right way."

Grabbing the shirt tucked into the waistband of his joggers, he shrugs it on. "Did you give her the lowdown on her restrictions?"

"Sure did," Grant says slowly, like he's not sure how much he wants to involve himself.

"And?" Dom prompts, looking at me this time.

"Take it easy and ice it," I summarize leaving out the bits I didn't like.

"That doesn't sound right." Dom frowns and looks back at Grant.

"Limited weight bearing, especially for the next week, no high-impact activities. The pool is okay. Same deal as when you sprained your ankle sliding into second."

"Thanks for looking after her. We better get you out of here." Dom hovers over me, reaching down to help me up before sliding the crutches towards me. His hand never leaves my bicep until I'm stable on my feet.

It's the same through the dark parking lot. And when he helps me into the truck. Under different circumstances, I would fight this, and not allow anyone to help. I've been strong for so long that anything less feels like failing. But all of my fight is gone at the moment, and as long as it gets me home to my bed, I'll go along with anything.

Leaning across my upper body he grabs my seat belt and buckles me in. I blink back at him, not realizing he'd already joined me in the car.

"Is there anything you need from your place for the night before we head to mine?"

That wakes me the hell up. "Uh-uh. Nope. Abso-fucking-lutely not."

"You heard Grant, someone needs to keep an eye on you tonight." He narrows his eyes at me looking more serious than I've ever seen him look. And damn it, even exhausted I can't deny it's kind of hot to see his assertive side. Or it would be if it were anyone but him.

"So come stay at my place. You have to go up and down the stairs at your place."

"Only if I plan on coming and going. Which I don't."

"What if there's an emergency? Are you going to wait for me to come over and help you?"

"No."

"Then it's settled. We're either both staying at your place or mine. You pick, but let me remind you there's only one bed at your place. And I'm not sleeping on the couch after playing a game when there's a perfectly good bed at my place."

"I'm not sleeping on the couch in my own damn place. Not today." As my frustration escalates, so does the volume of my voice.

"Hey. It's okay." Before I know what's happening, his large palm covers my thigh, squeezing lightly.

"No, it's not. Nothing is okay." Bordering on straight up panic I look at him silently pleading.

"Let me make this okay, just for tonight. Come to my place and you can soak in the tub—I'll give you space. Or we'll go to your place, even if it means I'm sleeping on the couch. Poppy and the girls would never forgive me if something happened to you."

There's an earnest concern in his voice that I hear so rarely from anyone but my best friends now that my mom is gone. Brianna gave me glimpses of it, but I never expected it from him, and I find myself caving to him because it just feels so damn good to be cared for. "No, you're right. It's silly for you to sleep on the couch. Go to your place."

"You're sure."

"Mostly, but if you ask again, I might take it back."

He rolls his teeth over his lips like it's killing him not to gloat. "Noted."

Other than helping me into the house and asking if there's anything else he can do for me in approximately a dozen ways, Dom sticks to his word and leaves me alone. In theory, that sounds splendid, but now I'm sitting here alone, going stir crazy. As tired as I am, I can't even think about sleep, not with the sweat and dirt from my ride earlier still clinging to me.

Pulling the hoodie over my head I set it off to the side. Next comes my tank top and sports bra, both too gross to wear later. Seated on the edge of the bed, I use my uninjured foot to lift my hips enough to slip my bike shorts and underwear down my legs. Annoyance creeps in as I look at the pile of dirty clothes. Another night of somehow ending up in *his* clothes.

What aggravates me more than anything is how comfortable they are. The oversized fit and softness you can only get when someone else breaks them in. A thrill races through me at the mere memory of the possessiveness that filled his chestnut eyes when they roamed over me in the hallway the other morning after seeing me in them.

Using the crutches I make my way to the bathroom and set them off to the side. The tile is cold against my bare skin as I sit on the edge and fill the massive tub. Swirling my hand through the water I test the temperature. When it's just below scalding, I add some lavender scented Epsom salts from the wicker basket next to the tub.

Martha would be so proud, and I can't even hold it against him because knowing he keeps it stocked for his mom makes it too damn endearing to use it as future ammo. Plus, after everything he's done for me since I moved, it would make me an asshole of epic proportions. It's almost like he cares. Like *really* cares, and I'm not sure what to do with that. It makes it that much harder to keep him in the box I put him in when I walked away. The one I convinced myself he deserved to be in because on the surface he reminded me too much of my past.

Carefully easing into the bath, I prop my bruised foot up on the side, but the edge digs into my swollen ankle, making pain shoot up my leg. I grab one of the rolled up fluffy white towels from the basket and slide it under my ankle. Much better.

Warm water laps at my skin as the tub fills. Switching on the jets, I sink lower, letting them work their magic on my tired body. Against my will, my mind wanders back to the man who came to my rescue today. Is he in bed already? Or is he wound tight after playing? Irrational jealousy has my teeth grinding together at the realization that he probably brings someone home after games to blow off steam.

With me here, that's obviously not happening.

That realization shouldn't make some of the tightness in my jaw melt away, but it does. It's just because I don't want to deal with whoever he brings home.

File that under lies I tell myself about the baseball player I'm not supposed to want.

Shifting in the tub to take some pressure off my ankle, a stream of water grazes my inner thigh. The pulsing sensation that accompanies it only reminds me of where I am. He would never know if I took the edge off. After a day like today, I deserve it.

Besides, he'll probably do the same. From everything the girls have told me, and from my own experience with the man in question, I know the postgame high that players feel is a very real thing. This time, when another jet of water hits my pebbled nipple, a delicious zing has me gripping the edge of the tub, and the pain tinged with pleasure tugs free the loose grasp I had on my self control.

Trailing my hand over my slippery skin, I cup my breast, heavy from the idea that I'm doing this under his roof. Being with him is not an option, but there's never been a question that he does things to my body. Things I hate.

Letting my head rest against the edge of the tub, I close my eyes, my mind already drawing on the memory of what he looks like under the spray from the shower. Is that where he is now, doing the same thing, or is he in his bed? The one he last had me in.

Shifting my pelvis I chase the pressure from the jet, letting it do the work for me. A whimper slips past my lips and then another as the pressure builds. His voice eggs me on as I imagine him pumping his hard length while he watches me.

With the warm jets making my brain malfunction, it feels like a missed opportunity that we never did that. His body is a work of art, sculpted from all the time he puts into it. Undoubtedly, it would've been hot as hell to watch him take matters into his own hands.

"That's it. Take what you need." I can practically hear him growl at me. His palm pressing down on my knee, he'd taunt, *"Show me how wet you get for me. That pussy doesn't look like it hates me."*

Blood pounds behind my ears as every muscle in my body tightens. I'm so lost in my pursuit of my orgasm that I almost don't hear it when my crutches slide down the wall and crash to the ground. And I certainly don't care enough to stop.

"What the hell." My eyes fly open at the rough voice. Standing in the doorway in nothing more than a pair of low hanging basketball shorts Dom looks wild. His hair is pushed back like he's been raking his hands through it, and his eyes are dark with lust and maybe a little anger. He looks from the crutches back to me.

With one hand on my breast, and the other between my legs, there's no hiding what I'm doing.

I should move, cover up, yell at him for intruding on my privacy.

But here's the thing: I've never been great about doing what I *should*.

Taking a step forward he looks down at me. "I hear whimpering and a crash. Now, imagine my surprise when I come running, thinking you've fallen, hurting yourself worse, and I find you touching yourself in *my* house. It better be me you're thinking of."

"And if it's not?" I push, my voice shaking when the jet hits that spot between my legs that has me seeing stars.

"I'll turn off these jets and remind you how good I am at giving your body what it needs." He moves another step closer.

"We're never doing that again." There's no conviction behind the statement, not with the pressure building between my legs again and the way he's watching me.

"No?" One more step.

"No." He's hovering over me now, right at the edge of the tub.

"Then tell me to leave," he says, adjusting himself through the thin material of his shorts. It's just as large as I remember. "Say it and I'll go. I'll accept that it was one time."

I bring my eyes back up to his, my heart pounding wildly against my chest as I work up the nerve for what I'm about to say. "Don't go. I want you here."

Fuck. His smile morphs into wickedly satisfied. "Tell me who you were thinking of just now."

Biting my lip I consider my options. Am I really about to do this after all the times I've sworn to him and myself that there was nothing between us? Nothing good can come from this, but my life is already a mess. What's one more time? It's not like it means anything, it's just an itch I need to scratch to get this little fantasy out of my head so I can sleep tonight.

"Words, Indie," he demands more firmly, dropping to the edge of the tub, and covering my knee with his palm.

Letting the weight of his hand help gravity, my knee falls to the side and I give him the truth. "You."

"Fuck. That's what I like to hear." I don't miss the way his voice turns all gravelly as his eyes land on the hand between my legs.

"Such an ego." My finger brushes over my clit making me shudder.

"Be careful, your sharp tongue only turns me on." The chuckle he gives me has me biting back a moan. "I need to know exactly what you were thinking that got you so worked up for me."

"Us . . . doing this. But to be fair, it started with a wayward jet."

"Don't blame the jets." His hand drops below the water. I should stop him. He's not supposed to be touching. Just watching.

Placing my hand over his I move it back up to my knee—giving me the illusion of safety. "I don't, I blame you. You just won't quit. You keep showing back up. Being in this house again, surrounded by your things. I can't control it. What am I supposed to do?"

"Maybe stop fighting it." His hand drops, grazing my inner thigh. My pussy clenches. *Traitor*.

"If you want me to keep going, your hand will stay where it was."

"If that's what you want."

"It is." The lie is more for me than him. "Take your cock out."

"No," he says with a shrug.

My mouth falls open in surprise. "Excuse me?"

"You'll get my cock again when you beg for it."

There's no holding back the snort that comes out of me at that. "Never happening." Just as the words leave my mouth, the jets kick up, catching me by surprise. It takes me a second to realize his hand is at the controls.

"Enough teasing, you've got me here, time to show me how hard you come when you think of me."

"God, you're such a cocky asshole." My words have no effect on him; not now that my hand is moving under the water, toying with my clit while the pressure from the jets helps me along.

"But I'm the cocky asshole you think about when you fuck yourself. And that's a win in my book. Slide your fingers inside that greedy pussy while you look at me."

"Oh, fuck," I groan, doing as he asks.

"That's it. Curl them the way I do, reach for that spot that makes you scream my name."

I wish I could say that it isn't exactly what I need, but it sends me reeling. My whole body tightens like a rubber band. Before I know what's happening, I'm lifted up and out of the water. It's incredibly gentle considering how quickly he moves. My ass hits the tile ledge behind the tub, my injured leg undisturbed. Dom is kneeling in the water, his shorts soaked, and his broad palm pressing my opposite leg me open for him.

"What the hell?" I ask, annoyed that he moved me when I was so close.

His eyes flash to mine looking so damn pleased with himself. "The water was getting in the way. I couldn't see you."

Everything about this should irritate me. The way he took me out of the moment, his hands on me, the bossy attitude, but in reality, the way he takes control makes the pulse between my legs pound harder. His grip on my leg tightens; he wants to see me like this as badly as I need him to.

"If I only get one shot at this, I want to see everything. Now slide those fingers back inside and give us what we both want."

I'm drenched from the prolonged edging, so they slip back in easily. Dom leans in close, placing his other hand on my knee, holding me open. Seeing him between my legs with all his focus on where my fingers work in and out has my pussy clenching and my back arching.

If it wasn't for his grip on me, I'd probably end up sliding back into the tub.

"That's it. So beautiful," he murmurs against the inside of my knee. "You're stunning when you fuck yourself for me—doing such a good job giving that pussy what it needs for me."

His stream of praise snaps the pressure coiling in my core. Everything goes black and tingles rain across my heated skin making me feel weightless. I vaguely hear the way his name tumbles out of my mouth, broken and needy. I'm too consumed by my release to dwell on it.

Fingers circle my wrist, bringing me back to reality. Without taking his eyes off of mine, he pulls my fingers to his mouth, running his tongue along them, until I finally come to my senses and take them back.

His tongue darts out licking his lips, looking smug as fuck. "The sweetest thing about you. Just like I remember."

"That was not part of the deal."

"Rules are overrated, especially when breaking them tastes like you." He leans back on his heels, rising in front of me. And dammit my eyes go straight to the tent in his shorts. From the way it bobs, I'm guessing he's not wearing anything beneath them. It would be so easy for me to reach out and test that theory.

As if he can hear the rebellious thoughts running rampant in my head, begging me to give him more, one side of his mouth lifts higher, giving me that lopsided grin. It shouldn't make my skin heat all over again. But it does, which is a problem, and all I need to shut down the needy voices in my head.

"Ready to beg already? I thought it would take longer."

"Fat chance. Now hand me a towel before I freeze to death."

After a beat too long, he reaches for a towel from the basket, shaking it out and draping it around me before he scoops me up.

"I can walk—" My protests fall on deaf ears as he continues turning sideways to get through the bathroom door.

"Actually, you can't. So let me just get you to bed safely before you slip trying to get out on your own."

"You're annoying."

"And you don't hate it as much as you pretend to, or you wouldn't have just let me watch you come with my name on your lips." With his knee on the bed, he sets me in the middle, looming over me. His eyes drop to my lips. For a second, I think he's going to kiss me. Instead, he brings his mouth to my ear and his free hand to his still tented shorts, gripping himself. "I'm going to go take care of this. If you listen closely, maybe you'll be able to hear me groan your name when I come all over my stomach."

"That level of detail was hardly necessary."

"I disagree. Last time you were here, I got you to picture me naked. Now you're thinking about the way I look with my fist around my dick after you let me watch you. You want this more than you let on, but don't worry, playing this game with you is the most fun I've had in a year."

Pushing off the bed he moves just out of reach, making a show of adjusting his cock. Then he leaves, flipping the lights off on his way out. Reluctantly I pull his shirt over my head accepting, once again, that it's my only option other than going to bed naked. But sleep doesn't come easy; not with my ears straining to hear any noise coming from upstairs.

Small miracles do exist because at some point last night exhaustion won out and my body gave in to sleep. The noises he taunted me with never came. Which is definitely not the reason I woke up on the wrong side of the bed.

Not at all.

That might be the throbbing in my ankle, or the fact that once again I can smell him everywhere; his scent clinging to the shirt I'm wearing and blending with the familiar clean fragrance of his sheets. If I wasn't cranky, maybe I'd ask him what brand of dryer sheet he's using because they smell too good for a single man.

The first thing I notice when I pull myself up to sit against the headboard is the glass of water and ibuprofen on the nightstand. The second is that my crutches are propped against the wall there as well.

Was he in here this morning or was it last night after—nope, not thinking about that.

Pushing away the landslide of memories, him on his knees in front of me, the way he taunted me with the promise that he'd make me beg for his cock. Like that's going to happen. Last night was it. Never again.

My sour mood improves marginally when the smell of strong coffee reaches me as I hobble towards the door, still slightly unsteady on the crutches.

Silence greets me when I step into the kitchen, which is always unexpected any time Dom is involved.

"Oh, Dommy-boy, you here?" The dripping of the coffee machine hints that he can't be too far. Movement outside catches my eye, so I crutch towards the sliding door to take a closer look. I almost trip when I get a clear view.

What seems like miles of muscles and tan skin glisten in the morning sun as Dom effortlessly hoists himself out of the pool, using the edge instead of the perfectly good stairs. With his back to me, he stands to his full height.

Oh my god. What the hell is he wearing?

Impossibly tight teal spandex cling to his ass, highlighting the perfect divots that grace each side. He bends to grab the towel at the side of the pool testing the scrap of fabric. There's a lot that sucks about my situation, but right now it's that I can't make a stealthy escape. If he turns around, he'll find me here gawking and I'll never hear the end of it, especially after last night. At the very least, I should look away.

Except what he does next has me entranced. Lifting his towel to the overgrown mop of golden brown hair, he runs it over his head, making every single ab pop off in spectacular fashion. His biceps and round shoulders flex with each pass of the towel. I am completely defenseless as I watch, knowing I'm playing with fire but not doing a damn thing about it.

Momentarily forgetting about my ankle, I spin, getting tangled in the stupid metal contraptions and lose my balance. My only saving grace is the oversized chair next to the door, which I'm able to dive into, keeping myself from putting weight on my injured ankle.

Once again, the clatter of my crutches falling gives me away, and moments later there's a still-wet Dom dripping on me as he leans over me.

"Enjoy the show?" He sounds smug as ever, but his brows pull together and his eyes roam over me, inspecting me for damage.

"I don't know what you mean. I'm just looking for help getting a coffee mug down."

A damp lock of hair falls forward when he cocks an eyebrow at me. "The mug I set out for you didn't do the trick."

Dammit.

"Oh. I didn't see that."

"That's weird. I set it right by the coffeemaker so you couldn't miss it. Grant told you to stay off your feet. Not to stand around like a Peeping Tammy while I swim. The shows are free, but at least take a seat so you don't hurt yourself."

Another droplet of water rolls off his hair, landing on my bare leg. "You're getting me wet."

"Glad to hear it. If you want some help taking care of that again, just let me know."

"What I need is a cup of coffee and a minimum of forty-eight hours without seeing your face." *Not true*, that annoying little voice in my head argues.

Shut up, you hussy.

"That's not very nice. I thought we shared a special moment last night." He mocks. "You'll be back for more before you know it."

"You're delusional," I say, rearranging myself in the chair and reaching for the crutches in his outstretched hand.

"There's a key by the coffee mug. The pool is yours to use anytime you want to rehab your ankle. Show starts at 7 o'clock every morning if you want to try to catch the full performance. On Wednesdays we swim naked," he teases. At least I think he's joking, but I can't be sure.

Not that it matters. I'll find another way that doesn't involve being alone with him.

"I'll drive you home. Just let me rinse off first."

CHAPTER 17

DOM

For the second time in twelve hours I'm gripping wood in the shower with Indie just downstairs. Her name pours out of me loud enough that she could hear it if she wandered up the stairs.

My muscles strain and my chest heaves as the last waves of my orgasm fade. Feeling less settled than I'd like after my solo session, I let my head fall against the tile. Warm water washes over me while my heart rate returns to normal. I finish my shower; the chlorine and the evidence of what I did swirl down the drain at my feet.

This is starting to be a real problem. I wish I could say that I'm ashamed, but I'm not. *Not after last night.*

All that lip service last year about how we were not worth repeating is nothing more than a lie she tells herself. I've suspected as much since she walked away. But now I know she was ignoring me because she wanted me— no, *needed* me. And I'm going to have so much fun making her admit it. Which is why I'm fine with resorting to more drastic measures.

This morning I was about to walk downstairs in my regular swimsuit—the pink one with Dean's face on it—when I remembered the weenie bikini still buried in the back of my drawer. A *gift* from my teammates during my rookie year.

To welcome me to spring training, they deemed the banana hammock fitting for a nobody that hadn't hit his first major league grand slam. I wore that bad boy with pride until I hit a bases loaded bomb right before the All-Star Break. Now it's got a new purpose, self-objectification to break Indie.

I meant what I said last night, the next time Indie wants me she's going to have to beg— preferably on her knees. I've spent a year trying to get her out of my system and failed miserably. As soon as her hands are on me, she'll have me wrapped around her finger, so she better damn well mean it. And nothing speeds up the process like exploiting her weaknesses by showing off her favorite parts of me.

Taking the stairs two at a time after my shower I half expect to find the house empty. To my absolute delight, I'm greeted by a stunning Indie—her curls pointing in every direction and her face free from make-up. Nothing is prettier than her sitting at my kitchen island sipping her coffee, and it hits me square in the heart.

She looks peaceful, with her eyes closed, sipping her steaming mug of tar like it's the best thing she's ever had. In truth, it's terrible. The smell is barely tolerable, yet I crave the bitter aroma because it means she's nearby.

"Look at how well you listened to my directions. I thought as soon as I left you alone, you'd call an Uber and bail."

"Trust me, I thought about it, but I didn't want this huge pot of coffee to go to waste. You never drink all of yours. You take one sip and get distracted."

"Huh . . . I never noticed." Hopefully her bullshit meter is as wrecked as her ankle. Pouring only a half a cup, I bring it to my lips, hiding my grimace when it hits my tongue.

The glint of gold metal dangling from the magnetic hook on my fridge snags my attention. I know an opportunity when I see one and there is no way in hell I'm passing this one up. Taking it from the hook, I cross the space to where Indie sits, and dangle it between us. "Take it. You'll be bored off your ass in two days, max."

"I'm not using your pool." When she doesn't take the key, I pocket it to give to her later.

"Why not? Afraid you'll see me swimming and do something stupid?"

"Like drown you? Yes, actually. You make me Dom-icidal."

Clutching my chest. "A crime of passion, no doubt. Don't use it, it won't bother me. Just don't go out biking or hiking and hurt yourself because you're too stubborn to accept help."

She sticks her tongue out at me and then takes a long drink of her coffee. Checking the time, I realize if I'm going to drop her off at home I need to leave soon to make it to the stadium. "Um . . . I need to get to the stadium, so unless you're going to hang out all day—which you can absolutely do—I need to get you home."

She stands and I take her empty mug from her, setting it in the sink. Her eyes move to my abandoned mug on the countertop. "Not going to bring your coffee?"

"Nah. I'll grab some from the stadium. Can't risk spilling it on the drive."

The ten-minute drive passes in mostly silence until we turn down her road and I say, "You really should have a doctor check your ankle, just to be sure it's not broken."

She mumbles something under her breath, letting me know she's not going to do that.

"What was that?" I pry, hoping she'll share what's going through her head.

"I'm just not really a fan of doctors, is all." She glances down at her lap but even without seeing her face I can hear the sadness in her voice.

"Your mom?" The urge to reach out and pull her into my lap nearly makes me cave. It's what I did the last time we talked about her mother's death. However temporary, there was a sense of intimacy and trust between us in the little bubble we created that night. One that burst the next morning when she made sure I was clear on where we stood. Each time she lets me help or confides in me, I feel a little of that trust being rebuilt.

I'm eager to get back to where we were, but if I've learned anything, it's that Indie needs more time to get to where I was then—where I still am now.

"That, among other things." There's no time to dig into the cryptic message because her apartment appears. She's going to try to bolt as quickly as she can, which is why I stashed the crutches in the back, leaving her at my mercy. "Wait there, I'll help you out."

I'm sure there's an eye roll I'm missing as I step out of the truck and grab her bike and the crutches.

"If you just give me the crutches, I can—"

Grabbing her waist, I lower her to the ground, keeping my hands on her while she finds her balance.

"That was unnecessary."

"Just let me help you, it makes me feel better. Besides, you know me, I'm the king of being extra."

Her eyes shift focusing on the bike behind me. "Well, since you mentioned it. Do you think you can put my bike in the garage for me?"

"Did that hurt?"

"You have no idea." Her nose crinkles. I'm sure it would only piss her off if I tell her how cute it looks.

Rather than risk being bitten, I bop her nose and back out of reach. "It looked like it might have."

What I don't expect is for her crutch to swing out and catch me on the ass when I bend to right her bike from where I laid it down next to the truck. The tap is barely enough to sting. But it still makes its mark on me. It's playful and that's one of my favorite looks on Indie, she twists her lips to hide her smile.

"There's a hook on the right side you can hang it on."

"I can do that, but I'm going to need something in return." Her eyes narrow. "Are you thinking about me naked again?"

"Forget it. I'll figure out how to put the bike away."

"No. I've got it. Just take the key." Prying her fingers from where they're wrapped around the crutch, I turn her palm up and press the key into it. "And when you get a wild idea, consider taking a swim instead."

"Fine."

"I think I like it when you do what I ask."

"Don't get too excited, Dom-a-zoid, I haven't done anything yet."

"Oh, but you will. That Speedo sealed the deal this morning!" I holler over my shoulder, wheeling the bike towards the garage, the new nickname lifting my spirits. Her bantering with me is a thousand times better than being ignored.

CHAPTER 18

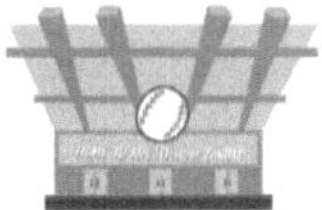

DOM

Everyone is heading to Draft to celebrate the Bandits beating the Rose City Roasters and the whole crew is waiting for me when I step out of the locker room. The girls have their heads together, leaning against the black brick wall and the guys are spread out on the couch, their focus on their significant others. At some point in the last two years almost all of my friends found love. Watching each of them turn into absolute simps for their women only makes me want the same thing more. Someday soon I'll step out in this hallway and find my firecracker waiting for me.

"I'm worried about her," Lilah whispers, her expression soft.

"She said she wanted to stay in." Poppy sighs.

"I know. I just don't like that she's alone. Maybe we should let the guys go to Draft and head to her place. You know . . . just check in."

Bracing my shoulder against the wall I casually scroll my phone far enough from the girls that no one suspects anything, but close enough to hear the conversation.

From what the guys have let slip over the last two days I know that Mia and Poppy got home late last night and spent most of the day with Indie. None of my friends were very pleased with me when they found out I knew about Indie's crash and didn't tell anyone.

With as much nonchalance as I could muster, I told them it wasn't my place. Who Indie wanted to know was up to her.

"Lilah, I get it. It's killing me to stay away too, but she's stubborn. And right now, bombarding her is only going to make her more withdrawn. I think we need to let her be," Mia says, siding with Poppy.

As Bri pointed out, I'm persistent as fuck and a little stupid for this girl. I know this plan could backfire but it's not going to stop me from trying. The girls had one thing right, Indie shouldn't be alone right now.

I slip out of the locker room before anyone can stop me, claiming I have a headache. I just have one quick stop to make on my way to her apartment. If I'm right, it'll be what saves me from getting my ass chewed out when I show up at her door uninvited, again.

Thirty minutes later, with a shopping bag dangling from my fingertip, I'm practically whistling as I wait at Indie's door. I'm about to knock again, but the telltale click clack of her approach finally comes.

"It's you." Her greeting is flat. Some people might be discouraged by the lackluster welcome, but not me. I'm hyper focused on the way *my* basketball shorts hang off her hips, leaving an expanse of skin exposed below the tattered hem of the thin tank top she's wearing.

Picking my jaw up off the floor my gaze moves to her face. The vibrant spark of life that belongs in Indie's eyes is missing. My firework is letting her fuse burn out and that bothers me—like really fucking gets under my skin. There's more going on here than just being bummed over her injury and I'm going to coax it out of her sooner or later. My sister tells me my inability to quit is one of my most annoying qualities. But when someone I care about is hurting it feels more like a superpower.

"It's me," I say, remembering why I'm here in the first place. "And I brought you something."

Dark hair falls over her eyes as she cocks her head eying the plastic shopping bag. "I'm not really in the mood for games."

"Well, shit." That sucks because that's exactly what I brought. "Are you sure? It's your favorite."

"Tell me about your mom." My lips graze the smattering of stars and planets inked across her collarbone. I know asking is risky, but it's been nagging at me since Indie told me she got the tattoo in memory of her. We've spent hours in bed exploring each other physically, but I want to know something deeper than how hard I can make her come on my tongue. Moving along her chest I kiss every dot of ink marking her skin until I reach her neck.

"My mom was everything, a personality as big as the galaxy and a heart that couldn't be contained within this universe. She was the center of my world, the calm to my storm . . . just all of it."

"Sounds like someone I know."

Her puff of laughter ruffles my hair. "You don't know me that well. And you didn't know her." There's nothing but admiration in her voice as her eyes grow misty. "She was endlessly giving and kind. Even when she was exhausted from chemo, she was there with a warm smile, playing board games with Poppy and I. Losing her broke part of me and I'm not sure I'll ever be the same."

"What was your favorite game to play with her?"

She hits me with a painfully beautiful smile. "Sorry. We all loved it. She played until the very end, even when she could barely move the pieces. Her head would be on the floor next to the board and she'd keep going until she knew whatever nonsense Poppy was dealing with at home was evened out by love and attention from her."

"And she passed that fierce loyalty on to both of you." My hand cradles the side of her face, tracing my thumb along her jaw. "Did you, or did you not, threaten bodily harm to Hendrix if he hurt Poppy again?"

Sucking her cheek like it's painful for her to admit that I might be right, she finally sighs and says, "Yeah, I did that."

"And you did it in your own terrifying way, I'm sure." I kiss the swell of her breast right over her heart. *"You might not be a mirror image of your mom, but those qualities you love about her, they're engraved on your heart."*

"I'm not so sure about that." Pulling away from my hand she rolls her head to the side looking out the window at the night sky.

My fingers trace the words inked into her stars. "That's fine, because I am, and she was too. Neither of us will let you forget how to soar, Firecracker." She stays silent, her throat bobbing as swallows roughly. Nothing good will come from pushing her, not yet. She might trust me with her body, but that bond doesn't extend beyond the bubble of this bed, so I change topics. "Do you still play?"

"The board stayed at my dad's. It didn't feel right to take it out of our home. Poppy and I used to play when she visited, but that happens less than it used to. Dad doesn't play and I can't bring myself to buy a board of my own."

She springs forward with cat-like reflexes that seem unnatural for a woman on crutches, and I hold the bag high, keeping it out of her grabby hands. My palm lands on her waist, steadying her, so she doesn't lose her balance. With all her flailing, the crutches are nothing more than wobbly kickstands. "Invite me in and we can play."

Tilting her chin down, she looks at where my fingers press into her warm flesh, her tank having risen in the commotion. One dark eyebrow lifts in a silent question. *Why are you still touching me?*

"Because I want to," is my silent reply.

Goosebumps scatter up her exposed arms when I lean in close. "Let me in and I'll make it worth your while. I have some of that terrible Neapolitan ice cream that you love."

"I'm inviting the ice cream in, not you." Relenting, she steps back, breaking our connection to let me in.

"We both know that's a lie," I say, setting the bag down and pulling the ice cream out. Without waiting for permission, I grab two bowls and a spoon and dish out the ice cream, taking it and the bag to the living room.

The scrape of her crutches follow me. "Is it? The ice cream is definitely helping, at least until you show me what's in the bag."

She'd probably be more comfortable on the couch playing the game at the coffee table, but I set the board up on the floor just like she and Poppy used to do with her mom. One by one I lay out the pieces giving her time to figure out her next move.

Slowly she sinks to the floor using the coffee table to steady her. "You bought *Sorry* for me?" The question is almost a whisper.

"No, I bought *Sorry* for me, but it's not as fun to play it alone." Unless she asks me to leave it here, I had every intention of bringing it home with me, because I wasn't entirely sure how she'd feel about having it here.

"Leave the yellow. It was *her* color." Emotion shakes her voice and her hand covers mine, stopping me, I let the piece fall back into the box, giving her hand squeeze.

"And what was your color?" I ask, pulling out the remaining pawns.

"Red."

"Then I'll be blue." Turning the board so we are lined up with our pieces, I set the ice cream in front of her, taking the bowl with the smaller scoop for me.

"Is this the most excitement you've had in the last two days?"

"You have no idea. I'm bored out of my mind. Poppy, Mia and Lilah have all stopped over. They mean well, but I can stand the hovering. It feels like they're babysitting me." Digging into her ice cream, she starts with the strawberry. "Speaking of, shouldn't you be out celebrating your win?."

"You watched my game?"

"Did you miss the part where I said I was bored? Plus those pants."

"Checking out my ass again. I knew that Speedo would work."

"How could I not? You can see the back of your red thong through them. Please tell me you're wearing it now. I could use a laugh."

"Sadly, I'm not. It needed a wash. But if you want to see me in a thong, go grab one—"

Cold, wet ice cream flies through the air and time seems to slow as I watch her mouth fall open in an *O*. It hits me in the cheek with surprising force. Across from me, Indie stares at her spoon, stunned, like she can't believe she just did that.

"Now you've done it." Catching the melting ice cream in my hand as it slides off my face, I pop it into my mouth and round the board game on my knees. Cautious of her ankle, I pin Indie to the ground with my body. "You make the mess, you clean it up."

Her chest stills, and the sweet laughter she was just gracing me with stalls out. For a second, I think I've screwed everything up by pushing her too much.

Then her tongue darts out and wets her lips. Narrowing her dark eyes at me, she pushes up on her elbows. The sticky residue on my cheek is forgotten as silence stretches between us. I'm all too aware of where our bodies are joined at the hips, the air growing thicker with each second that passes, neither of us moving.

Just when I'm about to pull back, unable to stand the growing tension, she threads her fingers through my hair and roughly tugs me toward her. Our lips nearly touch. They are so close it's killing me not to dip my head and take what I want. I'm about to break when she turns my head at the last second and runs her tongue up the side of my face, cleaning the ice cream from my cheek.

There's nothing conventionally sexy about her tongue on my cheek or the way she howls with laughter at the absurdity of it all. Yet, no one has ever looked as irresistible as she does under me, joy in her eyes and her smile unapologetically wide. She's completely pleased with herself and I'm here for it.

Before I can pull myself out of my stupor, she shoves me off her and peeks at her card, clapping her hands together, then she flashes me the eleven card and swaps places with me.

"This was a great idea. Nothing makes me happier than handing you your ass."

Pink that wasn't there when she opened the door tints her cheeks. She studies the card in her hand and hums, sounding lighter than I've seen her since she moved. She probably thinks I'm here hoping to get her back into bed, but Indie with her guard down and claws retracted, just being with me, is all I can ask for.

"You licked me. Does that mean you plan to keep me?"

"I don't believe for one second that you want to be kept." Her attention shifts to the game, her lips moving silently as she counts my spaces. "Besides, we've been over this. I don't date guys like you."

"You mean, handsome as fuck, but cheats at board games?"

"So you admit it." The side of her mouth quirks up and those dark eyes study me too long to be considered a passing interest.

"That I'm handsome? Obviously."

"That you're a scoundrel who can't be trusted?"

"Not going to dispute how good looking I am? I'll count that as a win." Using a gentle hand I brush my fingers over her bruise which has started to fade from an angry purple to green at the edges. "Scoundrel or not, you can trust me to come through when it counts. The offer still stands to use that key."

"I'm not sure I ever told you how much I appreciate you coming to get me the other day. And for this, it was unexpected and exactly what I needed. So, thank you."

"That's what friends do."

For once, she doesn't fight me on the label. She just hands me my card and rolls her eyes, letting me count out my spaces on my own. Just because her lips don't move doesn't mean she's not watching. Testing my theory, I take one extra space. "It's killing you, isn't it?"

"No clue what you mean."

"I've never really been a fan of rules where you're concerned." Especially the one that's keeping us apart. Slowly but surely I'm going to prove to her that she's wrong about us, that one night wasn't enough.

Driving home an hour later, one *Sorry* game lighter, I know, without a doubt, that this was where I needed to be tonight.

THE MYTH, THE MAN, THE LEGEND - DAD CHAT

DAD:

Don't leave me hanging. Did you get the girl?

DOM:

I'm working on it. She's a little prickly and she's going through some things. I'm just trying to be there for her.

DAD:

All you can do is show her the kind of man you are.

DOM:

I'm trying. I just hope it's enough.

DAD:

You know your mom put me through my paces when we first started dating.

DOM:

You asked her out five times before she finally agreed. I've heard the story.

DAD:

It's my favorite story. I would have asked her out a hundred times to get my chance.

DOM:

Mom's one of a kind. So is Indie.

DAD:

Maybe we can meet her when we come out at the end of the season.

DOM:

I hope so.

DAD:

Dottie wants to know if you're still going to help her with her homework tonight?

DOM:

Tell her of course, it's the highlight of my week.

CHAPTER 19

INDIE

For as long as I can remember, I've needed to be on the move.

After my mom's diagnosis, it only got worse. Sitting idle was physically painful, like my skin was being stretched by energy that had no way to get out. Biking was something my mom and I loved to do together. The sicker she got, the more I pushed it, riding on trails and longer distances. When I couldn't ride, I'd run or hike anything that got me outside and wore me out.

Usually it's enough to do the trick, especially coupled with anxiety meds, but sometimes the agitation wins out and that's when I end up being a little reckless. Not because I don't value my life, but because I need to feel something other than grief and panic. The adrenaline seems to calm it, at least temporarily.

Needless to say, I'm not adjusting well to this injury. So when Dr. Smith called after sitting around for almost a week to tell me they had a project they needed help with, I figuratively jumped at the chance to do something useful. Our meeting got off to a rocky start when she saw me hobbling in on crutches and insisted she look at my foot.

Now that she's confirmed it's not broken, just badly sprained as expected, and forced a boot on me to help me get around better, we are finally getting down to the reason I'm here in the first place—staffing a second location. Beyond that, they also need help to set up a volunteer structure for a future sexual assault crisis hotline that they are hoping to roll out later this year.

"It's a big undertaking, but I'm confident that we can meet the deadline. I'll start on it right away," I tell Maryann as she walks me to the door. As much as I protested the boot, telling her it was unnecessary, I've got to admit it's so much better than those crutches.

"I have no doubt. If you still have some time this evening, that support group is meeting in about—" She glances down at the delicate silver watch on her wrist. "Twenty minutes. That's just long enough to grab a coffee and make it back in time."

"You planned this, didn't you?"

The glint of humor in her eyes and wry grin give her away. She absolutely did this on purpose. "Only some kind of evil genius would do that."

"In that case, see you later, Gru."

Passing my car on the way, I drop off my crutches, since I no longer need them with the boot. I could just get in and go home, but after everything Dr. Smith has done for me, going to this meeting hardly seems like a sacrifice. Like she said, all I have to do is listen. It won't change anything.

There's not enough time to make it to Buns & Roses and back before the meeting starts, but there is a Dunkin' on the corner. If I'm going to sit through this meeting, I at least deserve a mid-afternoon pick-me-up. One plain cold brew later and I'm doing a lopsided stroll back into the clinic for the meeting.

Skipping right past the name tags, because I have zero plans to share today, I head straight to the circle of chairs. There's nowhere to hide, so I take the most unassuming spot I can find. With five minutes before the start, there are only a few open seats left and they are filling fast.

Just as the facilitator rises to pull the door shut, sneakers squeak on the tile, and there's a rushed apology as a woman who looks to be about my age cuts right through the center of the circle. Her light blue hair is cut into a bob and she's got a tiny hoop hanging from her septum.

"Hey, I'm Beck, mind if I—" Before the question is even out, she drops into the chair beside me. "Oh yeah, this is the spot."

"Uh, it's all yours," I say, offering her a half wave in introduction. "Indie."

I've always thought I had a lot of nervous energy, but Beck can't stop tapping her foot next to me. It doesn't stop until the facilitator calls on her. We are the last two to go and I'm no more excited to introduce myself now than I was ten minutes ago. The room is filled with cancer survivors, children of survivors, and those who have lost a loved one to cancer.

"Everyone knows me, so I'm just going to skip my usual song and dance to introduce my new friend Indie instead."

This takes me by surprise since the only thing she knows about me she already revealed, but if it means I don't have to introduce myself, I'm happy to give her the floor.

Shifting in her chair so she can study me for a moment she says, "Indie is a Leo, who loves adventure, hates cancer, and wishes she was on a tropical vacation instead of here."

Well, that was eerily accurate. "Close. I'm a Cancer by a date, but identify as a Leo. Ironic, I know. I love adventure, but it hates me right now," I say, wiggling my foot. "But the other two are totally true."

"And what brings you here today?" Beck asks, completely ignoring the facilitator, who's clearing her throat in an attempt to regain control of her meeting.

"Dr. Smith coerced me into coming, very nicely, but it was not how I planned on spending my day. My mother passed away from ovarian cancer when I was in college."

"Interesting. And why do you think she wanted you to come today?"

"Beck, let's not—"

"No, it's fine. I'll answer. That's why I'm here." Oddly enough, I mean that. Beck put me at ease making me feel like I'm talking to a friend instead of a room full of strangers. "I'm obviously high risk given my family history and I haven't done genetic testing. Maryann—Dr. Smith encouraged me to come today before I decide about testing."

"Ovarian, yikes, that's rough. Breast cancer mom here, double mastectomy for my eighteenth birthday. My sister and I both lost the BRAC1 lottery, and she's currently fighting pancreatic cancer."

"You're not really convincing me to get the test."

"Not trying to. That's up to you. Knowing she was positive made her hyper-vigilant about her health and it made me just give fewer fucks about everything that wasn't life and death. It all boils down to what you make of it."

"Do you regret it?"

"Nope, it's given me the freedom to live my life the way I want to—without fear. But it looks like you already do that." She glances down at my foot.

Yeah, I'm not so sure that's true.

Eventually Daphne wrangles the meeting out of Beck's grasp. By that point, my mind is spinning out of control. Heaviness where the boot weighs me down just serves as a reminder that there's not a damn thing I can do about it. I can't run to escape the turmoil boiling inside of me at Beck's story.

Remaining seated during the moment of gratitude at the end of the meeting is next to impossible, my skin itches and my mind races. I limp to the door the second we end, digging through my belt bag, blindly searching for my phone to call an Uber. Driving with this boot on doesn't seem smart, especially in my current state

Something cool and metal brushes against my fingertips.

Keys. Not just my keys, but Dom's too. Not that I planned to use it, but I added it to my ring so that I could return it the next time I bumped into him. Taking them out I examine them in my palm. Swimming might help work out the questions churning in my mind. It's really my only option unless I want to go home and stew.

But I can't do that. Driving with this boot strapped to my foot and my mind like a battlefield wouldn't be smart. Home is not where I want to be, anyway. I want to be outside biking or hiking until there's nothing left but boneless exhaustion. The stories shared in the meeting, this injury, and the constant pressure of the decisions I need to make are fighting against each other putting me into a tailspin.

Pocketing the keys, I enter his address into my phone. My hands tremble and it takes a few tries to get the car ordered. Three minutes has never felt longer as I watch the tiny car on my screen circle a block over, navigating the traffic and one-way streets so he can get to me.

When he pulls up to the curb, I'm practically diving into the car before he's fully stopped. That's how badly I need to get out of here, and the sideways glance he gives me in the mirror tells me I look as unhinged as I feel right now.

"Indie?" the driver asks.

I straighten, doing my best impression of someone who is not completely off their rocker. "Yep, that's me."

"Everything cool?" The amount of doubt in his eyes could fill an Olympic-sized pool.

Clearly, he's not buying the fake smile plastered to my face. "So cool. Thanks." *Not at all.*

The key I'm twisting in the lock fifteen minutes later doesn't make me feel any less like a petty criminal performing some minor B&E. Once I'm inside, I take the key from my ring and set it on the counter. This is a one-time deal.

Just like every other time I've been in Dom's house, it's nice and orderly, like his life. Somehow his place looks less like a bachelor pad and more like a home. A picture of his family in front of an actual white picket fence sits on the shelf. Longing for a life I've spent a decade grieving hits me, knocking me off balance. Next to it there's a photo of him and who I assume are his sisters in a photo booth, one on each side, kissing Dom's cheeks, draped in boas. I laugh at how ridiculous he looks with giant, bedazzled sunglasses perched on his nose.

In the center of the room is an oversized couch, big enough for all his friends.

"Oops," I mumble to the silent house when the navy-blue fringed throw pillow I run my fingers over accidentally falls to the ground. The man needs a little mess in his life, so I keep walking toward the wall of glass facing the backyard, pausing when I reach the patio door. There's one glaring problem with this spontaneous plan.

No swimsuit.

The Bandits are playing at home today. Something I only know because the girls would not stop talking about how thrilled they were to have a long home stretch. There's almost no chance he'll be home soon.

Just the idea of turning back now makes my palms clammy as I wrap my hand around the door handle and tug it open, stepping into the dry Colorado heat.

Even with the sun sinking lower in the sky, it's still stifling. Sweat gathers on my forehead, and that's all the convincing I need. Moving to the shade of the covered patio I grab a towel off the stack. There's wicker loungers spread around the pool; I pick one close to the edge and perch on the end, removing the boot. I wiggle my toes ignoring the twinge of pain and walk to the stairs slowly. Without the support of the boot my foot throbs with each step.

High shrubs surround the pool, giving me a sense of privacy that makes me brave enough to strip my shirt over my head. Next come the shorts. After a quick glance around to make sure I'm still alone, I peel them down my legs.

Getting caught completely naked, while unappealing, seems less uncomfy than riding home in a stranger's car, commando. So underwear go as well, creating a mountain of evidence that will give away what I'm doing if anyone finds me here.

Since I'm standing bare-fucking-naked in the backyard of a guy who I barely tolerate, I don't waste any time. With each calculated step, the sublime temperature of the water coaxes my body to relax. By the time I'm neck deep, everything feels a touch better—mind and body.

Using my arms since my ankle is still too tender to really kick, I pull myself across the water at a lazy pace. It's not the breakneck speed I'm used to when I'm biking or running, but after dozens of laps, my heart pounds against my ribs and my brain calms enough to process what led me here.

I flip to my back and float in the middle of the pool watching the sky morph from blue to pink as the sun sets.

Year after year, I go over the same decision, but tonight was the first time I've ever connected with the decision emotionally. In the past, it's always been about my mom and what she went through—a fast no.

Hearing Beck so candidly share her experience resonated in a way nothing else ever has. No matter how many doctors or nurses have tried to persuade me with statistics, anecdotes, or pamphlets, none of them have touched the impact the blue-haired pixie made on me. She was so sure of her decision. I want that for me. Peace in knowing, whatever the outcome.

Tears roll down the side of my face, mixing with the water, the magnitude of the decision settling over me like a rain cloud. If I do this, I can't un-know the results. Beck let it free her, but what if I do it and it traps me. Maybe that's why I've run from this decision every year.

CHAPTER 20

DOM

Nothing has ever been as beautiful and devastating as Indie naked and crying in my pool.

There was a notification from my security system that she was here when I pulled my phone from my locker after our loss tonight, but I wasn't prepared to find her floating, with her head tipped back and her face red from tears. Black curls float behind her in the clear blue water and her arms stretch wide, making her look like a broken angel; bared to me and vulnerable with everything below her breasts underwater as she drifts aimlessly through my pool.

It's not a conscious decision when I see her from the edge of the patio, her chest trembling as the strongest woman I know falls apart in front of my eyes. My shoes and socks join the pile of her clothes, followed swiftly by my shirt and joggers. Only my briefs remain when I lower myself into the water.

Not wanting to startle her, I whisper her name, laying my hand on her shoulder. "Indie."

She does the last thing I expect and doesn't hide from me. There's no yelling or snark when she turns in the water to face me with so much sadness.

Pulling her to me is as much of an instinct as going to her, because seeing her like this guts me.

It isn't until she wraps herself around me, her wet skin slipping against mine, that I question my character. Maybe stripping down was the wrong choice because my dick doesn't get the memo that now is not the time to take notice of the hot, wet woman in my arms.

One I've wanted since she walked out on me without looking back. "Do you want to tell me why you're topping off my pool with salt water?" I ask, doing my best to ignore the heat of her nestled right against my now semi hard dick. My efforts to keep him under control can only do so much—I'm not a magician.

"Talking won't help." Only the tracks from her tears remain on her stunning face as she sinks her fingers into my hair clinging to me like I'm the only thing that can keep her from drowning in her feelings.

"What do you need? Name it and it's yours."

"Make me feel something—anything but this." Her hips shift and she buries her face in the crook of my neck.

She's using me. I know it and she knows it, but I also know it's more than that. As much as she continues to deny it, there is this tether between us. One that keeps bringing her back to me; that she can't cut completely. "It's cute that you think you get my cock. I didn't hear you beg for it yet."

Fire rages behind those dark eyes just like I wanted. She asked me to make her feel something else and annoyance is just the start. Cutting through the pool I head to the stairs and adjust my grip on her, my fingers digging into her cheeks.

When I bought the house, one of the selling points was the privacy the backyard offered me. Especially this covered patio, although I never guessed that I'd have a naked Indie under me on the lounger. Which is exactly where she is now as I lower her onto the plush cushions.

"Where are you going?" She pushes up on her elbows and I can see the panic from earlier returning.

"Just grabbing you a towel."

"But I don't want a—"

"Calm down. There's no way I'm covering this perfect fucking body."

I turn back to find her with her arms folded glowering at me. "Didn't anyone teach you that telling a woman to calm down is the fastest way to a fight?"

"Yep. But I bet you taste even sweeter when you're mad, and I'm famished for a post-game snack."

If she's going to let me touch her, you bet your sweet ass I'm going to do it thoroughly. Grabbing her behind the knees I tug her down the chair causing a little shriek to come out of her. "Now get your ass down here where I can eat properly." I slip the rolled-up towel under her ass for support and straighten her injured leg so she's not tempted to use it. "Are you going to make me pin that leg down, or do you think you can control yourself?"

"That shouldn't be a problem judging by the amount of words coming out of your mouth when I told you I wasn't interested in talking." Threading her fingers through my hair, she tilts my head up to look at her. "Are you going to make me forget, or should I go find someone else?"

"You can try, but no one can do it as well as I can."

With a deliberate touch, my fingers graze the inside of her leg starting from just above where the yellow bruising fades away to her inner knee and back down. Each pass has her chest rising and falling a little faster.

Pain bites at my scalp when she twists her fingers in my hair. "I guess these pretty locks are good for something."

"The deal still stands. You can cut it anytime." Dropping wet kisses on her pelvis, I glance up to find her lips parted and her eyes clouded with lust.

"You were serious about that."

"As serious as I am about eating your sweet cunt." My teeth drag over her skin before I bite lightly. Whatever barb she's about to throw my way dissolves into a hiss when I bring my fingers down against her clit. "Hook that leg over my shoulder because I'm done fucking around. I've waited a year to bury my tongue inside you again, and I'm not wasting another second of it."

A string of nonsense is the last thing I hear before I lose myself in her. Just like I knew she would be, she's drenched, and not from the pool. My only regret about our time together before is that I didn't spend more time with my head right here. Missed sleep can be made up, but I'll never tire of her taste on my tongue, or how soft she sounds when she whimpers my name.

"You're a fucking mess. A beautiful disaster."

If this is the key to getting her to let her guard down, I'm going to treat myself every damn time she offers herself up. Because right now, with her ass in the palms of my hands and her fingers in my hair, she's not fighting what she feels for me. No, she's holding me to her like she doesn't hate the things she thinks I stand for.

Her voice cracks, breaking through the haze I'm in. "Fuck, yes," she hums, her grip tightening so that I'm forced to look up at her.

"You like my mouth on you, Baby?" I give her two fingers, making her suck in a sharp breath.

"W-want to know my favorite part?" The words stick in her throat.

"Tell me," I say, hooking my fingers just to see her squirm.

"It's the only time you stop running your mouth. And I plan to hold out as long as I can just to enjoy the extra few minutes of silence." She tries hard to hide it, but even the way she sucks her cheek can't conceal the twitch in the corner of her mouth.

"Just for that, I'm going to make you come fast and talk the whole time."

"Leave it to me to ruin oral with the hot baseball player." Her arm falls, covering her eyes.

Fresh with a renewed commitment to the cause, I drop my head and press my tongue to her clit, talking around it. "Nothing's ruined, but you realize you called me the hottest man you've ever met."

"No, I did—"

I cut her off, sucking her clit hard. "That's what I heard." So . . . talking like this isn't easy, but it's fun as hell to watch her roll her eyes at me, only to moan out my name a second later.

"Fuucck me," she draws out when my teeth scrape her clit.

"No can do, you know the deal." Her leg tightens around my shoulders, holding me to her wet center, covering my face in her. "Not holding out so well."

Each word is punctuated by a lick and a pump of my fingers. "It's okay, we aren't done yet. I'm still hungry."

Her walls tighten around my fingers, but I don't let up. Licking a stripe up her soaked cunt I pick up my pace pumping my fingers while she squirms beneath me. Her stunning face twists as her release tears through her. "That's it, now give me another," I demand, stroking her roughly.

She asked me to make her forget and when I'm done with her she'll be too tired to think of anything but how I made her feel.

"I can't."

"You can. Let go, Baby. Give me everything you've got."

Her back arches and the leg over my shoulder trembles. She's right there, so I pull her swollen clit into my mouth, letting my teeth graze it. This time when she moans my name it's paired with a warm gush, coating my face just like I wanted. It's not until she's pulling my head away, panting and begging for a break that I let my head fall to her stomach and catch my breath.

With the sun down and the temperature outside cooling, I scoop her up, leaving the pile of clothes behind.

When I step into the house and turn toward the stairs, she stops me. "Not up there."

And fuck if that doesn't mess with my head. Does she not want to taint our night together with whatever is happening now, or does she wish it never happened?

"Whatever you want."

"Couch." Her dark hair tickles my chin as she nods towards the living room. "It's not like you to be this humble about being right."

"That's where you're wrong. But I don't want to argue with you when I could have my head buried between your legs again. Unless you're ready to talk, that is."

She shakes her head, promptly burying it in my neck, and it's the most connected I've felt to her since our first night together—when she was wrapped in my arms, looking up at me like I hung the damn moon. Before she told me that she couldn't be with me and walked out of my life, taking away the future I could already envision. Now she's back, but I still don't know where that leaves us.

When I lower Indie to the couch, she brushes against my painfully hard cock and I groan, squeezing it through the wet material as I kneel between her legs.

"You're really not going to let me help you with that?" Her lashes flutter as her eyes drop from the bulge in my pants to the tattoo on my thigh. Like she can't help herself, she reaches out tracing the lines of it.

"It's yours anytime you want it." I shudder under her featherlight touch and her fingers dance higher, tracing Ares's helmet, until they are slipping under the damp fabric of my undies, making my cock jump.

"Most people probably think you're more like Aphrodite, with that pretty boy face and easygoing personality, and maybe you are in a lot of ways." Her palm flattens on the flank of my quad covering the goddess and her doves. "But the God of War was tenacious like you and he did the unexpected and gave Aphrodite what she was missing in her marriage to Hephaestus. People underestimate you in the same way, me included."

Her hand starts its path north again. Snagging her wrist, I stop her pursuit before she can snap the thin leash of control that I'm tenuously holding on to. "Are you going to let me take you upstairs and tell me how much you've missed this?"

"No." She swallows roughly as I lean over her on the couch, our lips nearly touching. Her eyes lower and for a second, I think she might actually kiss me. "I'm not."

"Then put those hands to use and play with your tits while you come all over my face again."

With one last glance at my lips, she covers her breasts with hands and kneads them.

"You listen so well when you're riding my tongue." Her eyes fall closed and a mumbled insult falls from her lips, but I count it as a win because she thought about kissing me, letting me take her to bed, and most importantly, she's seeing that I'm not the guy who hurt her.

CHAPTER 21

INDIE

Shimmying my legs, I try to work my blankets off. It's too damn warm, but the strangest thing happens: they huff, tightening around me. Because they aren't blankets. They're a strong, familiar set of arms that I've somehow fallen into again.

And boy did I fall, right into a bottomless well of bliss. This man is the maestro of my clit, a true virtuoso with his tongue. An oral ace. I swear I saw a bright light beckon me to it at one point when he had me pinned down to his pool lounger, doing his best work to make sure the only thing on my mind was how he devoured me. He wouldn't shut up about it and I only have myself to blame for that.

"Stop squirming or I'll hold you down and make you come again," my human blanket mumbles, his eyes still closed. His lips brush my forehead and I have to force myself to stay still because every instinct in me is telling me to kiss him, but that would send the wrong message.

When I finally tapped out last night and told him no more, he ordered us food, because as much as he likes to pretend he could live off eating just my pussy, it takes food to grow all those muscles he's working with.

With piles of chinese to share he turned on reruns of *America's Funniest Home Videos* and fed me bites of dumplings from his chopsticks between laughs at other people's expense. It was exactly what I needed to put me at ease; something I'm noticing happens more often than not when he's around. At some point I must have nodded off. Maybe all my assumptions about him are shortsighted, because he's nothing like my ex, Jensen. The only other people who've made me feel this settled are Poppy and my mom.

Brushing his too long hair back from his face, I stare up at him. What the hell am I doing? If anyone could hurt me the way my ex did, it's the baseball player sleeping soundly beside me.

It's not long before my eyes drift shut and I succumb to the exhaustion that's still bone deep from yesterday.

This time when I wake up, the sky outside is blue, and the warmth is coming from the sun beating in through the wall of windows behind me. The man who spent all night holding me is nowhere to be found. Slowly sitting, I look around. The shirt he pulled over my head last night isn't enough now that I'm alone in his house wondering where the hell he is. Next to the couch I find my boot and on the coffee table is a mug of pitch black coffee that makes my heart skip a beat. *Excellent.*

These acts of service are going to be the death of me. It's not until I'm bringing the coffee to my lips, jump-starting my senses, that I see the pile of neatly folded clothes and my phone on top of it. Another crack forms in the wall I keep around my heart.

This would be so much easier if he was the careless dick I expect him to be. But coffee made just the way I like it and my carefully gathered things waiting for me are stirring feelings I've worked damn hard to avoid for the last year. The more time I spend with Dom, the less I know. Confused and tired, my will to fight is at an all-time low.

Strapping on my boot, I grab my things and head to the guest bedroom to change. When I return, there's still no sign of him, so with my coffee in one hand and my phone in the other, I return a message from my dad asking me how my ankle is feeling. Next, I react to a few nonsensical texts in my chat with the girls. I'm about to check my email when my phone rings.

Dr. Smith's office number flashes on my screen. Glancing around, I decide to take the call outside in case Dom is still around here somewhere. The sun's already hot, so I head for the covered patio. Cushions and towels flung every which way from last night's fun on the lounger catch my attention and I almost go ass over teakettle into the pool. Avoiding the reminder of how good his hands felt on me, I course correct in the opposite direction.

"Hello," I answer tentatively, checking to make sure the coast is clear one more time, before I cautiously lower myself into the hammock on the edge of the patio.

"Hey, Indie! It's Maryann. I'm sorry to call so early, but I wanted to catch you before the clinic opens for the day."

"It's not a problem. What can I do for you?" I press my palm against my chest. My heart is hammering so wildly that I wish I would have picked the more stable loungers. Fear coils in my belly and my head spins. What if she's calling about an irregularity on my pap smear or something on the mammogram?

"First, I wanted to let you know everything came back normal on your tests and imaging." The breath I release is audible and I fold over, dropping my forehead to my knees. She's still talking, but nothing she says after that permeates the haze of panic still gripping me. After a few more deep breaths, the fog clears and I hear her say, ". . . tell me about the meeting. Was it helpful?"

"I'm sorry, Maryann. If anything you said after the update on my results was important, I'm going to need you to repeat it."

"Of course, dear. Do you need a minute?"

"No. I'm fine now. What was it you were saying?"

"I asked how the support group meeting was and if you'd given any more consideration to if you want to consider genetic testing at this time." There's no judgment in her measured words.

"The meeting was about as fun as the mammogram." Beck's blunt honesty from that day floods my memory. "But there was another woman there around my age who shared her experience, and it gave me a lot to think about. She seemed happy with her decision to do genetic testing, but it didn't stop her sister from getting sick. What's to say it would be any different for me?" My voice wavers when I add, "Maybe I'm just not ready."

"There are no guarantees in life. You and I know that better than most. I've seen patients go both ways and I've seen regrets on both sides. All you can do is make the best decision for you. If you're never ready, that's okay, Indie."

"I know my dad and best friend would appreciate it if I do the testing, but what if it comes back positive and I wish I would have never found out?"

"That can happen. This is something you need to do for you, not to please anyone else. It's a deeply personal decision," Maryann reminds me, sounding more like a friend than a doctor at that moment.

"You're not helping."

She chuckles. "I'm just here to give you information and arm you to make your decision. I'm not going to tell you what you should do, because there is no right answer."

The squeak of a tennis shoe has me whipping around in the hammock so abruptly that I almost flip it. Large hands wrap around my ribs, steadying me a second later, looking guilty as hell.

"I swear I wasn't eavesdropping. Not really. Or at least not on purpose," he whispers, dropping to his knees in front of me, his fingers playing with the hem of my shirt.

"Was there anything else you needed?" I redirect now that my audience has made itself known.

"Ah, Yes. We'd like to move the timeline up on the new clinic, and I wanted to see if you could come in later this week to meet the rest of the team."

"Yes. Absolutely. Just email me the time and I'll be there." My spirits lift in anticipation of having work to fill my plentiful down time.

"Excellent, and you'll let me know if you have questions about the testing?"

"I'll let you know."

Dom stays right there, his hands on my knees as Maryann and I say our goodbyes.

"I know that conversation was private, but I have to ask, are you okay?" Two deep lines crease his forehead and his hand hasn't stopped rubbing up and down my thigh.

Maniacal laughter crackles out of me and once again I'm sobbing in front of the one person I really don't want to see me like this. I'm not even sure why anymore. Every single time I've cried on Dom's shoulder, he's let me without judgment; never once throwing it back at me the way Jensen did. He's never called me dramatic or gaslighted me by brushing aside my feelings; it's the opposite. He gives me what I need in those moments—space, distraction, whatever he can do to make me feel better—he puts me first.

"Yeah, I'm fine. Everything is fine." I swipe at my eyes.

"Don't take this the wrong way, but it really doesn't seem like it. Are you sick? Genetic testing, mammograms. I'm trying to stay calm here, because the last thing you need is me adding to your stress . . . but I'm struggling." His voice cracks with the admission.

It nearly does me in, but I call on Maryann's words. This is my decision. Dom weighing in only adds more pressure that I don't need. If I'm not going to let my best friend and father weigh in, I'm certainly not going to let him. So I tell him the only thing he needs to hear right now. "Nothing to worry about. All my annual tests came back okay."

He doesn't look convinced, so I cover my hands with his and lower my head so we are eye to eye. "I'm overwhelmed and my emotions got the best of me, but it's good news."

"Okay." He releases a shaky exhale and then slowly lifts his hat from his head and pushes his shaggy, sweat soaked hair back, turning it around. Without the distraction of Maryann or my impending decision clouding things, I look at him, like *really* look . . . and holy shit.

If there was a moment I was going to break for this man, get down on my knees and beg for his dick like he keeps taunting me about, it would be now.

The holy grail of hotness is currently squatting in front of me in nothing but a pair of running shorts—the slutty kind with the little slit up the side that showcases his remarkably toned quads. The black ink of Aphrodite and her doves glistens in the sun. On its own the intricate ink is enough to make me dickdumb. It's a potent mix with his backward hat, and covered in a sheen of sweat. Like the traitor she is ,my pussy is cheering, pleading with me to make more reckless decisions.

"Did you find your coffee?"

Coffee. What's coffee? The only thing I want is a tall drink of him.

He catches me looking and unleashes a wicked grin. Pleased, smug, lopsided—it's catnip for my horny side. Shaking myself free from the dicktrancement, I sputter. "I did. I saved the rest for you. There's still half of a pot."

"Um . . . thanks. I'll grab a cup to drink while I get ready. So listen . . . I have a thing this morning at a nonprofit. Want to come with? I can introduce you to some people. Cruz volunteers at Saving Paws a lot and I need to swing by before I head to the stadium later this morning."

"Sure. I'll never turn down wet kisses." Later I'll tell myself it was the backward hat and tanned muscles that made me agree so quickly, not the desire to spend more time with him.

"Oh, I know."

"Gross." *Not gross.*

"You didn't think so last night."

Nope, I definitely did not, but I'm not feeding his ego. Especially not when I just agreed to spend the morning with him. He'll be absolutely insufferable.

CHAPTER 22

DOM

There's two ways this thing can go. She'll either be too distracted by the animals to notice my tiny, adorable manipulation and just soak up the experience. Or she'll realize that I didn't exactly give her the entire story about why we're here and kick me square in the nuts.

Either way, it'll be worth it. *Probably.* No, it will be, we both need the distraction after this morning. Her mouth told me everything is fine, but the state I found her in last night and again this morning makes me doubt how true that is. She might not be sick, but something is going on with her and I'm going to keep chipping away at those walls until she lets me in.

"Hey, Simone," I greet the adoption director for Saving Paws when Indie and I step inside the lobby. Concrete floors with the shelter logo stamped in the center gleam under the overhead lights. Indie looks around the space, her smile wider than I've seen it recently. A reminder of why I'm risking life and limb by not telling her what brought us here today.

"You ready for this? Today's the big day," Simone says, standing from her desk and grabbing a folder.

Indie looks between us, her brow wrinkling as she tries to work out what's happening.

"Simone, this is Indie Moreno. Indie, this is Simone. She's the shelter director."

"Nice to meet you." She holds out her hand, glancing at me before smiling warmly at Simone.

"Shall we go grab Ronnie before we sign the paperwork? I'm sure she'll be happy to see you."

"Let's do that. Indie, why don't you tell Simone about the work you're doing with some of the other nonprofits in the area?" I let my palm settle on her lower back as I guide her through the building, taking my time so she can keep up with her boot.

"What are we doing here?" she whispers.

"Right now, we're making introductions." Not a lie. I want Indie to focus on making a connection that can help make her dreams come true before I distract her with the real reason we're here. Turning her smile on Simone, Indie launches into her pitch about how she wants to help nonprofits.

There's a passion that I've only ever seen from her when she talks about her mom. Seeing my girl in action, I'm in awe of her. She's poised and professional. Her ideas to help the shelter, even on the fly, are creative and well thought-out. It's a new side of Indie and it only heightens the feelings I already have for her. I want to pull her closer and tell her how proud I am of her, but it will most likely make her run in the other direction.

"We should exchange information. The shelter could benefit from additional volunteers and the idea of co-hosting a volunteer fair sounds amazing," Simone says, when we stop in front of a kennel with a boxer who immediately perks up at having visitors.

"Hey, Ronnie, girl," I croon, stooping to her level. "It's our big day."

"I'll grab her leash and you can let her out," Simone says, leaving us alone with Ronnie.

"What is going on right now? This is Ronnie?" Indie's curious eyes flick from me to the dog and back again.

"I'm entering my dog dad era." To Ronnie's delight, I reach through the kennel with two fingers to scratch her nose. "She's just the goodest girl."

"Blink twice if you're being forced into something you don't want, sweet girl," Indie whispers from where she joined me on one knee.

"Nah. I won her over. Just like I plan to do with you."

Instead of volleying an insult back, Indie asks, "What are you going to do with her when you travel?"

"I hired a service to help when I'm on the road, plus I have a few neighbors that will help. She'll get three long walks and plenty of attention, but she's pretty chill. Simone helped me pick a dog that would fit my lifestyle."

"You've always wanted a dog."

It's the first time she's brought up any of the things we shared on our night together. The glee that rises inside me at that little fact is hard to suppress.

"Yeah, I have. It just took some time to find the right one." We might be talking about Ronnie, but I'm looking at her, hoping she's connecting the dots; I can be patient with things this important.

"I'm glad you found her." She tears her dark eyes from me and gives Ronnie her finger to sniff. "She's beautiful and so sweet."

"Sure is," I echo.

"Sorry, guys, I ran into a volunteer that needed my help. We're short-handed, again." Simone hands the leash to me and I unlatch the door, reaching in to hook it to her collar.

When she comes out, she goes right to Indie, burying her nose in her curls. I'm pretty sure Ronnie just secured her spot in the heart I'm vying for.

THE MYTH, THE MAN, THE LEGEND - DAD CHAT

DOM:

I present to you . . . Your grand-dog.
[Picture attached]

DAD:

Your mother will be thrilled that you've finally made her a Mimi.

DOM:

What the heck is a Mimi?

DAD:

That's what she wants to be called.

DOM:

I didn't realize she'd picked out a title.

DAD:

The moment she heard that you had a potentially serious suitor.

DOM:

A little early. I'm still working on it.

CHAPTER 23

DOM

"Dude, the dog is fine. Stop checking the camera," Hendrix says, glancing at my phone, where Ronnie is pictured sleeping peacefully on the couch.

"Help me out, Cruz. You check on your dogs," I whine, looking for backup from my captain, who's sitting across from me on the team plane.

"Mostly, I check on my wife. Think she'd let me install a camera for her?" He pulls out his phone tapping out a text and adds, "But for the love of God, stop giving her treats. Your dog dad guilt is going to make her throw up all over your house if you keep tossing her snacks with that thing."

"Whatever." Swiping up, I close the camera app and open my text messages. Along with her contact name, "Future Wife," there's a little picture of Indie and I snuggled up on the couch the other day that has my lips curving into a smile again.

"Leave the dog alone," Dean scolds from where he sits across from me.

Ignoring him I type out a message.

"Is that the girl from the housewarming party?" Hendrix asks.

I shake my head.

"Your sister, then?" He guesses.

"Nope." I leave it at that.

ME:

I hate to tell you this, but you have some competition as my favorite snuggle buddy.

FUTURE WIFE:

I wasn't aware I'd entered that race.
How do I withdraw?

ME:

Impossible.

FUTURE WIFE:

She's going to win by default.
Cuteness aside, I have no plans for a repeat.

ME:

You keep saying that, yet you still end up in my arms.

FUTURE WIFE:

Stop bragging, it's annoying.

ME:

Have a good day, beautiful. Don't forget the pool is yours anytime you need it.

FUTURE WIFE:

I won't.

ME:

Okay.

Two hours later, the plane lands in Phoenix and I'm still riding the high from my text exchange with Indie when we board our bus to the stadium for our first game of the three game series. I climb into the bus and my phone buzzes with a notification from the dog cam. What I see when I open the app doubles down on that feeling.

There's a spunky little firecracker sticking her tongue out at the camera while she limps through my house toward the pool in a pair of tiny shorts and her black swimsuit top that has me wishing I wasn't surrounded by my teammates.

Nothing can ruin my mood as we make the short ride to the stadium from the airport to practice before our game tonight. Not even the familiar voice that calls out my name when I'm on the field taking batting practice an hour later.

"My man. It's been ages." My minor league teammate slaps my back as I swipe my forearm across my forehead.

"Sonny . . . hey, man. How've you been?"

"Prime, buddy. Loving life since I got called up. I bet you are too." He elbows me in the side.

There's a reason this guy stayed in the minors longer than me after college. While I've done my fair share of screwing around, the game has always come first. Sonny never knew when enough was enough. We lived together for a year right out of college and since then I've kept my distance.

"How's your season going?" I ask, not really wanting to give up practice time to talk about his party habits.

"We should hang while you're in town, catch up. I know all the best spots to hit up postgame."

"Nah, I've got team stuff going on. But good luck tonight," I say, stepping back to finish my batting practice.

Rude? Yes, but I don't really care what this guy thinks of me, and I'm not interested in getting my ass chewed by Coach or Cruz for slacking off.

Exhaustion from the first two games of the series and eleven innings of baseball to lock in our win today against Phoenix has my limbs feeling like lead as I sink into my seat on the plane.

"Guys, he's got the phone out again. My money is on porn," Xavier says, dropping into his seat across the aisle.

There's been a pit in my stomach that isn't normally there when I travel. Leaving Ronnie sucked. The space between Indie and I sucked. Something is happening between us, but we're not in a place where we're calling each other or video chatting yet.

If it weren't for the dog cam, the whole trip would have been a total bust. But after that first alert when Indie stopped over, I was like a kid on Christmas morning, waiting for the next time she'd pop up on my camera. And she didn't disappoint, stopping over every day for the last three days to swim and play with Ronnie.

The guys keep catching me staring at my phone, watching the two of them cuddling on the couch or playing on the floor. All of them are jumping to their own conclusions about what I'm doing, but so far no one has figured it out and until Indie gives me some sort of indication that she's ready to stop denying her feelings for me, I'm not telling them a thing.

They can harass me all they want, it doesn't matter. Because each day I feel like I'm a little closer to getting everything I've wanted for the last year. Hell, she even sent me an unsolicited deck picture the other day. One with her and Ronnie sunning by the pool together, the black triangles of her swimsuit narrow and barely covering her. If I wasn't already down bad for her, that would have done it. My girl, sweet and sassy all at once.

I'm so fucking screwed.

Somewhere over New Mexico, my phone died and I was too tired to dig out my charger. So, I'm caught off guard—but not even remotely disappointed—to find Indie and Ronnie napping together on my couch when I get home.

Lowering my duffle bag to the ground, I quietly toe off my shoes, not wanting to disturb them. I make it maybe four steps before one of Ronnie's ears perks up and she turns her head, finding me. I'm sure she's going to wake Indie when her tail thumps against the couch, but she slides out from under her arm and stretches before she sits at my feet, waiting for me to greet her, like the good girl she is.

With one last look at the woman who's occupied every thought that wasn't devoted to baseball for the last few weeks, I pat Ronnie on the head, making a note to give her extra treats for giving my girl the peace she deserves. "Come on," I whisper before leading her outside.

CHAPTER 24

INDIE

Is this couch infused with some sort of sedative? That's the only plausible explanation for why I keep waking up here feeling more rested than I do after a full eight hours in my own bed. I refuse to believe it has anything to do with the owner of the house.

Speaking of the dopey owner, he's going to absolutely murder me if I don't find his dog soon. She was right here when I fell asleep. But I've called out for her and searched the house without luck. The backyard is empty too.

My throat is tight with panic when I see the duffle bag by the front door. They've got to be around here someplace. Sliding open the patio door, I check the backyard again. I'm about to give up when I hear him praise, "Such a good girl!"

Making my way around the side of the house I freeze when I see them. My hand comes to my mouth, stopping my laugh because I can't possibly interrupt this. A shirtless Dom is bent over with his teeth snapping at the water spraying out of the hose.

"You try." He holds out the hose and Ronnie mimics him, bouncing on her front paws as she tries to catch the water with her teeth.

Well fuck, this is not helping my brain convince the rest of me—my ovaries, my heart, all my instincts, really—that I should stay away from this man. Nope, my already weakening resolve snaps.

And it only gets worse when a moment later he lifts the nozzle above his head, sending rivulets of water cascading over his tanned muscles, making sexy rivers in the valley of his spine. Just like that, the endearing moment turns into something much more sensual that I'm sure will invade my dreams.

Backing away slowly, self preservation has me sneaking back inside to gather my things and slipping out the front door. When I'm safely down the block, I sit on the curb and order an Uber. The whole time I wait, I try to convince myself I'm not a coward, just a self-aware queen who knows when she's in over her head.

Delusional.

♥

An hour later, I've showered and distracted myself in as many ways as I can think of, but there is still that insistent ache between my legs. The same one that's been there since I metaphorically ran from Dom's house; ran from all the things that seeing him like that made me want. A future where we take Ronnie for long hikes, a white picket fence picture of our own.

Now I'm lying here, unable to sleep after barely escaping Dom's without doing something I shouldn't. Although I was tempted to ignore the text that came through from "Yours"—the contact name he entered himself—I knew it would only end with him showing up at my door. Which would defeat the whole point of leaving. So I reply with a vague text letting him know I'm okay and turn off notifications on my phone.

Thanks to the little show he unknowingly put on, I'm right back to where I was this time last year. Twelve hours of sex and pouring our hearts out to each other shouldn't have been enough to unravel everything I've learned about falling for guys that seem too good to be true. Yet that's exactly where we seemed to be headed after our one night stand. Except now I know he's not like the others. Dom's not cruel and cold like Jensen. Or the other guys in college who saw my sexuality as an obstacle to overcome, a phase, or worse yet, bragging rights.

Dom is kind and thoughtful. He's taken care of me when I've needed it, knowing me well enough to know how to make me give in and accept help when it's the last thing I want to do, but exactly what I need. And it feels good, so fucking good, to have someone who wants to take care of me for once.

This time I'm not sure if I can make myself walk away.

Tomorrow, in the light of day, I might hate myself for this decision, but right now I don't care. With a huff, I reach into my nightstand drawer and grab the one thing that comes close to the feeling of Dom's mouth on me and press the toy between my legs, letting the suction work its magic.

Sagging into my pillow, the relief is immediate. I'm climbing fast and hard, his face and body at the forefront of my fantasies. They blend together old tender memories of the way he touched me back then with the rougher, more demanding way he is with me now. Both spur me on, but part of me can't deny that I long for the moments that I've tried so hard to avoid.

Those locked away moments of him whispering how perfect I am against my skin; kisses, silent promises of more, have me shaking on the edge of losing control. The words he said last year when he thought I was asleep are what crack me wide open, stars bursting behind my closed eyelids.

"I feel like I've been waiting all my life for you, Indie Moreno."

Yep, definitely going to regret that in the morning. Not because it felt better than it should've, but because I don't hate myself for it. If anything it only makes me want him more, especially recalling those words that I locked away to protect myself for the last year. It's only a matter of time before I lose this battle I'm fighting so hard. Each day the reasons I've held him at bay fade a little more.

BINGO BITCHES DO IT BATTER

JANET:

Don't forget that lucky thong tonight. You're going to need it.

STEPHANIE:

Are you talking to me or the bat boy?

LARK:

We all know you prefer to go commando, you old pervert.

Dom removed himself from the thread

Janet added Dom to the thread

STEPHANIE:

Stop being dramatic. We'll behave.

JANET:

Speak for yourself.

DOM:

If you don't I won't bring the batch of cookies I made you using my mom's recipe.

JANET:

:::zips her lips:::

LARK:

Now you've done it. They're going to be kissing your ass all night.

STEPHANIE:

Such a nice tushy too.

CHAPTER 25

DOM

Our win against Atlanta this afternoon put us in contention for the wildcard race. With just four weeks left of the regular season, it's crunch time. Everyone needs to be at the top of their game for us to pull this off. And that would be a hell of a lot easier for me if Indie hadn't been avoiding me for the last four days.

Her texts have been short and sweet but she's avoided the house when I'm around, only stopping by to love on Ronnie and swim when she knows I'm at the stadium. Which by default means she's not coming to games with the girls. I know they're worried and I don't blame them, but I'm in no position to tell Indie what to do.

I'm giving her one more day and then I'm tracking her down. But first I have a bingo game to win. My ass is going to stay parked at my lucky table, my daubers lined up just how I like them, and my lucky thong nestled between my ass cheeks.

Surrounded by all my best girls I'm ready to take home another W today. Well, almost all of my girls. There is one notably missing; the feisty brunette who's ruled my thoughts for longer than I should admit.

Ronnie's at my feet and Nana Janet sits across from me. I'm flanked by the rest of our bingo crew, Lark and Stephanie. I met the two of them when I started volunteering at Sunny Acres and introduced them to Janet when she moved.

We're a ragtag crew, but with them by my side, I can't lose. At the front of the Sunny Acres Senior Center, Bev is calling bingo tonight. The longtime Bandits employee always entertains, whether she's slinging beers in the concession stands or volunteering as MC.

"Who's getting lucky tonight?" Bev asks over the mic, sending a chorus of cheers through the room. "I'm happy for all of you, really, but I was talking about the game. We all know what you get up to after. Just remember your safe word and if you can't remember it, write it on your partner's forehead or back, whatever tickles your pickle." Her teal bob swings around her shoulders as she looks pointedly around the room.

"Get the daubers ready over there. You're on a hot streak with that home run and that adorable girl at your feet. But I'm going to give you a run for your money," Hendrix's grandma instructs, a piece of cheese innocently slipping from her hand and landing at my feet for Ronnie. "Oops."

"Locked and loaded, Janet." I busy myself crafting an equidistant rainbow of brightly colored markers around my cards.

Bev's voice rings out across the room as she kicks off the first game of the night. "Y'all are in good hands tonight. I'll have you know, I'm excellent with balls, and the first one of the night is B13."

Grabbing my teal marker I dot the square on my board.

"My granddaughter's been asking about you again," Lark says, on my right. "She calls me every Thursday around breakfast since you took her to that housewarming party. I suppose I should thank you for that, but she says you told her it wasn't going to work because you were hung up on the one that got away."

I listen to the numbers, my eyes scanning the cards in front of me, dotting as we go.

"Um, yeah. That's true." I glance up to find Janet staring me down with her eyebrow raised. *Shit.*

She can't know who we're talking about. If Dean and Mia never got together last winter, Indie would have taken the story of that night to the grave. As it is, they're the only two of our friends that know any of the details about that night. The others have guessed, but as far as I know, Indie hasn't even confirmed it to Poppy. Such a fucking temptress, the way she played me and Dean off each other.

As if Ronnie can hear my thoughts, she whines, burying her nose under her paws.

"Look at you. Just one more and you'll be the first winner of the night. Some people have all the luck. That pretty face, a well-trained dog, and a bingo win. Didn't anyone ever teach you to share?" Stephanie pushes her glasses down and looks over them at me.

I cough at the irony of that question considering where my mind just was. "Did you make that chain yourself, with Bandits' colors just for me?" I nod to the beaded strand her glasses are attached to.

"And cocky too. I guess you can't be perfect." She hmpfs and one bony finger presses her glasses back into place. "This is for Xavier. He's got what the kids call junk in his trunk."

"Ouch! Taking shots at my personality and my tushy, Steph," I tease, daubing my winning number. "Bingo!" My voice breaks through the chatter of the Senior Center.

"Not again," Fiona groans from the table over. "Janet, I told you to stop inviting him. He's a distraction and a lucky SOB."

"Mind your business, you busybody. He's one of the girls. I'm not kicking him out and you can't make me," Janet chirps back.

With my winnings for the night signed over to Saving Paws, I head back to the house, a little more spring in my step after a night well spent. That spring turns into a full-blown gallop when I see the car parked in my driveway.

Putting the car into park in the garage, I look over at Ronnie, who's watching me expectantly, and pat her head. "She's back, girl."

CHAPTER 26

INDIE

Warm water glides over my body, but it has nothing on the heated look on Dom's handsome face when I breach the surface of the pool. Just like the first night I swam here, I find him waiting. Only this time, the look he's wearing tells me I'm in trouble. His light brown eyes swirl with darkness and the playful smile he normally wears is dripping with sinful intent. The moon casts shadows on his face that give him a dangerous edge, like he's a thief in the night, and I'm pretty sure I'm the prize he's about to steal.

Yep, so much trouble.

With my ankle feeling much better the past few days. I'm still rocking the boot but tonight I'm testing it out by actually swimming instead of just floating through the water. Pulling myself through the pool, I stop in front of him and rest my forearms on the pool's edge.

He looms over me dressed in a pair of dark jeans and a white short-sleeve button up with tiny—are those troll dolls doting his shirt? Dropping to one knee, he tips my chin up to look at him. "Couldn't stay away for long, could you, Firecracker?"

My heart is still pounding against my ribs from the swim, and with the way his attention burns through me, it isn't going to slow anytime soon. The look he's wearing now is a familiar one.

It's the same way he looked at me right before he sank into me the first time, with resolve. His jaw is firmly set with certainty, like he understands my nature better than anyone else ever has.

"I'm not sure there are words to explain how badly I need to fill you, Firecracker, to make you mine. You don't need fancy declarations, do you? I think you know, the same way I do."

His thumb brushes over my bottom lip, and I tremble. Every word he just said resonates, making my core coil with need. I've never needed anything like I need him. It's crazy and reckless. I get the feeling that fighting it won't do us any good. I'm giving in, just this once.

"Yes. I'm yours for the night."

Disappointment flashes in his eyes.

"I can't do—it's all I have to give you." Doubt creeps in as soon as I say it, but he can't hurt me if I only give him this one night. "If you can't handle—" The words die on my lips when his mouth crashes against mine.

"I can handle it. I can handle you. For the record, I think you're lying to both of us right now, but that's okay. By the morning, you'll be so thoroughly fucked that I'll be etched deep within you. Every time your legs shake and your back bows, it's me you'll think of. I'm going to fuck you like this is more."

The air is thick as I stare up at him, lost in memories. He holds his hand out between us, waiting, it's the same stalemate that started this whole thing when asked me to dance. Over the last year, I've asked myself repeatedly if I regret those three letters. The ones that sealed my fate. When I replay it in my mind, my answer to him is always the same, a resounding *yes*.

And now I know why, this thing between us isn't going away. Now the only questions are, am I brave enough to give him everything I couldn't then? And will he make me regret it if I do?

This time if I place my hand in his, it means so much more because there is no escaping back to Chicago. He's right here, and he's shown me time and again he's not giving up on me.

My fingers brush against his as I place my palm in his hand and he helps me out of the water, lifting me onto the pool deck and into his arms.

He leans in close, his nose running up mine. When an overpowering flowery scent hits me, I almost gag on the distinctive smell of perfume. Fighting to calm the anger burning me, I rear back and see the lipstick on his collar. It's clear as day, right next to a troll with purple hair, a bright pink smear of damning proof.

My palms flatten on his chest and I push, almost stepping right back into the pool when he doesn't move. Red-hot rage only spikes higher when his grip tightens on me keeping me in place.

"I can't believe I fell for your good guy act. So damn convincing, too." My cheeks flame with heat that reaches the tips of my ears. Such a damn fool.

"I'm not going to ask you to calm down because I'd like to stay alive, but I'm going to need some context here."

The calm response only pisses me off more, making me want to march off into the night. But I can't exactly do that. I eye my boot and clothes by the lounger over his shoulder, planning my exit.

"Why the hell do you smell like cheap perfume and have lipstick smeared all over your collar?" Venom is dripping from my voice, and my hands on his chest ball into fists. Anger and embarrassment combine into an inferno that burns just below my skin.

"That would be Janet and Lark's fault. It was bingo night."

My nails dig into the palms of my hands and my eyes close, the embarrassment still there but now aimed right back in my direction. I'm the asshole. He was doing something incredibly thoughtful and I'm over here painting him as a villain again.

"Both are over seventy and very much in love with better men than me."

"Bingo night with Poppy's grandma. That explains the trolls." I bury my face in his shirt, but he's not having it.

"Baby, look at me." Taking my chin between his finger and thumb, he holds me captive. "You got one thing right, I'm a decent guy, Indie. I know you've been hurt, but I'm not like that. There's no one else I want more than you. Not today, not in the last year, not in the years before we met."

CHAPTER 27

DOM

Just like that first kiss, I wait for her to make the move. To prove to me she's not just using me as a distraction. There's a lot I'll put up with, especially from this woman, because she's worth it. That being said, I need to know that she heard me when I laid it out for her, that she's not running from her fear—we're in too deep now for that.

"You're annoyingly persistent." Smoothing her hands up my chest they loop behind my neck.

Her eyes drop to my lips and it takes all my willpower not to duck my head and steal a taste because we've been here before, with me thinking we were in it together, only for her to leave. I've been waiting for this kiss for months; there were times when I thought it wouldn't come. Now that it's right here in front of me, I almost can't believe it. My palms sweat and my stomach flips like it's my first kiss all over again.

"I'd say it paid off."

Her tongue darts out, wetting her lips, and I can't tear my eyes away from that one little movement.

"You think so?"

Fuck, this girl is stubborn.

"Mhmmm . . . because you're about to kiss me and then I'm going to spend the rest of the night torturing you with my fingers and mouth until you finally beg for my cock. Unless you're planning to run again because this time, when I fuck you like we are more, we will be."

Her quick intake of breath is the last thing I hear before she pulls me down to her and takes my mouth just the way I remember, with wild abandon and passion. Our first kiss was nearly perfect, but I'll never forget this one because she's finally giving herself to me, and not just for the night.

Our lips work together, making up for the months we missed. Indie presses closer, her wet swimsuit soaking through my clothes. When she chases more, I open for her, swallowing the contented sigh she makes as our tongues brush. One sweet sound is all it takes to break me. My hands travel down her body tracing all her curves and slick skin before I grip the back of her legs and lift her.

Taking the hint, she wraps her legs around my waist. I walk us right past the lounger, into the house, and past the couch, heading for the stairs. I pause at the bottom step and she pulls back for a moment. For once, there is no war waging behind those eyes. She presses her forehead against mine, dipping her head in a resolute nod.

"Fuck yes," I growl against her lips—each step, each kiss closing the gap between our past and what we can be.

Her hands work the buttons on my shirt as I move us to the bed, my lips never leaving hers. If I have my way, there will be a lot more kissing, because of everything I've missed this last year, being able to kiss her is at the top of that list.

Maybe it's because she so rarely shows people her softer side, but when her lips are on mine, she melts, giving me access to a vulnerable side that feels like it's just for me. These last two times we've been together, she kept that part of herself from me. But right now, each kiss feels like a promise that she sees more for us.

It's a race for skin, all frantic hands and trembling fingers. She pushes the shirt off my shoulders and I tug at the strings holding her top in place, making it fall away. When her hands reach for the button on my jeans, I stop her, needing a second.

"You need to be sure, because if we do this, it means something to me. I need to know that this isn't you just playing games, using me as a distraction." My heart sinks when she pulls her hand from between us. But when her expression softens and her fingers graze my jaw as she cups my face, my world rights itself.

The pad of her thumb brushes along my cheekbone, and I can see the truth in her eyes when they slowly lift to meet mine. "It's always meant something to me."

Removing my hands from the one still on the button, I watch as she works it free and pushes the fabric down over my hips so I can step out of them.

"I really hate this tattoo." Her pupils dilate and her voice is raspy. Even as she says it, her eyes never stray from the ink.

"It seems like it. That's why I always catch you looking at it. You just don't like that it makes you want to take my dick for a ride." Letting my finger drift over her jawline, I push a wet curl behind her ear.

"It certainly doesn't hurt, but that's not why I want you right now."

"And why do you want me right now?" I need to be certain that we are on the same page.

"Because when I'm with you, everything else disappears. For some stupid reason, you and your dick calm the storm raging inside me. I can't explain it, but *we* make sense. You soothe my wild heart. The happy, easygoing nature that drives me nuts transfers over to me and I can just *be*."

"You know how much I love it when you compliment my cock, but right now I'm going to pretend you left him out of it. All I heard was you finally admitting that you want me."

"Mhmmm. Do you really want to leave him out?" she asks, pulling me closer by the waistband of my briefs.

"In a heartbeat, if it means that you admit you like me as much as you like him."

"I-I don't hate you, isn't that a start? And I let you take care of me, which is more than I ever thought possible. Then there's the fact that I can't seem to stay away. None of it makes sense. I guess I'm just sick of fighting it."

"A start isn't good enough. Not where you are concerned, but you're close to admitting what we both know."

"And what's that?" she asks as I drop my lips to her neck.

"You."

Bite

"Like."

Kiss

"Me."

Suck

"What would make you think that?"

"The way you kiss me. How I'm the person you call when you need something. That no one is forcing you to be here and yet here you are, again."

Dragging her up the bed with me, I kiss my way down her chest, taking my time with each nipple, sucking the tight peaks into my mouth. As much as she complains about my shaggy hair, she can't seem to keep her hands out of it. If she ever cuts it, I'm going to miss the way she tugs on it, especially when I do something that drives her wild.

"Dom, please. I want you."

"So glad to hear that, but I'm not ready yet. I promised to eat this pussy, and I meant it. Besides, that didn't quite sound like begging, but you will be soon." Reaching between us I tug her swimsuit bottoms to the side and swipe my fingers through her slick center. "Judging by how wet you are, you like the sound of that."

"Oh, shit," she moans when I push two fingers inside her. My cock aches and the friction from sliding down the bed does nothing to calm him. Kneeling at the end of the bed I drape her thighs over my shoulders. Moving intently, I peel her bottoms down her long legs before I lick a hot path right to her center.

"I'll never tire of the taste of you. No one would believe me if I told them how sweet my girl is, but that's a secret I'll take to the grave. This is all mine, and I'm not sharing these pieces of you with anyone."

"God, I hate how hot I think that is. What are you doing to me?"

"If you have to ask, I'm obviously not doing my job well enough. I'll have to try harder." I suck her clit into my mouth, forcing a broken, ragged noise from her throat. She's close.

"Dom." My name on her lips is a plea for more.

"Yes, Baby." My fingers reach for that spot inside her and press, the move has her clenching around me.

"I want you," she cries, her nails scrapping my back, trying to force me from my happy place.

"And you're going to get me. But first I need you to come for me." Those magic words and one flat drag of my tongue over her clit, is all it takes for her to lose herself to her release, thighs trembling on my shoulders as her back bows off the bed. "That's it, Baby. So perfect when you let go of control."

"You make me feel out of control. You have since that first night. It was all too much, too fast. I did that once before. Falling hard and fast for a boy who said all the right things. I couldn't trust my instincts when they had been so wrong last time, but he wasn't even half the man you've shown me since I moved here."

"Careful, it almost sounds like you're admitting you like me." I crawl up her body, stopping to lay a kiss right over her still wildly beating heart.

"I do like you, Dom. What the hell are we going to do about it?"

"Let's start with you telling me how badly you want my dick so I can fuck you, and then we can figure it out, together."

She rolls her eyes, but there's plenty of heat behind the sassy reaction. "Admitting I wanted you wasn't enough, you need me to stroke your ego as well?"

"You want to stroke him . . ." I roll my hips over her still sensitive clit making her eyes flutter shut and her mouth fall open. "Then yes, I need to hear you say it."

"Please, Dom. I need you inside me." The husky voice she uses and the way my name rolls off her tongue will be burned into my memory forever

"So polite about it too. You want this dick, Baby?" Another pulse over her center.

"No, I need it. A year without . . . we are well beyond want," she says on the edge of coming apart for me again.

"It's yours." I push up on my elbow, taking her hand in mine and slipping both under the waistband of my underwear. Together, we stroke my hard cock. "Fuck. I've been dying to have your hands on me again."

"Could have fooled me with how you held me off, but I get it. I'm sorry for not seeing what was in front of me sooner. Something that feels this perfect can't be bad, right?" I try not to focus on the remaining insecurity in her voice. If she needs me to keep showing her that I'm the man she needs, it's fine. I had no plans to stop.

"Well, I'm not holding you off any more and right now I need to be buried so deep inside you, you never forget what it feels like to take every inch of me."

I shudder at the loss of her hand squeezing me, but it's quickly forgotten when she slides the briefs over my hips, helping me work them down my legs. She's just as eager as I am.

Now that we've made it here I'm having a hard time processing that this is actually happening and need to be certain I'm not dreaming, so I brush her hair behind her ear and kiss her, taking my time with each caress of my tongue against hers. The steady rise and fall of her chest under me and the slight sting when her fingers twist in my hair are enough to make me believe this is real. I'm finally getting the second chance I've been holding on to for the last year.

When she shifts under me, my hard length slides through her heat and I groan, absorbed in the feel of her skin against mine

"Hold on—fuck," I drag out, panting because she's already gotten me so worked up. I lean back on my heels squeezing the base of my cock. "Damn, you're so fucking beautiful. I've missed this—you."

"Then why aren't you inside me yet?"

"Condom," I croak out.

"Oh." Her face falls for a second and my heart drops. "I never forget protection and I was ready to just let you . . ." Her voice trails off.

"If you're not ready, we can wait," I say, pausing with my hand halfway to the nightstand.

"No, that's not it. I just . . . you just make me crazy. I want you. This. All of it. Please."

That's all I need to hear. I'm pulling open the drawer and sheathing myself a moment later. Resting on my forearms I kiss her nose and notch myself at her entrance. She doesn't wait for me to move, tilting her hips to meet me and sighing when the tip sinks inside her.

The only thing I want more than to sink all the way inside her is to torture her a little first. So I pull back, loving the way it makes her whimper and the fire in her eyes. She hooks her leg over my hip.

"You want more of me?"

The nod she gives me won't do, even with the coy way she bites her plump lower lip.

So I push in again, only giving her a fraction of what she needs and then withdraw.

A harsh breath skates over my heated skin as she sighs. "Please, Dom. Fuck me. Give me all of you."

The shift between us is immediate. Her words lock it into place, like two tectonic plates shifting and forever altering the landscape of our relationship. "All you had to do was ask." This time I sink all the way in, shuddering when her tight heat wraps around me. I fuck her slowly, with long drags of my cock until we are both barely hanging on, panting and sticky with sweat. Leaning down I take her mouth, quieting a string of curses as she tightens around me when I press my thumb to her clit. With each pass of my finger over the sensitive spot, she clings to me, and her tits press into my chest.

"Oh hell, Indie," I growl, everything around us fading away until it's just the feel of her tight heat draining my own orgasm from me. My cock twitches inside her, filling the condom until there's nothing left to give.

For a minute, the only noise is the swift whoosh of our beating hearts. Indie is the first to speak, pressing soft kisses along my neck, my pulse still hammering beneath her lips. "Begging might just be my new favorite hobby." Her soft chuckle turns to a contented sigh when I ease out of her to take care of the condom.

"You begging for my dick is a core memory for sure, but anytime you want something from me, all you have to do is ask."

"Noted," she says, patting me on the cheek.

"Just, um . . . give me a second to take care of things." My eyes keep finding my way back to her as I cross the room to the bathroom to dispose of the condom and clean up. If she bolts again, I'm not sure what I'll do. I've always let things roll off my back, but losing her right after I finally got her back would stick with me.

When I return with a washcloth in hand, she lets me take care of her. She would never admit it, but I can see the nerves in the way she pins her swollen bottom lip between her teeth.

"Don't hurt those lips. I like kissing them too much for you to chew a hole through them," I warn, shooting the cloth into the hamper like a basketball.

"I'm just not sure what to say."

"Then maybe you can just answer a question for me. Do you want to stay the night?"

"Yes."

Relief washes over me with the immediate answer.

"And will you let me make you your coffee in the morning without making a run for it?"

"Also yes." This time she smiles and everything is right in my world.

"Let's just start there. We can take it one step at a time. You spend more time here, I spend more time at your place. When I'm not on the road, you let me take you out on a proper date."

"That sounds perfect."

"Good, now how about you beg for my dick again and this time I'll fuck you like you made me wait a whole year to have you again. Hard and dirty."

Her pupils flare at the heat behind my words. She better believe I mean it. I might be patient, but this girl put me through the fucking wringer.

"Please, Dom," is all she says before I pounce on her.

There's a smile on my face when I wake up the next morning, the spot on the bed next to me still warm, but when I reach for the body beside mine I'm met with wiry hair that feels nothing like Indie's smooth skin.

Panic takes over and I shoot up, scaring the shit about out of Ronnie, who jumps off the bed and runs out the door. It's not until I hear the shower running that the alarms ringing in my head go silent.

She didn't leave me.

Maybe both of us still have some healing to do to trust each other.

I'm pulling on a pair of basketball shorts and a clean t-shirt to start her coffee before I need to head to the stadium when I hear a sob that I can't ignore.

CHAPTER 28

INDIE

Sobs shake my body against the cold tile of Dom's shower. My meltdown started quiet enough that I thought a shower might calm me down. But it only escalated with each intrusive thought that assaulted me, bringing me to my knees. Dom, having to watch me go through cancer treatments, my dad and Poppy at my bedside, me surviving but something happening to one of them. All of this being for nothing because he walks away when he realizes I'm not worth the work.

I don't hear him come in over the sound of the water and my sobs, but suddenly his arms are pulling me into his strong chest.

"Baby, look at me." He takes my tear-streaked face in his hands, trying to tilt my chin up, but I don't let him. I'm not ready.

Last night was everything. I went in with open eyes and no delusions about what was happening, but Dom doesn't know what he's signing up for and that's not fair.

We spent hours talking that first night, he knows what losing my mom did to me. But he might not be prepared to do it himself. There's this little voice inside my head saying that this all could be temporary, that I could be more than he bargained for. Maybe it's that or my impending period, but I'm a fucking mess.

"Indie. I need you to tell me what's going on. If you're scared . . . or having regrets." He flinches like those words physically hurt him and that's what does me in because even though I fought this tooth and nail, the last thing I want is to hurt him. "Talk to me, please."

"Nothing like that." I sniffle, my hands smoothing over the gray Bandits shirt that's now stuck to him. "Oh god, you need to get to the stadium."

"I'm not leaving here until I know you're okay. Please tell me why you're so upset?" he begs, still cradling my face.

"This is not a short discussion, but remember when my doctor called the other day?"

"Yes," he drags out, sounding weary of where this conversation is going.

"I'm okay," I promise. "I've always said no to genetic testing, but I met someone at a support group my doctor recommended. It's given me a new perspective. I've put it off for years, but I think I need to do it. That's what started all this." I wave to my sore, swollen face.

He pulls me from the floor and into his arms, ducking his head so he's eye level with me. "But you're okay?"

"Physically, yes. Mentally, I'm a wreck."

"Nah, you're perfect. But what do we need to do to get you out of here?" His lips find my forehead in a kiss that does more to chase away the tears than anything else I tried.

"Just conditioner."

"Turn around and tilt your head back." He spins me by my shoulders without waiting for a reply. "But I'm keeping my clothes on so we don't get distracted before we finish this conversation."

"You're going to wash my hair?"

"Yep, and it's going to be so amazing you're never going to want to do it yourself again."

As soon as his fingers sink into my hair working the product through, I know it's the honest to god truth.

"What does this testing all entail?" he asks, focusing his attention on the base of my skull, rubbing circles with his thumbs as he massages the product into my hair.

"The testing itself is simple. After the consultation to talk through family medical history and testing limitations, it's really just a blood test. A potentially life-altering blood test, but it's not physically invasive."

"I'm coming with you."

"Excuse me?" I turn so fast I slip on the wet floor and almost take both of us out, but when I see the steely look on his face, I know the fit I was about to pitch is pointless. To most people he might be the happy-go-lucky centerfielder for the Bandits, but he's shown me another side, one that feels like it's only for me—thoughtful, protective, reliable. I've got the best of both worlds.

Closing my eyes I suck in a deep breath. I want him there, but pushing him away is second nature at this point. "What if you're on the road?"

"I'd really appreciate it if you make it for when I'm not, but I'll be there either way." He steps into my space, backing me against the wall.

"Why?"

"Because this is important, and I want to support you."

"Okay."

"I like it when you're agreeable. Now rinse." He steers me back under the water.

"I'm going to get out and change. Finish up and we can talk while you drink your coffee."

When I get out, we go over his schedule for the next two weeks and pick a couple times that work for both of us before he leaves.

CHAPTER 29

DOM

"Cutting it close," Dean says when I skid through the door to the locker room just in time to avoid a fine. I keep my head down and start getting ready at my cubby, but I can feel his dark eyes on me.

"I like it when you're late. I got your favorite parking spot today," Hendrix piles on. When I look up and see the picture of him and Poppy from New Year's Eve hanging in his locker, the guilt hits me.

I respect Indie's desire to keep her medical decisions personal for now. But she has so many people who care about her. The girls are at the top of that list, right below her dad. Mostly it just makes me sad that she won't let them help her. Which means I can't confide in my teammates.

"My alarm didn't go off." My grumbled lie makes me hate this whole situation even more.

"Bullshit. It's either the dog or a girl. Which one has you on a leash?" Braxton Hayes asks, butting in.

"Be respectful. These guys choose to be leashed because they know they've overextended the fielding position," I snap back, feeling defensive.

"What the hell are you talking about?" Xavier asks.

"It's the baseball equivalent of out-punting your coverage," I explain as I tie my cleats looking up to find five pairs of eyes staring down at me.

"He's trying to say our girls are all too good for us," Dean says, closing his locker.

"That doesn't make any sense." Braxton shakes his head, following Dean towards the field.

"He's actually right, it just doesn't have the same ring to it," Cruz says, patting me on the back, leaving just Hendrix and I.

"Everything okay? You seem . . . less you."

Things are so far from okay. When I woke up to an empty bed this morning, I thought the worst, but the truth I found in the shower was more heartbreaking than I could've imagined. My hands ball into tight fists at my side and I have to fight to keep my breaths even. I want to punch something, rage about the unfairness of it all. More than anything, I want to wrap Indie in my arms and create a bubble around her to keep this all away. To protect her, to protect the future we've just started to build. None of this is fair. Indie's already endured so much with losing her mom and she could have to face that same cruel battle. My stomach twists with just the thought and I think I might be sick.

Swallowing down the bile, I look up from where I'm staring at the cement floor and find Hendrix waiting, his arms crossed and his head cocked. I'm so close to breaking, to crumbling here on the bench and telling him just how not okay I am. Because I'm barely holding it together and the only reason I haven't lost my composure yet is because Indie needs me to fight with her.

Don't get me wrong, she's more formidable than anyone. She could do this on her own, but I won't let her, no matter how hard she pushes, and I know she will at some point. Not because she doesn't want me, but because she's terrified of how this could hurt me. My girl's been fighting on her own for too long already, and now that she's let me in, she'll never face another battle without me there to help take some of the blows.

It takes everything in me to shut off all the warring emotions and tell the biggest lie of my life. "Yeah, it's fine. They were right. I lost track of time playing with Ronnie this morning."

There's doubt in his narrowed eyes, but I shrug, standing to head out to the field.

"Is it lame of me to admit I was kind of wishing it was a human girl? You deserve to find someone like we have."

"Don't worry about me. I've got everything I need." At least that is the truth.

♥

In the three days since I found Indie falling apart in my shower, I've learned more than I ever cared to know about ovarian cancer and the different types of BRCA gene mutations. I've read studies in medical journals, I know the early symptoms, the survival rates for the different variations. If it's available online, I've read it.

Early this morning I woke up in a cold sweat from a grim nightmare; one where Indie found out too late about her diagnosis and I lost her. Every complaint of a stomach ache or being tired is going to trigger me to think the worst. I'm terrified of what could happen, which is how I found myself at the stadium before breakfast this morning. All this fear and worry needs an outlet because Indie needs me.

The pitching machine reloads the balls and I wipe the sweat from my forehead with the sleeve of my shirt before hauling my bat back up and getting in my stance.

I've lost count of how many buckets I've taken at this point and my arms are heavy with fatigue as I load, coiling my body tight, and stride towards the machine, crushing the ball back at it. Over and over again. I repeat those steps until I'm out of balls and have to wait on the machine again.

The folding chair creaks under the weight of me dropping into it and I pull out my phone, scrolling to my dad's contact information, he'd know what to say. Before I can hit the call button, the green light on the machine catches my eye and I drag my bat along with me as I push up from the chair.

"Take another round and I'll bench you." Coach Wilson's gruff voice barks at me.

"I'm fine." It's not in my nature to argue with a coach, in fact this is the first time I've ever done it, but I'm not exactly thinking clearly.

"The hell you are. You're a mess, Duran, and you're done here. What the hell has gotten into you?"

"Can't a guy put in some extra reps without getting grilled."

"This isn't extra reps. This is punishment. I've watched you take hundreds of balls without as much as a break to catch your breath."

"You don't know what you're talking about." That nagging sensation to open up to someone is in the back of my mind begging me to tell him what I'm up against.

"You're the happiest guy on the team. Cruz might be the captain, but you are the backbone. Whether they realize it or not, everyone on this team looks up to you. When things get hard, you keep everyone going. If someone is having a bad day you're the first to pick them up. My job is to know everything I can about my players, and the man in front isn't the unburdened Dom we are all used to. So tell me what's got you in here killing yourself."

I tell him everything, barely maintaining my composure through it. Pouring all my fear onto the concrete floor in front of both of us and when I'm done he pulls me into a hug and I let the floodgates open. It's the temporary reprieve I need so I can be strong for Indie.

♥

DOM:

I thought you weren't going to hide from me.

FUTURE WIFE:

I'm not. I've been over three times this week.

DOM:

During my games to see Ronnie.

FUTURE WIFE:

I'm just a little overwhelmed since
I made the appointment.
Give me a few more days.

DOM:

You shouldn't be dealing with this on your own.

FUTURE WIFE:

I'm not. I have Ronnie and your notes.

DOM:

You get two more days. I'm not leaving for
this road trip without seeing you.

CHAPTER 30

INDIE

The clack of nails on the wood floor speed towards me when I step inside Dom's front door. "What have you got for me today, Ronnie-girl?" Coarse fur brushes my legs while my favorite companion circles my feet, only plopping her butt on my foot after three spins in each direction. Big brown eyes look up at me expectantly, waiting for me to remove the note from the tiny pocket sewn into the firework print bandana she's wearing.

Only Dom would turn his dog into the world's most adorable carrier pigeon, tucking sweet notes into a handmade dog accessory that I'm sure one of his bingo ladies made for him.

"Those shorts you wore yesterday. So hot!!! Do me a favor and make sure you bend over in front of the dog cam again so I can tell you which I like better. I hope you're ready for me tomorrow, Baby, because I'm not waiting four more days to see you."

"Don't look at me like that," I say, when my snort has Ronnie tilting her head. "Your dad is a fool." Some of the notes have been filled with sweet concern, or dirty promises, but all of them are a reminder that he's here for me.

Walking through the living room, I pause, Ronnie's toys are spread out on the ground in an "X" right in front of the camera.

"An absolute fool," I repeat, before I bend down, picking up her favorite ball from the center and standing. "Let's go girl." I look over my shoulder and give the camera a little smile before I straighten. My belt bag vibrates against my hip and my hand digs for my phone. I can't stop the grin that spreads so wide it makes my cheeks hurt.

YOURS:

Close call. I need a review from New York.
Play it back, please?

ME:

I don't think that's a challengeable call.

YOURS:

My game, my rules.

ME:

Aren't you supposed to be practicing or something?

YOURS:

Agua break but this was worth
getting yelled at to check my phone.

YOURS:

No boot?

ME:

Nope, it's feeling much better.
Still no biking or running, but I can walk on it.

YOURS:

Good things happen when you follow directions.

ME:

Don't get used to it.

YOURS:

I wouldn't dare. You going to watch me tonight?

ME:

Maybe.

YOURS:

There'll be a quiz later.

Ronnie darts out the door in front of me heading straight for where the backyard opens up beyond the pool.

"Don't get too excited. I can't throw as far as you're used to." She just thumps her tail, waiting. "Yeah, you don't care, do you?"

My intention wasn't to stay the night when I came over earlier, but after playing with Ronnie and going for a swim, the last thing I want to do is drive home. This couch is too comfy and being here with Ronnie, surrounded by Dom's things, just feels right.

I've cut myself off from everyone for the past week to avoid dealing with all the overwhelming emotions that have been plaguing me since I decided to get tested. My lack of social life after moving has raised some suspicions, but I'm just not ready to talk about this with anyone else yet, so I've been blaming my hobbit tendencies on the need to focus on work.

It's not totally a lie. The new volunteer database I'm creating for the clinic, Double Play, and Saving Paws, before the recruiting event they're co-hosting later this year, is keeping me plenty busy.

All I want now, after all that time alone, is Dom. So instead of driving home and turning on my TV, I take the stairs up to his bedroom with a container of Chinese that I had delivered, change into one of his shirts and turn on the game, immersing myself in all of him I can get at the moment.

By the ninth inning, I'm fighting sleep and losing quickly, the soothing smell of Dom on the sheets lulling me into a relaxed state.

I vaguely recall feeling the bed dip before being wrapped up in a warm body.

"You're here." It's barely a whisper, but the low rumble is like a magnet for me.

"For some stupid reason, I missed you," I mumble, turning into his warmth.

"I missed you too, Baby. Now go back to sleep." One kiss to my forehead and his heat behind me is all it takes for me to fall back into a peaceful sleep.

♥

"This is so much better than waking up alone in bed," I say sleepily, when two thick fingers lazily toy with me as the sun comes up over the mountains outside. Dom has one hand down the front of my underwear and the other cupping my breast through his shirt.

"Couldn't agree more." His voice is husky with sleep and desire. Goosebumps ripple across my exposed stomach and his hard cock presses into my back more persistently when his lips search for mine.

Spreading me open, he plunges one long, thick finger into me and I immediately want more. "Fuck me. Just like this," I plead, reaching for the hem of his shirt that I'm still wearing from last night and pulling it over my head.

"That's my girl." He adds another finger layering hot kisses on my neck. "I love hearing you ask for my cock."

"I need it. Please." Reaching behind me, I pull him out of his briefs. Stroking his hard length before placing it between my already damp thighs.

"Baby, you can't do that." He rocks his hips, coating his length with my slickness, sounding pained by the restraint he's using. "I want you bare. Just the idea of filling you up with my cum has me on edge." Teeth clamp down on my shoulder, a punishment for the way I'm torturing him.

"Oh." I gasp, when he pushes forward his head nudging my clit. "We can't. I haven't been on the pill long enough."

"That's not the detractor you think it is."

"Wh-what?" I ask, sure I didn't hear him right over my screaming ovaries.

"Relax, I'm not trying to knock you up. We need time to figure this out, but the idea of it is really fucking hot. *You* carrying *our* baby? Yeah, I don't hate that at all."

He drags his cock backward over my clit again and I lurch forward, reaching for the nightstand where he stashes his condoms.

"Condom, now," I squeak.

"You don't like the idea?" he asks with a laugh. I roll my lips together. "Or do you like it a little too much?"

"Let's not gloat. Put the condom on and fuck me."

Thankfully, he follows directions flawlessly before running out the door for practice.

CHAPTER 31

DOM

"Marry, Kiss, Kill. D.J. Tanner-Fuller, Stephanie Tanner, or Kimmy Gibbler," I ask, playing with a wayward dark curl. Ronnie snores at our feet, her favorite pastime followed closely by a game of catch. My favorite pastime is quickly becoming these peaceful moments alone with my girl. The ones where she's not busy busting her ass to get her work done and I'm not rushing off to the next practice or game. Where all our worries about the future seem to slip away for a while and we can just *be*.

"We're talking about the *Fuller House* era, right?" She eyes me over her shoulder. I've got her tucked under my arm on her couch. The Bandits played an afternoon game, and I came straight here. Other than Ronnie, who Indie's been spending more time with when I'm at the stadium, she's still brushing off everyone else. Somehow, the girls talked her into a girl's night tomorrow while the team travels for a road trip. Knowing they'll be around, even if they don't know what's going on with her, is a relief.

"Of course. What kind of person do you think I am?" I tug on that same stray curl, teasingly.

"Just checking. Don't get your panties in a twist. Kiss Stephanie. Kill Kimmy. Marry D.J. What about you?"

"I prefer undies, but whatever." She rolls her eyes, tempting me to put her on all fours and spank the attitude out of her. But I choose to soak up these simple moments, the same kind that made me want more that first night. We might poke at each other, but no matter what we are talking about, it just flows. From that first night, it felt like I'd found my best friend in Indie. "Kiss Kimmy. Marry Stephanie. Kill D.J.," I answer, not needing to think about it.

"Poor D.J., what did she ever do to you?"

"D.J.'s too tidy for me. I like someone that keeps me on my toes. She's predictable." Leaning forward I grab the remote from the coffee table, switching off the sports highlights and pulling up a streaming service. "Want to watch a few episodes of *Is it Cake?*"

"Sure, just let me call my dad real quick. He should be done with his village meeting. You get it ready."

"Are you going to tell him?"

"Not yet." She stops in her tracks, her head tilting to the side slightly and scans my face for a reaction carefully, like she's expecting me to be disappointed. Her shoulders sag with relief when she doesn't find anything but genuine concern.

I wish she would tell him. I've encouraged her to do so, but only because I want her to feel supported by more than just me, especially when I'm gone as often as I am.

Her soft lips brush my cheek. It's an innocent kiss, but it makes me want to pull her back for more. Before I have the chance, she grabs her phone and disappears through the sliding door to the balcony. While she's catching up with her dad, I scrounge for snacks. You can't watch a baking competition without sustenance of your own.

"Ooh cookie dough. I could fuck with that," I say to Ronnie, who followed me out here and is currently stationed at my feet looking adorably spoiled as she waits for a snack. "None for you, little lady." I pop a few bite-sized pieces in my mouth and move on to making popcorn, pouring some M&M's into the bowl.

I'm halfway back to the couch, chewing on another piece of cookie dough, when Indie slips back inside.

"What are you eating?" Something ominous creeps down my spine in the cool way she asks. Like she knows exactly what I'm eating and there is no right answer to this question.

"Cookie dough," I say wearily, dropping to the couch and shaking the container for her to take a piece.

"My emergency cookie dough that I got from the food truck downtown for when I start my period tomorrow and want to murder you instead of Kimmy?" Her arms cross under her chest, drawing my attention to her breasts.

Nope. Not the time.

"Oh, shit." Trying to hide the nearly empty container, I pull my hand back, but it's too late. She leans over, peering in. "I'm sorry. I'll get you more. The exact same kind and then some."

"And when do you plan to do that? Your flight leaves at the crack of dawn," she challenges, taking the container from me and returning it to the fridge.

"I don't want to die. I'll figure it out." It might not be wise, but I've always been dumb for this girl, so, I come up behind her and wrap my arms around her. If nothing else, maybe it will distract her.

A short, sharp snort comes out of her nose, then she relaxes against me. "You're too pretty to murder. Plus, I'm not sure my ankle is ready for running from the law yet."

"See, you say those things and I hear, 'Dom is boyfriend goals.'"

Her back vibrates against my chest as she gives into a full-bodied laugh this time. "That's weird. I don't remember agreeing to be your girlfriend. And now that you've eaten half of my snacks for my stay at the Red Roof Inn, I'm not sure I ever can."

"Fuck, Baby. You drive a hard bargain, but if it's an orgasm you want to convince you, it's an orgasm you'll get."

"That's not what—nope, actually, you know what, I'll allow it."

"Wait, really?" I ask, stunned that she's just going with this.

"You're kinda cute, and I have no doubt you'll replace that cookie dough in that over the top manner that only you are capable of. Besides, I told my dad about you, so now you're stuck with me for a while."

"You told your dad about me?" The bright smile she grants me when I turn her in my arms nearly knocks me off balance. *Such an adorable pain in my ass.*

"Well, he already knew you from when you hijacked my phone after I hurt my ankle, but yes."

"So I'm your boyfriend," I draw out, booping her nose.

"Only if you stop singing it like that . . . and I still want that orgasm."

Spinning us, my hands go to her waist and she lands on the counter with a squeal. "Now is probably when I should tell you that my dad knows all about you too. We have a whole text chain dedicated to me updating him on my progress towards winning you over. He's your biggest fan."

"You do not."

"We very much do. He loves that made me work for a chance." My hands drop to her hips teasing the waistband of her shorts.

"What are you doing?"

"You took away my snack and I'm still hungry."

"Oh my god. I can't. You're ridiculous. I take it all back." Even as she says it, her hands thread through my hair. "You're just trying to distract me from the fact that you and your dad have been plotting against me. I never stood a chance, did I?"

That's it, Baby, hold on.

"Nope," I say, dragging her shorts and undies down her hips and getting to work.

NAUGHTY SLIDERS & TACO SLUTS

POPPY:

Ladies! I'm calling for an intervention.

MIA:

Is this about Lilah and Cruz getting it on in other people's houses?

LILAH:

We haven't done that in months. It seems like Mia is our new exhibitionist. Ride any gondolas lately?

MIA:

I wish. Although he did sneak me into the locker room a few weeks ago.

POPPY:

Well, that is hot as hell. This problem trumps that.

INDIE:

What could possibly out rank locker room sex?

POPPY:

You.

INDIE:

That seems drastic.

MIA:

She has a point.

LILAH:

You've been quiet since moving. Is everything okay?

INDIE:

I know, I'm sorry. I'm still just getting settled in. I'm excited to see you all tomorrow.

POPPY:

And this is why we need an intervention. Something is up.

MIA:

I agree with Poppy, you've been unusually withdrawn.
You know we are here for you.

INDIE:

I know and I love you guys for that.

CHAPTER 32

INDIE

"Explain to me again why we are meeting at Dom's to watch the game," Poppy quizzes me from the other end of the phone, which is on speaker. The girls are supposed to meet me there in thirty minutes and I'm still getting my shit together. By getting my shit together, I mean stress eating the rest of the cookie dough that Dom opened the other day.

"It's nearly ninety-five degrees out and he has a pool with a TV. Do you need more of a reason to have a frozen drink and watch your man play from a pool with your best friends?"

"Are you sure it's not an aquarium? Because I smell something fishy."

It's not that I don't want to tell her, I do; keeping her in the dark feels like a betrayal. I just want to get this over with all at once instead of telling everyone individually. "If this interrogation continues much longer, Mia and Lilah are going to be left waiting outside because they beat us there. And they are bringing the margarita mix, so I should probably get going."

"Dammit, you're right." She sighs.

"I know."

"I still have questions. Don't think I'll forget just because margaritas were involved."

"Again, I know." This time it's me sighing into the phone as we hang up. I toss the now empty container of cookie dough, which isn't as tragic as it sounds because, as promised, Dom found a way to pack my freezer full from his early morning flight yesterday. As of this morning, my stock is more than replenished. Chocolate chip, double chocolate, peanut butter, snickerdoodle and M&M. He also had a heating pad and tylenol delivered. I had no doubt he would come through but it still made me question why I fought this for so long.

Luckily, it's been a pretty easy period so far and I haven't needed the last two emergency items, but the gesture was very much appreciated.

Like I predicted, Lilah and Mia are both waiting when I get there and are all over me as soon as I step out of the car.

"You have a key?" Mia asks, stunned.

"Did you think we were going to do a little light B&E today?" I twist the key in the lock letting them into the house. One that feels more like home than my own apartment over the last few weeks.

"No, I just assumed you had a garage code or something. A key is so tangible."

"And it's a lot harder to change the locks than just resetting a code. She's right, it's a big deal," Lilah adds.

"Your brother gave Poppy a key so she could water her plants and they barely knew each other." I drop to my knee, giving Ronnie some love when she trots up to me.

"And now they're getting married," Lilah reminds me, before joining me to scratch behind the dog's ears.

"Can we just give me a break until Poppy gets here? I'll tell you all anything you want to know then."

"Anything?" Mia salivates at the potential for gossip.

"Within reason." Walking toward the living room, I find Ronnie's collection of toys haphazardly strewn across the floor in front of the dog cam.

Bending to pick one up, I ask, "Did he train you to do this?" Behind me, the contraption whirls mechanically and I whip my head around just in time to see it spit out a treat. "Of course he did."

"So . . . you want me to make yours a double?" Lilah asks, unpacking the bag she brought.

"Yes . . . No, actually. I don't want to drown." And I also want to be sober for my FaceTime with Dom after their game.

Poppy walks in a few minutes later, with Nana Janet following close behind—a tray of brownies in hand—and we all follow Ronnie to the patio, wasting no time sinking into the water, eager for a reprieve from the heat.

"She's such a cutie," Nana says, floating up to where Ronnie and I are sharing an oversized float that Dom bought for this very reason. Perking up at the sound of her name she nudges me with her nose demanding ear scratches.

"And she knows it." I indulge her with a laugh.

"Must get that ego from her owner. It's awful nice of him to let you come and go as you please. Last I heard, you could barely be around him without sparring."

"He gave me a key when I hurt my ankle so I could use the pool."

"And?" Lilah asks, paddling over from where she drifted across the pool.

"I started spending time here, and no one was around to keep me from doing something stupid." I huff out an exasperated sigh, and just go for it. "It turns out I actually enjoy doing stupid things with him, so I kept doing them, and now I have a boyfriend."

"But he's a baseball player," Poppy says, so loudly and shrilly that Ronnie rolls off the float. She swims over to the steps where she climbs out, shaking off and sauntering over to the grass to find a quiet spot in the sun.

"It didn't take long once I gave him a chance and realized that's not all he is. He lets everyone think he's just this carefree, goofy guy, but he's yet to let me down when I need him."

"So all that back and forth for the last year was just foreplay?" Janet asks, sipping on her margarita.

"Maybe it was." Even I can admit that throwing barbs back and forth was never about hating him. It was about driving away all the feelings that made me uneasy. But the bickering and banter, his sharp tongue, and the way he didn't back down for me was always exhilarating.

"I've always been a big fan of foreplay," Lilah adds, looking down at her wedding ring.

"Is that why you ignored the sexual tension with your best friend for years?" Poppy pokes.

"It certainly made for a memorable time when we got together." She tips her head back, letting her body sink further into the water and soaking up the sun.

I hold up my drink, clinking it to hers, a silent agreement that emotional edging makes for hotter sex. *Every. Single. Time.*

When the team takes the field a few minutes later, we all float closer to the TV screen hanging on the outside of the covered patio and anchor ourselves with our heels on the patio's edge. Sipping from my non-alcoholic drink I try to hide that I'm practically giddy over the prospect of watching my boyfriend play. This man made my heart do a complete one-eighty over the last month.

Brick by brick, he's dismantled the wall around my heart that I built to protect it from who I thought he was. He might still be the silly, carefree baseball player I met last year, but he's also reliable and thoughtful.

And sexy as hell in those pants.

"Why is Dom wearing a red thong under his pants?" Poppy asks, splashing some water at me.

"They're two games out from making the playoffs. He's become a little obsessive about making sure he has luck on his side." Just another quirk I never expected to be so endearing. There's something about the way he carries himself, so sure. I always thought it was arrogance. In truth he's anything but arrogant. Confident, yes. Self aware, definitely. He knows his strengths and plays those up, but he's the first to make fun of himself and admit his weaknesses. Besides, he might be the most thoughtful man I've ever met. You can't be arrogant and incredibly kind, can you?

"He knows those pants are basically see through this year, right?" Mia asks snorting. "Remember when Xavier slid into home back in May and shredded his?"

"I thought he was going to give us all a peek of what kept Kristy coming back for more after all the times she's said she was done," Lilah adds, her chin tipped up to the sky.

"Have you ever known Dom to shy away from anything? He knows you can see his lucky thong. He just doesn't care, especially if it helps them win."

"No one likes a challenge more than that man," Janet agrees, giving me a little wink.

"Did you just call me difficult?"

"If the shoe fits, lace that bitch up darling." She holds up her cup. "Now float me another drink and a brownie."

By the seventh inning, we are all out of the pool and nervously pacing in front of the TV. The Bandits are tied with their division rivals, the LA Diablos, and we all know how important this win is if the team wants to keep their postseason hopes alive.

It's two scoreless innings later when the top of the Bandits lineup steps up to the plate. Hendrix starts the inning off with a blooper into right-center that drops just short of the outfielder.

Poppy grabs on to my hand, squeezing it hard. "Don't you dare go for two," she yells at the TV as her fiancé rounds first, skidding to a stop and diving back just in time for his fingertip to grip the edge of the base before the tag comes down.

Dean is up next; his jaw is set and his cleats dig into the dirt as he waits for his pitch. The first pitch is a fastball and he's behind it just a hair. The pitcher tricks him with a curveball on the next pitch for a strike. Stepping out, he refocuses, before taking his spot in the batter's box again. After fouling off a few in row, he strikes out, swinging on a slider.

Lilah stops the steady pattern she was pacing on the patio and stands in front of the TV, watching as her husband traces two letters into the dirt. A J for his late brother, followed by a D for her, just like he does every game. With intense focus, he watches the first two pitches before swinging at one he likes and sending it down the third baseline, all the way to the corner.

While the outfielder is digging it out, Hendrix and Cruz advance to third and second base.

Nerves crawl up my spine as Dom walks to the plate. His trademark smirk melts away and his muscles coil, poised to strike. I know that look well, and it has me clenching my thighs together, hoping no one notices.

He doesn't take his time and wait or battle like his teammates. Instead, he sees something he likes on the first pitch and swings away. It pays off. The ball goes flying over the outfielder's head and clears the fence, ending the game in impressive fashion. I don't even realize that I'm making a spectacle of myself until I realize that every pair of eyes is now turned on me as I throw my hands in the air, cheering wildly.

"Oh, I love this." Poppy laughs, wrapping her arm around my shoulder. "You're a Bandits WAG now, and you're just as crazy as the rest of us."

Yeah, I think I am, and I don't hate it at all.

When the girls clear out after the game, I could take Ronnie with me and go home—I probably should—but I don't. Instead, the two of us head up to his bed and wait for him to call. With the dog settled on the floor at the end of the bed, I scroll my email while I wait.

When the phone rings, Dom's face takes up ninety percent of the screen—the contact photo he assigned himself on display. He's sweaty from his workout and his honey-colored hair is held back by . . . holy shit . . . how did I not notice that the bandana he's been wearing all season matches the one he had made for Ronnie?

I study the picture more closely, trying to remember the first time I saw him wearing this pattern. I think back to the games I've watched. He's had it since I moved, for sure. He was wearing one in Chicago as well, and I vaguely recall thinking he was ridiculous for wearing one with fireworks when it wasn't a holiday. I'm such an idiot. The fireworks were never about Memorial Day or the Fourth of July. Snapping out of it, I quickly answer the call before it goes to voicemail.

"Oh fuck, Baby, you're in my bed. You don't know how much I like that." He's seated at the end of his bed, the unremarkable white sheets and beige hotel walls visible behind him.

"Ronnie wanted to stay here tonight," I say, causing her to groan from where she lazily lays at the end of the bed.

"She did?"

"Uh huh," I lie.

"Did Ronnie also dress you in my shirt for bed?" he asks, the corners of his lips turning up in a knowing smile.

"No, that was all me. I missed you and this smells like you." Inhaling, I bring the shirt up to my nose. "Did she dress the two of you in your matching bandanas?"

It's annoying how perfect he looks with that crooked smirk tilting his lips. So damn pleased with himself.

"Took you long enough to notice."

"Is that a superstition you picked up from Memorial Day or the Fourth?"

"Nope."

I swallow the lump in my throat. "How long have you been wearing it?"

"Lark made it for me at the beginning of the season. I've been wearing it regularly since then, Firecracker."

"Why?"

"You know why. I've never kept my feelings for you a secret."

"That scares the shit out of me, Dom; how fearless you are in your belief that things will just work out."

"I'm not fearless. Nothing scares me more than the thought of losing you."

My chest splits open with his admission. He's been my rock, making sure I'm okay day after day, but this is taking a toll on him as well. He just hides it better. I wish I could take that pain away from him the same way he does for me. I know from losing my mom that I can't. He's made his choice by being with me.

"If it bothers you, I won't wear it."

"No!" I practically scream. "Don't do that. It doesn't bother me. I'm envious of how hopeful you are. I wish I could be more like you. It's one of my favorite things about you. It's just one of the reasons this works."

"You don't need to be like me, Indie. Let me balance out your wildness. Lean on me for my faith. Talk sense into me when I'm not being serious enough. We're a team. That's how relationships are supposed to work," he says, moving until he's settled against the headboard, his bare shoulders tanned and still showing some scratches from the last time we were together before I left. *God, that's hot.*

"You make it sound so easy."

"With you, it is. That's how I knew I wanted more when we first met." He exhales, looking at me seriously. "I know things aren't always going to be easy. I'm going to annoy you. You're going to get snarky with me. It's going to take everything we've got sometimes, but the decision to put in the effort is never going to be the hard part. Not for me. I know what I want and it's you."

"I want you too." He's right about that much, now that I'm being honest about wanting Dom, being with him is effortless. He's quickly become my best friend.

"Since we are getting deep, how are you feeling?" he asks.

"Oh, um, fine. The cookie dough was delicious. Thankfully, my uterus is sparing me the dramatics of trying to murder me from the inside out."

Warmth washes over me when he chuckles, even through the phone it affects me, coasting over my skin like a gentle touch and making me miss him more. "Glad to hear it. If that changes, my freezer is stocked as well. But that's not what I meant." The smile on his face fades, replaced by a look of concern. "Are you feeling okay about the blood work tomorrow?"

"Oh, *that.*" Like I could have forgotten. It's been haunting me since I made the appointment. I'm still not sure if it's the right decision, but I'm going through with it.

"We get in early. I have some meetings at the stadium after we land, but I'll pick you up, just like we talked about."

He's insisted on coming and driving me. It goes against all my instincts to let him help like this, but I know I shouldn't shy away from the support, even if it feels foreign.

"Yeah, okay," I say. "Nice game tonight," I add, desperate to take a step back from the heavy conversation. "The girls noticed your thong."

"Well, duh, I wear the shit out of that thing."

"So humble. How'd I get so lucky?"

"You want me to put it on and remind you just how cocky I am?" He wiggles his eyebrows. Something so ludicrous has no right looking as hot as it does.

"That's it. This relationship was fun, but it's over now."

"You couldn't quit me if you tried. Now tell me more about your nigh—" Banging in the background interrupts him mid-thought. "Hold on, that's probably room service." He stands from the bed, phone held out in front of him as he walks. I hear the locks click and confusion crosses his face. "What the hell are you doing here?" he asks, stepping back from the door.

From my limited view, I can see the guys filter in without waiting for an invitation.

"Seems like we have company," Dom says, his normally sunny disposition souring at the intrusion.

"Never stopped you before," Dean grumbles, sticking his head in view of the camera. "Hey, Indie."

Without acknowledging his friend, I tell Dom, "So, I told the girls tonight. I hope that's okay."

"Fuck yeah it is. I've been dying to shout it from the rooftops," he practically cheers, dropping onto the side of the bed.

"You want to deal with this and call me back?" I ask through a huff of laughter.

"No. I want to talk to my girlfriend, but Blanche and her gabbers aren't going anywhere until I fill them in." Hendrix proves his point by dropping on to the bed next to him.

"You have fun with that."

"I wanted to have fun with you," he grumbles and then we say a too-quick goodbye.

By the time Dom calls me back, I'm asleep, and the next time I hear from him is the following morning when I wake up to a panic-filled phone call because storms have them stuck on the tarmac.

As much as I try to assure him it's okay, he's already beating himself up over a situation that's completely out of his control. I'm still filled with anxiety over going alone, but he's done so much for me and I want to protect him from his own guilt. I reassure him it's okay and I can go on my own, dreading it the whole time.

Hours later, I'm alone in the sterile waiting room of the clinic, twisting the hem of my t-shirt in my hands until it's stretched beyond repair. I swipe my sweaty hands on my shaking thighs and try to focus on anything but how badly I want to walk back out the door. It's the fear talking, and I'm done letting it win.

Dom took off just over two hours ago, and promised to come straight here, but there's no way he's going to make it. Being this close to the postseason, they have the team at the stadium almost nonstop—reviewing tape and putting in extra time with trainers to stay on top of their game. Any hope I've held onto is dashed when a nurse steps into the lobby from the back and calls my name. With one last glance towards the entrance, I stand, resigned to being here alone.

I'm halfway across the room when the door to the waiting room bangs open and a red-faced Dom rushes in. I'm so relieved to see him I could cry, but he's got his arms around me before I have the chance.

I bury my face in his shirt and suck in a deep breath. When he kisses my head and whispers, "I've got you," all the nerves melt away. And he means it because his hand never leaves mine, not when he holds the door for me, or when the medical assistant ties off the rubber tourniquet and draws my blood.

CHAPTER 33

DOM

I've never felt as out of control and frustrated as I did sitting on that tarmac. Even Dean noticed, asking repeatedly if everything was okay because I couldn't stop checking the time. Now that I'm here, my whole body is still rumbling from the leftover adrenaline.

Indie might think I'm just being a dutiful boyfriend holding her hand, but my grip on her is the only thing keeping me from losing it. She fought her attraction to me with everything she had, convinced that I was this unreliable playboy, and I almost gave credence to all of that by missing this appointment.

Even if it was out of my hands, even if she said she understood, I couldn't give her a reason to doubt me. Not with something this important. Not when we've come so far.

"Dr. Smith will be in to see you shortly," the medical assistant says with a sweet smile, gathering up the tubes she collected.

The kind gesture doesn't do anything to calm the way every muscle in my body is pulled tight like a rubber band, and seeing those vials in her hand has them close to snapping. Judging by the way Indie's eyes dart around the room, never settling on me for more than just a second, she's feeling the same way.

"It was silly of you to race over here. It was just a little blood," Indie lies. There's nothing silly or little about what she's going through today.

"And pass up an opportunity to pretend I was Bowser racing on the rainbow to get here in time? I don't think so." I give her the smirk I know annoys her and it does the trick. Using the arm that doesn't have a bandage wrapped around it, she smacks my bicep, her fist bouncing off my arm. Fuck it. I give my muscle a flex and trap her hand in mine, bringing it to my lips.

"So damn ridiculous, that's what you are."

"You always forget to add the '—ly good looking' to the end of that."

"Modest too."

"All I hear is you naming all the things you like about me."

"Mhmm. I do—"

There's two sharp knocks on the door before Dr. Smith pokes her head through. "Ready for me?"

"That depends on how painful you're going to make this."

"The painful part is over. We've already gone over the consent, risks, and potential outcomes. I just wanted to check on you and make sure you don't have questions about what's next." She looks between us, her eyebrow raising at Indie. "And who is this?"

"Yeah, aren't you going to introduce your boyfriend?"

The eye roll that earns me is one for the record books, so much attitude.

"Maryann, this is Dom."

"Ah, the irritating one that rescued you. Seems he charmed you after all."

"As a matter of fact, she was just about to tell me how much she liked me before you walked in."

"Well, don't let me interrupt."

"Don't we have some medical things to cover?"

"So shy, this one. She's not quite ready to admit that she's head over heels for me, but we're working on it."

"Oh, I like him." Dr. Smith laughs, pulling a rolling stool towards us and perching on the edge of it.

"Everyone does. It's really annoying."

"Endearing," I fire back.

"So test results?" Indie asks, the grip she has on my hand finally loosening. Blood rushes back into my fingertips, making my skin prickle.

"We should have them back within the next two weeks."

I ask the question that has kept me awake most nights since I found out what Indie's facing. "And if it's positive?" Emotion seeps into my voice, and this time it's Indie that's reassuring me with a light squeeze of her hand.

"You don't need to worry about that."

"The fuck I don't." I tear my gaze from Indie, wincing at Dr. Smith, who's leaning forward watching us with curiosity. "Sorry, but can we have a moment?"

"Of course. But Indie's right, you should try not to worry about that for now."

Only I'm not sure that's what my girlfriend meant.

When the door closes, leaving us alone, I turn to Indie, my hands framing her face. "Make no mistake, I'm in this. It might be new, but I didn't wait an entire year for you to come back to me just to push me away out of some misplaced effort to protect me. You can't scare me away, you can't protect me."

"You don't know—"

"No, *you* don't know. I might be the team puppy, the happy-go-lucky guy, but that doesn't mean shit. My golden retriever will turn to a grizzly bear on a dime for you. Do you understand? I'm here no matter what the results say. And if it's—I'll do everything I can to make sure you're okay. You *can't* push me away. I won't let you."

She presses into my hands trying to turn away.

"Not happening. Answer me."

"Yeah, I hear you."

This isn't over, not by a long shot. I've proven her wrong about how she sees me once, and I can do it again.

Standing from the chair I cross the room, wanting to finish this conversation so I can show her just how wrong she is about this. Opening the door, I stick my head into the hall, finding Dr. Smith leaning against the opposite wall.

"We're ready for you," I tell her, leaving the door open and rejoining Indie in the vinyl chairs that are doing nothing for me after hours on the airplane.

She takes her seat on the chair, wheeling it closer and leaning in to talk directly to Indie, and I'm immediately grateful that she found Maryann. She doesn't sugarcoat things, she just dives back in, leading with compassion.

"*If* the test comes back positive, we'll use that information to decide on additional screenings and prevention."

Prevention. That could mean surgeries and tough decisions about Indie's future—one I hope to be a part of. My Google search after I found her in the shower led me down a dark path of what-ifs. And while I don't know what role Indie will allow me to play in all this, I wanted to feel equipped to support her.

If Coach Wilson hadn't found me in the batting cages, my hands blistered, my emotions raw and given me an outlet for all my worst fears, I wouldn't be as level-headed today. Each day after practice since, he's been waiting with a bucket of balls. Silently supporting me as we load the machine together and he stays close in case I need an ear.

Most days I follow him to the cage and hit until I can barely lift my bat, because my arm being numb is better than me being angry or numb. Indie needs me to come through for her and I can't show up a shell of the man she needs.

After a few more minutes of talking about what to expect and how to deal with the wait, I follow Indie out of the clinic to her car. Her fingers wrap against the door handle, but she doesn't open it. Instead, she rests her forehead against the side of her car for a moment before she turns back toward me.

And I can see it, that same resigned look she had earlier, the way her arms cross over her chest protectively. She's rattled. She's shutting down.

Before she has the chance to make up an excuse or offer me an out, I step into her space, tilting her chin up. "If you're about to give me some bullshit excuse for why this can't work or tell me to walk away, save your breath. Listen carefully because I don't want to repeat myself again. I'm not walking away. Nothing you can say will change that. No test results. No procedures. Nothing."

After staring back at me with a hard expression I'm sure mirrors mine, she opens her mouth and closes it.

"Now, if you're done trying to chase me off, I'd really like to kiss you," I say, brushing my nose along hers and making my scary girl soft under me.

"Yeah, okay."

"Not the resounding 'yes' I was hoping for, but I'll take it." Kissing each corner of her mouth first, I take her lips slowly. It's tender and unlike any kiss we've shared, and it's not until her fist twists my shirt, pulling me closer, that I sink inside her mouth. When our kiss is bordering on indecent, I pull back just enough to rein myself in. "Leave your car here. I'm taking you home."

"What about me leads you to believe that I'll respond well to being told what to do?"

"My arousal alarm is telling me you will this time."

Heat from the huff of air she releases hits my neck. "Oh god, I'm afraid to ask," she says.

But all the fake sass in the world can't hide the way her pulse jumps under my palm. "You're lying, Firecracker. You're turned on by me telling you what to do. You crave feeling out of control, you're an adrenaline junkie, and you want me to strip you of the need to think—take all the decisions away and let you drown in your own pleasure. You can't run off and do something reckless with that ankle freshly healed, so let me be your danger for today."

She licks her lips but stays silent.

"Are you getting in my car, or should I slip my hand into those shorts and prove my point?"

Pushing against my chest, she backs me up and leads the way to my car, opening the door and getting in without a word.

She doesn't break the silence until I'm turning out of the parking lot. "Now would be a good time to channel your inner Princess Peach."

"Why's that?" I ask, glancing over to find her face flush with as she watches me.

"Because if you don't, I'll make you pull over to take the edge off in the back seat."

"It's cute that you still think you're in charge here. I thought I made it clear that I'm calling the plays."

"Like the pretty boy face, and nice guy personality weren't enough, now my body's decided it's hot when you act assertive. It's maddening, honestly."

"You need to ease the tension. Go for it, but the rest are mine," I say, my cock pressing against where the seatbelt is restraining it.

"I can wait," Indie says with more certainty than I've heard from her all day.

"There's my girl." My hand covers her bare knee, coaxing a whimper out of her when I slide it upwards, letting my pinky travel under the hem of her cutoff denim shorts.

"I hate you."

"No, you don't, but you will when we get home and I edge you for saying that."

"You won't," she says, her hand covering mine and holding it there, high enough on her inner thigh that I can feel how hot she is. My eyes stray from the road just long enough to see the dare in her smirk. "Because you want it just as bad as me."

I refocus on the road, determined to get her home in one piece. "That might be true, but you've underestimated me since we met. I've proven you wrong about a lot of things already; you need to understand that I'm still so much more than you believe me to be."

"Dom." Her voice softens, instantly tugging at my heart, because it's so rare that she shows that side of herself freely.

"Don't lie to me, and don't try to make me feel better," I say, turning onto my street.

"I'm not."

"That's lie number one. Any more, and I'll make you regret them."

The hand that still clutches mine wavers like she might withdraw it, or move it, but I can't be sure which. Flipping my palm up I drag hers along as I pull it back toward me and kiss the back of it.

Once the car is parked, I click the button, closing us in the garage. The ride here was fucking torture and the time it would take to get her inside is longer than I want to wait to have another taste of her.

Reaching over the console, I cup the back of her neck and pull her to me. "I hate away games," I say, against her mouth before I nip at her bottom lip making them part and giving me the access I want to kiss her—exploring, reacquainting myself as she does the same.

"Stupid car," Indie says, trying to get closer but unable to without climbing into my seat.

With one last kiss, I break our connection and unbuckle. Rounding the front of the car, I step up to her door just as she opens it. My hands grip her waist maneuvering her out of the way and shutting it with my foot as I turn us towards the gym I have set up on the other side of the garage.

"What are you—" Her words turn to a squeal as I lift her, wrapping her leg around me as I make the short walk to the weight bench and sit with her in my lap.

"Showing you just how not sweet I can be. You keep underestimating me and I'm not going to let you use it to push me away. I can handle this, just like I can handle you."

"You don't know what you're getting into. Hell, I don't even know—"

"Fuck, Indie. I know every terrifying statistic about what could happen. I know that the five-year survival rate is forty-nine point one fucking percent. That you'll have to decide about having kids if your tests come back positive, that you'll have to make other decisions . . ." I say, burying my face in her neck and soaking her in. I might be strong but I'm not bulletproof, and the idea of her having to go through surgeries, even if they reduce her risk, is enough to shred the suit of armor that I'm donning to show her what I'm willing to endure for her.

"Why?"

"Fuck, don't you see what you do to me? What you've done to me since the moment we met? When I look at you, I see the future I've always wanted. One with someone that will keep me on my toes, and no one does that better than you. I can't imagine ever waking up beside you bored, because as much as you love adventure, to me, *you're* the adventure."

"And what if we find out that the future you want is in jeopardy next week?"

"We'll deal with it together. I'll take every second I have with you, Indie. And right now, I want to spend those seconds showing you that you don't get to make all the decisions." My hands move to her hips, pulling her against me so that every inch of me is pressing into her through her shorts. "First you're going to come for me just like this, the way you did in the car the first night. Then I'm going to strip off your ruined panties and have some fun with you before I finally fuck you into believing that I'm here to stay."

"I want to believe that—I really do." Her words are fractured as I rock her center over my hard length.

"Aren't you sick of fighting it? Just let me be there for you through this."

"I'm scared."

"I know, Baby, I am too. But we both know we are better together. You make me stronger. I make you less scary. Like two halves of a whole." Tugging her shirt free from where it's trapped in her waistband, I use one hand to inch it up the side of her rib cage before she pulls it off the rest of the way. "So impatient. You can get naked as fast as you want, but you can't force me to rush."

My hand follows the curves of her body, brushing the underside of her breast with my thumb. I continue up her sternum and trace the column of her throat until I hook my thumb under her chin, and hold her delicate neck in my hand, forcing her to stop and really look at me. "When you're scared or unsure, you come to me. You tell me and I'll remind you that you don't have to be strong. That I can be strong for you." Pulling the cup of her baby blue lace bra down, I trace her taupe nipple with my finger, making her shiver. The soft color looks so damn sexy on her. Indie's brave and formidable. Though I would never show it, she intimidates me at times with her strength. But she's not without warmth, I've seen it firsthand in the way she nurtures her friends, in the generous spirit she has for her work and the compassion she infuses into it, in how she is when it's just us in the early morning hours, and with Ronnie.

"I don't enjoy being coddled."

"No one said anything about being coddled." Dropping my mouth to her nipple I suck hard, forcing a whimper from her parted lips. "I would never coddle you. But I take care of what's mine. And you are mine."

"Who's going to take care of you? I see the way you try to shield me from the worry and hurt—the heavy armor you carry. What happens when it wears you out?"

"Then we will lean on each other. But for now, you're going to let me take care of you, starting with this flawless fucking body that I want to play with until it can't take anymore. Sound good?"

"Uh, yeah," she says, sucking in a gulp of air, when my mouth finds her other breast, nipping at the swell of it. "I think I can manage."

"That's it, Baby. Now you're getting it," I praise when she takes over canting her hips, precum leaking from my cock.

"There's no one else I'd let use that nickname."

I'm almost positive she's still trying to fight with me, but I can't be sure with the way her eyes flutter shut and how she arches her back, forcing her tits into my face.

"Good, because no one else gets to call you that. Only me."

"Only you," she agrees, her fingers sifting through the strands of my hair as she chases her release. I wanted her to come for me the same way she did that first night, but this is infinitely better because this time I get to keep her.

"You going to let go for me now?" I ask, matching her rhythm as I roll my hips to meet her.

"So good," she mumbles, her head tilting back, as my name spills from her lips. After, her lower body stills as laughter rumbles out of her.

Confidence has never been in issue for me, but the girl falling apart in my lap right now has me questioning myself. When she finally stops, there are tears glistening in the corners of her eyes. All my insecurities forgotten, I bring my hands to the side of her face, my thumbs wiping the moisture away.

"I can't believe I let you do that to me in front of Dean."

Standing from the bench, I turn toward the full rack and set her in front of it, my hands working the button on her shorts free. It takes all my patience to carefully slip them down her legs and over her feet. Even with all my annoyance at his name on her lips right after I made her come, I can't stand the idea of being too rough and hurting her freshly healed ankle.

"Look at you—soft lace, flushed skin, and all fucking mine. Flawless. Beautiful. Strong." Stepping up behind her, the backs of my fingers run down her arms, making her skin pebble in their wake. When I get to her hands, I thread my fingers through hers and place her palms on each side of the rack. "What a shame that you ruined these," I say, my thumb gliding under the lace that's riding high on her hip. The pads of my fingers dig into her thigh as I reposition her, so she's partially bent over, her arms extended in front of her and her ass out.

Dropping to my knees behind her, I pull the soaked blue fabric to the side. "Who did this to you, Baby?"

"Y-you did," she stumbles over the admission when my knuckles brush her heated center.

"That's right. Me. No one else. Unless you were thinking of him while you were riding my lap."

"Never," she says, spreading her legs further.

"Are you sure about that?" I withdraw my touch.

"He was never the one I wanted," she pleads almost desperately as she shifts on her feet.

"Damn straight." Working quickly, I grab two of the resistance loops hanging from the rack. "Now, are you ready to have some fun?"

"What kind of fun?" She looks over her shoulder, eyeing the elastic bands.

"The kind where I play with your body until you're begging me to put you out of your misery." Bending on one knee I use a girth hitch knot to secure the band to the rack on one side and do the same on the other, twisting the ends to shrink the loop before I slide each of her feet through. It's high enough that it won't stress her ankle and loose enough that it's only really giving the illusion of being restrained. "Comfy?"

"Uh sure, do I need a safe word?"

"Do you want one?" I ask, standing behind her.

"No." The word catches in her throat when my fingers glide the thin blue straps off her shoulders. "You're my safe place to land. I don't need it."

Any sign that she's not thoroughly enjoying the lack of control and I'll stop—she knows that; it's there in the trust in her eyes as she looks at me over her shoulder. Something I wasn't sure I'd ever see from her and that I'll never take for granted, which is why I find myself leaning in for a kiss. Our lips brush each other in a promise that we're in this together.

"You can't distract me with sweet kisses," I say, my lips slowly moving down her neck.

"You kissed me."

"You say tomato, I say potato."

"That is not at all how that phrase goes." Her back shakes with laughter as I kiss my way down her spine.

"Says you. Now quit arguing." Her flesh ripples when my hand comes down playfully on her ass. I have to bite down on my lip to stop myself from doing it again and again. My lips cover the red mark I left behind, softening her moans.

"Oh, shit," she cries when I give in to need and leave a matching mark on the other side.

"Shit is right, you're soaked for me." Parting her slick center I chase down more of those sweet little whimpers, my tongue flicking over her heated core, dipping inside her for a taste. Wrapping one arm around her front I find her clit, toying with it lightly.

"Harder."

Without stopping, I tsk, my mouth still working her from behind. "You still don't understand that you're not in charge." My words are muffled, and the only indication that she's heard me is a grumbled curse. I've got all night to pry the control out of her hands. She bucks back into me when my fingers come down hard on her clit, giving me the perfect excuse to press my tongue inside her. Fuck yes.

"Stop trying to control everything and let me enjoy my meal. I have no problem keeping my head between your legs for hours, if that's what it takes."

Alternating between my tongue and fingers, I build her up slowly before backing off.

"Dom!"

"You're trying to rush me again. And I won't have it." She shivers when I blow on her hot center, seeking me out impatiently.

Her pained whimpers make my balls ache enough that I give in, sealing my lips over her clit. Time slips by as I enjoy the hell out of myself, feasting on her to the chorus of her noises growing more urgent.

"Don't stop," she cries.

Judging by the way her legs are shaking, she'll be pleading with me to let her come soon. Which is probably a good thing because as much as I'm loving every second of this, my dick is painfully hard between my legs and if one of us doesn't cave soon, I'll be making a mess in my pants.

I apply a little more pressure with my thumb, rubbing circles that have her knees buckling.

"Yes, thank fuck." It's a strangled appeal that borders on panic.

When I pull my hand away, I can feel her frustration in the way she sags back against me. She's close to begging me for what she needs, so I wait, my hands resting on the outside of her knees, my nose coasting up the back of her leg.

"Dom. Please. I need to come. I can't take it anymore. Please let me come—fuck."

"When are you going to learn that all you have to do is ask? Was that so hard?"

"Wh-what?"

"I've got you. You just have to ask for help and let go of the control you hold so dearly. Fall and let me catch you," I say, standing behind her, fishing a condom out and shoving my pants down.

With one thrust I'm rooted inside her, groaning against her back at the relief of her warmth squeezing me. Her climax is so sudden that I end up having to loop my arm around her waist to keep her upright.

"That's it. See how good it feels to let someone else help." Setting a painfully slow rhythm I pulse in and out of her, trying to stave off my own release, which is not far off after all the time I spent with my mouth on her, denying my dick any part of the action. When I can't take it any longer, I give in to the tension winding down my spine, making my balls pull up tight and switch to punishing strokes that have both of us slick with sweat and gasping for air.

"This body was made for me. The way you squeeze me. So damn good," I grunt out, my words rough and raw as my cock swells inside her, my orgasm bursting free and making my vision go black. It's always so damn good with her. Nothing has ever felt like this.

"You really would have let me come right away if I'd asked?" Indie asks between ragged breaths after we come down from our high.

"Of course. When have I not given you something you asked for?"

"You're an ass," she says without any of her normal bite.

Shifting beneath me, she's finally steady enough that I can reluctantly untangle our bodies and take care of the condom. Then I squat to help her out of the bands, holding on so she doesn't topple to the ground. "Mhmm, but I'm your ass. And right now, I'm making decisions and there's a bubble bath on our dance card."

"A bubble bath?"

"Yep."

"Like you and me together?"

"Mhmm. All that slippery skin. What could go wrong?"

"Don't even think about trying to slip it in without protection. I still need backup birth control for a few more days."

"But do you?" I ask, giving her my best puppy dog eyes.

"Yes, two sets of those brown eyes working against me is more than I can handle right now." The laugh she gives me as I scoop her up in my arms, carrying her towards the bathroom, comes easy and hits me hard in the chest.

Not that I should be surprised, everything this woman does has that effect. I just hope it doesn't take her too long to catch up to the feelings that are now much more than an infatuation for my teammates to tease me about.

245

CHAPTER 34

INDIE

Ronnie whines at my feet as I shift on the couch. Agitation rolls off me in waves, making it nearly impossible to sit still, but I have too much work to do to blow it off for a hike. I'm sure she'd rather be at home. I don't blame her. Who wouldn't? But staying there for this quick three-day road series seemed a tad clingy.

Dom didn't seem to think so. In fact, he practically begged me to stay at his place, but I'm going to assume it had more to do with playing voyeur with his dog cam than it did with anything else. Dealing with the constant emptiness that seems to surround me since he left is enough. I don't need the existential crisis over why I miss him so much first thing in the morning when I wake up in his bed alone on top of it.

I mean, I know *why*. I'm just not ready to admit it. Not to him or myself. Admitting it makes this all very real. And the last time I let myself feel that it ended with me broken. This time would be so much worse.

God, I sound like a brat. These are first world problems. Instead of my whiney internal tirade, I should be grateful that the Bandits schedule allowed

Dom to come home for my appointment. Going from a game on the west coast to one on the east means one day in Denver between the series. That little detail kept three days from turning into eight days apart, and I'd have gone through my appointment alone. I'm not sure without him physically there reminding me that it's exactly where he wanted to be that I wouldn't have succeeded at pushing him away.

"Maybe a short walk isn't a terrible idea." Ronnie's ears instantly perk up at her favorite four-letter word. I can't help but laugh as she circles her own body, turning herself into a black and brown donut of excitement. This girl never fails to make me smile, even with the inner turmoil over missing Dom and waiting for the dreaded phone call from Dr. Smith. It seems that she's a perfect match for her owner, and in turn, me.

INDIE:

Your dog is ridiculous. [Photo Attached]

YOURS:

Nah, she's perfect, just like her momma.

INDIE:

I did not birth this furry thing.

YOURS:

Biology isn't important. She loves you. You love her.
We're a family. My mom is thrilled.

INDIE:

What in the purple dinosaur are you smoking?
You know they drug test baseball players, right?

YOURS:

Just high on life, Baby. Enjoy your walk.

INDIE:

How'd you know?

YOURS:

I'm her dad. I know her walk face. Suck it biology.

INDIE:

You're a weirdo is what you are.

YOURS:

Your weirdo.

INDIE:

"Weirdo," I tell Ronnie with a laugh, clipping her leash on and letting her pull me through the door. Even from across the country, he managed to make me smile and lift the grumpy hazy I was stuck in, just like he always does.

"Wait, he did that in the garage?" Delilah whispers between a fit of giggles, her cheeks pink as we huddle around a table at Buns & Roses a few days later.

I nod my head, heat crawling up my cheeks at the fact that I actually just shared that, but I got caught up in the moment. They were goading me about how mind-blowing the sex must be if I've gone from being annoyed by his every move to anxiously awaiting his return. Only they don't know it's so much more than that. My heart must have doubled in size since I moved here because right next to Poppy and the girls, Dom has carved out his own spot. One he earned each day by making me smile when it felt nearly impossible.

"Maybe don't throw stones in glass libraries, Lilah," Mia says, lifting a dark brow at the blonde who's now hiding her face behind her hands.

"I admit nothing." The words are muffled as she avoids all the watchful eyes.

"Why doesn't anyone ever rail me into next week in interesting places?" Willa asks, sounding dejected beside me.

"I can't be sure, but maybe it's because you're either home, studying, or here," I guess. The girl is dedicated, that's for sure, and hot enough to have people banging down her door, but she's not giving out her address.

"Have you considered studying in the school library?" Poppy chimes in. "The book I'm narrating has a scene where the hockey player goes down on his study table partner in the stacks. When his teammate catches them, he stays to watch."

I almost choke on my coffee, and Mia pats my back knowingly.

"Just a few more months until graduation and then maybe I'll have time for sex. In the meantime, send me all your best toy recommendations."

"You came to the right place," Poppy says, rubbing her hands together, looking positively giddy.

The bell above the door chimes, drawing Lilah's eyes there. There's a squeal, and then she blows past me with a gust of air. I pivot in my seat. The sight of Dom standing in the doorway steals my breath. His still-too-long hair is framing glowing amber eyes which are zeroed in on me. My knuckles turn white as I grip the table. It's the only thing keeping me from sprinting across the lobby and making a scene like my friends are right now.

None of the other couples seem to notice the standoff we're locked into. They're all too busy with each other to see that neither one of us has moved.

All it takes is a smirk and a crook of his finger for my resolve to turn into a pile of rubble at my feet. Pushing away from the table, I'm halfway across the lobby and in his arms before I have time to second guess the decision.

"That's better." His deep voice shoots straight to my soul, soothing all the unsettled parts. He lifts me by the backs of my legs and turns, walking us out of the coffee shop without stopping to say goodbye.

"My phone and keys," I manage to say between kisses.

"How bad do you really need them?" His steps slow, but he never stops.

I pause, seriously considering leaving them behind, and then I remember the call I'm waiting for.

"I got it," he says, bringing me along for the ride and pocketing both before returning to his mission to get me out of here.

"Leaving so soon?" Poppy asks, from where she's tucked into Hendrix's side.

The two-finger salute I give her behind Dom's back only makes her burst out in laughter.

"Just try to make it inside the house this time," Willa calls as we push through the door.

"Were you bonding over how well I dicked you down the other day?" he asks, the shock and amusement mixing as he sets me down in front of his car. Only instead of opening the door, he pins me there with his hips, waiting for me to respond. With his mouth hovering just above my lips, he surrounds me. The spicy scent that always clings to him wrapping around me and his hair falling in manly curtains around my face, making it feel like we are in our own bubble, not a busy downtown street.

"Maybe." I nibble on my lip. "Is that a problem?"

"Shout it from the mountain tops, Baby. You can brag about how well, and often I eat that sweet pussy anytime you want. Loudly too."

"And to think I missed you."

"Fuck yes. Mark it down in the history books."

"Or how about you kiss me and then take me home?" I say, no longer interested in the coffee I abandoned at the table.

The only thing I want now is to soak up his easygoing nature. Just being around him is a sedative to calm my anxious mind and body. Especially with the phone call from the clinic shadowing my every move. Our coffee date this morning was a temporary distraction, but they don't know what I'm facing, and I want to keep it that way. I don't think I could stand it if they started looking at me with pity and fawning over me like I was already sick.

"Under one condition." His voice is deep and velvety, infused with a sultry amusement. To think this time last year, I would have pretended it was one of his annoying qualities instead of turning to putty in his hands.

"What's that?" I ask, fully expecting something filthy. The door to Buns & Roses shuts behind Dom but I don't bother looking up to see who it is.

"We go to your place so that I can see Ronnie."

"That dog has got you wrapped around her finger."

"Just. Like. You." He punctuates each word with a kiss peppered to my nose.

"He looks good on you," Poppy hums as she walks past, tucked under Hendrix's arm. It seems like they have the same idea, not stopping on the way to his car.

"Damn right I do," Dom fires back, opening my door and helping me into the car.

Dom drops into the driver's seat a moment later and checks traffic before pulling out. "Did you and the girls get to enjoy your coffee before we barged in?"

"We were just getting into some quality girl talk before you showed up."

"Oh shit, do I need to take you back?"

"No. Don't," I say, a little too quickly. Making his cocky smile light up the whole damn car. "It's alarming how quickly you go from charming to annoying."

"Don't get mad, Baby. It's cute that you missed me. I missed the fuck out of you too." His calloused palm fits itself with mine and we stay like that, our linked hands resting over his knee, as he pulls away.

It's the little things with Dom, the ones I never expected, that make me turn into a puddle for him. Like the way he holds my hand as he drives us to my place, as if it's not a big deal. Jensen always hated holding my hand—he said it was childish. I linked Dom and my ex together in my mind early on and spent so much energy making Dom out to be something he never was. Sometimes I still have to remind myself that they are nothing I like.

"How are you feeling?"

It's the same ambiguous question he's asked me every day since the blood draw at the beginning of this week. Mostly I've pushed him off, insisting I'm fine, but today I'm tired of pretending. Maybe it's the warmth of his hand on mine that makes me feel safe enough to admit my fears, but I can't hold it back any more.

"I'm scared, Dom. Every day that I don't hear from Maryann, it gets a little harder to keep the anxiety from taking over. I'm working as much as I can to try to distract myself, but it's still there, in the back of my mind, all the time."

"I hate that I wasn't here for you." He squeezes my hand, his jaw hard and his knuckles turning white on the steering wheel.

"You were, more than I've ever let anyone else be. And it's not your job to face this for me. Only I can do that." It's not even a lie to ease the obvious guilt he's feeling, it's one hundred percent the truth. Other than my dad and Poppy, when my mom passed, I've never given someone else this much access to the real me; to my fears and worries. But I can see how it's affecting him even if he won't admit it. He hides it behind jokes and lavishing me with affection, but I've noticed the lines at the corners of his eyes from not sleeping and the early morning batting practice or extra runs.

The rest of the drive is mostly quiet. Every time I glance over at Dom, I can see his wheels turning. When he feels my eyes on him, he gives me a tight-lipped smile. It's nothing like the easygoing, panty-melting smile he usually tosses around.

There's barely enough room for me to turn the key in the lock with Dom hot against my back. Fumbling with the lock, I finally get it open and he's guiding me through the door so fast that my head spins trying to track our movement. Lowering to one knee, he pulls me down to sit on his thigh and keeps one arm firmly around my waist. Like he's afraid to let me go out of fear that I'll slip away from him. Ronnie skids across the floor, crashing into him.

My stomach flips at how she burrows her wet nose into his neck like she can't get close enough. *Me either, girl.* This feels right. *We* feel right; the two of us laughing in the middle of my kitchen as Ronnie's tail thumps against the linoleum. This girl was meant for us, and right now, she eases the pain in the way only she can with sloppy kisses and her happy wagging tail.

"My two favorite girls. Life doesn't get any better than this. I think the three of us could use a nice long hike and maybe a picnic. What does my goodest girl think?"

I will not get jealous of a dog. I will not get jealous of a dog. I will not get jealous of a dog.

Repetition makes the mantra finally sink in and I notice Dom watching me. He's carefully waiting for my reaction more than Ronnie's. The polar opposite of me, she's clearly hyped based on the puppy sprints she's doing between us and the door on a loop. I'm less excited. It's not that I don't want to hike, it's exactly what I need, but I'm worried that it's not what he needs.

"What do you say, Firecracker? Want to spend the day exploring with me?"

"You must be exhausted. We don't have to do that." I shouldn't still be shocked that he's putting my needs first. It's been a constant since I moved. It's just one reason why I fall a little deeper each day. Someone else is finally taking care of me. I've been the lone soldier in this battle for too long, and with Dom by my side, I feel like I have a whole army at my back.

"Never too tired to spend time with you."

"But we could do that here." The lump in my throat tightens at the words, fighting my attempts to talk him out of this.

"Something tells me you need to get out of this apartment more than I need to sleep. Besides, I took a nap on the plane. Dean even sang me a lullaby." Seeing the easy smile I'm so used to back on his face has my shoulders dropping away from my ears.

"He did not."

"You're right, it was Cruz."

That I find a little more believable. "Fine, take your girls on a walk, you crazy man."

He stands us up, his lips finding my neck before he goes to my fridge. "I'll make some sandwiches. You go get ready."

I glance at the jean shorts and t-shirt I'm wearing. Perfect for coffee, but not so practical for hiking. "Did you have a trail in mind?"

"There's a state park about thirty minutes from here that has a nice loop that's hard enough to take your mind off things, but still gets cell reception—just in case—and no scrambles that might re-injure that ankle."

It's exactly what I need. My ankle is healed, but it's not quite ready for the strenuous mountain biking or trail running I'm used to. Swimming and sex with Dom have been good alternatives to take my mind off things when my wheels just won't stop spinning, but I can't deny I'm on edge. "Get out of my head," I tease, rounding the doorframe to get changed.

"Nah, I think I like it here." A smirk pulls up his lip as he works in the kitchen, pulling lunch meat and cheese out of the fridge to add to the selection of fruit and vegetables he already grabbed.

Dressed in a pair of spandex shorts and a sports bra, I rejoin him in the kitchen to find him packing the sandwiches and snacks into a small insulated bag.

"I thought we could use this for water and lunch," I say, laying down the daypack that I use when I hike. "And don't forget a bowl for Ronnie," I add when I take a seat at the kitchen table to put on my trail runners.

He holds up one finger before producing a small bowl from the pile of stuff. "I grabbed her some treats for lunch too."

"Seems like you thought of everything."

"I'm more than just a good time." He's teasing, yet guilt sits heavy on my chest for how harshly I judged him when we first met.

Pushing up from my chair I cross the kitchen and wrap my hand around him from behind, kissing his back. "You're so much more than that. Thank you for not giving up on us. For not being the self-centered, playboy I wanted you to be when we first met. For being my lifeline, my friend, *mine*."

Pulling the cord to cinch the backpack closed, he turns in my arms. "I'm glad you made me earn it because you're worth the fight."

"I don't know about that." All my doubts about how my test results affect this future he sees between us tunnel in on me. My brows pull together and I open my mouth to tell him, but he's already there, forcing my eyes to his and making me think twice about what I was about to say.

"It's my job to remind you every damn day that you're worthy of a partner who puts in the work." Those dark eyes flick back and forth between mine until I finally nod, letting go of those destructive thoughts. "Let's get out of here."

Dom fills the ride with stories about the road trip and the games they played. When the sign for the park turn off comes into view, my cheeks ache and it's hard to believe it's been almost forty minutes already. But that's how it is with him. His charismatic personality sucks you in. You can't help but be happy when he's around. Resisting is pointless. Trust me, I tried so damn hard.

He parks in a shady spot near the trailhead saying, "This trail has a really gorgeous overlook that we can have our lunch at before heading back." Then he jumps out, opening the back door to let Ronnie out and coming around to do the same for me.

"How are you feeling about your chances at a wild card spot?" I ask when he leads us out onto the trail, Ronnie leading the way, nose in the dirt.

"With the schedule we have, and the way everyone is playing, I think we have a serious shot. We just need to stay healthy and focused." His voice is steady and rich, filled with confidence, but when he glances to the side and scraps his teeth over his lower lip, I can tell there's more.

"That's amazing. What's the 'but'?"

"There's no 'but.'"

"Don't get shy on me now. There's something."

"My parents are coming into town to watch the last series of the regular season."

"That's nice for them to be able to do that. Will your sisters be with them?"

"They will." He huffs out a breath. "And I'd like you to meet them."

My feet stop moving, rooting themselves to the ground like the wildflowers around us. Next to me Dom's arm is yanked forward as Ronnie keeps moving, completely unaware of the significance of the moment or that her owner is no longer moving.

"But what if—"

"No what ifs. They are dying to meet you. In fact, they've asked every time we've talked in the last few weeks."

Nervous laughter bubbles out of me. Given the events that transpired that night in the car, I have to ask, "Details?"

"Just that I want my own version of what he has with my mom and that I was still very hung up on the one that got away. He reminded me that the best things are the ones you have to work for and he was right."

"So sweet details?"

"Did you really think I would tell him anything else?"

"Just checking."

"If it makes you feel better, my parents don't know anything about what happened that first night. Not the picture in the club, or that Dean had it buried."

I swallow roughly, letting my eyes flutter shut and soaking up the memories that flash through my mind of that night. Me in his lap, my skirt bunched up around my hips, soft sensual music pumping through the interior of the car, his hand gripping my hip as he helped guide me over him.

When my eyes open, Dom is right there, staring down at me with a wicked glint in his eyes that tells me it's not the mountain lions I should be afraid of. If anything is going to eat me alive, it'll be him. Not surprising, the man lives to eat and I'm his favorite meal.

Slowly, he steps us backward off the trail until my back is pressed against the rough bark of a tree trunk. "You can't bite your lip like that out here."

"My lip?" Old me would be embarrassed by how breathy and desperate I sound for him. New me is just accepting that this is who I am now.

"Yeah, Baby. You were biting your lip."

"I hadn't noticed," I comment, struggling to focus with his hard muscles under my fingers and his thigh pressed between my legs.

"Were you thinking about how good it felt when I made you come after you played cat and mouse with me all night, pretending that I wasn't exactly what you wanted? What you needed."

"Yes." No point in lying. It's exactly what I was thinking of.

"That night is etched in my memory. Everything before then is hazy and everything after—technicolor. Even the time apart because I knew I was coming for you. You gave me a glimpse of something I've always craved and it was no longer just a fleeting feeling but a tangible, real thing. A person—my person. My future."

The night was magic, and I'm not talking about the stars he made me see on the ride home—or several times after—but the in-between. Being up all night, fighting sleep, because you want to soak up every second of time you have with that person. The flowing conversation, the seamless way we just fell into each other. You hear about it all the time in movies or books, but I've never found that with anyone else and doubt I ever will.

"You're sure it's not just because you were feeling cocky about showing Dean everything he was missing?" I tease, my hands smoothing up the hard planes of his chest.

"Definitely a highlight, but no." Heat and admiration swirl together in his eyes.

"And it wasn't how you settled me over your lap once the driver pulled out of the club parking lot and whispered in my ear, 'You wanted to play games, give him a show he'll never forget.'"

His throat bobs as he swallows when my lips graze the side of his neck. "It wasn't that, or the way you pinned your knees on either side of my thighs and looked over your shoulder at him as you started rocking your hips."

"You did not like that," I comment, and his chest vibrates against me. The roughness of the tree bites into my skin as he crushes his body to mine.

"And I still don't like it," he practically growls at me, his hand finding the side of my neck and tilting my head back. "You've got a thing for being watched? Is that why you're baiting me out here where anyone could find us?"

"Not for being watched, but for driving you crazy."

"That you do. Are you going to call out my name when I roll my hard cock over your clit until you're panting in my ear, telling me you're mine, just like you did then?"

A branch cracks somewhere nearby, causing Ronnie to shoot up from where she's sitting at Dom's feet and ending our charged stroll down memory lane. It's probably a good thing considering it felt like we were dangerously close to saying things that I'm not certain either of us are ready for.

"Come on, Firecracker, you're not getting it on the trail where anyone could see what's mine."

He steps back and I follow, not wanting to lose the weight of him, but in the light of day, right on the trail where anyone, park ranger included, could find us, is more of a risk than even I'm willing to take. "Fine," I grumble, picking up the pace, hoping to redirect the blood back to my heart and dull the heavy ache between my legs.

For the first time since I fell off my bike, I'm able to really push myself outside the pool and I chase that feeling for the rest of the climb to the overlook. Letting it wash away the anxiety and the lingering horniness from earlier. When we stop at the clearing, Dom wraps his arms around me from behind. His lips brush my temple, and his heart beats almost as fast as mine against my back.

"It's stunning."

"Sure is," he replies quietly.

Glancing over my shoulder, I find his eyes on me. "I meant the view."

"Me too. What else would I be talking about?"

"Ass," I tease, trying to wriggle out of his hold.

"Now that you mention it . . ." He steps just enough to glance down between us. "Yeah, that ass is stunning too. Although you have some sap stuck to it."

"And whose fault is that?"

"Yours. I can't be held responsible for what happens when you look at me like you might climb me like a tree."

I roll my eyes and relax back into his hold.

"Feel any better?" The tone he uses is soothing and calm, but there's a hint of urgency that underscores how deep his concern runs.

It's confusing as fuck to love being taken care of this way and simultaneously hate it. I want it for me, that presence I've missed in my life since my mom passed, but I hate it for him because I remember what it's like to be on the other side. The never-ending worry that comes along with caring for someone like my mom . . . like me.

"This helped. Thank you for thinking of it," I tell him, choosing not to get sucked into the worry and just be.

His chest caves underneath me with the deep sigh that rushes out of him. "I hope you worked up an appetite, because I made us a feast."

"I've seen what was in my fridge. A feast feels like a stretch."

"Prepare to be amazed," he says, shaking out a blanket we grabbed from his car and spreading it out for us.

We sit down, side by side and he starts unpacking the bag, setting everything between us on the blanket. When I think it's all there, he reaches in one last time and pulls out a small box.

"Is there a rabbit in there too? That didn't come from my apartment."

"Nope. I grabbed it yesterday from the bakery by our hotel and snuck it in when you were changing."

"What is it?"

"Open it and see."

I slide my finger on the tape that seals the box shut and open the top. When I see the chocolate and caramel, layered over the shortbread crust, I smile because it's straight out of my childhood. I've never been a fan of cake and my mom used to make these for me anytime there was something to celebrate. I have to roll my lips together to keep the emotions from pouring out of me. "Twix Cookie Bars?"

"I'm not sure if they are the same as what your mom used to make, but I tried one the other day and they taste just like you described, sweet and salty—just like you. So I figured it was worth a shot. And we have so much to celebrate.

"We do?"

"You got rid of the boot and you're finally giving me a chance to make you the happiest woman on the planet."

That makes me snort—loudly. Bittersweet laughter takes over and I crawl into his lap, careful to set the box out of harm's way.

"I've tried so many times to recreate these and every time I end up crying over the mixing bowl. These look just like hers. Thank you." I crush my lips to his, kissing him with every ounce of admiration that's pumping through my body for this man. And for the first time, I voice the words I should have said weeks ago. "I'm sorry that I ever made you feel like less than the man you are. It was never about you. You're nothing like I thought you would be."

"Putting in the work was never a hardship. Being yours is a privilege, one I was happy to earn and I'll keep earning."

"My only experience being in a relationship with a man was nothing like this. It was my only serious relationship, and because it was such a disaster I never gave anyone else a chance. My ex was actually the worst, and for a long time I didn't date men. I'd hook-up now and then . . ." The hold he has on me tightens. "Calm down. We both know you're not a saint."

"It doesn't mean I want to hear about your past partners."

"Yeah, well, ditto. But I think you need to know this. Or maybe I just need to say it to move on. You know, stop letting it hold me back. For us."

"Proceed," he says through gritted teeth, only loosening his hold a fraction.

"Other than Bri, I've kept things casual. Our relationship was too new to be serious when I moved. The guy I dated in college was an athlete. Everyone knew him and he *loved* being revered. He was always throwing up high fives when he walked around campus. It was hard not to get sucked into his charismatic personality when he set his sights on me. Eventually, I stopped fighting it and for a while, things were good. Then my mom's cancer came back. I needed him, or I thought I did. But he didn't want to stop having a good time to console his girlfriend—didn't understand why I wasn't in the mood to go out. I brushed it off. Told myself he worked hard and deserved a chance to blow off some steam without having to deal with my trauma."

"Fucking asshole. You were devastated, and rightfully so. "

"Oh, it gets worse. I'd just come out to my friends on campus before we started dating and was upfront with him about my sexuality."

Dom's jaw is clenched so tight I swear I hear his teeth crack. I bring my hand to his face and stroke along it, weaving my fingers into his hair.

"He didn't seem to care at all, just kind of shrugged it off. It was too easy and I should have known better. I was stupid."

"Uh uh," Dom chides.

"You don't even know what happened."

"I know you, and you are not dumb. You trusted the wrong person because you're a good person." His lips brush the inside of my wrist.

"I gave him years of my life. I thought he was the one, but he waited until my mom was in hospice to tell me I wasn't the kind of girl he saw himself marrying. Dating the bisexual girl was a fun experiment for him—I was a notch on his bedpost, a game. See if you can get the queer girl to date you, maybe she'll let you have threesomes. A fucking joke for him and his buddies."

"What the hell." The vein on the side of his neck pulses angrily, but I have no anger left to give Jensen. The piece of me he's held onto for so long is mine again, and it's so damn freeing. Dom erased so many of my scars without even realizing it. Pressing my lips to his, I kiss him softly until the tension eases from his body.

"It's fine—I mean it's not, not even a little, but he doesn't hold any power over me anymore. That's what I'm trying to tell you. He was a selfish prick. From how he broke my heart when I needed someone the most, to how he treated my sexuality as a game. But he doesn't get to cloud my judgment where you are concerned. Not anymore, because you've shown me you're nothing like him."

"Give me five minutes alone with him," he grits out.

"Someone needs another kiss." Dom doesn't even crack a smile at my attempt to ease the tension radiating off of him. "I can't help you with that. I have no clue where he is or what he's doing. He transferred schools the next year. Poppy cleansed him from my phone and socials. Not that I wanted to check up on him after what he did, more to protect me from an ambush when I opened my apps."

"You said he was an athlete at Lakeside?" I can see him mentally cataloging the players he knows trying to put the pieces together.

"Mhmm, but I don't want to talk about him anymore." Reaching over I grab the dessert box, Ronnie watching my every move. Taking a bar, I bring it to my lip and bite off the corner, chewing it slowly. The groan doesn't so much slip out, as I let it fly free, distracting Dom from his worries the same way he's done for me. Out of the corner of my eye I see the brown and white paws scooting closer. "You should try this." I hold it in front of him to take a bite. The set of his jaw eases as I bring the bar to his lips.

Hit bites the corner, his eye never leaving mine. "Already tried it." He drags his gaze down my body, setting me ablaze little by little. "But you know what I'm dying for a taste of?" His cock swells between us, and I don't have to use my imagination to figure it out. This man would live between my legs, never coming up for air if he didn't have to play baseball.

"Are you getting hard watching me eat dessert?" I try to keep my tone light, but the effect he has on me with just a glance is devastating. And the smile that tilts up the corner of his lips when I stumble over my words just makes it worse.

"My favorite treat is sitting in my lap, moaning obscenely. What do you think?" His hands smooth up my thighs, thumbs hooking in and tracing the juncture where my thighs and hips meet. Next to us, Ronnie groans and buries her face under her paws.

I swallow, my throat suddenly dry. "That we should finish lunch and break land speed records to get home."

CHAPTER 35

DOM

Fucking perfect, that's what Indie is and I'm livid that someone treated her the way her ex did. He's a prick, and I'd like nothing more than to be the one to put his head through the outfield wall. Indie might have succeeded in temporarily distracting me, but it doesn't negate how angry I am on her behalf.

At least the view is phenomenal while I stew. Each step Indie takes in front of me makes her ass bounce. She hops over rocks and roots, picking her way down the narrow trail back to the car. Honestly, the rhythmic bouncing is the only thing keeping me from losing my shit. I'm not a fighter, but fuck, if I thought she'd tell me who hurt her, I'd be ringing his bell as quick as I could charter a flight to find him.

Indie seems completely unbothered. Like getting it out was enough to heal the damage he did. I'm pretty sure she would have sprinted back if it hadn't been for her recently healed ankle. This gorgeous girl could have anyone she wants, and she's picking me . . . and my tongue. But after that rare heart to heart, it feels like we are both finally on the same page. Her page is much more relaxed than mine after our conversation, but I'm glad to bear the burden. She deserves the break.

"Careful," I warn when she skids around a corner. I lunge forward, my hands landing on her hips and tugging her back into me to steady her before she can lose her footing. Her contagious laughter echoes through the trees, and she gives me a look over her shoulder that's so happy it makes my chest squeeze. "You're fucking stunning."

Only two things are stopping me from tossing her in the backseat and burying myself inside her. The dog watching us creeps me the fuck out, and a rushed car quickie isn't what I'm after, not when it feels like her walls are finally down.

"Is it just me or was that drive back lo-longer?" Indie sputters when my lips find the spot on her neck that makes her eyes roll back in her head. She's pressed up against the wall in the entryway to my house as I let my hands roam over her, mapping out the way she feels in my arms.

"Should have just made the dog close her eyes and had you ride me in the car the way I wanted you to," I tell her, finding my way under her tank top and up the side of her rib cage.

"Weird. I swear you said you were hungry."

"Famished." Lowering her feet to the ground, I follow the same path, my knees landing on the ground in front of her.

"I like the way you look down there, kneeling at my feet." Nails scrape across my head as she pushes my hair back off my forehead, tilting my head back. "This was my favorite way to imagine you when I couldn't get you out of my head for the last year. On your knees, begging for just one more taste. I never dared to admit, even just to myself, that I wanted more too."

"That fantasy of yours got one thing wrong," I tell her, my palms covering the miles of silky skin she has on display, not stopping until they are cupping her cheeks under her shorts.

"Which part is that?"

"One more time was never going to be enough. I would've been begging for a lifetime with you."

Her eyes widen and her hand wraps around the base of her neck. She looks like she's at the top of a rollercoaster. There's the awe of being so high, along with the fear of the fall. "I'm not sure I'm ready for that."

"I'm a patient man, and being on my knees for you is one hell of a way to wait." After a temporary detour to grab her ass, my hands reach the waistband of her shorts, pulling them down her legs, only to find her bare underneath.

"They have a liner." She shrugs in explanation.

"Is this like that thing girls do with pockets?"

Breathy laughter bubbles out of her. "What?"

"When girls wear a dress with pockets and they need everyone in a fifty-mile radius to know."

"I'm familiar with the phenomenon, but why are you?"

"Two sisters."

"Right. They're going to like me, aren't they?" No one would ever describe this woman as vulnerable, but in this moment, her raw unguarded insecurity has me desperate to put her mind at ease.

Leaning forward I kiss her stomach. "They're going to want to keep you as much as I do. But do you really want to talk about them right now?"

Her dark eyes flare. "No. I want you to show me what it feels like if I let you keep me forever."

"Fuck, yes." I hook her leg over my shoulder and run my tongue along her slit. There's a thump above me that sounds like her head falling back against the wall, but I don't stop to check. "You okay, Baby?" I mumble against her sex.

"Never better."

"You say that now, but I'm just getting started." Proving my point I tease her clit with my tongue.

"More please," she gasps, pulling me to her.

Giving her more has never been the problem; it's whether or not she would accept it. But something is different tonight. "Is this what you want?" Walking my fingers up her inner thigh, I run my fingers along her seam.

"I want you inside me," she purrs, her heel digging into my back.

"Like this?" I ask, pressing two fingers into her heat.

"It's not enough. I need your cock."

"Not until you come for me."

Pain zings through my scalp when she pulls my head back. She shakes her head, swallowing almost fearfully.

"Tell me, Indie. I'll give you anything you need."

"Just you, Dom. All of you," she begs, her words splintering when I curl my fingers.

My heart stutters in my chest, and for a second I think it might give out on me. Still at her feet, the lines of her face are soft, the fear gone. This isn't a game, it's not something she's trying on for size. She's right here on the precipice with me, ready to fall. Vulnerable, open and so fucking stunning. I thought it was there earlier when she opened up about her ex, but I see it now clear as day. She's all in. "I need your words."

"I want you bare. Nothing between us."

I'm on my feet, bringing her with me in an instant. There's no way in hell I'm doing this with her pressed up against a wall like some desperate quickie.

As I walk us past Ronnie's bed, she doesn't even lift her head, exhausted from the hike. Thank fuck for that.

With Indie still clinging to me, I lower her to the end of the bed and she goes up onto her knees, kissing me deeply, taking control as she tugs my shirt up, breaking away just long enough to get it over my head.

"Indie, slow down."

"Can't. I need this." Her lips are already brushing against mine again as she pushes at the waistband of my shorts. "Need you."

"Fuck, don't I know it, but we've got time," I say, my hands coming to the side of her face, stopping her, surveying if it's fear or something else driving her.

She nods, slowing her pace. "It's just . . . No one's ever made me feel the things you do. Sometimes it feels like it could all slip through my fingers."

"I won't let that happen." I push her back on the bed and stretch out over the top of her.

"These still need to go," she says, slipping her hand into the back of my shorts, but she lacks the panic-laced urgency from a moment ago.

"And they will, but first, I need to finish my meal."

She hisses when my teeth graze her nipple on my path down to her pelvis. "You don't have to—"

I silence her with a raised eyebrow. "You wouldn't take my life's greatest pleasure from me, would you?"

"Ridiculous," she huffs before she turns to putty under me with one swipe of my tongue.

"Judging by how soaked you are, I think you like it, too."

"So damn much."

My fingers slide in easily, curling and pulsing; working her back up to the panting mess she was in the hallway before she asked me to fuck her with nothing between us. My cock throbs at the reminder and I press my hips into the bed, seeking out relief. "I'm going to need you to come for me now, because I'm not too proud to admit that I'm not sure how long I'll be able to hold out with this perfect pussy wrapped around me and nothing between us."

"Dom." Her cries are borderline feral as she grips the sheets, her hips lifting. Pushing her back down, I keep my palm pressed to her pelvis and work her clit with my tongue. She comes apart with a curse as her thighs close around my head.

Crawling up the bed I lower myself so my lips brush against her when I say, "Taste yourself and tell me if you'd get sick of this. I'd give up baseball if it meant I could start and end everyday like this for the rest of my life."

She lifts, sealing her lips over mine. While we work each other into a frenzy with our mouths, she wraps a leg around my waist, pulling me in and scooting her hips until I'm lined up right where she wants me. "Fuck me, Dom."

"Say no more," I tell her, thrusting into the most perfect pussy. She stretches around me, her tight heat almost more than I can handle. "This is where I was meant to be. This pussy was always mine. You were always meant to be mine." I ignore the primal need to pull out and drive myself back inside her, claiming her until she's screaming my name. This moment is one I want to imprint on my very soul, never forgetting a single detail.

"I'm yours," she repeats, pulling me forward with her heel, burying me as deep as she can. And when I give my hips a shallow thrust, her mouth falls open and her eyes roll back. "I can feel you everywhere like this. Oh god. It's so good."

And it is. I've never felt anything like it. Gritting my teeth I battle the tension already crawling down my spine, threatening to end this far sooner than I would like. The she-devil underneath me notices and her lips tip up in a devious smile before she tightens around me. "You're playing a dangerous game, Firecracker."

"What's wrong?" Her voice drips with a sweetness that we both know she would never use outside of mocking me.

"If you're enjoying this half as much as I am, I'd think twice before doing that again." Snaking my hand between us, I press my thumb to her clit, pulling a shaky exhale from her.

"This?" she asks, clamping down so her muscles squeeze me again. It's enough that I have to slow my movements.

"Fuck, Indie," I growl, circling her swollen clit, hoping she's close because I'm hanging on by a thread, as sweat beads along my brow.

"Shit," she groans, her facade cracking and the cocky smile slipping as she digs her nails into my shoulder.

"That's better. Two can play this game, Baby." I lower my head, sucking her nipple into my mouth. "Tell me you're close."

"Fill me, let me feel you inside me," she says panting through each word and my restraint snaps as my body coils tight. "That's it. Take me with you when you go." Stars burst in my peripheral as I reach the point of no return.

She tilts her hips up adjusting the angle to get what she needs as I pound into her, my mouth and fingers working in tandem to get her there with me. When her eyes flutter closed and her back bows, I take her mouth, kissing her as my dick pulses inside of her—filling her just like she asked.

Fuck, I want to do it again.

CHAPTER 36

INDIE

Rolling to my side, I turn into the warm body beside me, the delicious ache that blooms between my thighs a memento from last night. Thankfully, the back-to-back road trips and the late game today allow us to wake up together, instead of him rushing off to the stadium for meetings or practice.

It's the last morning we will get like this with the end of the season and a playoff berth in reach for the Bandits.

The stiffness settling in my bones tells me it's late, but my phone is still in the entryway from last night, and it's worth the pain to soak this up for a few more minutes before I track it down.

Brushing the hair off of Dom's face I study him. The first time we woke up like this after that infamous car ride home, I did something very similar, but the ending was not nearly as sweet.

There's a delicious heaviness that's settled over my limbs that can only come from many orgasms. Rolling slowly to my side, I'm met with warmth in the form of a hard body and that languid feeling turns to a satisfying ache that makes the last twelve hours rush back to me.

I don't need to open my eyes to know the hot, hard body I'm currently nestled against is Dom Duran. Trouble. Fun trouble, but the kind of trouble I vowed never to allow into my life again.

Yet, from the moment his lips touched mine, being near him felt like coming home. No one has ever pursued me with the dedication that this man has. Not only that, but he spent more time getting to know me physically and emotionally than anyone ever has. There's something about his personality that puts me at ease and had me spilling all my secrets between mind-numbing orgasms. So many orgasms.

His arms tighten around me and he hums contentedly, his breathing steady as he sleeps soundly behind me. My hand covers his and I sink into the embrace, imagining what it would feel like to wake up feeling this safe, this secure, this cherished everyday. When his hips shift and his impressive erection pokes me from behind, my eyes fly open, landing on the one thing that could pull me out of my idyllic daydream faster than anything else.

His jersey.

Seeing it here, now, after everything we shared last night sends me crashing down to earth, all the pieces of my soul shattering on the ground as the cruel reminder taunts me.

My failure at staying away from him is almost laughable. Or maybe it would be if the truth of being wrapped in his arms in the morning wasn't twisting itself around my spine, coiling tighter until nothing is left but fear.

I can't do this.

Panic takes over, each shallow inhale coming too quickly after the last. My stomach flips dangerously in my stomach. I need to move. I need to get away.

Like a coward, I slip out of bed, making a beeline for the fancy coffee machine in his kitchen, already knowing my plan—coffee and flee.

This was a mistake. One that becomes more obvious as I make my way through his magazine-ready house. Everything here is too perfect. It's all a facade to trick you into thinking you can have it all. Just like with my ex, Jensen.

He was the same. Picture perfect on the outside. I fell for this once before— the boy-next-door with the picturesque life. He made me feel wanted and then he destroyed me when I needed him the most. After one night, I already feel too much for this man. The power he has over me could crush me, and I'm not so sure I would recover from it, because even with everything I've been through, part of me still wants this. But the part where the fear lives is louder.

I steady my hand to start the coffee. Each drip from the machine makes me jump as I wait for the Uber I order to arrive. I'm an asshole, sneaking out without saying goodbye, without an explanation.

With my coffee in hand, I watch the time on my screen tick painfully slow. Four more minutes. My head whips to the stairs, where Dom stands stock still on the bottom step, looking rumpled and confused in nothing but a pair of low hanging shorts.

He pushes a hand through his messy hair, his exhale audible. "You're leaving." It's not a question.

"Did you expect me to stay and play house with you?" I cringe internally at the sharpness in my tone. It was my default setting with him before last night, and now it just feels cruel. "This was fun, but I've gotta get out of here before Poppy realizes I'm missing." Not any better idiot.

He crosses the kitchen stopping right in front of me so I have no choice but to face him. "Can't have that, can we?" His tense words hit the mark. I take one last drink of my coffee, glance at the car arriving on my phone. "Let's talk for a minute before you run out."

"There's nothing to talk about. You knew this was a one night deal." I give into the part of me that wants to stay for just a moment, his chest warm and firm under my palm.

"The fuck it was. I've done one-night, this was more and you know it." His jaw clicks as his teeth move side to side.

"That's all it can be. Please don't make me regret last night. Let me go." My heart cracks open at my plea.

"Is that really what you want?" His fingers cover mine and I pull back, afraid that I won't be strong enough to walk away if I don't.

I hesitate a beat, warring with myself, but when I see hope creeping into his dark eyes, I break us both. "Yes."

"I'll give you space for now, but I'm going to prove you wrong someday. You'll see this isn't over." Resolution is written all over his handsome face.

Last time I panicked, running from him, from what I thought he was. He was never a mistake.

Now there's nothing but easy contentment and so much admiration. And something else too, a feeling deep in my soul that I'm not ready to acknowledge yet. But with every passing day, it makes itself known a little more, building to the point that I know I won't be able to ignore it much longer.

With one last look, I brush my lips against his forehead and ease out from under the weight of his arm. Shuffling my feet over the hardwood floor I stop, resting my head against the door frame and watch the slow rise and fall of his chest for a minute before I pad down the stairs and into the kitchen.

The reflection of the sun on the stainless steel coffee maker catches my eye, and I pause. "Coffee first," I say to Ronnie, who tilts her head at me when she looks up from where she's sleeping on her bed in the living room. "Then I'll let you out and find my phone."

With the coffee going, I open the door to the back porch and let Ronnie out, moving on to finding my phone. My purse is sitting on the table by the door to the garage, where I dropped it last night in the middle of a heated kiss with Dom.

Fishing it out, I open it up and move back to the door to check on Ronnie, who's already waiting to come back inside.

"You can come back in, but don't go waking your dad up. I think I wore him out last night," I say, letting her back in. When two bulky arms wrap around me from behind, I almost jump out of my skin.

"I'm already up, Baby. But don't listen to her, Ronnie. You can wake me up anytime."

"Are you a damn ninja? Make a little noise and stop eavesdropping on our girl talk. That could have been private," I tease leaning back into him, the warmth from his bare chest calming my racing heart.

"What are your plans for today?" he asks.

"My proposal for the new volunteer program at the Pride Foundation is due next week. I'm going to work on that. And I have some more grant research to do. Your girl's gotta start collecting a paycheck soon."

He hums, and it tickles my ear. I think he's got more to say, but he stays silent, enjoying the mountain view with me for a moment before he asks, "Is that coffee I smell?"

"It is. Everything okay?" I turn in his arms. This man doesn't hold back, he says what's on his mind and I can tell that's not what's happening right now.

"Yeah. Fine."

"You're lying."

"I am. And in this case, that's for the best. It might be keeping me alive."

"Talk." I place my hand on his chest. Not pushing away, but just holding them there.

"I really don't think that's in our best interest. You're a lot less stabby with me these days and I like it that way. Me telling you that you make the worst coffee on the planet might end that."

"But you make your coffee the same."

He shakes his head. "I make *your* coffee the same."

"What?" This feels like a deflection from what was really on his mind, but now I'm intrigued.

"I make coffee like that because it's the way you like, although I can't fathom why." He shudders.

"But you drink it too." My brows wrinkle. I've seen him drink it.

"Do I?" He chuckles, making my blood heat the way only he can.

"Wait, you never drink it, do you?"

"Nope. I dump it as soon as you leave," he admits.

"Look at that, boy wonder isn't perfect after all—" My phone rings, cutting me off.

I glance down and see the clinic number flashing on the screen, freezing immediately. All the fun forgotten as terror turns my blood to ice in my veins.

I'm not ready to know. I'm not ready for everything to change.

When I don't move to answer, Dom takes the phone from me and accepts the call, putting it on speaker. "Hello," he says. His voice is fuzzy and distant, but I can still hear the pain in it—see it etched in the lines of his face.

"I think I have the wrong number. I'm looking for Indie Moreno," Dr. Smith says.

"Right number, this is Dom. She's here with me, but she's having a little trouble talking right now." Smoothing his hand over my hair, he squats, so he's eye level. "Indie, Baby, can you talk to Dr. Smith for me?" His voice cracks as he struggles to keep his composure.

"Maryann, I'm here," I croak out, my throat dry.

"Indie. I'd like you to come into the office."

My world collapses in on itself. Dom's arms band around me keeping me upright as my chest constricts, making it impossible to breathe, to see, to do anything other than fall apart. This is it. The reason I always put off testing. Everything is about to come crashing down around me.

"We'll be there soon." His gravelly voice barely registers as he disconnects the phone and takes over.

Somehow he gets me into the car, never leaving my side as he calls Coach Wilson and a few other people. Some of it's about him and some about me. The one thing I pick up from the calls is that he never calls any of the guys. I hear everything but nothing penetrates the haze of despair that I'm drowning in. Everything is distorted, like I'm underwater as I stare out the window, not focusing on anything as the city passes us by.

When he parks the car in the lot, his hand covers my knee. I feel him squeezing and I know he's talking, but I still can't focus. It's not until he comes around to my side of the car, opening the door, unbuckling me, and putting both hands on my face that the world starts to come back into focus.

"You need to go. You can't be here," I say in a blind panic, only now realizing that he needs to get to the stadium.

"I'm not going anywhere, Indie. Coach knows I'm dealing with a personal matter."

"But you have a game. You can't—" Tears stream down my face. This isn't supposed to be his life. I'm messing it all up.

"Listen to me carefully. There is nowhere else I need to be today but here with you. Understood?"

I nod, but I'm not sure I do. Why would he give up everything he's worked for his entire life for this mess?

"I need you to look at me." His thumbs smooth over my cheekbones. "Do you see me?"

"Yeah," I say, sniffling before I find his amber eyes.

"That's it, Baby. You're going to let me be here, right?"

"Please don't leave me," I say, collapsing into his chest.

"Never," he murmurs into my hair.

We stay like that, locked together in the parking lot for a few minutes, until I finally pull back. "I'm ready."

CHAPTER 37

DOM

Sitting in Dr. Smith's tiny office with my trembling girlfriend, I'm only now noticing how sterile and cold it is. Squeezing Indie's hand, I use my other hand to drag her chair closer. If I think this place is scary right now, she must be out of her mind.

There's a knock at the door and I turn my head to see Dr. Smith come in, her lips pressed into a thin line. Instead of taking a seat behind the desk, she pulls her stool around, sitting on the other side of Indie and taking her hand.

"Just tell me," Indie says, her voice heartbreakingly defeated and completely void of any emotion. She's broken, numb, and it's fucking killing me.

"Your test was positive for the BRCA 1 mutation."

All the air is sucked out of the room, leaving me feeling lightheaded, but somehow I keep my voice even as I ask, "What does that mean?"

Indie turns to me, a single tear rolling down her cheek, her dark eyes guarded. "It means an exceedingly high risk of breast, ovarian, fallopian, and a whole host of other terrible cancers. Still sure about staying?" There's a bite in her tone that I try not to take personally.

"If you want me to leave, security will have to drag me out," I tell her, brokering no argument with my equally harsh tone. "I know the statistics. What I want to know is what's next."

"That depends on what Indie wants. There are a lot of big decisions, but none of them need to be made today."

"I already know," Indie says, shocking us both. My mouth opens to argue, but Dr. Smith is right, this is Indie's show now. I just hope she decides to fight like hell because I can't lose her.

"Take some time. Nothing needs to happen today," Dr. Smith tries again.

Next to me, Indie shakes her head, brushing away the tears and sucking in a shaky breath. "I want to schedule surgery." There's resolve in her voice and I'm so fucking proud of her for fighting, but she needs to be sure. These surgeries have life-changing impacts.

"Baby—"

"No, Dom, it's what I want."

Letting go of her hand for the first time since she got out of the car, I turn her chair so she's facing me. "This is your decision, and we'll do whatever you want. I'm not trying to talk you out of anything. Fuck, you're so goddamn strong. I want to fight right alongside you, but I need you to be sure." I pause, making sure she's listening before I emphasize, "I'll be here for all of it. No matter what."

"I'd like to just impress one more time that you don't need—"

Indie turns back towards her friend and colleague. "Maryann, I know. But I'm telling you, I won't change my mind," Indie says, her voice stronger now. "My mom never got this chance. She fought with everything she had, but she didn't have this. And I do. Give me the best chance to have the future I want. Let me fight."

"Okay. Well, what about freezing your eggs? Have you given that any thought?"

I hold my breath waiting on Indie's answer, but it doesn't come. She looks back at me and then back at Dr. Smith. "Can you give us a moment?"

"Yes. Take as long as you need. Text me when you're ready for me to come back." She squeezes Indie's hand before she stands, giving us the room.

When the door shuts, Indie stands from her chair, moving to my lap. "I'm not ready to have babies yet. But that means you'll never be able to have kids with me without help from IVF or a surrogate."

I pull her down so our foreheads are touching. "As long as I get to keep you, the rest is just icing on the cake."

"Are you sure about that?" Her fingers sink into my hair, holding us together.

"Yep, and I've got a plan." Let's just hope she doesn't hate it.

"A plan?"

"Yeah, Baby, a plan. I've been researching for weeks. I meant what I said, all these decisions are yours, but I've got a few thoughts if you're willing to hear them—willing to do this together."

She texts Maryann and we talk through the next steps, get a recommendation for a fertility specialist and a surgeon for when the time comes.

Maryann wraps Indie in a hug, and we walk hand in hand out to the car. The rest of the afternoon is filled with chaos as we check things off our to-do list. Researching insurance options—all of which suck—and looking at calendars to plan out how we can make this work, all of it needs to happen quickly if I'm going to be there to help her through this first obstacle, seeing a fertility specialist with just a week left in the regular season.

It takes me pulling a few strings, and a vague call to Lara who knows just about everyone in the city, but she's able to help get us in to see one of the best fertility specialists in the area.

The next afternoon, after a conversation with Coach and filling him in on the latest developments, I'm able to sneak out between meetings and pregame warmups to meet Indie at the fertility specialist for an ultrasound and more blood work. It's the first step so we can start the process of freezing her eggs.

It doesn't take long for me to realize that this whole process would be nearly impossible on her own. The paperwork alone is enough to leave you seeing double, then there's the information overload and the bills you know are coming. Indie is smart as hell and more driven than most but this all would have been a huge burden to deal with alone.

Our game that night clinches our place in the postseason, something I've chased my entire career. But it's not what's on my mind when I leave the stadium. No, the only thing I want is to get back to Indie and Ronnie, who are watching the game together at her place.

"Are you coming out to celebrate at Draft?" Xavier asks, surrounded by Dean, Mia, Poppy, Cruz, Hendrix, and Delilah.

"Not tonight, I gotta get home." It's not exactly a lie, but none of them know the reason behind why Indie's not feeling well. They all just assumed she's got a bug and since Indie's not ready to tell anyone, I haven't corrected them.

"I hope she's feeling better," Delilah says.

"Are you sure we can't bring her anything?" Poppy asks for the third time, sounding a little hurt.

"I'll ask her again. She'd probably love a text to let her know you're thinking of her," I add.

"Or maybe we'll all just show up at the door, soup in hand," Mia threatens.

"Have you met Indie?" Poppy jokes.

"Yeah, maybe not the best idea," I agree half-heartedly.

When I walk through the door to her apartment thirty minutes later, I find her curled up in a ball on the couch. Her eyes are red and unfocused as ESPN highlights play in the background. I drop to my knees, pushing the hair out of her face.

"What's going on?" I softly stroke my hand over her head.

She shifts under the thin blanket that's draped over her, sitting up and making the material slip off down her body, exposing an ivory corset with a sheer panel down the front. "I wanted to surprise you when you got home, but even with this on I don't feel sexy, just bloated and gross from the injections."

"May I?" She shivers when my fingers graze her thighs, freeing the blanket from where it's pooled around her waist, revealing a matching pair of strappy panties. "Fucking stunning. No one else does what you do to me. Don't doubt that for even a second, but if you're not feeling it, I'll run you a bath and thaw out some cookie dough. This outfit…" I bite my fist taking in the soft fabric that hugs her per curves. "Gorgeous just like you, but I'd take you in sweats any day of the week."

"I just wanted to thank you for everything you've done, but then I started crying for no reason and it all snowballed from there. Now you're here and you should be out celebrating. Instead, you're stuck home with a whiny version of me that I don't even want to be around."

"I'm right where I'm supposed to be. Are you kidding me? I get to come home to a damn vision in lace and mesh on the couch."

"You like it?" She sniffles scooting forward on the couch, making room for me between her legs.

My hands land on the tops of her knees. "Like it, I more than like it, Baby. I've never seen anything more perfect." She toys with the thin gold ring on her pointer finger, spinning it in circles.

"I had this whole plan in my head. You were going to love it."

"I have no doubt. Want to tell me about it?" I ask, my thumb rubbing over the inside of her knee in slow, rhythmic circles.

"It might be more fun if I show you." Her hands come to the side of my face, and she leans forward, kissing me slowly, pressing her tongue into my mouth. Each swipe builds her confidence back up until she pulls back and gives me my first look at the spirited woman I'm used to.

"I'd love that, but I don't want you to do it for me."

"This is just as much for me. I need this, Dom."

"I'm yours," I reassure her, standing from where I was kneeling at the couch, but when I hold out my hand to bring her with me, she doesn't take it. Instead, she drops to her knees in front of me. I groan, instantly hard, and about to come in pants at the sight of her on her knees for me in *this* outfit. She looks ethereal and I can't get enough of it. "You want my cock in that pretty mouth, Firecracker?"

"I do."

"Fuck yes you do, and so do I," some primal part of me roars at her words.

"Then take it out for me." She looks up at me, her eyes shining with confidence now, and works my belt loose. Her hand covers me over my briefs and I hiss in a breath through my teeth when she squeezes me. "See how hard you make me. I always want you, that'll never change." My thumb runs over her bottom lips and I pull it down. "The whole damn world is at my feet right now and it's so fucking perfect."

My cock springs free, bobbing against my stomach when she tugs my briefs down. With her mouth open, she sticks her tongue out flat and I grip the base of my aching dick. Looking up at me through her dark lashes she pulls me forward by my hips, feeding herself my cock, inch by inch.

Jesus, this woman is going to be the death of me. No one is stronger, more beautiful, or a better match for me. She takes everything she can until she's pulling off and alternating working me with her hand and licking around the crown. When I hit the back of her throat, I'm barely hanging on. I try to tug her off, but she shakes her head.

"You're killing me," I groan. The need to be inside her is beating like a drum through my body, but she's not stopping. If anything, she's doubling down, swirling her tongue and sucking harder. "I can't hang on," I say through clenched teeth.

Fucking finally, she pops off, her fingers still wrapped around my shaft.

"If you can't fill my pussy with your cum, fill my mouth." Her eyes are filled with wicked delight, and I'm blown away by all of it, but mostly how thoroughly she's taking her power back. So much has changed in the blink of an eye, and even though we can't have sex during this step in the process of freezing her eggs, she's not going to let that stop her from taking what she needs.

"Jesus," I choke out, pushing her hair out of her face. I have to roll my lips together to stop the stream of words that are fighting to get out. Not because

I'm not ready to say them, or even because she's not ready to hear them, but because right now, with her on her knees licking her lips at the sight of my cock, it doesn't feel like the right time. "Are you going to let me spill every drop down this pretty throat?" My fingers brush over her cheekbones before anchoring themselves at the base of her neck and giving it gentle squeeze.

Her lips tilt up in a devious smile and she puts me back in her mouth, then places my free hand on the back of her head. My resolve unravels and I give her what she's asking for, pumping in and out of her hot mouth until my thighs are burning and she's swallowing all of me. "Fuck, Indie," I pant out.

When I slip out of her mouth, she kisses my thigh before letting her forehead rest against my tattoo. As soon as I'm steady enough that I'm sure my legs are going to work, I'm pulling her up off the ground and into my arms.

"Let me take you to bed and take care of you now."

"You just did. You gave me my confidence back."

"So you're saying you don't want an orgasm?"

"Have you ever known me to say that?" she asks, her legs wrapping around my hips.

"No, I haven't. Besides, I heard they can help with the discomfort."

"So you're saying it's good for my health?"

"Practically doctor recommended," I tell her, carefully navigating the narrow hallway to her bedroom with her in my arms.

"Can't say no to that." She laughs, brushing my hair out of my face. "We really need to take care of this hair."

"Are you ready to cut it for me?" I ask when we step into the bedroom.

"Maybe, but that seems risky. It could be unlucky."

"Damn, you're right. I guess it's going to have to wait," I say, dropping her on to the bed and stepping back to take in the full effect of the lingerie. My woman is a fucking smokeshow, I already knew that.

"Did you get this just for me?" I ask, leaning over her and running my finger over the ivory strap.

"I got it for us. Everything changed so fast. You've put me first every step of the way, and I let you. We deserved some time to just stop and enjoy each other after the last few days."

"You know I'd do it all again in a heartbeat. I have no regrets."

"And Coach is okay with the time you're missing this close to the postseason? What about the guys? They must be asking questions."

"Let me worry about the team." The guys have noticed, but so far they are giving me space. My lips cover hers and the kiss that I mean to be reassuring quickly turns heated.

The next morning while Indie is still in bed, I roll out to start the coffee the way she likes it, and get ready to head to the stadium for a full day of practice and meetings before our game tonight.

With the drip of the coffee going in the background, I let Ronnie out and turn on yesterday's baseball highlight while I wait. The photos spread across the end table catch my attention. I hadn't noticed them last night, but I was a little distracted.

Picking up the box I place it in my lap, carefully replacing the pictures in the box for Indie where they are safe, stopping every few pictures to examine the photos of a younger Indie with her mom. Poppy's even in a few.

At the bottom of the pile is one that's bent. Indie looks like she's probably in college, maybe a senior in high school. I smooth the photo out to put it away, but I have to blink when I see who else is in the picture: Jensen "Sonny" Phillips.

"What are you doing?" Indie asks, her voice shaky. I look over my shoulder to find her standing a few feet behind the couch in nothing but my shirt, her arms crossed protectively over her chest.

"Just cleaning these up so they didn't get wrecked." I glance back down at the picture in my hand, already knowing the answer to the question I'm about to ask. "Why do you have a picture of Sonny?"

"Who?" She stops behind the couch looking over my shoulder. "Are you talking about Jensen?" she asks, her mouth tilting into a frown. Reaching over my shoulder she takes the picture from me, folding it back and then forward again. She repeats the motion a few times while rounding the couch and dropping to sit next to me. Carefully ripping along the crease, she separates the two halves of the picture. Setting the half with her and her mom back in the box on my lap. "I should have done that a long time ago."

"He's the one that hurt you, isn't he?"

"Yes, he's the ex from college," she says slowly, clearly not sure why this matters.

"That son of a bitch," I seethe. "He's always been a shithead. Only we called him 'Sonny,' not Jensen, when I played with him in the minors. A nickname from the veterans, probably because he was so immature. We roomed together our first year until I moved out."

"Wait . . . what? I need coffee for this conversation."

"I've got it." Pushing up from the couch, I give myself a second to process. I know enough about Sonny to know he'd make a terrible boyfriend. The asshole who hurt her, the one that made it so hard for her to trust me, is my former friend. Granted, we weren't friends for long, but I lived with the guy. We shared countless beers together and bonded over baseball and life. Grabbing her a mug I pour her a coffee and return to my spot beside her on the couch.

"Do you still talk to him? Are you friends?" The cup cradled in her hand shakes against her knee where it's resting.

"No. He was a wild card when we lived together, and was constantly making the wrong choices. I moved out because I didn't want to be associated with him once I saw what he was really like."

"So you still don't talk to him?" She sips from her coffee and I want to pull it away so she can't hide behind the cup.

"I saw him a few weeks ago on the road in Phoenix. He asked me to do something after the game. I blew him off."

"I didn't even know he was still playing."

"I hate that someone hurt you like that. I hate even more that it was him." Taking the other half of the picture from her, I ball it up. "I think I'll use him for batting practice today."

"Have at it," she says, resting her head on my shoulder. "I can't believe I ever thought the two of you were anything alike."

"Proving myself to you was an honor. No one should ever treat you the way he did, and now it's my job to make sure no one else ever does."

"And believe it or not, I'm okay with that."

"Look at us growing and evolving." I kiss the top of her head as she sips her coffee. A happy Indie in my arms first thing in the morning is the best way to start my day. "Can you do me a favor?"

"Anything." She hums.

"Take my credit card. It's on the counter. I know you have your own money but it'll give me some peace of mind when I'm traveling knowing that you have it. With all the bills coming up—please just take it. There's not a lot I can do for you, but this I can."

"If it will make you worry less, I'll take it, but Dom, you've done so much already—more than I could have ever asked for."

"Fuck, it's hot when you're agreeable."

"Don't lie, you love it when I argue."

And she's not wrong. I really do.

CHAPTER 38

INDIE

This week has been a cyclone of activity and there's no end in sight. Not enough people talk about the toll medical trauma can have on a person. Growing up my parents shielded me from it. Being on the other side of it now, I can tell you this shit is awful and the exhaustion I feel has nothing to do with my actual appointments. It's everything else, the financial burden, hoops the insurance companies make you jump through, decision fatigue. It all adds up and makes surviving even harder.

My hand trembles as I raise the eyeliner to my lids, hovering above my lash line. I set it down, shaking out my hand and picking it back up. It's just his parents and sisters. It's not like I'm meeting the president, I remind myself.

It's not helpful because honestly, this feels monumental, maybe even more so than meeting a head of state. Dom's already at the stadium and I'm sitting with the girls tonight, so I won't even have to face them until after the game. I'm being ridiculous. I know that, but can't help it. And more than anything, I wish I could call my mom. She'd know what to say to calm me down. Like she always did, she'd give me perfect advice to calm my nerves without telling me what to do.

These damn hormones are screwing with my ability to keep it all together.

With my curly mane tamed and light makeup I'm hoping will cover the dark circles from the last couple days,

My phone rings with a FaceTime call that I'm not expecting. "Aren't you supposed to be out on the field warming up?" Instead, he's in an office I recognize from when I hurt my ankle. That day feels like a lifetime ago. *So* much has changed since he came to my rescue.

He pushes his hand through his hair. "Just wanted to check on how you're feeling." Worry creases his forehead. He's given me autonomy over decisions about how we handle this, but I know he'd prefer I tell the girls what's going on. He wants me to have support, but with him by my side I already feel like I have everything I need.

"A little sore." I shrug. I've been poked and prodded nonstop since meeting with Dr. Smith. Fortunately, things lined up with my cycle, so I could start the hormone injections a few days after the first appointment with the fertility specialist. I've yet to ask, but I'm positive even getting in to see them was helped along by Dom dropping his name.

"Fuck, Baby, I'm sorry. I'm going to try using ice on it first tonight and I looked up some relaxation techniques that might help." Dom hangs his head, and I wish I could be there with him. Guilt has been eating at him since yesterday over the bruises on my stomach from where he gave me my first shots for the egg retrieval process.

"Dom, are you kidding me? I couldn't have done it without you. I expected it to hurt. We'll figure out what works together."

"That doesn't mean I have to like it," he grumbles. It kills me that my problems have made my happy-go-lucky man so stressed, especially with the additional pressure of the postseason starting in just two days.

"I'll let you kiss it better later tonight when I see you after the game," I promise. "Can you do me a favor?"

"Anything, you know that."

"Good. Make sure you do a few extra stretches for me before that game. I think it'll really help me feel better."

His rich laughter is enough to dull the aches I'm feeling from the injections.

"Are you objectifying me?" he scoffs with faux horror.

"Yep." I'm not above resorting to his methods of banter and humor to coax him out of his guilt.

"It'll be a hardship, but I think I can manage."

"Have a good game. I'll be waiting for you afterwards."

"Fuck, I love that." There's a knock on the door behind him. "Gotta go. See you soon."

Shit, I've gotta get going too. I shove my feet into a pair of sandals and grab my bag to head to Poppy's so we can ride over together.

The team secured their spot in the postseason already, which means the pressure is off tonight. This game doesn't impact their season other than what kind of momentum they carry into their first series. Still, I'm so nervous for Dom and not just because his parents are going to be there, but because they are playing Phoenix. If they were just a rival, it would be one thing, but now that he knows who Jensen is and with the added history between them, it feels like the lit fuse to a bomb just waiting to go off.

Maybe I'm worried for no reason. Jensen doesn't know I'm in Denver, let alone who Dom is to me. Plus, Dom is basically the most laid back person on the planet. I'm sure it's just my already frayed nerves, married with the fact that I'm meeting his family tonight.

My fingers tap out a too fast beat to the radio on the drive to Poppy's and by the time I pull into her driveway, I'm seriously considering turning around and going home to cry into my pillow.

"Hey," Poppy says, greeting me at the door with a smile.

"Hey," I reply with a lot less enthusiasm.

"What's wrong?" She reaches out, looping her arm over my shoulder and moving me inside. The simple gesture has tears pooling in my eyes. "Are you still not feeling well?"

My throat burns with the lie I'm about to tell. "Just jittery, I think."

She bites her lip, looking like she'd rather do anything but say whatever is on the tip of her tongue. "Um. I'm not sure I should tell you this. But I feel like I should warn you, in case you don't already know."

Oh. I hadn't exactly forgotten about my ex playing for Arizona. A fact that Dom reminded me of earlier, so I wasn't caught off guard by seeing him tonight. It's just with everything else going on, it's not my biggest concern. "I already know that Jensen will be there," I tell her.

"So you're nervous about meeting the family?" she asks, tilting her head to the side. It reminds me a little of Ronnie, which makes me laugh. What the actual fuck is wrong with me?

"Yeah, it's a big step."

"Do you think it's too soon?" My normally loud best friend rubs my back, her voice filled with quiet concern.

I actually snort out a laugh at that one. She's going to think I'm crazy. Maybe Dom is right and I should tell her everything if for no other reason than her not thinking I'm losing it. I will tell her, just not tonight. "No, it's not too soon," I finally say.

In the grand scheme of things that Dom and I have gone through together, tonight should be a cakewalk, and maybe it would be if I wasn't pumped full of hormones.

"Is everything okay with you?" She eyes me cautiously, her eyes sweeping over me. "Something's been off since you moved. Are you not happy here?"

"No, that's not it." I take her hand in mine, desperate to reassure her. "Living closer to you is everything. I'm happy, promise, just in my feelings today. But you know what always cheers me up? Baseball pants."

"Okay, now I know something is *very* wrong. Who are you and where is my best friend?"

"The butts were never the problem and they definitely aren't now. Are the rest of the girls meeting us there?"

"Don't think I didn't notice that deflection." She checks the time on her phone. "Shit, we've gotta get going or we'll miss warm-ups."

"What the hell are we waiting for? The stretching is the only reason I'm going." I grab her keys from the hook and toss them to her.

"No, it's not." She catches them, leading the way out the door to her car.

"Fine, there are other reasons too," I admit opening the passenger door.

The traffic gods take pity on us and we are in the stadium before the guys come out onto the field for warmups.

We take our seats along the outfield wall, the same seats Poppy and Delilah have been sitting in for the past few seasons. Tonight we take up half the row with Janet, Marv, Mia, and Willa joining us as well.

Mia and I are talking about her upcoming book release, when Poppy lets out a high-pitched whistle next to me as the players run out onto the field.

Cruz is the first to spot his wife, blowing her a kiss. Next, Dean kisses his fingers and points to Mia. Such a secret softie, that one. Hendrix jogs out to center field and winks at Poppy, who's screaming her face off at him.

We're a spectacle, and I'm sure everyone in the section is watching the chaos unfold. But I don't notice because when Dom takes his spot, legs spread, he bends forward at the waist, stretching. Laughter bubbles out of me because that damn red thong is visible, clear as day, through his pants. After a few extra deep stretches, he looks over his shoulder and wiggles his fingers at me, blowing a giant bubble, before he pops up and joins Cruz and Hendrix in playing catch.

Willa leans across Mia to ask, "Have you ever made him wear the thong for you?"

"What do you think?" I ask, holding my hands out towards him. "Have you met this man?"

She simply holds out her hand for a high five and I give her one without a second thought because my man looks good in those baseball pants, but him in a thong, well that's something I'll never forget. Maybe because I laughed so hard I got the hiccups.

"I'm so nervous." Mia's knee bounces against mine.

"No one wants to lose the last series going into the postseason and Phoenix won't take a loss lying down tonight," Delilah says, sounding like a seasoned pro compared to the rest of us. Which makes sense since she's come to almost every home game for the last four seasons.

"Plus, Phoenix has a chip on their shoulder after being so close to making the postseason and getting knocked out by their loss to the Boston Revs earlier this week," Willa says matter-of-factly.

All of us turn to look at her.

"What? Just because I'm not sleeping with one of them doesn't mean I don't know the sport." She pops a peanut in her mouth chewing. "But if any of those rookies happen to be single, I wouldn't kick them out of bed for eating biscotti."

"You can do better than a rookie. What about the new assistant manager?" Janet says, pointing to where Miller Murphy is standing against the dugout talking to a few of the coaches. "That man looks like he knows a thing or two about how to use his bat."

"Can we not? I'm right here," Marv says.

"And yet you still love me."

"That I do." He kisses the back of Janet's hand, settling it into his lap.

A few minutes later, we all turn towards the outfield scoreboard for the national anthem. The first few innings are scoreless, with not much action coming out of either team. But the Bandits get their bats going in the top of the fourth inning with a single from Cruz with two outs. Hendrix drives one into the gap and it takes the left fielder too long to chase it down, leaving Cruz room to score.

The momentum is short-lived when Dom pops one up resulting in the third out and leaving Hendrix on second. Just as Willa predicted, the Roadrunners come out ready to even things up.

My heart is in my throat when Jensen comes up to the plate. It's the second time today I've had to watch him bat, and it hasn't gotten easier. If anything, the anxiety builds more each time I spot him out there. I was much happier not knowing where he was or what he was doing. Seeing him share the field with Dom makes me hate him even more.

Chewing on my thumb I watch nervously as the Bandits pitcher shakes off Xavier's sign, not liking what he's seeing after throwing two balls and one strike. By the time the pitch smacks the leather of Xavier's glove, I'm practically sweating.

Mia leans close, whispering, "You okay? You don't look so good."

"Fine, just not used to how warm it is here yet. And no damn breeze." I tug at the collar of my tank top.

When the next pitch is thrown and Jensen strikes out I feel like I can breathe again, especially now that he is back in the dugout, out of my line of sight.

Not today, Douchelord.

For the next few innings, both teams advance runners but strand them before anyone can score. It's frustrating as hell. With the score still one to zero in the eighth, I'm unraveling at the seams when Dom steps into the batter's box. "Come on, come on," I chant quietly to myself while he gets set in his stance.

"He's got it," Mia says, taking my hand and squeezing.

He's laser focused up there, completely zoned in. I feed off his energy, wanting it as bad as he does. He watches the first pitch curving away and steps out of the box, his bat under his arm, and readjusts his elbow guard. The same concentration is etched into his features.

This time when the pitch comes down the middle, he swings, sending it over the shortstop's head, the ball bouncing in the grass before the outfielders can get there to make the catch.

"Hell fucking yes!" I scream, probably a little too loudly, but oh my god am I proud to call this man mine.

The hit only gets him a single, but with Dean following him in the batting order, Dom breaks away and steals second, sliding headfirst before the catcher can get the ball to Arizona's second baseman. He pops up from the dirt, brushing his pants off and I swear the smile on his face lights up the whole stadium, or maybe that's just because I'm fucking gone for this man.

"Look at that smile," Poppy sings.

"Right?" Why do I sound out of breath?

"Oh honey, she wasn't talking about him." Janet laughs, reaching across her granddaughter to pat my knee.

Heat crawls up my cheeks. I never blush. That's Lilah's thing. "There's a baseball game to watch. And it's out there." I point to the field where Dean is still staring down the pitcher, his face serious.

"Gah. He looks so good when he gets all grumpy like that." Mia sighs next to me just as he swings the bat, sending the ball down the first baseline. The outfielder runs up on it, scooping it up and firing it back to the Roadrunner's first baseman, getting Dean out. It's enough to put Dom firmly into scoring position.

"Nice hit, Baby. Way to advance the runner." Mia stands, clapping and pointing at Dean as he jogs back to the dugout.

Xavier struts out to the box next, looking over his shoulder to where the most of the WAGs sit and shaking his head. "What's up with that?" I wonder out loud.

"Kristy probably didn't show up to the game again," Poppy comments.

"I don't know why he keeps chasing her," Mia says, shaking her head. "Wait, is he going to bunt?"

"Looks like it and Dom's fast enough to make that play," Lilah agrees, scooting forward in her seat just as Xavier drops his bat to bunt, killing the ball and placing it perfecting midway down the first base line and just fair.

As soon as he makes contact with the ball, I'm on my feet yelling for Dom to run and making a complete fool of myself, but I couldn't care less, because the man that's worked his way into my heart crosses home plate and scores.

The top of the ninth brings the energy in the stadium down a few notches when Arizona scores with a one run homer. With two outs and the game on the line, we need a quick out to end the game.

"When did baseball get so nerve-wracking?" I ask no in particular.

"About the time you fell in love with one of the players?" Poppy comments offhandedly, not taking her eyes off the field.

Well fuck, now I feel like I might throw up for a whole other reason. The fertility drugs are playing games with my emotions and I'm not sure what's real anymore or what's being amped up because I'm pumped full of hormones.

Dom puts me out of my misery, making a routine catch when the batter sends a fly ball in his direction and ending the game.

Or maybe not, I swallow, because now it's time to go meet the family; his parents, who by all accounts, are perfect and still very much in love, everything he wants to be. And his sisters, who he would protect with his dying breath.

What if they hate me? Or worse, what if they love me but think Dom is risking too much by being with me?

"Hey, you'll be fine. Dom worships you. He's been calling you his future wife for over a year at this point. You have nothing to worry about," Mia reassures me.

Grabbing my drink, I take a sip trying to cool the emotion burning my throat. "Not helping," I say, a crazed laugh sneaking out. These damn hormones have me going from nearly crying to panic and back again in mere seconds.

Dom is the definition of a man obsessed. I know that. I've always known that, but all of this suddenly feels so overwhelming. Poppy throwing out the "L" word and it feeling very right. Mia letting it slip that Dom has been manifesting me as his wife for over a year. His family waiting in the wings to meet me. What if this all goes horribly wrong and is ripped away before I get the chance to really enjoy it? Because that's what I want more than anything, to let this man love me the way only he can, for as long as he can.

Willa, Marv, and Janet left right after the game, so it's just Delilah, Mia, Poppy, and I snaking through the corridor to the family waiting area. Each step has my heart beating harder than the last.

Reaching out I grab Poppy's arm stopping her. "I'm just going to duck into the bathroom."

"Okay, I'll come with you."

I shake curls whipping my face. "No." Forcing a smile, I add, "I'm fine, just too much lemonade."

"If you're sure."

"I need to do this on my own. Just give me a second to collect myself."

"If you decide to run, text me. I'm an excellent getaway car driver," she says, trying to lighten the mood.

"No running." It's the first thing I've said since we left our seats that I'm sure of, this man is my future.

"Okay. See you soon." She squeezes my hand. Then leaves to catch up to Mia and Delilah, who are further down the hallway, where it opens up to a waiting area outside the locker room.

Ducking into the bathroom, I beeline for the sink, washing my hands with cool water before patting my face with them. "Stupid hot flashes," I murmur, bracing my hands on the sink and looking at myself in the mirror. "They're family, Ind," I tell myself.

Pulling up my big girl panties, I step out into the hallway, but before I even clear the doorway, I hear a laugh I'd know anywhere. One I never wanted to hear again that makes my stomach heavy and my neck tense.

"Well, well, what do we have here? You looking for me?"

Chills crawl up my spine at the mocking tone he uses as he steps closer. I should walk away. I should shout for one of the girls, but I freeze up.

"No, it's not me you're after. It seems you want a Bandit." He reaches out, his fingers pinching the badge hanging from my neck. I yank it back.

"Don't touch me, Jensen," I seethe quietly.

"Oh come on, which one is it?"

"None of your business." I look down the hallway, not sure what I'm hoping to find, but it's empty. The girls are probably right around the corner and none of the guys appear to have left the locker room yet. There's no one coming to rescue me.

He moves quickly flipping the badge over so Dom's name and number are visible on the pass.

"Dom Duran. Interesting." He laughs and a cold sweat covers my skin. "I bet he wouldn't mind at all if you came back to the hotel with me instead. I'm meeting up with a pretty little thing I met at the hotel bar last night. I bet she's just your type. We could have some fun, for old times sake."

Bile climbs up my throat. How did I ever think I loved this horrid man?

"Fuck you," I spit back. Turning towards my waiting friends I don't look back. My fists are balled at my side and I'm shaking when I get to the end of the hallway.

Mia spots me first, her brows pulling together in concern, so I plaster a smile on my face and join her. Followed quickly by Dom's family and my cheeks heat at how eagerly they wave me over.

"You must be Kelly. Hi, I'm Indie," I say to the woman tucked under the arm of a man that looks like an older, albeit still handsome version of Dom.

"I am. This is my husband Nick. And I think you might be my favorite person ever," she says, with the same easy smile her son so often wears. "Just as beautiful as the picture Dom sent us too.

"Of course he did. And thank you so much, but I can't imagine what I've done to deserve the title." The tension from my encounter with Jensen still lingers in my voice.

"Outside of baseball, I'm not sure my son has ever had to work quite as hard at anything as he has with you."

"Someone has got to keep him on his toes," his dad adds.

"So you're happy that I made your son's life more difficult?" Nervous laughter spills out of me.

"God, yes. Ever since he was little, things have come easy for him. When he met you, he had to work to keep your attention. If you have kids someday you'll see it's a balancing act. You want them to thrive, but not skate by. Earning the things we want only makes it that much sweeter."

"This way. You never take for granted what you've had to fight for," Nick adds, looking down at his wife.

I feel him behind me before I see him, and my body recoils against my will, still on edge from seeing Jensen. "You guys aren't scaring her away, are you?" One hand gripping my hip, he leans around me, kissing his mom on the cheek. When Dom's warm scent surrounds me I relax a fraction.

"No, we want to keep her," Kelly says.

"I'm not going anywhere." I lean back, and strong arms wrap around me. It's comforting, calming, exactly what I needed.

"Where are the girls?" Dom asks, looking around the small room.

"Daelyn took Dottie to get ice cream across the street. I told them we'd meet them there," his dad says.

"I could fuck around with some cookie dough ice cream. What about you, Firecracker?"

"Dessert before dinner. Why am I not surprised?"

"I am who I am," he says, making everyone laugh. Yes, he is, and it's one of my favorite things about him. "You guys go ahead. We'll be right behind you," Dom says to his parents. The rest of the guys have slowly joined us in the waiting area, but only Mia and Dean remain. Everyone else has already left.

"You ready for this?" he asks when his parents disappear. If Mia and Dean think he's talking about anything other than dinner with his family, they don't let on.

"Have a good night," Mia says, leaning in to give me a hug while Dom and Dean bro hug at Dom's insistence.

"Yeah, let's get it over with," I groan as he pulls a small cooler bag out of his backpack and leads me to a small privacy room opposite the locker room, closing the door behind us. Kneeling at my feet he grabs a little ice pack. "Hold this on your stomach for me."

He's so serious as he applies the sanitizer to his hands, then pulls out the powder and liquid he needs to mix together for the first shot and gets to work. With everything ready, his warm hand covers my cold one removing the ice pack. "I'm sorry," he says, looking up at me before swiping the antiseptic pad over the injection site.

"I hate this one," I grumble as he pinches the skin, injecting the medicine.

While I hold a piece of gauze over the injection site, he gets the next one ready. This one is easier on both of us. It's a pen, so it's less daunting and it hurts less.

When he's done, he removes the tip and puts it in the sharps container before turning back to me and kissing my stomach like he does every time. The hardest part about these shots isn't the pinch, it's seeing him take it so hard. This man, who I pushed away for so long, earns a bigger piece of my heart with each injection. He's made all of this just a little less daunting by taking care of me, bringing my shots, and just being him.

My throat grows tight, and I can feel the tears burning my eyes. The sudden swell of emotion that threatens to take me under has nothing to do with pain or the hormones. I get it. It took me a while, but I finally understand. Deep down, I think I knew all along that Dom was this good, this kind—made for me. He's always known, and it seemed impossible—terrifying—that he had so much faith in us. When I kept pushing him away. Somehow he saw what I couldn't and I'm so fucking thankful he never gave up, because I can't imagine doing any of this without him.

Hand in hand, we walk out of the stadium and across the street to find the girls sharing a banana split. His parents each have their own ice cream cones. I half expected to find them sharing a malt with two straws.

Daelyn makes it her mission to embarrass Dom with childhood stories. And in true Dom fashion, none of it gets under his skin, but that doesn't stop the two of us from laughing until my stomach hurts.

Dinner is more of the same, but this time it's Dottie telling jokes that have the whole table struggling to breathe. Hours later, I'm dead on my feet when Dom and I walk back to the car to head home.

"I feel awful that they are staying in a hotel."

"Don't. I'm not mad about it and neither are they. After sharing you with them all night, I want you to myself."

"Okay," I say with a yawn, too tired to argue with him on this. This man has fought so hard for me it's about time I just give him a break. "Take me home, Dom."

CHAPTER 39

DOM

Blue bruises peek out between the thin tank top and pair of cheeky panties she wore to bed last night. A reminder of everything Indie's already faced. With my hand that's not wrapped around her, I rub my knuckles over my sternum trying to ease the ache they cause. Deep down, I know bruises could be the least of our worries, that injections and needle pokes could be part of our future forever. I'm fucking terrified, but no matter what happens, I'll fight for this woman, for our future, with everything I have.

Easing the blankets back, I move my body down the bed. With my upper body propped up by my elbow, I dust my lips over the bruises on each side of her belly button.

"I'd take this all away if I could." It's on the tip of my tongue to confess everything I'm feeling to the silent room when she stretches under me, her hand finding my hair like it always seems to.

"Don't pity me, Dom," she warns.

"I don't pity you. Pity is something you feel for the weak. You're the strongest person I've ever had the privilege of knowing. So this isn't pity, it's love."

She sucks in a harsh breath and I'm afraid I screwed it up by even using the word. But then she does the last thing I expect and scoots down the bed to meet me. She might not say anything in return, but I can feel it in the way her lips move against mine. Whether or not we've said it, she feels the same.

I groan against her mouth. "How much do you think Coach will fine me if I'm late this morning?"

"Too much. Go."

"But I don't want to. You deserve an orgasm first thing in the morning."

"How will I ever manage?" She twists away from me, stretching to reach the nightstand where she stashed one of her vibrators.

"You're the devil, woman. How the hell am I supposed to leave now?" I sound pitiful, and I'm not even a little ashamed.

"Happy, knowing that I'm self-sufficient and satisfied."

"I don't like it." Lie. Would I rather be here watching? Hell to the yes, but I would never deny this woman anything.

"Don't be jealous of a toy. All my orgasms belong to you. It's your name on my lips every time I come."

"Not helping," I grit out. Visions of Indie coming with my name pouring out of her dance in my head, clouding my judgment.

"Was I supposed to be?" She shrugs. "How about I hop in the shower with you and take care of you the same way you've taken care of me?"

"I thought we agreed I couldn't be late." I push off the bed. "Besides, do you really think I would come without getting you off too?"

"No, definitely not. Cold shower then?" She looks so damn innocent batting her eyelids at me, still clutching that damn toy which jumps to life, humming in her hand. "Oopsies." Realizing that it's not helping, she turns it off and shoves it under the pillow.

"A menace."

"Your menace."

"Mine," I echo, leaning over the bed to give her another kiss.

"You're going to be late," she whispers against my lips. Reluctantly I leave her to shower and when I come back, she's up and making coffee. Still rumpled and sleepy from bed she holds out a travel mug for me. I take it hesitantly and she rolls her big chocolate eyes in return.

"Trust me."

Lifting the cup to my lips I sip it, waiting for the bitter taste but it's rich and smooth with a healthy pour of creamer. Just the way I like it.

"Don't worry, mine is still as thick as motor oil, even if it's decaf."

"I'll see you later?"

"Yeah." She stares down at her coffee cup, the teasing smile gone. I'm already cutting it close, but something is off. Her lips turn up a little too quickly. "I'll see you this afternoon. I'm excited about lunch with your mom and sisters. See you at the stadium." She pushes up on her toes kissing me before steering me towards the door.

"Is everything okay?" I try one more time, checking the clock over her shoulder.

"Uh huh. I'm good, promise." She's not, but I can't force her to talk to me and I need to go. Knowing that she's heading to meet my family soon is about the only reason I'm able to force myself out the door for the drive to the stadium.

The hallways leading to the film room are empty and I'm going to be late even without getting Indie off. Cruz is standing by the door to the auditorium about to pull it shut when my hand stops him.

"Is this going to be a regular thing?" Damn, he's a little scary when he goes into captain mode. Tough love from him is like your parents telling you they're not mad, they're just disappointed.

"Nope," I say, trying to skirt him to find an open seat.

"Over here." He nods towards the back row where there are two empty seats at the end.

Great, now he's babysitting me. Dropping into the seat I set my bag down between my feet.

"Coach said you've got some stuff going on, but he wouldn't tell me what. Are you going to tell me?"

"Nope."

"Are you in trouble?"

"Nope."

He shakes his head. "You know, you remind me of my brother."

That has my attention. Cruz's brother passed away four years ago. He was a pitcher and his death haunted my teammate for years until he finally got some closure last season.

"You two would have been unbearable together. Too much energy, always happy. Everyone loved him. Just like you. If you need help, you'll let me know, right?"

"Yeah. I will," I concede.

"Good, now stop being late. I don't like having to be a dick to my friends." He pats me on the back a touch harder than necessary.

"I wasn't late." I sigh.

"You were." He points to where Miller Murphy is standing at the front of the room waiting for us to shut up.

After the team meeting and reviewing tape from last night, I head to see Grant for a little preventative work on my hamstring. After stealing home last night, it's a little tight. Nothing concerning but with the postseason I don't want to chance it.

Mid-session, there's a knock on the door. Hendrix pokes his head in, and I wave him in.

"Getting involved in other people's business isn't normally my style, but my fiancée is worried about her best friend and, since you two are basically living together at this point . . ."

Probably not the time to tell him we are indeed living together, even if all of her stuff hasn't made its way over.

"Just ask what you want to know." My words come out harsher than intended, and I'd like to blame the pressure Grant is using, but it's not the only factor here. Keeping all of this from everyone is harder than I thought it would be, but I respect Indie's decision.

"Is she okay?"

I let my forehead drop to the table with a thud. "Can you be more specific?"

"Poppy's worried that she's sick. My money's on you knocking her up." I lift my head up and whatever he sees on my face shuts him up.

"Not pregnant, not sick," I say, wishing I wouldn't have let him in.

"And then there's you missing meetings and a game."

"Hendrix," I snap.

"Okay, Indie's fine. I'm leaving." He backs away from the table like he's trapped in a cage with a tiger and honestly, that's how I feel right now too.

Grabbing my phone from the table I fire off a text to my dad.

DOM:

Watch out for Indie today, she seems skittish this morning.

DAD:

10-4

The game has barely started and my body is still riddled with the tension that's been building all day. It's the bottom of the second inning and that prick Jensen is catching today after only batting as the DH yesterday. I preferred him on the bench, where I didn't have to interact with him.

Standing in the on-deck circle, I'm like that caged animal back in the trainer's office. Only now I'm coiled and ready to pounce with him this close to me. Tearing my gaze off of my former roommate, I focus on the pitcher. Cruz's bat cracks with the sound of the ball coming off it and he takes off for first, barely beating out the throw from the shortstop.

Toeing at the dirt, I grind my back foot into the batter's box. A low whistle comes from behind me and I try to tune it out, concentrating on the pitcher.

"Enjoying my leftovers, Duran?"

How the fuck he knows Indie and I are together is beyond me, and I'm not in any position to figure it out. The pitch comes and I swing and miss. Grinding my teeth together I step out of the box, readjusting my elbow guard and exhale a deep breath.

"Better luck next time," he sneers.

My hands twist on the bat and I sit back waiting for my pitch, channeling all these relaxation techniques I researched for Indie.

This time, when I swing, the ball and bat connect almost perfectly, sending it all the way to the fence. It doesn't have the juice to make it over the wall, but it's deep enough that the outfielders aren't able to make the catch.

When I stop running at third, I know there's no way I'm ending this inning without scoring. Call me petty, but stealing on Jensen would make my whole damn season.

Dean strikes out and I don't get a chance to make a break for it, but I taunt the shit out of the douchey catcher with a healthy leadoff every chance I get.

Biding my time, I wait for my opportunity as Xavier takes his turn at the plate. The next pitch is a slider that ends up in the dirt and Jensen misses the block, giving me the opening I'm looking for.

One goal in mind, I take off diving for home and brush the plate with my fingers. Jensen barrels into me as I slide across the plate. He hits me hard, but with all the adrenaline pumping through me, I hardly feel the jarring hit.

I look at the ump and see him signal safe. Groaning, I reach for Xavier's outstretched hand and let him pull me up. "That's skill, not luck," I say, brushing myself off. I see red when Jensen pushes my catcher out of the way, rips his mask off, and gets right in my face.

"Be proud of yourself all you want for scoring on me. Just remember I scored with your girl first. She was always an easy lay. Not worth that trouble, but that's your problem now."

Blood pounds in my ears and I cock my fist back, not thinking twice before it connects with Jensen's face, taking him down to the ground. Even as I hear the home plate ump yelling, "You're out of here," I don't have an ounce of regret.

Xavier tries to pull me back from where I'm bent over Jensen, but I'm not done. "You were never going to be enough for her. That's my whole damn world you're talking about. The next time you talk about her like that, this won't end with just one punch. I'll make you eat your fucking teeth."

I spit in the dirt next to Jensen, who is wiping the blood dripping from his lip before I'm dragged off the field by Cruz and Dean. Storming past Wilson I head straight for the locker room. My night is far from over, but I won't be going back out on the field and I probably just ruined my shot at playing in the postseason.

Worth it.

She's worth everything. I just hope Indie sees it that way.

CHAPTER 40

INDIE

My hand flies to my mouth when Jensen collides with Dom at home plate. It's a late hit. I don't even know if that's a thing in baseball, but it was fucking dirty. I vaguely hear Kelly gasp beside me and Daelyn clings to my arm on the other side of me, sliding Dottie under her arm.

"Oh, no." Kelly sighs as the two of them get in each other's faces. It's like a slow motion train wreck.

"Don't do it, son," Nick says, his arms around his wife.

The sound of Dom's fist connecting with Jensen's face is louder than any hit in the park today, and I'm not even sure if it's real or in my head. Tears prick my eyes when I see the anger twisting Dom's face. This is not who he is, and I did this to him.

Oh god. I've ruined him. And even if I can forgive myself, will he be able to forgive me?

The ump signals the ejection that we all know is coming and I suck in a shaky breath, looking from his sister to his parents. All four of them have their heads hung.

I wipe my sweaty palms on my skirt, the same one I wore that first night. This is not how the night was supposed to go. Fidgeting I tug on the silky teal fabric that suddenly feels too constricting. Tonight should be a full circle moment. Me at the game with his family and wearing his jersey a year after I told him we had no future. The same outfit except instead of wearing a borrowed Harrison jersey, tonight I'm surprising him by wearing his for the first time.

"I'm so sorry. This is all my fault," I admit quietly.

It's Dottie who speaks first. "No, that was definitely my idiot brother."

"I have to agree with my daughter. My son has never done something he didn't want to," Kelly adds, shifting away from Nick and placing both hands on my shoulders. "I don't know what's going on with you two. Dom has never been one to keep secrets. As a matter of fact, he's pretty terrible at it. There might be things you two aren't ready to tell us, and that's fine." She points at Dom, who's disappearing through the dugout door. "But his feelings for you are written all over his face and he's not trying to hide those."

"He makes the same face I make when I see puppies," Dottie says. "I think that means he loves you."

"Dottie," Daelyn scolds.

I drop into my seat so I'm eye level with her. "That's a relief because I love your brother." I look at Nick and Kelly, not sure what's next. "Should I go find him?"

"No, sweetheart," Kelly says, pulling me in for a hug.

"I know you want to, but he's going to be busy for a while. He'll watch the game from the locker room and have to talk with his manager and agent at some point. Give him time to sort those things out. We'll go down after the game," Nick explains.

"I'm sure he wants to see you more than anything, but it's not a great idea," Kelly adds.

My phone pings with a text.

NAUGHTY SLIDERS AND TACO SLUTS

POPPY:

Are you okay? I can come to your seats.

ME:

Dom's family has me. I'm okay.

MIA:

Will we see you after?

ME:

I'm not sure.

LILAH:

He's going to be okay.

POPPY:

Just let us know what you guys need.

Sitting through the rest of the game sucks, especially when the Roadrunners take the lead. On the bright side, Jensen strikes out in all his remaining at bats. So that feels like a tiny slice of karma.

"What's going to happen now?" I ask, directing my attention to Nick, during the bottom of the ninth.

He presses his lips into a thin line, and I'm not sure he's going to tell me.

"For christ's sake, Nick, she's not going to break. Answer her."

Remorse flashes in his amber eyes, so much like his son's. "You're right, I'm sorry, Indie. It's unlikely he'll play in the next series. Depending on how the team does that means his season could be done. He'll be fined, but he's never had issues before, so that should be the end of it."

Much like last night, the walk down to the family waiting area is daunting, even with Kelly's reassurance that everything is going to be okay. But I don't know how it could be, based on what Nick told me.

The normally packed waiting area is empty. We left our seats before the end of the ninth so we could get out of here if Dom was ready to go. Call me a coward, but I was hoping he'd be ready, so I didn't have to face our friends. If his teammates have figured out that I'm the reason for his altercation with Jensen they aren't going to be pleased with me. The last thing I want is to cause more drama tonight.

He doesn't make us wait long. Everyone is just getting comfortable in the leather chairs when he steps out of the locker room—his eyes on the floor and his jaw tight. I stand to go to him, but his mom holds me back. "Give Nick a second and then he's all yours. Trust me."

Nick puts his hand on his son's shoulder and bows his head. They keep their voices low, but it's mostly Nick talking and Dom shaking his head. "I think your girl needs you," Nick says, and Dom finds me over his shoulder, looking remorseful.

His family hangs back, and I go to him. "I'm so sorry, Dom," I say, the words rushing out of me, choppy and weak. "This is all my fault. If I hadn't—"

"No," he starts, but I'm on a roll. My arms wrap around myself protectively.

"They're going to suspend you—you're going to miss out on the postseason. How can you even look at me?"

"Indie, Baby, stop" His voice is soft, calm, so damn full of affection. He pulls me to him gently cupping the back of my neck until we are forehead to forehead. I can't help but to lean into him even if it's the worst thing for him, like my body knows how thoroughly he owns me. A pain like I've never felt crackles through my whole body, he could break my heart right now and I'd never recover. Even with the deep ache in my soul, I wouldn't change a thing. Loving Dom is the best thing that's ever happened to me.

"It's okay, Dom. You deserve more—better. I'm sorry I put you in this situation."

"Indie! Stop. Stop talking for a second. Stop apologizing. Please." His lips cover my face in kisses. But his jaw is tight like he's holding back. One shuddering breath later and there's fire in his eyes when he pulls back to look at me. "You. Are. *My.* Wife. And I love you. Stop trying to give me an out. Stop blaming yourself for something you had no control over. Jensen disrespected you and I won't hear anyone speak about my wife that way. Not today, not ever. They can fine me, bench me, fire me and I'll still pick you every time.

There's a chorus of gasps behind us, way more than just the three that were there a moment again.

"You love me?"

"Of course I love you. I married you, didn't I?"

Tears roll down my face, but Dom won't stand for that and his thumbs brush them away.

"You really love me."

"I do, but so help me Indie if that jersey has my best friend's name on it like it did last time..."

"You'll do what?" I ask, stepping into him, matching the heat he's putting off as his eyes rake over me.

His lips graze my ear. His voice is a warning, dangerously low, "Just because I told you I'm in love with you doesn't mean I won't turn that ass red for wearing someone else's name."

"Well, shit. Now I almost wish I would have borrowed a jersey instead of buying one of my own."

"Show me." A screech leaves me when he spins me around by the hand. I glance over my shoulder, and find him standing there stunned, one big hand is dragging over his jaw. He steps forward pushing my hair over my shoulder. "I've been manifesting you as my wife for a year and damn, Baby, our last name looks good on you."

When I face him again there's a challenge in his eyes, like he's daring me to say that I married him for anything other than love, because he knows that's bullshit, even if this is the most frank conversation we've had about it outside of our vows. "I love you, Dom Duran. Had things been different, I might have made you wait more than two months, but I married you because my husband is the best man I've ever known. You're it. You've been it since that first night. I was just too scared to see it."

Me wearing his jersey might do it for him, and I admit it's hotter than I expected, but I can't focus on anything other than the necklace peeking out of his shirt. My fingers dance down his neck and follow the gold chain, pulling it from his shirt. Our simple gold wedding bands hang between us.

"And you look hot wearing my ring, *husband*."

His lips crash down on mine, and applause erupts around us. It's cheesy and ridiculous and perfect, because after everything we've been through our love deserves to be celebrated.

"I have so many questions," Poppy whispers behind me. "But mostly, I'm just really fucking happy for you two."

"What did I miss?" Dean asks, when he steps out of the door next to us.

"These two assholes got married in secret," Mia says, reaching for her boyfriend.

"No shit. I'm happy for you, kid." Dean smacks my husband on the back, displaying more affection than I've ever seen from him outside of Mia.

There's so much more we need to tell them, especially the girls. I've blamed my mood swings on the hormones and I'm sure they aren't helping, but the secrets have been eating at me and it's time to come clean. I can't protect them from this any more than my husband can protect me from cancer.

We will have plenty of time, just us girls when the guys leave for the Division League Series the day after tomorrow. Right now, I just want to get my husband home.

"Ready to go home, wife?"

Hendrix and Cruz choose that moment to join us.

"What the hell is going on? Who made my fiancèe cry?" Hendrix barks, going straight to Poppy.

"They're happy tears." Poppy sniffles, letting him wrap her up.

"These guys can fill you in." With my arms looped around Dom's neck, I wave at our friends and Dom's family, who I'm positive also have some things they are dying to ask.

"Mom, Dad. Are you guys good waiting until tomorrow to ask your questions?" Dom asks, kissing my forehead.

"Why don't we bring you and your wife breakfast in the morning?" Kelly says, her face lit up with a smile. She crosses the room pulling me into her arms. "Welcome to the family, Indie. I love this for you two." Switching her attention to her son, she pats his cheek. "You're going to be an excellent husband. Just remember, she's always right."

At least I know she's on board.

"Tell me something I don't know."

CHAPTER 41

DOM

Punching my wife's ex and getting benched right before my team made it to the postseason for the first time since I was called up wasn't on my bingo card for this season. But neither was getting married and I wouldn't change a fucking thing about either of them.

Jensen deserved so much more than a single punch to the face, both for the way he treated Indie back then and for the things he said tonight.

Indie stops when we get to the car, both of her hands coming to rest on my chest and moving up until her hands are in my hair. "Are you okay? That was a hard hit. What about your hand?" she asks, her uneasy gaze flicking over me.

With the way Jensen crashed into me, it's a miracle one of us wasn't hurt. Those kinds of hits always mean delayed pain though. When I wake up tomorrow, I'll probably feel like shit.

Right now though, with this woman in my arms and everyone knowing that she's mine not just as my girlfriend but my wife, nothing else matters.

"Never better, Baby."

"That seems like a stretch." She's looking at me like I'm crazy.

"When are you going to understand that you're the most important thing in this world?"

She ducks her head and a dark curl falls in front of her face. We have a lot to talk about. This marriage started unconventionally, but there's nothing about it that's fake.

Pressing my lips to hers, I open her door, taking her hands and helping her in the car.

After I start the car and back out of the stall, she links her fingers with mine and we make the drive home in a comfortable silence. Even with everything we need to figure out between us, our friends and families waiting to be brought up to speed, and the impending implications from the team over my actions tonight, I know we will be okay.

Shutting off the car, I follow Indie's lead when we get home. After a quick greeting from Ronnie, we let her outside. When the lock clicks into place after the dog has taken care of business, Indie leads me upstairs.

My wife takes a seat at the end of the bed and drops her head into her hands, looking utterly defeated. Taking a knee in front of her, I run my hands up her thighs.

"Tonight was all my fault," she says, and the anger from earlier creeps back up, my body growing stiff at her feet. "I'm not trying to give you an out. I don't want you to run away, but you deserve to know everything."

There's almost nothing this woman could say that would send me packing. "Say whatever you need to, but I doubt it will make a difference."

"Yesterday, when I was coming down to meet you after the game, I saw Jensen."

She certainly has my attention. I'd wondered how he knew about the two of us, but in the heat of things it didn't really matter, not once he started talking about Indie. "You did?" I ask, keeping my voice even.

"He spotted me coming out of the bathroom alone. The whole thing couldn't have lasted more than thirty seconds, but he was disgusting and overly interested in what I was doing there. I should have told you last night—"

"What do you mean he was disgusting?" I ask, alarm bells going off.

"He grabbed my arm and said some things."

With a calm I definitely don't feel, I take her hands in mine examining her arms. If he hurt her, that punch I threw earlier will be the least of his worries.

"He didn't hurt me," she says, looking far steadier than I feel. "He can't hurt me."

"Tell me what he said." I can't explain why I need to know, but I do.

She looks away, her eyes angry and fixed on the wall behind me.

"You don't have to." I waver, not wanting to put her through more pain than she's already dealing with.

"It shouldn't matter what he said."

"But it does, and it's one of the reasons I love you. You're passionate and fierce. You don't put up with shit from anyone, not even me. Feeling a certain way about seeing him doesn't make you weak or give him power. It's just who you are."

"First, he insinuated I was there for him. Which was bad enough, but then he grabbed my pass and saw your name. I didn't want him to know—to taint what we have." My voice shakes with anger. "He mocked my sexuality—and our relationship—telling me you wouldn't mind if I came back to his hotel for a threesome. It's the kind of shit I expect from him, but I hate that he made me question things even if only for a second."

"Why didn't you tell me last night?"

"It happened right before I met your parents, and I didn't want to cause any drama. I just wanted to enjoy the night. Later, when we were alone, I was embarrassed that I let him talk to me that way. That I let his words affect me at all. I'm used to handling things on my own. I'm sorry I didn't tell you."

"This is one-hundred percent a *him* problem, not a *you* problem. If I'd have known—"

"Yeah, that's another thing. What the hell were you thinking, fighting with him? You can't fight my battles for me. I'm a big girl."

"That's where you're wrong. You don't have battles anymore. *We* have battles."

"Because I'm your wife?" Her lips tilt up in a smile that makes my dick perk right the fuck up. He needs to tone it down because with her upcoming egg retrieval, I can't make love to her the way I want to right now.

"I'll never get sick of hearing you say that."

"What about, 'I love you, husband'?"

"You're fucking killing me, woman."

"So we're doing this?" she asks, her eyes shining with tears.

"Were we ever not doing it?" I ask, dragging her to the edge of the bed so I'm wedged between her legs and my arms are around her hips.

"We're doing it out loud, and for real?"

"Just like I told you in the courthouse earlier this week, you're the only one I want for the rest of my life. I've known since last year that this is what I wanted. It didn't quite happen the way that I expected. Loving you out in the open is the only way I want to do this from now on."

"Good, because it was never about the insurance for me either. You make me feel things no one else ever has, and I can't imagine getting through these last few months without you. You're infuriating and crazy. But you love me better than anyone else ever has, and I don't want to hide that because of how it happened. Quick or not, what we have is real and perfect."

"Do you think it's time we come clean with your dad?"

"Yeah. He deserves the truth and more importantly I want him to know."

We call her dad together, she tries so damn hard to keep it together, but when her dad's voice starts shaking as he asks questions about her plans for surgery, my girl falls apart.

"Come with me," I say, standing from the floor and holding my hand out for her. When she places it palm down in mine, I lead her to the bathroom, grabbing a towel and my grooming kit. I strip my shirt over my head and place the towel over my shoulders, unzipping the black bag and handing her the scissors. "I think it's time for a fresh start."

"You're kidding right, I'm not cutting your hair." Her fingers ruffle the long strands. "Besides, I kind of like it this way."

Twisting, I grab the clippers and add a guard. "In that case, just clean up the sides, wife."

She rolls her eyes at me. "If it sucks, don't come for me."

"I'll always come for you." I wiggle my eyebrows at her in the mirror as she turns on the razor.

She chuckles. "Like I said, infuriating. Just remember who's got the power right now." Her lips tilt up in a mischievous smile while the electronic buzz grows louder as she presses it to the base of my neck, sweeping before rocking it away.

♥

The next morning when I wake up, there's a text from my mom letting us know they'll be over at ten with breakfast. I already know they will be supportive, but I can't say the same for the league official who I'm supposed to call in a few minutes.

Following the game last night, Wilson sat me down and asked for my side of the story. The league will issue a ruling on what, if any, disciplinary actions I'll face. Compared to bench clearing brawls, what happened last night is pretty cut and dry.

Leaving a sleeping Indie in bed, I sneak down the stairs into my office, each step emphasizing the strain on the right side of my body from the collision last night. Whatever the outcome of this meeting, I'll deal with it. After what Indie shared last night about her interactions with Jensen and how it affected her, I just want this to be over. Dragging it out will only hurt her more, the last thing she needs is more stress.

"Hey, Dom," Jillian, the representative for the player disciplinary board, says when the call goes through.

"How's it going this morning, Jillian?"

"I expect my morning is going better than yours."

"Actually, I don't have any complaints. I woke up beside my beautiful wife and we are having breakfast with my parents soon." My agent would probably slap me upside the head, but it's the truth. Jensen's a douche and misogynistic prick. He deserved much more than what I gave him.

"I heard from your coach that you were recently married when we talked this morning. Congratulations. He also told me he didn't believe you should be suspended based on your actions and the events that triggered it."

That surprises me, Wilson's a man of few words and reading him isn't always easy. That he went to bat for me, or really for Indie, makes the respect I already have for him grow.

"If you expect me to tell you I'm remorseful, you'll be disappointed."

"Honestly, after hearing from Wilson, Xavier Kingsley, and Tom Kellerman, I didn't expect you to. I knew Wilson and Kingsley would have your back, but Kellerman's statement backs up what the other two said. Jensen was baiting you the entire time at bat. He was actually apologetic that, as the home plate umpire, he didn't step in sooner."

"He had no way to know that it was more than just one player chirping to get under another's skin at the time," I say.

"Can you tell me exactly what happened?"

And I do, from the moment he put his hands on Indie in the hallway until I was dragged off the field.

"I appreciate your time today and your professionalism. Not everyone is as understanding during these discussions. We should have a decision later today or tomorrow," Jillian explains. "That being said, you should prepare yourself to fly with the team when they leave for the League Division Series in Atlanta."

One obstacle out of the way, some of the tension I've been carrying since last night lifts, making my shoulders ease away from my ears.

"I hate decaf," Indie whines to Ronnie as she pours herself a cup of coffee. She still hasn't heard me approaching and continues talking to the dog, her tone softening. "But if it means your dad and I can give you siblings in a few years, it's worth it."

Damn, I wish I would have gotten that on video. "I can't fucking wait to see you growing our babies." She jumps, almost spilling her coffee, when I come up behind her and wrap my arms around her.

After consulting with the fertility specialist, along with the surgeon who will do her procedure after the egg retrieval, she decided she wanted to retain her ability to get pregnant through IVF. As long as there was nothing to indicate that she should have a full hysterectomy, which she will eventually have when we've had kids, she wants the chance to experience pregnancy.

Surrogacy isn't off the table. We've talked about it at length, and if that's what needs to happen, we are both open to that option. Indie is already grieving being able to conceive naturally, so I just want to support her however I can. And right now, that means we're both drinking decaf.

"Are you done with your call already?"

"Mmhmm," I mumble into her neck, inhaling the smell that is so distinctly her—sweet like honey, a little floral and that hint of spice that makes it so Indie. My cock thickens when she relaxes back into me, exhaling a contented sigh.

"Aren't you parents and sisters coming over?" It doesn't stop her from bringing her hand to the base of my skull and raking her nails through the much shorter hair on the back of my head. She kept the top long, trimming the back and sides into an impressive fade considering it was her first haircut.

"We have time," I say, taking the coffee from her and setting it on the counter. With nothing but one of my old shirts on, there's nothing stopping me from slipping my hand under the fabric and running my calloused hands all over her flawless skin.

Her chest rises and falls in time with mine as my finger coast along her ribs, and when my thumb brushes over her already tight nipples, she sucks in a breath. "So sensitive."

"Want me to stop?" I ask, cupping her full tits gently.

"God, no. Feels good." The words come out rushed and needy

"Perfect. I live to make you feel good."

"How long do we have?" she asks, her voice uneven as I slip my other hand inside her panties.

"Let me worry about that." Dropping my hand to the hem of her shirt, I bring it over her head slowly, relishing each new inch of skin exposed to me. "Hands on the counter, wife."

Her fingers grip the edge of the marble and I pull her hips back, making her back arch. With morning sunlight streaming in, she's fully on display for me.

"I want your hands on me," she whines, pushing her ass back further.

The temptation is too strong. I bring my hand out down on her ass making her skin ripple and the cheek glow pink. "So impatient. I want to look at you. So fucking beautiful it hurts, especially with my handprint on your ass and your greedy pussy soaked for me."

She looks over her shoulder at me in mock indignation. "Is that anyway to talk to your wife?"

"That depends." I smooth my hand over her hip and down between her legs, my fingers easily sliding over her hot center. "Feels to me like my wife liked it." Her knees fold in, knocking together when I push two fingers inside her. "Let's see how much."

My other hand comes down on the opposite side making her clench around my fingers. "That's it, squeeze me, Baby. Show me what a dirty girl you are."

"So close. Again," she cries, begging for my hand, abandoning the playful banter.

I want to see her shatter so completely. "Pinch your nipples for me," I tell her.

Keeping one hand braced against the counter, she brings the other to her tits, gasping at the added sensation. And when my hand comes down again she cries out, her hips pressing back, riding my hand as her walls flutter around my fingers.

"That's it, wife, so good for me." My cock is a steel spike in my shorts, stretched up tight against my stomach as I watch her shake through her orgasm in the middle of our kitchen.

She sets her head down on the counter as I slowly withdraw my fingers, my arm hooked around her to hold her up.

Helping her stand, I turn her around in my arms, taking her lips. "I love you so damn much." I mutter before I slip my tongue inside her making her melt into me.

"I love you. Please tell me we have time for me to taste you."

"More than enough. They'll be here in forty-five minutes."

"God, I married a shithead," she says, sinking to her knees.

"That may be so, but you still want this cock."

Her pink tongue swipes across her lips as she looks up at me with hungry eyes. "Like I want my next breath."

"It's all yours," I say, as she takes it out, licking around the crown. I like to think I possess some level of self-control but when Indie's fingertips dig into the flesh of my ass and tug me forward, making me bump the back of her throat, I'm a man on the edge.

She gags around my cock but doesn't let up, holding me there. I ease out when her grip loosens, and she sucks in a gulp of air. "You want me to take this mouth the same way I just took your pussy?"

With my cock lodged in her mouth, all she can do is look up at me and nod. My hips snap forward pushing to the back of her throat again, making her eyes water. "You take my cock so well." I pulse there for a minute before I pull back, giving her a break.

Each time I nudge the back of her throat, she swallows, bringing me closer to the edge. Like a fucking goddess on her knees, she moans around my cock. "Drain me and I'll take you up to the shower and give you another on my tongue."

Whether it's my promise of another orgasm in the shower or just her competitive spirit, she ramps up her efforts, sucking hard and moving one hand from my ass to my balls, rolling them in her palm. Instead of holding me in her mouth like I expect her to, she pulls off, one hand wrapped around my base as the other goes to her breast.

My balls pull up tight and dick twitches in her hand. She leans forward, taking everything I have to give her, and looking like the dirtiest thing I've ever seen as my cum covers her perky tits. "Jesus, Indie."

CHAPTER 42

INDIE

Forty-five minutes sounds like a lot of time until your husband insists on going down on you in the shower after washing your hair and takes his sweet ass time. Now I'm rushing to make myself presentable with the ten minutes I have left and I'm not convinced that one shower was enough to wash away the evidence of all the filthy things we did this morning.

After the last twenty-four hours—hell, after the last two weeks—we deserve mind-altering orgasms. Let's just hope his family thinks the pink staining my cheeks is from the sun during yesterday's afternoon game and not from the memory of him coming all over my chest.

I've read that the hormones for the egg retrieval can do funny things to your body like make you more turned on. It could be that or it could just be that I really wanted my newly outed husband to mark me in a very hot way. We'll never know, but if anyone ever finds out, I'm blaming the shots.

With my hair still damp, I make my way back downstairs just in time to hear the front door open.

"Hey guys, come on in," Dom says, holding the door for his dad, who's got a carrier of coffee in his hand.

"Decaf? What the hell, Dom," Daelyn says, shoving a bag of food at her brother's chest.

"Oh, um." Why is my voice coming out all quiet and meek? Clearing my throat I try again. "That's actually my fault."

"Leave your brother alone," Kelly chides, following Dottie in.

Taking the bag from his mom, Dom glares at his sister. "You can set those down in the kitchen, Dad."

We all file in through the kitchen and exchange a round of hugs. Nick and Dom pick through the food, distributing it at the table as Kelly and I grab napkins and the girls love on Ronnie.

"So . . . You're like my sister now, right?" Dottie says, as she scratches the fur behind her ears. And then she looks over at me. "Or actually, you're my sister and she's like my niece or something. Right? Oh my god. I'm an auntie," she gushes.

"Yeah, kiddo. I am," I say, my eyes finding Dom across the kitchen. "And I'm sure you're going to be an excellent aunt."

"Are you going to make us eat before you tell us how this happened?" Daelyn huffs her arms crossed.

"What is her deal today?" Dom asks Kelly, who looks like she's about ready to throw the roll of paper towels she's holding at her daughter.

"You got married, and I didn't even know you had a girlfriend. There was no wedding and the groomsmen would have been *so* hot in the tuxes. You basically robbed me of the best night of my life."

"I'm sorry." Dom snorts. "There definitely won't be a big wedding now." Then he freezes, turning to me. "Wait, did you want a wedding?"

I press my lips together, holding in my laughter at the look of panic that crosses his face and just shake my head.

Kelly sits and everyone picks up on the silent message, taking a spot at the table and passing out food from the pile in the middle of the table.

"So, no wedding. Anything else you want to tell us?" Nick eyes the decaf coffee in my hand.

Dom throws his arm around my shoulders in a protective gesture. "Indie's not pregnant, if that's what you're fishing for." And swear I see Kelly deflate just the tiniest bit at the news.

"But yeah, there is more to the story than just a quickie wedding." Dom releases an exhale and looks at me for permission. After I cut his hair last night, we talked about how much we wanted to tell everyone. With the team going on the road for the postseason and surgery coming up, I know it's time. All I need is Dom, but I want the support of our friends and family too now that I've had some time to come to accept everything.

"My mother died of ovarian cancer when I was in college." A chorus of sympathies interrupts me. "Thank you. Recently, we found out through genetic testing that I inherited the mutated genes that make it more likely that I could get cancer. Dom and I had just started seeing each other, but he stuck by my side through it all." I turn my head and find him watching me, his forehead creased with worry. "He's been amazing."

"Indie had to make a lot of decisions about what to do with that news and she decided to get surgery, but before she can do that, she needs to freeze her eggs if she wants to become a biological mom someday." His eyes flick towards Dottie.

"Like how we had you, kiddo," my mom says, ruffling my little sister's hair. "Made with love and science."

The reaction to the next part is what I'm the most worried about, but I swallow it down and pick up where Dom left off. "When I moved here a few months ago, I quit my job and have been working with non-profits since. The clinic I was going to is one of those, but with the test results, I was going to need a more extensive team and insurance," I explain, glancing down at the table.

"There was no way I was letting her give up the work she's doing. It's too important. And I already knew she was it for me. So I convinced her to marry me."

"You make it sound like it was easy." I laugh remembering my initial response when he brought it up. "I thought he'd lost it and told him there was no way in hell I was marrying him just for insurance."

"But you weren't," he reminds me.

"No, I wasn't." I sigh. "He asked me to picture my future. One year from now, five years, ten years, twenty. No matter how far out we got, he was still there by my side."

"You tried so hard to resist me, but it's just not possible," he teases. "The day after we got her test results, we went to the courthouse."

"I wish we could have been there," Kelly says, a smile on face and her eyes glistening.

"That was the only thing I'd change," Indie says, her hand covering mine. "But if you'd like, we can show you."

"Indie brought a tripod, and we recorded the whole thing," he says, his face lighting up the same way it did when I set it up in the courthouse.

Like he was shocked that it was something I wanted to be able to look back on. Dom wears his feelings on his sleeve, he always has, even when he doesn't say the words, you can read it on his face. I knew he was coming for me after our first night together. He never let me forget it. But the way I fell for him—I didn't see that coming. Sure, the banter was hot. And the sex was unbeatable, but I had myself so convinced that he wasn't what I needed right up until he was the only thing holding me together.

He's my home plate. All the other reasons to marry him were non-existent when I walked into that courthouse with him last week. There were no other base runners forcing me home. It was just me and him, doing what felt right. For the first time in what feels like forever, I wasn't running from something. I was running to it. So yeah, I wanted a video to share with everyone and to look back on when we're old and gray, probably still bickering on the front porch surrounded by our grandchildren.

Kelly is the first to stand from the table, coffee in hand. "Thank you, Indie." She walks around the table and wraps her arms around me.

"Let's go to the living room and I can put it on the TV," Dom says, joining his mom and standing to lead us all to the oversized couch.

Dom's parents share the chaise at the end of the couch, his mom's head resting on his dad's shoulder. Daelyn takes the opposite side, her legs crossed as she scoots back into the corner. Dom pulls me down next to him in the middle of the couch so my legs are crossed over one of his muscular thighs. With everyone else settled, Dottie stands in the middle of the room, surveying her options. Ronnie circles the spot at Dom's feet before plopping down and that does it. Dottie skips over snuggling up to Ronnie and Dom.

With everyone seated, Dom starts the video. Even with the awkward angle of the camera and my nose scrunched as I set it up, you can see the happy glow in my cheeks.

"I always knew we'd be here," Dom says, coming up behind me.

I laugh. "You knew that you'd marry me in the courthouse?"

"No, I knew that it would be you, and I manifested the shit out of it." His face falls for a second and now he's thinking about how we got here.

Putting my back to the camera, I turn in his arms. "None of that exists today. This is about me and you."

He kisses me softly, his lips brushing over mine, once, twice, before a throat clears behind us. The justice of the peace waits with a patient smile on his face.

"Sorry, I think we are ready to start," I say, smoothing my hands down the white sundress I picked out for today.

"I've been ready for a year."

"You have not, stop it." I lightly smack him on the chest and he covers my hand, bringing it to his mouth and kissing my palm. He shrugs and leads me to the center of the room. Taking our place in front of justice of peace.

"Dom and Indie, you've come here today to join two souls in a beautiful union, to build a life together on a foundation of respect, loyalty, and commitment to each other. This ceremony is a symbol of that bond and the shared vision you have for your future. Do you have vows you would like to read to each other?"

"We do," Dom answers, clearing his throat. Fingers intertwined between us, he looks at me with so much reverence that tears well in the corner of my eyes before he's even said anything.

"Indie Jane, I've spent my entire life in awe of the love my parents shared. It's one of the few things in life that's evaded me. While other things have come easy, this tested my patience. The woman that lit up my soul wasn't ready for the future I saw for us. But like all things worth having, working for your attention, and eventually admiration, was time well invested. I stand here today a better man because of the partner I found in you."

He clears his throat before continuing.

"As your partner, I vow to nurture our bond, respect you above all else, and honor the path we walk together. Through the twists and turns life throws at us, I promise to be your compass through the unknown, offering you direction, or just a pat on the ass when the hill seems too steep to climb. I promise to be a stellar pool boy for years to come, and to pick up all the dog poop after the snow melts. To always stock cookie dough when it's shark week and build a life filled with fun and laughter, even when things get hard."

There's so much love in his honey eyes when he looks at me.

"With every breath I take from this day forward, I choose you: as my wife, my lover, and my hiking partner."

I'm not a crier, but there is no holding back the tears that spill over my lashes. Sniffling, I let them fall, focusing only on the man in front of me. The one my heart beats for.

"Dominic Duran."

"Um . . . you know that's not my name, right?"

"I think I know my soon to be husband's name." I wink at him.

"Dom, no one's ever understood me to the depths you do. Since the moment we met, you've had the ability to read me. It's impressive and terrifying, much like your tenacity. Standing here with you today I'm filled with immeasurable gratitude and joy, all because you refused to give up on us."

Emotion wells up inside me, making my voice crack as I start. "I welcome your vows and accept them into my heart. Embracing not only your promises *but every facet of who you are. Your optimism, loyalty, and kind heart won me over despite my best efforts to resist your charms. I vow to treasure the person you are now and always. The same way you do for me."*

Dom squeezes my hands reassuringly, and I continue.

"I can't tell you what the future holds, but there is no one else I'd rather face it with, bad jokes and all. Inevitably, there will be times where life isn't perfect, but with you as my husband and partner, it'll be as dynamic and extraordinary as you are."

His eyes are misty now as the Justice of Peace begins his part.

"Dom, as you place this ring on Indie's finger, may it be a symbol of your enduring commitment and a reminder of the love and partnership you share. Let this ring serve as a daily affirmation of the promises you have made to each other, and may it be a constant reminder of the bond you are creating today."

He repeats the same sentiment when it's my turn to slide the simple golden band onto Dom's finger. On the other side of her son, Kelly sniffles. When the Justice of Peace announces us as husband and wife and our kiss plays back, I join Kelly, my own tears landing on Dom's shirt.

Damn, hormones.

"Thank you for sharing that with us," Kelly says, pulling both Dom and I into a hug when we stand to finish breakfast. "It was a beautiful ceremony."

After we finish eating, the girls take Ronnie for a walk as I get to know my new in-laws. It's surreal. The morning flies by and before we know what's happening, it's time to say goodbye so they can catch their flight home.

CHAPTER 43

DOM

"Slugger," Montana calls out, holding his hand up for a high-five.

He's not the only one that thinks he's funny. Braxton Hayes puts his fists up and pretends to dodge punches as I pass. The team plane is a minefield of questions and snarky remarks from my teammates as I walk down the aisle to find my seat.

Once I make it past the rookies, who are relegated to the front where management and the coaching staff sit, the chatter dies down. The middle of the plane is much more subdued, maybe even a little peeved. I haven't seen the guys since after the game and our texts have been limited as I waited to learn my fate, spent time with my family, and met with Indie's surgical team.

My best friend stands, holding out his hand for a hand for fist bump. "I'm glad you're here even if you can't play in the first game. Now sit down and tell us what the fuck is going on."

"Such a warm welcome. How could I not?" I'm forty percent joking. Coming from Dean, it's practically a love poem.

Indie told me I could fill the guys in as long as they let her tell the girls, which she's doing today. I rub the gold ring on my finger. Across from me, Xavier's eyes drop, tracking the movement. Catchers don't miss a thing.

"You're really fucking married?" He laughs, like he can't wrap his head around it.

"Yep."

"Congratulations," Cruz says, earnestly holding out his hand for me to shake.

"Thanks. Listen, I know you guys have questions. You're all basically foaming at the mouth for the gossip and while I applaud you for keeping it together for this long, you need to keep this to yourself at least until after the game tonight when Indie has a chance to talk to the girls."

"Oh shit, I was mostly kidding about you knocking her up," Hendrix says.

My jaw clicks with irritation. I've probably done the same thing a hundred times, but until you're the one going through something like this, you don't realize the impact those kinds of comments can have.

"Or not," he adds carefully.

"Not pregnant." I push my hair back from where it's fallen over my forehead. "A couple weeks ago, Indie had genetic testing done. The results weren't great. She carries an inherited gene that makes it much more likely for her to develop cancer, like her mom."

"Fuck," Dean draws the word out.

"Yeah. That pretty much sums it up," I tell him, before I go over what the testing meant for us and everything we are facing, to make sure that Indie has the best chance at a long, healthy life.

"She's gone through a lot in the past two weeks. Learning that she could have to battle like her mom did was hard enough, but the treatments and surgeries, that shit is expensive as hell. I couldn't stand by and watch more of her dreams be taken away. I already knew she was it for me, so I offered to help the best way I knew how."

"By marrying her?" Hendrix asks, sounding a little more doubtful than I'd like.

"It wasn't like that. I mean, okay, it kind of was when I first came up with the idea. But it's so much more than that. She needed the insurance. And yes, marrying me helped with that, but I was already head over heels for her. This just accelerated that timeline."

"Not to be a dick, man, but does she feel the same way?" Xavier asks.

"Dude." Cruz kicks his shin making him flinch.

"I just want to make sure he's not going to get his heart broken."

"She was a half step behind me when I suggested it. But she's right there with me now. Indie's not great at accepting help. She never would have married me just for the insurance. Her stubborn ass would have gone out and gotten another job with insurance to try to cover it while she continued trying to build up her portfolio of freelance work."

"You obviously know your wife better than I do." Dean smirks, and he's lucky I'm required to be a boy scout right now or I might put him in a headlock for that. "But Mia said something similar after the game. That whatever happened, Indie needed to be all in or she would never have gone through with it."

"She might be reckless in a lot of ways, but never with her feelings for you. She fought those hard," Cruz contributes thoughtfully.

"Is she going to be okay?" Hendrix asks, his eyes filled with a genuine concern.

"I really fucking hope so, because I can't lose her." My voice breaks and I fight to keep my composure. "My wife is tough as hell, but we're doing everything in our power to make sure I can annoy the crap out of her until she's old and gray."

CHAPTER 44

INDIE

There's a gentle breeze in the air, a telltale sign that fall is coming, but my palms are clammy as I walk up the path to meet the girls at Mia's. I'd love to blame hot flashes, but I'm not deluded enough to pretend it's not also about the fact that I feel like I'm walking into a firing squad. A very friendly firing squad whose ammo is just a boatload of questions.

I wipe my palms on my jeans, unsure if I want to be the first one here or the last. Or I could turn around and run, except it would have to be a fast walk and they'd definitely catch me, *stupid restrictions*.

Nope, there is no other choice but to woman up and face them. It's time. In our group chat earlier, Mia told everyone just to let themselves in. So I do just that, walking through the kitchen and following the sound of voices to the back patio.

I'm the last one here, and there are four sets of eyes on me as I join them at the outdoor table where Poppy, Mia, Willa, and Lilah wait. I take the open spot between Mia and Poppy, leaving Willa and Lilah on the other side of the table.

"Hey," I offer in greeting as I pull my chair forward, wincing when it scraps loudly.

Poppy's hand covers mine, flipping it over in hers and rubbing a thumb over the simple gold band. "You got married and didn't tell me." She tries to hide it, but there's a hint of pain in her words.

"I never imagined it would happen like this, or quite so fast," I tell her, covering her hand with my other one and squeezing. "There's a lot I need to tell you, and I'm sorry if any of it hurts you. That was never my plan. A lot happened all at once and I needed some time to come to terms with it." I laugh weakly, realizing I sound like a broken record.

When I look around the table, everyone is waiting for me. Maybe I was wrong about the firing squad. Mia's brows are pinched as she studies me with concern. She's always been the most observant of the group.

I shift in my chair so I'm looking at Poppy for this part. It's going to hit her the hardest. "I had the genetic test done."

Her face pales, and her eyes go wide. "When?"

My throat is dry when I try to answer her and I have to swallow to get the words out. "Two and a half weeks ago. The results came back positive."

Her head drops to where our hands are still joined and her back heaves. I watch my best friend struggle not to fall apart and my heart splinters. This is why I didn't want to tell her. My mom's illness impacted her almost as much as it did my dad and I. She was more of a mother to Poppy than her own was. I wanted to protect her from this as long as I could, the same way she tried to do when Jensen broke me.

"It's going to be okay. I've already met with my doctors. Dom helped me make a plan. We're going to be okay." My hand rubs circles over her back and she slowly lifts her head.

If she's still hurt that I kept things from her, she doesn't show it. "Tell me the plan," she says, sounding stronger. More like the friend that kept me from withering away to nothing when my mom was dying.

When your world comes crashing down around you, time does this funny thing where it seems to stand still. It's like you're trudging through it in slow motion and the world passes by at light speed. I think back to that day two and a half weeks ago when a simple blood draw upended everything and that's where I start.

"Dom was with me for the blood draw, and every step of the way since. He put baseball aside to be there when I needed him, not caring if he got in trouble. No one I've dated has ever given that much of themselves to me."

"The game he missed," Lilah remarks, putting the pieces together.

"That was the day I got the results back. I was useless. There's no way I would have retained any information or made it through that appointment without him there."

"I'm glad he was there for you," Poppy says, wiping the tears from her cheeks.

"Once the initial shock of it waned, I knew I wanted surgery. I want the chance my mom never had; the future Dom and I have planned out. I want it all; every fucking second that I have, and I want it with him."

"Do you have surgery scheduled?" Willa asks, chiming in for the first time.

I shake my head. "That future I mentioned includes having kids with the man I love." Poppy's grip on my hand tightens. "Slow your roll, babe. I'm freezing my eggs, not getting pregnant. Don't you think a new husband is enough adventure for one week? Once we get through the retrieval, I'll know the timeline for surgery."

"I hate to ask, but this marriage came out of nowhere. Are you worried at all that you are letting the emotions of all this cloud your judgment?" From what I know of Willa, she's practical and to the point, so I'm not surprised that she's the first to ask the question I'm sure has crossed everyone's mind.

"No." Everyone but Lilah seems equally shocked by the sureness in my answer.

"How'd it happen?" Poppy asks, tilting her head to the side.

"When we found out, he went straight into business mode. We had so much to figure out and once I started processing all of it, I realized I was going to have to get a job with insurance. He wouldn't hear it."

"He could have just helped cover the costs," Willa points out.

"He could have, but it wasn't just about the money or insurance." I rub my temples trying to figure out how to explain that the man I wrote off as a mistake ended up saving me more than once. "The past two months have been the hardest of my life; barring my mom being sick. Except for one thing—*Dom.* When I gave in to him for a second time it didn't take me long to realize that by forcing myself to avoid how he made me feel was only hurting both of us. Turns out he's everything I needed and what I wanted."

"So he just proposed?" Mia asks.

I tilt my head to the side thinking about that day. For the first time since I got here, everyone stops with the questions and listens while I recount how the non-proposal-proposal happened.

Exhaustion is etched in the lines of Dom's handsome face, in the set of his dark eyes and the slump of his shoulders. His golden brown strands are a mess because he's been tugging at his hair for hours as we sit side by side at his kitchen table researching fertility clinics, the best surgeons, insurance, trying to line up his calendar with my cycle, everything. The one thing we haven't talked about, that's at the front of my mind, is how I'm going to do this without giving up my dreams.

One thing that is clear, this is going to be expensive without insurance coverage. I almost broke at the stress in his voice when the topic of medical proxy came up.

"Hey. Are you okay?"

He's been checking on me all day, staying strong while I fall apart, but right now he's quickly fraying and I can't blame him. It's a lot; more than he should have to deal with, but I don't dare tell him that.

Dom pushes his chair back and takes my hands. "No, I'm not. I'm trying really fucking hard to be, but I'm not." His voice trembles as he voices his truth. "And I need to say something. You're probably not going to like it. You're going to think I'm nuts, but I can't get it out of my head."

"I already think you're nuts." I try for a joke, but the spirit just isn't there.

"Marry me."

That's it, two words that change everything. I blink back at him, stunned, wondering if I misheard him.

"What?" I choke out.

"Everyone will think we're crazy, but I don't care. I've been calling you my future wife behind your back for a year. Let me take care of you. Give me the peace of mind of knowing no matter what, I'll be able to support you in every way."

"You're right. That is crazy." So why does my heart skip at the idea? "You shouldn't do this because you're scared."

"Baby, scared doesn't begin to cover it. I'm fucking terrified. But that doesn't change the fact that this is what I want. The thought of you getting sick—" The fear in voice tears at my heart. "You are what I want. Life is short as it is. I want every moment I get with you, and I don't want to wait just because people might question our decision. Think about it. What do you want out of this life? Tell me I'm not there when you picture yourself and a year from now, five years from now, ten? If it's not me there with you, I'll drop it and just cover all the costs."

It makes so much sense when he says it that way. I bite my lip, weighing the pros and cons in my mind, picturing my future. Every single image I conjure he's front and center, right there with me.

"Let me help you keep your dreams alive while we face this together," he says, again.

"Okay." The fear that should be there given the circumstances is missing— gone for the moment. And I know it's because I've fallen hard for this man. Even though I fought it with everything in me, he owns my heart.

When I'm done, they all stare at me, blinking back tears of their own. "Now, are any of you comfortable with needles? Because I'm going to need some help, I don't think I can give myself the shots I need later."

Pinks and orange paint sky, the sun dipping below the horizon when we move inside to watch the game. There's no way I can administer the medications I need myself, but it feels like an invasion having anyone but my husband do it after everything we've shared the last few weeks.

Still, I let Lilah hold my hand while Poppy gives me the shots. Mia and Willa do their best to distract me with commentary about the game. The Bandits are losing terribly to Atlanta.

Frustration twists my husband's normally cheerful face into a grimace as he sits on the bench, dressed in team warmups instead of his uniform, his legs crossed at the ankles, and his arms folded over his chest.

Normally I'd be gawking over the way his biceps strain against the dark material of his sweatshirt, but all I can focus on is how miserable he looks. The game ends in a Bandits loss and all I want to do is teleport home so I can video chat with my husband. To make sure he's okay the same way he always does for me.

Ronnie's waiting for me, paws clicking against the wood floor as she dances around my feet excitedly. "I know, girl," I tell her, dropping to my knee to scratch behind her ear. "Let's get you outside so I can talk to your dad."

The breeze blowing in from the mountains swirls my curls around my face and I push them back, watching and laughing into the darkness as Ronnie does sprints back and forth across the yard before she slows, circling her favorite spot and doing her business.

Like her dad, she's been all over me for the last two weeks, like she can sense I need her more now. I don't need to look behind me as I climb the stairs to know she's on my heels. It's where she always is now, her cold, wet nose brushing against my calf, so I don't forget she's there if I need her.

Even when I silently undress in the bathroom, the tub filling with hot water, my phone waiting for Dom to call, she's laying in the doorway with her head on her paws watching me. "You're the sweetest voyeur ever." I chuckle at my own joke as I slip below the surface of the water.

Water clings to the ends of my hairs as I let the warmth sink in, soaking away the constant sting around my belly button from the daily shots.

Only seven more. Every day is a countdown to the egg retrieval.

My phone rattles against the tile as it rings with the call I've been waiting for. I answer on FaceTime, careful to angle the phone so it doesn't reveal too much in case he's not alone.

"Fuck, Baby, I miss you." My husband sighs. "Do you always answer your phone naked, or was that just for me?"

"Only ever for you," I answer, distracted. One of those biceps I noticed earlier flexes as he leans back against his headboard tucking his arm under his head. This time I can't tear my eyes away because my husband is shirtless and the serious look on his face makes this water feel like it's boiling.

He looks like I felt all those times when I was about to implode and I came to him for help, for distraction, for him. Because whether or not I realized it, the force that pulls us together was always at play. We never had a choice in the matter. The game of cat and mouse we played for the last year was always going to end with us together.

"Right answer." His voice is rough and my blood heats at the way he looks at me, his eyes dark. I reach out, turning the water to cool, and cup some in my hand to run over my chest and neck.

CHAPTER 45

DOM

"That was a rough game. Are you okay?" she asks, or at least I think that's what she says. I'm solely focused on the rivulets of water dripping down her neck, following the same path my tongue takes to get to her sensitive breasts.

"Mhmm." Not my most intelligent answer, but can you really blame me? I'm completely dumbstruck by how gorgeous my wife looks, dark curls loose and skimming the water.

It only gets worse when she props the phone up, taking the hair tie from her wrist and tying her dark curls up on top of her head, making the round swell of her breast rise and flashing me a sliver of her nipples. That muted mocha has become my favorite color.

Warm laughter from her end of the call instantly lifts my spirit as I run my palm over my jaw. "See something you like?"

"I like the look of you relaxed in our house." Technically she hasn't moved in, not for a lack of wanting to, we just haven't had the time to get her stuff moved from her apartment. That hasn't stopped her from hauling a suitcase over and staying every night for the past week.

"This bathtub is the eighth wonder of the world. It's almost like you built this house with your future wife in mind," she jokes.

"I've always known what I wanted. Well, before I met you, I knew that once I had a love like what my parents have, I'd settle down. So yeah, I guess I did."

"You're one of the good ones, husband."

Right now I'm not feeling like it. Watching from the bench as my team got demolished, knowing I could be out there helping was brutal. I still can't bring myself to regret punching Jensen, and that will never change, but I'm tense as hell.

"How'd it go with the girls tonight?"

"Fine." Her shoulders drop below the water, sagging in defeat. "Poppy was hurt. She didn't say as much, but I could see it in her eyes. I just needed some time to process, and I think she understands now."

Every cell in my body aches to be there with her. I want to wrap my arm around her and take away her stress. "Sounds like neither of us had the best nights, but seeing you, hearing your voice, makes it all worth it."

"You know what might make it a little better?" She traps her lip between her teeth and my cock knows that look. It's all it takes for him to go from semi to fully erect. That's how it's always been with us. Everything is just more. The heat between us burns hotter. The ability to annoy each other is unparalleled, and our love is a force to be reckoned with.

"Tell me what you need."

It's her way of taking care of me. For all the times I've distracted her, used how well we work together to help her when she needs to get out of her head, my wife is doing the same for me now.

It's a flip on our normal dynamic. We work together, both of us know when to switch from teasing to sweet, and I've never questioned that. I'm man enough to admit that right now I need this, her taking care of me. Helping me forget about riding the bench today and worse, not being there physically when she needs me the most.

CHAPTER 46

INDIE

Gravity pulls me to my stomach and I groan in pain from the new position. It takes me a minute in the dark to figure out that a dip in the bed is the reason for my discomfort.

"Shhh." The warm body beside me soothes. Even barely conscious, I sag into him, clinging to his hard body after five days without him. "What's wrong, Baby? Is the trigger shot making you uncomfortable?" His voice is hushed, like he's trying not to wake me more than he already has.

"Yeah," I grumble softly, curling around him, desperate to find a comfortable position. The heaviness in my stomach has had me tossing and turning since I laid down in our empty bed.

Our bed. I'm still not used to that.

"The shot wasn't terrible, or maybe I'm just used to it, but the fullness is . . . awful. I hate it Dom," I groan, allowing him to see the rawness of it all.

He kisses my head, and I sigh into his chest. Not feeling any better, but having him home from the series in Atlanta making this suck-fest easier to stomach. We have barely seventy-two hours before he has to board another plane and head to Chicago for their next stop on the road to hopefully win a world series.

While the rest of the team flew straight from Atlanta to Chicago, he chartered a flight home just to be here for my egg retrieval procedure tomorrow. Or is it this morning? "What time is it?"

"Three, go back to sleep. You need your rest for tomorrow."

It's a short procedure, barely fifteen minutes, but he was adamant he would be there when he found out that they would put me under.

His big palm covers my back, rubbing slow circles on it until I drift off in his arms.

Hours later, I wake the same way, only this time the sun is streaming through the blinds and creating shadows on the most handsome face I've ever seen. His chest rises and falls in a steady rhythm as I watch him sleep, knowing he has to be as exhausted as me from his games and the cross-country flight to be here this morning.

"I can feel you watching me." The scratchy voice hits me right in the heart and his grip on me tightens. "Is it time to leave for the clinic? Did I sleep through my alarm?"

"No, the sun woke me up and now I'm just watching you like a creep. Past me would hardly believe it."

"Past me always knew this is how we'd end up." His warm breath fans across my head as he huffs out a laugh. "Not you being a creep, but us together."

"I knew what you meant."

His chest vibrates against me as he continues to chuckle over his own joke.

"You're ridiculous," I tell him, a smile tilting up my lips despite still feeling miserable.

"You married me." Is his sleepy response.

"That I did."

He watches me through lidded eyes and asks, "Are you feeling any better?"

"Not even a little," I admit, looking down at my bloated stomach.

"Since you can't eat, do you want to go for a walk before we leave? Maybe moving will help."

Moving doesn't help, it doesn't hurt either. But nothing I do eases the discomfort. Thankfully, the procedure itself isn't bad. I'm in and out within an hour of arriving and the Gatorade they give me afterward is life changing. Unfortunately, that bloating has turned to cramping and even just getting to the car from the clinic is a struggle.

Poppy would have gladly helped me today, but having Dom here is a relief. The after-effects are worse than I imagined.

"Take it easy, Baby," Dom says, as he helps me into bed when we get home.

"Will you lay with me?" I ask. "You can put on a movie or something," I add nervously.

The moment he crawls into bed with me and presses his forehead to mine the minty scent of his toothpaste takes hold and I know it was silly to be worried. This man has put aside his life for me time and time again over the past three months to make sure I'm taken care of. Laying with me while I recover from a procedure isn't going to faze him.

"You couldn't keep me away if you tried," he says, crawling in behind with the utmost care not to disturb me.

The next twelve hours are rough, but things improve when I wake up two days later feeling human for the first time since he got home. It only gets better when the clinic calls to let me know we have ten mature eggs. It's a great number, but we will still need another round if we want any chance of having more than one child using my eggs in the future.

It's a problem for another day because Dom and I only have a few hours before he leaves again for Chicago. The plan is for me to join him for the second or third game of the series, depending on how I'm feeling.

CHAPTER 47

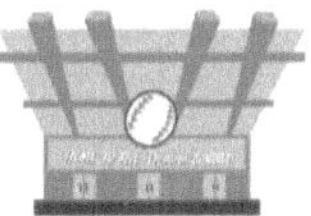

DOM

"Since coming back from his one-game suspension at the beginning of the postseason Dom Duran has helped his team battle back to end up here in Chicago tonight for the League Championship Series. Demi is on the field with him to hear firsthand what he thinks about tonight's match-up."

Demi Wilder from ESPN stands in front of me, a megawatt smile on her face, as the crew passes it down to her for the pre-game interview.

"Tell us what we have to look forward to tonight, Dom."

"Hey, Demi. We're thrilled to still be playing and I'm ready to make some contributions out there to help my team take this season as far as we can. The guys are pumped and win or lose, it's a great night for baseball."

Tonight, I have an even greater incentive to play my ass off. My wife made the trip. Not only that, but after the game this afternoon we're getting dinner with my father-in-law.

"We're eager to see what the Bandits can do with their first playoff run in the last decade. With the series tied at three wins each, it's sure to be an exciting game," Demi says, before switching off her microphone. "Good luck out there tonight. I'm rooting for you guys. My dad grew up in Denver and even though I wasn't raised there, I'm a long-time fan."

I glance over my shoulder to find my wife sitting with her dad behind our dugout. "That father-daughter bond is really something." Her eyes track my stare.

"Mhmm. Nothing like it. Enjoy the game tonight, Dom. Looks like you have some big fans here," Demi comments before crossing the field to speak with the Chicago players.

Jogging over to the netting that runs along the third baseline, I crook my finger at Indie, calling her to me. She skips down the stairs, an uncertain look on her face.

"What's going on?" Her brow furrows adorably when she stops in front of me.

"Can't a guy just want a good luck kiss from his wife?" Hooking my fingers through the netting I snag her jersey, the one with our last name on it and drag her to me, our lips connecting in one of the small squares. "There, now everyone here knows you're mine," I say, a little roughly from how she affects me.

"Go win your game." She chuckles against my lips and I feel the vibration of that little laugh everywhere because it's light and airy—happy. Which has been rare since Indie came back into my life.

"Are you my prize?" I tease, keeping her close as fans fill in the seats around her.

"Sure, hit me a home run and you can have me anyway you want me tonight." It's a whispered promise just for us.

"Coming right up." I step back and hit her with a wink.

We didn't win the game, but the home run I hit in the top of the eighth helps to soothe that sting. But what helps even more is the look on my wife's face as we sit across the table from her dad after sharing a meal in a Downtown Chicago pizzeria as he watches the video from our wedding. Both their eyes are brimming with unshed tears.

"I love you," I say quietly brushing my lips over her temple.

"Thank you for everything you've done for my daughter," Samuel says, looking up from the phone.

"No need to thank me. Getting a second chance with your daughter was the greatest gift of my life. I've never had to work as hard for anything, but I'd do it all again in a heartbeat, because she's always been it for me."

"Either way, I'm proud to call you my son-in-law. Not just anyone could've gotten Indie to accept help the way you did."

"You two know I'm right here," Indie huffs.

"You'd never let us forget," her dad teases, reaching across the table to squeeze her hand.

"Don't you have a curfew?" My father-in-law glances down at the watch on his wrist and gives me a knowing smirk. "You better get going if you want to make it back in time."

Indie pouts, and it's so fucking cute it hurts. My wild card of a wife hardly ever pouts, not even when I was giving her shots or she was rocking that boot after hurting her ankle. "I'll come by the house tomorrow morning for a little while before the game. We can go see Mom together." She meets him halfway around the table, letting him wrap her up in a bear hug.

Following behind her I clap Samuel on the back, pulling him into a hug as if this is the first time we are meeting. It's not, but my wife doesn't know that. At my request, my father-in-law met me for breakfast this morning so that I could fix something that's been bothering me for the last three weeks.

"Text me when you're home safe," Indie says, making her dad scoff.

"Isn't that my line?"

"Yeah, well, I've got this one to walk me the two blocks back to our hotel. You, on the other hand, have to drive an hour home alone. So let me fret, old man." His response is a grumbled reply I don't quite catch, but I'm almost certain it's lamenting how he ended up with such a sassy daughter.

There's another round of hugs before we go our separate ways. Indie's arm is looped through mine as we walk down the sidewalk, heading back towards our hotel.

Confidence is never something I've lacked, yet an inexplicable wave of anxiety washes over me as we approach the park near the hotel. It's the perfect place for what I have planned.

"Let's walk through the park." Pulling Indie along with me, I have to focus on the effort not to walk too fast and blow this whole thing, ruining all the planning it took to make this perfect for my wife. The wife I know loves me, I silently reassure myself as we get closer to the spot I picked out.

"Look, there's a little trail there," Indie says, pointing to the opening in the trees just like I knew she would.

I stop us in the middle of the path, pulling her into my arms so that we're face to face. "Want to go on an adventure with me?"

"Always." The simple response comes without an ounce of hesitation and tamps down my nerves.

It's a short walk to the small clearing. In the center of the open space, there's a deserted pond and a wooden dock for fishing. With the sun dipping low in the sky, it casts her in the most stunning glow. Other than the swan couple on the pond, it's just the two of us, and it feels poetic, because for the last three months it's been us against the world.

Taking both her hands in mind I drop to one knee, only slightly concerned that I might end up with bird shit on my knee. But even knowing that risk, it's worth it.

"Indie Jane, we may already be married, but you and I have never done much according to convention. But I want to fix that because I want it all with you, without skipping any of the steps. Baby, you're the best thing that's ever happened to me and I couldn't go one more day without seeing this ring on your finger, where it belongs, right next to the one from our wedding."

I release Indie's right hand and fish out the tattered velvet box her dad passed on to me this morning with tears in his eyes. This ring means more to Indie than anything I could buy her on Michigan Ave.

Tears are streaming down her face when I open the box and she drops to her knees in front of me. With the box in hand, I cup her cheeks, wiping away the salty tears the best I can. "I love you, Indie, now and always. You didn't get the proposal you deserved, one worthy of our love, and I'm sorry for that. I hope this makes up for that, but just in case it doesn't, I promise to tell you every day all the reasons I choose you as my wife."

She nods through her tears and I take her hand between us, slipping her mom's ring on her finger. "Perfect."

"I love you, Dom Duran. I would marry you all over again every day for the rest of my life, with or without a proposal. But this ring, carrying my mom with me all the time as a symbol of our love, is more than I could have ever asked for. Thank you."

Our lips meet and I lose track of everything but the feeling of her in my arms. We cling to this moment, to each other, to our future. Each caress of her lips against mine feels like that first kiss, filled with a lifetime of possibility.

After everything we've been through in the short time since we got together this summer, you'd think it would make us jaded about life, but it hasn't. Now Indie runs to me instead of running scared. She helps keep me grounded and I like to think I make the hard stuff a little easier on her.

When we break apart, the sun is below the tree line and I'm cutting it close to the very curfew her father mentioned and even if I wasn't, my wife is still wearing our last name on her back, my rings on her finger and I want nothing more than to get her alone.

Is pairs speed walking an Olympic sport? Because I think we might have just earned a gold medal. Not even five minutes after leaving the park, I have Indie pressed against the cool metal wall of the elevator.

My mouth works down the column of her throat, devouring her like a starved man. Let me say, on record, that I'm not complaining, but I haven't been able to properly fuck my wife since we've been married. And right now, with her in my jersey after re-proposing, my dick is about to rip through my pants to get to her. Couple that with the incentive she gave me if I hit a home run and I'm a fucking goner.

With each ding of the elevator climbing a floor, it gets harder not to hit that red button and slide inside her, here and now. That last chime echoes like a bullet going off and I lift her by her waist, her legs winding around me as we make our way to our room. Her hands are in my hair and her lips find my neck.

Fumbling my key over the sensor it slips from my hand but by some miracle the light turns green. I push through the door, kicking the key inside and letting the door slam shut.

There's a thud as Indie's back hits the wall but my wife just groans when I press her against the wall with my pelvis. "I've been thinking about all the different ways you could have me tonight since that homer hours ago."

"That must have made for a very long night. Especially since I still haven't decided how I want you." I pop the button on her jeans, dragging the zipper down slowly as I kiss her neck. Lowering her to the floor I peel the jeans down her long legs as she helpfully toes off her white sneakers.

Taking my time I slide my hands back up her legs, stopping where her jersey meets the tops of her thighs. I pinch the fabric of her jersey between my fingers. "Undo the buttons for me, but leave it on while I decide how I want to fuck you." My voice is gruff and demanding, in complete opposition to how I sit at her feet.

Her eyes fall to the buttons as she works them free, one by one. Each one that comes undone is the most exquisite form of torture and with my hands still on the backs of her legs, I can tell it has the same effect on her. Goosebumps blossom across her stomach and heat radiates off her as undoes the last one.

"Fuck, Baby, you're stunning." Brushing my thumbs over her hip bones, I split the jersey. All the bruising has faded, the shots, the appointments, the procedure is nothing more than a memory. With her in nothing more than a few scraps of dark teal lace, it's easy to forget that she still has another round of stimulation and retrieval before her upcoming surgery. "It almost seems a shame to bend you over this desk and take you from behind."

There's a sharp intake of breath that makes her stomach cave in as I kiss a path up her torso, coming to my full height in front of her. Dark curls fan out, tickling my chin as I spin her around in my arms and walk towards the desk. My hands don't leave her body, finding the swell of her breast and the curve of her hip. Neither does my nipping at the crook of her neck and dragging a soft moan out of her on the way.

Both of us are breathing hard, panting from how badly we need this. I thread my fingers through hers and place them palm down on the desk. "Stay like that while I look at my wife and decide if this is how I want her."

Glazed over brown eyes find me over her shoulder as I step back. Ignoring the pull to be close to her, I run my hand over my jaw and I take her in. Dark curls stick out in all directions, swollen red lips from kissing on the ride up here, those five letters sewn on her back, but the thing I can't tear my eyes from is that ring on her finger. The one that should have been there from day one.

My wife is wild, a force of nature, and she looks it right now, her legs spread and her hands on the desk as she waits for me to decide how to fuck her. "Is this how you want me?" It's a dare, a test of my willpower.

"Hard to say." I step in close again, my hands going to her waist, and my fingers dipping under the teal lace riding high on her hips. "I think I need a closer look. Take these off and sit on the desk for me."

Desire slashes through me when she presses her hips back, the globes of her ass brushing over the hard length of me as she shimmies out of her undies. She reaches back, sliding them in my pocket and spins so she's facing me.

Climbing on to the desk, she bats her eyelashes and asks, "Like this?" This woman is toying with me, sitting on the desk, naked from the waist down, her knees pressed together. So much has changed since we met, but this hasn't. And hope it never does, she still loves to give me a hard time every chance she gets.

"Spread your legs, wife. Show me how wet you are waiting for my cock."

Not one to back down, Indie pins her plump lip between her teeth and smooths both hands down her thighs, stopping when she gets to her knees and parting her legs for me. Keeping those big brown eyes glued to me the whole damn time.

Without missing a beat she covers her pussy with her hand blocking my view and slips a finger inside her heat. Her breath shudders as she pumps it in and out a few times her eyes roll back. One of us whimpers at the suctioning sound it makes when she pulls it away and I couldn't even tell you who made the desperate noise.

My fingers circle her wrist, holding her hand captive and lowering my head to suck the slick digit into my mouth. This time I'm certain it's me that makes the appreciative sound. How could it not be? I've spent more time on my knees for this woman. She's the prayer on my lips each night, the cause I fight for, my whole damn universe. And she tastes like heaven on my tongue.

"This is a start. Maybe I'll camp out here between your legs for a while, getting my fill and then take you on the bed, that perfect ass up in the air, before I strip you bare and make love to you the way I've been dying to since the moment you said I do."

"Less talking, more doing." She sucks on her cheek, her eyes lit with the thrill of this game we play with each other.

"Would you like a hand necklace to go with that mouth? Or maybe I'll stuff your mouth full of my fingers so you can't interrupt my meal."

"If that's meant to be a threat, it's not working." Opening her legs up wider, she leans back, nodding toward the floor. "Unless you're waiting for me to leave a puddle on this desk, so the hotel staff knows exactly what we got up to."

"Fuck me," I say, once again I find myself on my knees for my wife. With one hand between her legs, the other wraps around the slender column of her neck and holds her like that, zeroing in on the spot that makes her clamp down on my fingers.

"Oh god, Dom," she whimpers, her hand covering mine, holding it there as her pulse pounds under my grip. "I need you," she pants, her body shaking now like she's trying to hold out.

With one last long languid lick, I remove my fingers from her hot center and lift her from the desk carrying her to the bed. "Ass up. Show me how badly that pussy wants to be filled." I make a show of slowly undressing as she gets into position, her face turned to the side so she can watch.

It's obscene, wild curls sticking to her face, my jersey riding up her back, swollen sex on display for me. And she's just as affected as I am, her chest heaves with the effort to keep it together just waiting to be filled.

"Please." It's a plea that I can't ignore. Fisting my cock, my knees hit the end of the bed. Her back arches that whimpered cry, turning into a feral moan when I run my knuckles over her dripping seam.

"Please what?" I ask, my fingers kneading the flesh of her ass.

When she doesn't tell me what she needs, my hand comes down on her cheek, spurring her to cry out, "Fuck me."

"Was that a request or a reaction?"

"Both," she whines, pressing into the palm of my hand as it smooths over the red mark.

"Good, because I need to be inside you."

"Condom." She reminds me when my crown brushes over her center. There's a flash of sadness in her eyes.

"It's keeping you safe. So you can be old and wrinkly with me," I whisper, pushing the hair off her shoulder, where her jersey is sliding down her arm, and kiss the tattoo that wraps over it.

"Just hurry," is her unsteady reply as I rush to grab the foil packet from my duffle bag.

Once I'm covered, my hand wraps around her hip and I sink inside her, groaning at the feel of her hugging my cock. "So good. So perfect. Fuck, I missed this."

"Yes. Give me every inch of you."

That's not a request I plan to deny. "Baby, I'm going to need you to help me get you there so I can flip you over and make love to you."

"Teamwork makes the dream w-work." The joke is muffled by the way her face is pressed to the mattress as her fingertips brush against where we are rooted together. With her hand working between her legs, it only takes a few deep thrusts before the telltale sign of her release starts. Red lips part on a moan and her legs tremble, struggling to hold her position.

When I've rung every drop of pleasure from her, I pull out, easing her on to her back and peeling the jersey off her sticky body.

"You're too far away." Grabby hands reach out for me as I toss her jersey to the side.

"I want to see you wearing nothing but my ring. Take the bra off," I tell her, pushing the strap down her shoulder.

Her fingers work the clasp, and her breasts spill free, giving me exactly what I wanted. Her palms flatten against the white sheets and she pushes herself up to sitting. "I think I've let you be bossy for long enough. Come sit against the headboard and hold me while I make love to my husband."

Just like that, she flips our dynamic and I'm crawling up the bed to her. Which tracks because I'd crawl over broken glass for this woman. Although I'd much prefer our current situation with her naked nipples pebbled, ready to straddle my lap and ride me while I tell her how much I love her. "Never going to say no to that."

Finding her hips, my hands coast over them, wrapping around her to hold her close, like she asked, while she sinks down on my length.

"Always so perfect," Indie sputters as she stretches around me, taking me slowly.

With each shallow thrust, she takes more of me and her perky tits bounce in my face, taunting me. Drawing closer I pull one peeked tip in my mouth, sucking. That only makes Indie throw her head back, arching into me, pressing closer.

Releasing her from my mouth, I kiss across her chest to the other side, my lips pressing against her wildly beating heart. "You own every piece of me. I love you, Indie."

Her arms that are braced on my shoulders move so her fingers are in my hair, angling my head up so I'm looking into her adoring eyes. "And my heart only beats for you."

To most people, our marriage probably seems rushed, but I've been waiting to hear those words from this woman for the last year. And there was a time when I didn't think she would ever say them, when I thought her fear would win. Every time she says them I cherish them, the same way I cherish what we have, a love like I always wanted, but uniquely ours. One that will stand the test of time because we balance each other out. There's a mutual trust between us because we both understand what the other needs. Most importantly, we would both burn down the world for each other.

She rides me slowly and her brown eyes disappear behind dark lashes as her lids flutter shut. "Need more."

"Your wish is my command." I bend my knees behind her, urging her closer as I grip her waist and thrust up into her, bringing her down hard. Each punch of my hips drives her higher.

Pain bites into my scalp as she tugs at my hair and seals her lips over mine, kissing me with the same urgency of my frantic rhythm. Her body goes stiff in my arms, every muscle straining when her release comes. I give up my fight, letting go when she collapses against me, both of us covered in a sheen of sweat.

CHAPTER 48

INDIE

Hot sand burns my bare feet, the tiny grains slipping under my toes as I tiptoe down the beach. The sun and sand have nothing on my scorching hot husband. Miles of carved muscles and tanned skin are wrapped in tight spandex the color of the ocean. It only makes me more grateful for our quickie wedding because this man is a catch and he's without a doubt mine.

Thank god he booked us a house with a private beach because I've grown very attached and I'm not interested in sharing him with anyone else this week. After the Bandits got knocked out of the postseason, another round of hormones and a second successful egg retrieval procedure, we deserve this break just the two of us before my surgery later this month.

Even with what's looming ahead of us, I've never been happier, freer, or more at peace. And it has everything to do with the ridiculous man snoozing on a Ronnie print towel next to me. He helped me let go of my past and made me stop running from my fear. It's the greatest gift anyone has ever given me, a future worth fighting for.

"Wake up, sleepy head," I whisper, rolling the ice cold bottle of water over his shoulders. "Your wife is ready for an adventure and she'd hate to go without you."

"Mhmm. I'm supposed to be relaxing. It's the off season."

"One little bike ride won't hurt you," I say, joining him on his towel when he rolls to the side.

"How about I just take you back to bed and worship this body instead?" His fingers glide under the string of my bikini tracing the curve of my hip.

"Tempting, but we have plenty of time for that and only a short window with bike rentals. Now, let's go."

"You're right. I can't have you facing off against those flying squirrels yourself. I know all about the trouble you like to get into on your own."

"I'm never going to live that down, am I?"

"Baby, you parked your bike in a tree and blamed your sprained ankle on one of the forest's most innocent creatures. What do you think?"

"Innocent my ass," I huff.

Standing and tossing the towel over his shoulder, pulls me with him, his hands slipping under the white bikini he gifted me, palming my ass right under where "Mrs. Duran" is embroidered. He lifts me and I wrap my legs around him, letting him carry me up the beach..

Somehow we manage to rinse off in the outdoor shower with only a brief interlude, where Dom's fingers slip between my legs and I detonate for him in record time as he tells me all the ways he's going to worship me when we get back from the bike ride.

We finish getting ready just as the guide pulls up in the shuttle to take us north to Las Catalinas, where there are some of the best mountain biking trails Costa Rica has to offer. Because I don't think the new general manager of the Bandits, Miller Murphy, would appreciate me breaking one of his best players, we are sticking to pretty basic trails today. Believe it or not, I'm one-hundred percent okay with that. Gone are the days where I chase an adrenaline high just to feel something.

I glance at my husband, who is holding the shuttle door open for me, much to the annoyance of the driver, and my heart skips a beat. These days, I feel everything as it comes. There's no running or shutting down what my heart wants.

We don't waste any time unloading our bike and starting our ride. Dirt splatters cover my legs, sweat coats my body, and my heart drums out a punishing beat in my chest as I follow Dom up the incline. Despite not having a fucking clue what he's doing on a mountain bike, he insisted on leading the way. He's actually not half bad, which shouldn't surprise me. My husband's never met an obstacle that he can't leap blindly over.

Ahead of me, Dom leans his bike against the railing at the edge of the overlook, taking my bike from me and doing the same as soon as I dismount. We hang our helmets on the handlebars and stand side by side, catching our breath from the climb.

"Wow!" White waves crash violently over jagged rocks and cliffs below us. Houses and tan beaches dot the rugged coastline.

"This was worth leaving the shower for," Dom says, his hot breath ghosting over my neck when he pulls me into his arms.

"Sure was," I agree.

"I want more of this, Indie." My husband says going still behind me. "Promise me you'll always fight. No matter what happens, you won't give up. Because I want a life filled with memories like this one. You're the love of my life, and I can't do this without you."

I turn in his arms, fighting back tears when I see his watery eyes. "You made me want to fight. Before you, I was hiding—barely living. You opened my eyes and made me face it all. How I felt for you, the way I was running from my past and my future at the same time. There's no going back now. Loving you changed my outlook on everything. I'm still scared, but I know you'll be there to help every step of the way, and that makes it all okay." I kiss his lips, letting my eyes fall shut. "So yeah, I'll fight if it comes to that. I'll never give up on the future we have together, because this life is worthy of millions of memories, just like this one."

With the soundtrack of pounding waves in the background, we stay like that for a few minutes, just soaking it all in before Dom's lips find the crown of my head, giving me one more kiss before we strap our helmets back on and ride back down to the waiting shuttle.

EPILOGUE

DOM

Shaking off the snow I step into the atrium of the Bandits stadium. Today it looks nothing like it does in the middle of the baseball season. And instead of being here for practice or a game, today, I'm my wife's coffee bitch. And I wouldn't have it any other way.

There's a sea of people buzzing around the evenly spaced out tables, including Lara who is busy helping with set up. Each table is home to a display about one of the five charity organizations here today. Soon, the rest of the available space will be packed with people interested in volunteering for one of these organizations. They'll get to speak with current volunteers and full-time team members about the mission of each organization and the types of volunteer work they can do.

In the middle of it all is my brillant wife, commanding everyone's attention as she gives directions to finish the set-up and ensure the event runs smoothly.

I wait off to the side while she finishes doling out assignments. I'm beyond impressed with everything she's accomplished in the last six months, but I never doubted she'd pull it off. Still, my wife has transformed right in front of my eyes, from the woman who ran from her fears, to someone who faces them head on.

From the moment she got her test results back she's battled with every cell in her body for the life she wants and I'm just really fucking lucky that she saw me as part of that future when I asked to her to imagine what it would look like.

I make my way to the heart of the atrium, where she's finally alone, and hold out my hand. "One black coffee, jet fuel, fully caffeinated, just the way you like it."

"My hero," she coos, playfully. "Now, where are your minions?"

"If by minions you mean teammates, they should be here in a few minutes."

"Perfect. I can't wait to order them around. It might just be the highlight of my day."

"I'm sure it will be, but why don't you come sit with me for a few minutes first? Get off your feet while you have the chance."

If looks could kill, I'd drop dead here and now.

"You promised not to coddle me. It was in your vows."

"No, it wasn't."

She shrugs, bringing the coffee to her lips. "I'm fine, Dom. It's been weeks and the doctor cleared me, but it makes you feel better, I promise not to lift anything heavier than this coffee cup."

"Reconstructive surgery is no joke, Baby. Just be careful."

"I'll sit for five minutes and enjoy this coffee with you, but as soon as there are Bandits here to boss around, break time is over."

Taking her hand in mine, I lead her to a little alcove, one I know has a chair waiting just for her, because I called the stadium this morning and spoke to the head of facilities myself to make sure it would be there.

"Happy?" she asks, when I pull her down onto my lap.

"For now," I tell her honestly. I'll be watching her like a hawk until the moment I get her home. She's slowly returned to work over the last three weeks, but today will be her busiest day by far since her breast reconstruction three weeks ago. I know she's strong. I've witnessed just how strong countless times in the past six months, but I'll always fight to protect her, even if it annoys the shit out of her.

"Want a drink?" She holds the coffee between us, a devilish grin on her face.

"No fucking way. Not even Lilah can make that tar taste good."

"I won't tell her you said that. It could put her over the edge in her state."

"You're a menace. She had to plug her nose while she made that so it didn't trigger her morning sickness."

"Shit, really? Now I feel like an asshole." Indie looks genuinely remorseful. It almost makes me feel bad.

"No, not really. She just had Mikey make it."

"You're the worst. Can you believe that by the start of next season, Cruz and Lilah will have a baby, and Poppy and Hendrix will be married. Maybe Dean will finally ask Mia to be his wife and then we just need to find Xavier a girl, now that he kicked Kristy to the curb."

"Indie Duran, do you love love as much as I do now?"

"No one loves it as much as you do. I just feel bad for the guy. He's always third wheeling it or getting stuck babysitting the rookies." She laughs, checking the time on her watch. "Five minutes are up. Let's go see if your goons are here."

When we walk back out into the atrium, Dean, Xavier, Cruz, Hendrix stand together in one group while Braxton Hayes, Montana Jones, and Dash Thomas stand a few feet away looking hungover and like this is the last place they want to be. Between the two groups is Miller Murphy looking like he's not sure where he fits into all this.

"Oh boy, this is going to be fun," Indie says, handing me her coffee cup and rubbing her hands together.

"Vivi, Willa, and Beck," Indie hollers to where the three women are huddled together at one of the tables. They all stand and stroll over. "We're going to split these guys up into groups and you can give them all the down low on each nonprofit, the work they do and volunteer roles available. They won't be registering new volunteers, we just want them to be able to direct people to the correct tables as they greet them."

After giving the group of newcomers her speech about the purpose of the event and introducing them to the three women, she splits them up. Sending the rookies with Beck and Vivi, Miller with Willa, and taking the rest of the guys herself.

I could recite the facts about each of the five nonprofits in my sleep, but I tag along just to see my wife in action. When Xavier looks at his phone for the dozenth time in a matter of minutes, I almost smack it out of his hand.

"Xav, what the hell?" Indie says, before I have the chance to bark at him for not paying attention.

When he looks up, his face is pale.

"Kristy's pregnant."

"Fuck," Hendrix groans next to him, the air whooshing out of him when Cruz backhands him in the stomach. "I mean congratulations."

"Do you need to leave?" Indie asks with genuine concern.

"Um, no. She flew to her parents in Tennessee. There's nothing I can do right now."

"Okay, if you're going to stay, I need you to put the phone away. You have nine months to prepare for the baby. I need you for the next three hours."

"Two months."

"Excuse me?" This time, it's me getting the glare from Cruz.

"Apparently . . ." His eyes drop to the phone in his hands, his brows scrunched. "She's—um she's due in two months and is just telling me."

"It's really okay if you need to leave, Xav," Indie assures softly.

With his lips pressed together and a shake of his head, he puts his phone away and pretends to focus, but I'm sure his mind is anywhere but in this room. At least until the future volunteers file in, because once they do its nonstop activity, until we close the doors three hours later.

Pride swells inside me as I squat in front of my wife, who is finally sitting down again while my teammate and our friends help clean up the space. "You're incredible. Truly, Indie. This event is going to have such a big impact on these organizations for years to come. Vivi just gave me the final count, and they added two hundred new volunteers to the roster for Double Play. Beck said the hotline, clinic, GSA and Saving Paws had similar numbers. Your mom would be so proud of what you built."

Her head drops into her hands and lets out a shaky exhale. "I did it."

"Yeah, Baby, you did."

BONUS EPILOGUE

INDIE

FORTY YEARS LATER

"Happy Birthday, Baby. Seventy and more stunning than the day I met you," Dom says, as he walks across the front porch of our house, a cupcake in one hand and the other shielding the candle sparkling on top of it. A breeze blows the swoop of gray hair off his forehead.

"Are you having an episode? We can't break out the cupcakes before everyone gets here. They'll riot," I tease.

"Let them. We've earned the right to do whatever the hell we please and I want a moment with my wife before we are overrun with family and friends. Lord knows once the grandkids get here you'll forget I exist." Dom leans in close, holding the chocolate cupcake between us.

"Stop it. You're just as wrapped around their grubby little fingers as I am." I blow out the candle, closing my eyes; wishing for health and happiness for my loved ones. There's nothing else that matters. I have it all, everything I ever dreamed of.

My husband pulls out the candle for me and I take a bite before he steals one of his own.

"Getting them wasn't easy," he says, running his thumb along my bottom lip, cleaning the chocolate frosting from it.

"But it was worth it." Every needle poke, every failed IVF cycle until we finally got our oldest. Even the scare we had after I delivered Farrow was worth it. A full hysterectomy led us down a different path to get Vienna and Blake.

"I'd do it all again because you're happy and healthy, we have a beautiful family, and amazing friends who helped build this life."

The first of many cars that will roll up to celebrate with us today parks along the curb, when they get out Hendrix holds open the gate of the white picket fence for Poppy. Without my childhood friend this family wouldn't be complete. She carried Vienna for us—a gift I'll never be able to repay.

"Happy Birthday, Ind," Poppy says, kissing my cheek when she joins me on the porch swing. "Oh chocolate." She pulls a piece off and pops it in her mouth.

"Lilah and Cruz were right behind us," Hendrix tells Dom. "He's the slowest driver ever."

"And even grumpier in his advanced age," I joke.

We owe another piece of our family to them. Lilah carried our youngest Blake for us to complete our family.

Car after car rolls up, our family filling the yard with squeals and giggles as the kids and grandkids arrive, filling my heart until it feels like it might burst.

"You okay, wife? You've got a little something . . ." Dom says when he takes the spot next to me on the porch swing a few minutes later, his hands find my face and wipe away the tear trailing down my cheek.

"Couldn't be better. Just taking it all in." I lean my head against his shoulder and together we watch the joyful chaos unfold as kids chase each other around and their parents struggle to rein in their little ones after the ride.

"You've never been one to sit on the sidelines, don't tell me you're slowing down."

"Not a chance." I kiss his neck and then stand from the chair, holding my hand out for him. "We've got lots of life left to live, think you can keep up old man?"

"You know I can. Now let's go squeeze those grandbabies and fill them with sugar."

"I love you, Dom," I tell him with a laugh.

"Forever and always, Indie Duran. I love you."

THE END

WHAT'S NEXT?

OTHER BOOKS BY LO EVERETT

MILE-HIGH HEARTS SERIES:

All on the Line - Poppy & Hendrix

All or Nothing - Delilah & Cruz

Calling it Safe - Mia & Dean

Passed Ball - Xavier

TIMBERLINE PEAK:

SMALL TOWN ROMANCE WITH HIGH ADRENALINE HEROS

Fool Me - 2025

Chase Me - 2025

Ruin Me - TBD

Keep Me - TBD